EARLY PRAISE FOR

# An Uncommon Bond

"Jeff Brown has done it again... Within your hands is another magical master-piece. If you are ready for a whirlwind of radical honesty, bare-boned intimacy and the raw dissecting that MUST go into Sacred Relationship then read on. A jewel of the highest order." —ANAIYA SOPHIA, author of *Sacred Sexual Union* & co-author of *Womb Wisdom*

"In *An Uncommon Bond*, we are shown love as a relentless force within the universe, acting on the lives of the two main characters to crack open their hearts that their souls might come home to each other. And we recognize their story as our own. Written with passion, honesty and wisdom, this is an uncommon book." —PHILIP SHEPHERD, author of *New Self, New World*

"Jeff Brown elegantly weaves an evolutionary romance in *An Uncommon Bond*. Whereas most love stories end with "happily ever after," Jeff takes us beyond the fairy tale and into the grounded spirituality necessary to truly meet the Beloved, both within ourselves and in our relationships. He is a master wordsmith, engaging and enlightening us with his whimsical word-play as we watch the journey unfold between Lowen and Sarah, the story's "Scar-Crossed Lovers." Armed with his witty-wise lexicon and his deep understanding of human nature, Jeff presents a new paradigm of relating that is essential to the healing and growth of our society." —CANDICE HOLDORF, actress and author of *From 6 to 9 and Beyond: Widening the Lens of Feminine Eroticism*

"An Uncommon Bond is both evocative and riveting, wrapping its way around the heart and soul of anyone who ~~is~~ involved or interested in a deeper type of love t~~hat~~ common sense and connection. Jeff Brown b darkness, the confusion, and the elevation xquisite merging of two people who were ~~transf~~ormational and transcendent relational experi ~~exceedi~~ngly eye opening, shape-shifting and profound, I will never again look at the beautiful possibilities of love the same as before." —VICTORIA ERICKSON, author of *Edge of Wonder*

" In this beautifully written prose, Jeff Brown weaves powerful teachings and wisdom into a vulnerable tale of love, pain and truth. While reading, I experienced an integration of my heart and mind that opened a channel directly to my soul. I believe that with every vulnerable and raw truth told, each of us is uplifted into a timeless place where there are no words—just experiences of the soul. Thank you Jeff for taking me there." —KELLY MCNELIS, founder of Women For One; www.womenforone.com

"Jeff Brown has put into words the glory and anguish of love that all of us who have loved know so well. His words burrow into my heart. I feel him. I feel me. I feel our common experience in a way that expands my own personal understanding and gives me new ways to think and talk about the love in my own life. In addition, Jeff draws out of his experiences wisdom that honors these experiences and elevates his awareness. So often when we have had pain in love, it is easy to point the finger and deny our own part in the creation of the challenge. The male character's willingness to take responsibility and take a hard look at his patterns leads to his enlightenment and enlivenment. This approach is inspirational. Anyone dealing with deep heartache over love lost can follow his tracks to come out the other side. And what is on the other side is reason enough to take the journey through the heart of darkness. I am delighted I got to take this journey. In my own relationship with my beloved, Tomas, we have hit some rocky patches and have had to take hard looks, too, at our patterns. What Jeff is sharing in his juicy and powerful book is what has worked for me and Tomas. It has been through our willingness to see ourselves more clearly that we have worked through our own dramas. What a gift to have Jeff's book to inspire, support, and illuminate the path of relationship, and how to navigate it more honestly, and successfully." —JOAN HEART-FIELD, PhD., author of *Romancing the Beloved: A Sacred Sexual Adventure into Love*

"Jeff Brown holds a mirror up to the dance of the masculine and the feminine in this fearless look into the everyday rise and fall of relationships. A realistic and honest view of the true meaning of soulmates." —JILL ANGELO, author of *Sacred Space: Turning Your Home Into a Sanctuary*

# An Uncommon Bond

Jeff Brown

ENREALMENT PRESS,
TORONTO, CANADA

Published by Enrealment Press
PO Box 64
Acton, Ontario
Canada L7J-2M2

Cover photo by Colette Stevenson (www.colettestevensonphotography.com)
Author photo by Paul Hemrend
Cover and book design by www.go-word.com
Publisher logo by Brad Rose (www.facebook.com/GetSeenGraphics)
Printed in the USA

From the book *The Power of Now*. Copyright © 1997 by Eckhart Tolle. Reprinted with permission from New World Library, Novato CA. www.newworldlibrary.com

From *Love's Glory: Recreations of Rumi* by Andrew Harvey, published by North Atlantic Books, copyright © 1996 by Andrew Harvey. Reprinted by permission of publisher.

From *The Essential Rumi*, translated by Coleman Barks, published by Harper Collins, San Francisco. Copyright © 1995 by Coleman Barks. Reprinted by permission of Coleman Barks.

From Achterberg, Jeanne (1998). *"Uncommon Bonds: On the spiritual nature of relationships."* ReVision 21(2): 4-10. Reprinted by permission of ReVision (Jürgen Werner Kremer).

From the poetry collection *Hope is a Traveler*. Copyright © 2015 by Susan Frybort, published by Enrealment Press.

Publisher Note: The writings of the female character (Sarah Harding) in this book are taken from the writings of Susan Frybort. Some are intrinsic to the poetry collection noted above, and others from words written by her to the author of this book, Jeff Brown, as part of their personal correspondence. Reprinted with her permission.

Library and Archives Canada Cataloguing in Publication

Brown, Jeff, 1962-, author
    An uncommon bond / Jeff Brown.

Includes bibliographical references.

Issued in print and electronic formats.
ISBN 978-0-9808859-5-8 (pbk.).--ISBN 978-0-9808859-6-5 (pdf)

    I. Title.

PS8603.R68394U53 2015        C813'.6        C2015-900292-3
                                             C2015-900293-1

I dedicate this book to Rocketdog, to Bubbi Perlove, to Susan Frybort, to all the women who have loved and endured me, chiseling away at my armored heart with their beautiful offerings, opening and preparing me for the conscious relationship journey.

I also dedicate this book to the brilliant Jeanne Achterberg, whose heart-echo lives on. You were right, Jeanne—there is a far more profound universe waiting for us in the heart of love's magic. I can only hope that you are there now, held warmly in God's embrace.

And to all of you here and now, who are braving this new relational path, on your way to the next paradigm of enheartened consciousness, I wish you a transformative and magical journey. May you arrive at your next destination with your heart wide open, ready to embrace the next stage of wonder.

# Note to the Reader

This is a work of fiction. Names, characters, places and incidents are the product of the author's imagination or are used fictitiously. Any resemblance to actual events, locales or persons, living or dead, is entirely coincidental.

Note on the word "God": When used in this book, the word "God" is not a linear, limited or limiting definition. It is not guilt or shame associated, not religiously affiliated, not affixed to any particular doctrine. It is an open-ended term that can be interpreted and applied in whatever way you personally relate to and identify with it: Divinity, Higher Power, Goddess, Nature, Unity Consciousness, Source, Truth, Infinity, Wholeness, to name only a few. Whatever feels true for you. The author is himself an avid explorer of the God concept, and his perspective changes as his experiences inform and expand his consciousness. What he identified as God through a more individualized lens, is entirely different from how he came to understand God through the eyes of love. Perhaps God morphs as we morph, or, perhaps we are seeking an understanding far beyond our comprehension.

Near the back of the book you will find a 'Love Dictionary' composed of words and terms that were 'hearticulated' in the following story. They include "Uncommon Bonds," a term created by Jeanne Achterberg to describe the relationship phenomenon at the heart of this book.

The telling of the story of uncommon bonds creates a new myth for relationships that involves the evolution and transformation of our being. The bonds may well be the threads in the matrix of humanity, and in the final analysis, the only thing that endures. We who have had bonded experiences can see ourselves as two of the many lights in the interconnected web of all life, and as these lights burn brighter in synchrony, we shake and move and transduce the filaments of the web so that the material universe is changed, subtly perhaps, but changed, nonetheless.

—JEANNE ACHTERBERG

There are two types of double stars.
The pair that appear close,
but are in fact at different distances
and are an optical double.

And there is the binary.
The pair that are mutually attracted
and bound to one another
by forces of gravity and motion.

You must find your counterpart in the heavens.

—SUSAN FRYBORT

# An Uncommon Bond

I met her when I most expected it. I felt Sarah entering my heart weeks before we met in real time. She was quietly everywhere—a distant flute, a subtle shift in wind direction, a whisper of longing that called me home. I felt her in my bones, in my breath, in the sudden and inexplicable lifting of my weary spirit. She was orbiting me, close at heart, eagerly awaiting our cosmic reacquaintance.

Let there be no doubt: all love connections are not created equal. Some bonds are simply practical. Others are blindly rooted in pathology and old traumas. Still others are opportunities to heal and have essential needs finally met. And some have a mystical quality from the first meeting. Pure and simple. Apparent from the first out-breath. Unmistakably sacred. God rising on the wings of their love. This is how the timely and the timeless become indistinguishable—when love meets God deep in the heart's inner temple.

Does this sound insane? If it does, that's okay. Great love is the most exquisite kind of madness, an asylum of delight. Enter its gates and divinity rises into view.

Like all synchronistic delights, it's only madness until it happens to you.

# 1

## Divine Preparation

L et's begin in the beginning, when I was preparing myself for this great adventure. There is always a preparation phase before great love comes. Sometimes it's a gentle one, sometimes it's a harsh one. Mine was downright ugly. Perhaps this is the way the universe works—it deals you an ugly hand before it deals you a beautiful one. The trick is trusting the beauty when it comes. It may never come again.

As much as I want to tell a love story that doesn't include conflict, I can't. War has framed my life from the beginning, influencing and permeating every step of the journey. I have lived war, I have loved war, and, even when I let it go, it has come back to reclaim me. We all have a way of being that we are here to outgrow. War is mine.

I was born on a battlefield in suburban Toronto. From the outside, it didn't look like a place of battle, but suburban homes seldom do. In a well coiffured sub-division, it had two rocking chairs on the sweeping front porch, a small man-made waterfall, and a sweet lavender garden that covered most of the front lawn. You would think that the Buddha lived there, it was that peaceful.

Inside, there were three warriors. My histrionic Scottish mother screamed night and day, while my passive-aggressive Jewish father wavered between immobilizing depression and menacing attack. When their attacks on each other proved unsatisfying, they channeled their frustrations in my direction. They needed a punching bag more than they needed a son, and I unconsciously obliged. Although they

1

named me Lowen, they actually called me "the mistake" behind muffled walls. I wasn't the daughter they had longed for.

We spent the first 17 years of my life in battle. If we weren't screaming at each other, we were screaming at our neighbors and relatives. The quiet times—infrequent as they were—were mere respites from our habitual way of being. Once everyone got a chance to rest and refuel, the arguments began anew, stocked with more ammo. Both as a necessary defense, and as a perfect reflection of my male conditioning, I turned to armor as a way of being. With 'never surrender' as my mantra, I navigated the battlefield with panache.

At the same time, I was a complete mess inside. There are few things more confusing than going to war with parents who are diminishing you, particularly when you are very young. If you fight for your dignity, you risk losing the love you need from them to develop. If you don't fight back, you lose your self-respect and your development is stifled. How very confusing—to have to fight for your right to be here against the very people who brought you into existence.

### The Abandonment Dance

When I finally escaped the clutches of my war-torn childhood, my forays into intimate relationship weren't much better. I had imagined I would find some refuge in the arms of the feminine, but instead found that old habits die harsh. Each of my first intimate relationships seemed to magnify yet another unresolved issue, most of which I would have rather kept buried.

Soon after fleeing the war zone, I met my first girlfriend. A tenderhearted social worker, Naomi would come by with peppermint foot massage cream and pumpkin pie ingredients, hands at the ready. She wanted nothing more than to love me. She didn't stand a chance. Whenever she reached for me, I ran away. When she backed off, I ran after her. Ne'er the twain shall meet.

At the heart of our dance was an abandonment wound of radical proportions. Emotionally rejected by my mother, I was certain of only one thing in this world: my inherent unworthiness. If Naomi loved me, she lost all credibility. If she exhibited signs of disinterest, she rose to immediate prominence in my inner world. If only I could get her to want me again, if only I could win her love, I could heal the wound. A perfect plan—until I won her over again, and immediately lost interest. Fractured by a distancing mother, I couldn't bear to be left, even if I did the leaving. Crazy-making!

For many years, this wound shaped my relationships in its own image. Naomi was merely the first reflection. After she wisely gave up, I commenced a lengthy relational cycle that reflected both polarities of the wound in perfect measure. About half the time, I was the distancer, pulling away from kind women who simply wanted to love me. After only a short time in their arms, I became bored with their availability and lost my sexual charge.

The rest of the time I was the fuser, chasing unavailable wildcats as they sprinted off in the other direction. Their detachment actually ignited my sexuality, unconsciously turned on by the illusion that I was gaining the favor of my inaccessible mother. If I could bed the wildcat, I must be a worthwhile human. Of course, the ass was always greener on the other side. The moment they surrendered to my charms, I began looking over the fence for the next conquest. One way or the other, I was designed to avoid intimacy at all costs.

It took me many years to realize that everyone involved in the abandonment dance was living out their own baggage, even the kind and connective women who seemed so perfectly available for love. Although they appeared to have a greater capacity for intimacy than I did, the fact that they danced with my unavailability suggested otherwise. They wanted me for the same reasons I wanted the wild ones—as a reflection and perpetuation of their unresolved issues. It's no accident that we were on the same dance floor together. We were all looking for dance partners in an empty ballroom.

### Love-Proof Vest

No matter where I was on the abandonment continuum, there was a common thread—invulnerability. It came in countless forms: constricted musculature, evasive communication, detached sexuality, repressed emotions. Those who chased me knew it well. The moment they thought they had me, they immediately confronted the armor that encased my tender heart. My love-proof vest was impenetrable in form, crafted as it was with frozen feelings and congealed rage. Love relationship demanded surrender, but willfulness, conflict and armor were all I knew.

Despite my gamesy ways, I was able to do one thing with conviction—study. In each of my first three years of university, I made the dean's honors list. In my second year, I won a bursary for writing an award-winning essay on emotional healing. God knows I wasn't ready to actually do any healing, but I was ready to write about it. Funny how that works. Funny how we come at things conceptually first, before life pushes us to experience them in real time.

Just before my final year, I applied for law school. Although my LST and grades were strong, I was certain that I would be rejected. I wasn't. I got into all six schools that I applied to. I decided to go to Osgoode Hall Law School in North Toronto the following autumn. I felt a deep desire to fight for the rights of the disenfranchised. If I couldn't find fairness in my family, perhaps I could find it for others in the courtroom.

Ignited by the stresses of study, my anger began to infiltrate my love connections. Violence was not an issue, but emotional abuse became a common occurrence. With no sense of how to express my anger in a healthy way, I took it out on my girlfriends. Not surprisingly, I specialized in women with terrible self-concepts. I shamed them, as I had been shamed. Nasty business.

One of the primary ways that I avoided vulnerability was drama. Intensity was habitual and easily mistaken for aliveness. If I wasn't having powerhouse sex with a woman, I was having a pointless argument with her. I loved the thrill of the chase. I loved make-up sex. I didn't understand the difference between connection-avoidant intensity and intensity that is sourced in love's light. My heart was aflame, but it wasn't open. I was too busy starting fires.

### Rear-view Mirror

And then the universe sent me my karmuppance in the middle of second term law school. Melanie was a trauma survivor with nipples of gold. From the moment I saw them, I was lost to a primal suckfest that lasted for months. So intoxicated by her projected mama breasts, I failed to notice that she was a pathological liar and a thief.

Her specialty was my specialty—intimacy avoidance. But she was much better at it than me. She would seduce me with her sensuality, then slip out the exit door just before morning, leaving her edible scent all over my bed sheets. The faster she ran, the harder I chased. Then, when I was sure she was truly gone, she re-appeared with her nipples on her sleeve, beckoning me home to Mama. What three-year-old cares where Mama had gone, now that she is back? Just give me the nipple, now! I was ensnared at my own game.

How easy it is to mistake the primal for the passionate.

Melanie was the perfect nexus of all my issues: abandonment, betrayal, drama, objectification. But she went one lie too far. I took her for an abortion in downtown Toronto. I paid the fee. She asked me to wait in the car. Twenty minutes later, she came out with her eyes moist and tender. She looked me straight in the eye and said, "I'm so sorry Lowen—twins." My knees buckled. I had paid to abort my twin children. We drove back to the apartment, and I beat myself up all afternoon.

That night I had a dream. My long dead Uncle Bernie came to me and said, "She has the money in her wallet."

Money in her wallet? I don't understand.

But, of course, I did. For weeks, I wouldn't touch her. I couldn't admit what I knew out loud, but my body knew everything. The body never lies. We may misinterpret its message, but it always speaks the truth. My body knew why she asked me to wait outside. It knew that she staged the abortion to get the money. No doubt she told them she had chickened out, and they returned the money to her. No doubt she had said "twins" to me as some kind of over-compensatory smoke-screen. I was caught in the grips of madness.

The next week, the tsunami rose to a crescendo. We were driving down the highway after an all-night battle. I was at war with my knowing. She was at war with my knowing. We began to argue, and I confronted her about the abortion. She was startled. How could I accuse her of such a thing? Then she tried to jump out of the car. Better to die than admit the truth. I grabbed her just in time.

I pulled over and got out of the car. I walked to the roadside and fell to the ground with a heavy thud. *This is love? What the fuck do I know about love?* I began to weep—the first time I had cried in years. Then I drove right home and contacted a therapist. The great gift of Melanie. I needed things to escalate into insanity before I could even begin to look in the rear-view mirror.

## Exit: Healing Road

That summer, I requested a one-year sabbatical from law school and began my healing journey. I knew I had no choice—my stuff was catching up with me. I couldn't focus on my studies with so many relationship dramas dominating my days. On a conscious level, I wanted to heal so I could be a more effective trial lawyer. On an unconscious level, I wanted to heal so I could finally taste love.

I got a part-time job at a downtown bookstore, and devoted the rest of my time to my healing process. With my therapist's support, I slowly became acquainted with my emotional life. I went deep into the process, recognizing how the battleground that had been my home had forged an entirely warped lens on reality. A master of self-evasion, what I identified as reality was a fragmented patchwork of defenses and disguises. They were no longer serving me, but they were all I knew.

At some point, a wave of repressed emotion broke through my armor, demanding expression and release. As I plumbed the depths of my despair, I shed one layer of pain after another. My inner world was like a series of reservoirs, each holding a different wave of emotional memory behind them. When one reservoir burst, another soon appeared. This phase went on for many months—the first of many essential release phases.

At the heart of the inner work was an attempt to form a well-constructed self, essential to sustaining healthy connection: *Solid me, solid we.* Growing up in that war-zone had left me with a completely bifurcated self-concept, either boastfully egoic or dreadfully self-loathing. What I needed was to learn how to live in the middle—neither King nor trash, but healthily human. Without a balanced sense of self to land in, my forays into relationships couldn't possibly sustain themselves. The key was to construct a healthy foundation to relate from.

By year's end, a little light shone through the fissures in my heart. The light was fragmented, like I was fragmented, but there was enough of it to invite my optimism. I began to feel a measure of joy creeping into my inner landscape, a sliver of "yes."

The next two years of law school included a cornucopia of intimacy adventures. Connections came in many forms: practical, playful, sensual, intellectually charged but emotionally barren, wildly dangerous. They lasted one evening, one weekend, or many months. I relished the opportunity to know myself in different ways, depending on the tenor of each dynamic.

Although many of the women I connected with called me "commitment-phobic," the characterization didn't resonate. I didn't feel afraid. I just felt ill-prepared. I intuitively knew that I had so much to learn about connection before I could really hold one together. I needed an array of experiences first.

My therapist didn't agree. He felt that I was playing a cat-and-mouse game with my intimacy: "You want to commit, but you still associate commitment with your childhood prison. Are you afraid you will never escape if you commit?"

One afternoon, he labeled me with something he called "The Unavailable Available Pattern." It's where you convince yourself (and others) that you are available for relationship, but you always find a way to stop short. That stopping short can manifest in many ways: choosing unavailable people, looking for excuses to run, focusing on a lover's imperfections rather than their appealing qualities, getting lost in the excitement of ecstatic possibility until the first glimpse of real vulnerability sends you packing. It's the addiction to possibility and the fear of intimacy all rolled into one.

I left him and found a new therapist, one with a more soulful lens. Yes, I had a bevy of issues, but not every choice I made was rooted in the neurotic psyche. Sometimes there is something much deeper going on. Sometimes there is a knowing that cannot be explained in psychological terms. I had the oddest sense that I was heading somewhere, rather than avoiding something. That I was preparing the soil for something plentiful. Who can criticize that faith?

## Conscious Dating

After graduating and opening my own criminal law practice, I became more deliberate in my relational choices. I thought of it as conscious dating. Instead of walking through every open door, I stood back a little, contemplating the steps I was about to take. Whenever I was set to explore deeper, I brought it into my therapy, working through the emotional material at the heart of the decision.

I soon began to manifest relationships with a greater capacity for emotional intimacy. Reflecting this shift, I experienced a burgeoning interest in romantic love. Although still cautious, I crept out now and then with flowers and chocolates in hand. And sometimes, while having sex, I even felt the heart and genitals meet for a moment, before they scurried back to their separate corners. Up to this point in my life, my genitals were primarily pleasure-seeking missiles, looking to land somewhere soft before quickly returning to their hiding place. The idea that a physical union between two souls could open the God-gate was still well beyond my imaginings, but there was progress.

And now and then, I would actually get a vision of a woman waiting for me up ahead. I didn't see her face, but I sensed her presence, as though she was encoded in the cells of my being. Sometimes I would hear her in my dreams, like a heart-song that rises through the ether with your name on it. Wishful thinking, or prescient visions? Time would tell.

At the same time, I still carried a deep cynicism where love was concerned. It threatened my organizing system, the hyper-vigilant way of being that had served me well. It was one thing to be vulnerable when alone, something else entirely to trust another to hold my heart safe. It felt safer to drop in for a visit now and then, before returning to my man-cave for a good night's sleep.

Of course, this resistance wasn't simply a reflection of childhood wounding. It was also a function of cultural conditioning. I had been taught to equate manhood with invulnerability—one eye on the door, one eye on my weapons. How to surrender to love with a pistol in my hand?

### On the Hunt for God

After years of therapy, I began looking for God (whoever God was). I wanted something more than healing the mother wound. I wanted the Divine Father himself. Healing was a wonderful thing, but then what? What was on the other side of those mountains of emotional debris? What was the outer edge of human possibility? Where lived pure consciousness? How to drink from the God-root?

I looked for God everywhere. I hunted for him on the yoga mat, the meditation cushion, the Camino Pilgrimage. I looked for him in the heart of a disciplined meditation practice, energetic clearings, mantra and tantra. I looked and looked, but something was missing.

What was missing was connection. Not surprisingly, I was seeking God in the same way that male warriors had since the beginning of time: in my aloneness, in my isolated mind, on a meditation cushion separate from humanity. It was just me, and me alone, seeking the maker while the womenfolk were tending to the relational world. Even when I was sharing tantric delights, I had no template for mutuality. She was on her adventure and I was on mine. God was not somewhere we go together. He was at the end of a long, heroic solo journey through enemy territory.

But was it God I met alone in the wilderness, or just his pale imitation?

I soon came to question detachment as a path to enlightenment. In its healthiest forms, I got that it was a wonderful place to visit, a reminder of something beyond our localized perceptions, a peek into a vaster reality, an opportunity to distinguish between that which serves us and that which derails us. But taken too far, it felt more like self-avoidance masquerading as enlightenment. If this wasn't so, then why did I fall right back into triggers shortly after getting out of my meditation cave and re-engaging with the world? And why did I feel more bereft of feeling as my practice deepened? Was this meditation or medication? The New Earth or the New Mars?

Frustrated in my quest, I began to look for meaning in another direction. Although my tendency to isolate was still prominent, a deeper longing for relationship began taking up space inside me, pushing up against my armor from the inside out.

I soon began to crave love. Out of the blue. I suddenly felt frustrated by its absence, as though it had been a treasure stolen from me while I was asleep. *Was it?*

Although talk therapy had been helpful to this point in the journey, I sensed I needed something deeper if I wanted to manifest real love. Dialoguing with a therapist played into my heady and strategic nature. At some point, it became another courtroom where I was trying to outsmart the opponent. I had to go deeper.

I began to explore more body-centered approaches to emotional healing in the hopes of excavating deeper layers of unresolved material. The exploration began with a massage therapist who adeptly worked through layers of holding in my musculature for two hours per week. Although I was by no means muscle-bound, I was heavily armored, like an impenetrable fortress. As she peeled the armor, older and older memories emerged, muscles with a story that needed to be told.

To accelerate the de-armoring process, I began doing session work with a body-centered psychotherapist. After four years of regular release sessions, I felt a deep letting go inside my heart. It's like I had gone back down the path of my life and reclaimed a lost piece, one that held a key to my awakening. I felt lighter, softer and more genuinely available to the moment. Never mind detaching from the wound-body—immersing in it was the key to my salvation.

One afternoon, I went into the woods with my heart open and bared and actually asked for love. I walked miles from civilization, in the midst of a wild rainstorm, carried forward by a determination that defied reason. I arrived at a rambling brook, one I had never seen before but that felt entirely familiar. (Are locations encoded in our destiny, too?) It was getting dark and the branches were clanging in the wind. There was an ominous energy, an oddly inexplicable combination of destruction and passion.

I got down on my knees beside the brook and said aloud: "My

spirit is tired of stumbling this earth alone. Please bring me love. Please..." The warrior within chastised my vulnerability. The lover being birthed beneath my armor celebrated.

I had actually asked the universe for love before, but never with this depth of conviction. To this point, the universe wouldn't take my calls. It seemed my soulular phone plan wasn't activated yet. Or perhaps I hadn't paid my karmic fees yet. Whatever it was, it knew I wasn't ready for the great crack open, the grand teaching. My heart was still too protected, my relational patterns too unstable. I needed more inner prep work to clear the lines. So they sent me substitute teachers, preliminary lessons on the path to readiness. No sense planting the cosmic seeds in an ill-prepared field. Better to prepare the soulsoil for a real good harvest.

### The Call of the Beloved

As my inner work deepened, serendipitous events occurred to support my opening. Suddenly, I was bumping into people I had parted from at moments of tension, relationships that still weighed heavily on my heart and needed resolution. And they weren't encountering me at random moments. They were walking into me just after I had thought of them, in the oddest of places. Even the carpenter who showed up to install hardwood in my apartment was from my unhealed past. I had bumped into his sister the week before. My intuition told me that I was no arbitrary tourist in these encounters. The universe was busy with me.

Soon, everything within and around me felt like it was shifting. There was a kind of crispness in the air, a poignancy, like the way it feels before a storm, or before a breakthrough experience comes your way.

Around this time, I began to dream about a petite blond woman, sensations of deep abiding love. I couldn't see her face, but I could sense her presence beside me, walking together down sacred pathways. A karmic knot was loosening around my heart. I began to feel more and more certain that great love was coming into my life soon. How to articulate this knowing in human speak?

Before I knew it, the call to tenderness permeated my armored working life. It first happened in the middle of a rigorous cross-examination. I was going for the jugular when I was suddenly overcome with compassion. Never before had I felt remotely kind in a courtroom. Never before had I lost my focus in the heart of a trial. It was as though a presence had filled the room—a soft, open invitation to humanize this warrior charade. The presence wasn't other worldly. It moved from the inside out, like an encoded path that had always been there, waiting patiently for its moment of revealing. *Lay down your weapons*, it said. *Open your heart...*

I walked home that day, disillusioned with the life I had created. Suddenly, trial law seemed like little more than a perpetuation of my childhood battleground. How had I not noticed? Why had I thought it would be different? I was now 36 years old with a growing practice—two secretaries and an eight-month-long trial list—and it all felt like the same old war. I wanted a deeper life, I did. I wanted something sweet.

I began to feel a throbbing sense of restlessness. I had extracted so much from my healing processes, but now what? I was healthy and successful, yet I was still walking this planet alone. I felt comfortable in my own skin, yet I longed for the feel of another's skin upon mine. I longed to meet the woman of my dreams. She kept coming to me in my sleep, but where was she in my waking life?

One night, after yet another dissonant day in court, I knew I had to get away. A retreat of some sort. Something to give me a clue as to what's next. I asked the universe for a sign, and two soon appeared. That night, I dreamed I was hiking the mountains around Boulder, Colorado. I had been there once before, at a holistic lawyer's conference, and always wanted to return. The next morning, a young woman knocked at my door, soliciting donations for her local yoga studio's *seva* mission. I had no idea what a *seva* mission was, but her peaceful energy inspired me to go on-line and search for a yoga workshop to attend.

The first to come up was a five-day yoga conference in Boulder. I clicked on it and knew I had to be there. As I hit "submit" to register for the retreat, I felt an electric current pulse throughout my body. It was crystal clear. Something was waiting for me in Colorado.

I wanted to share my excitement with someone. I immediately picked up the phone and called my best friend. "Daniel, I have news for you. I'm leaving for Colorado tomorrow."

"Huh?... Why?"

"I'm going to meet the great love of my life."

"Oh, yah. Sure."

"No, I am. I really am," I said confidently.

"Fly safe, loverboy," he said, chuckling like a mad monkey.

I guess it was a secret for me alone to treasure.

# 2

___

# An Undress Rehearsal

I began to look for her almost as soon as I arrived at the conference. I wandered around Boulder between yoga classes, earnestly scouring the women that walked past. I scanned cars, cafés and bookstores, somehow imagining that my willful nature would yield results. Is it *you*? How about *you*?

I arrived back at my hotel after an exhausting night of searching and noticed the phone blinking.

A message. I pressed play, and heard Daniel's familiar voice:

"Hey buddy... So, she land on your head yet? Better look up."

I smiled at his playfulness. But I didn't doubt my clarity. I knew something he didn't. Her imminent arrival had been announced in the great hall of my heart.

Ignoring him, I fervidly resumed my search the next morning. Almost immediately I bumped into a woman I had known in Canada. We had kissed once before, and never saw one another again. As we walked and talked through the town, I wondered, *"Is it you? It doesn't feel like it, but perhaps if we spend a little more time together, we can craft a soul connection."* We all know that story. After one uninteresting lunch together, I called myself on my own game and went back to the quest. *Where are you, breath of my heart?*

I had never experienced such a compelling faith in something this intangible. As a long time pragmatist, I believed it only when I saw it. I didn't *feel* it into form. But this was meaningfully different. It felt so certain, like I had stumbled upon a pre-encoded blueprint that had been buried for decades. All I had to do was step firmly in its direction, and believe.

## Smiling Eyes

After a few days on the prowl, I began to feel conflicted. I was torn between the willful mantras of positive thinking: "Ask for what you want and you'll get it" and "Believe it into being"; or a more subtle interface with reality.

I had moved mountains in my life with my warrior spirit, but could love be summoned in this way? What state of being opens the gateway? Does determination connect two destined souls, or does it actually sever the lines? What brings love home?

And then I did something uncharacteristic. I stopped looking. I surrendered. All the healing work I had done had apparently left an impression. Hunting for love only made love seem further away. With my will actively engaged, I could no longer feel her coming. Perhaps love needs an opening to receive it.

It was a good learning, one I would no doubt soon forget.

On the final day of the workshop, I slept through the first class. I wasn't particularly interested in doing more yoga. How many downward dogs can one man do? I stumbled out of bed mid-morning, and went for a long slow walk along Boulder Creek. It was a perfect spring day, and the bubbling creek kept me good company. When I hit the edge of town, I felt a strong impulse to continue walking all the way to the Flatirons, the sandstone mountains at the edge of Boulder. Then I remembered there was one more class that afternoon—a talk on the five Buddhist precepts. Those darn Buddhists, always spoiling the fun. I sat down on a fallen tree trunk to ponder my next steps.

Within moments, a red cardinal came flitting past me, almost close enough to touch. He was eerily large for a cardinal, and completely unconcerned about my presence. A bird on a mission, I watched him racing from tree to tree for some time, as though he was looking for something he had lost. Perhaps he was.

I decided to head towards the Flatirons. After a few steps in their direction, I suddenly turned right around and headed for Boulder to make my final class. Walking rapidly, I was a man on a mission. I was not sure why—it wasn't any kind of conscious decision. Perhaps it was the cardinal's quest that reminded me of my own. Perhaps.

I arrived a little early and sat in wait outside the classroom. After some time, I shifted my position and looked to the left. There, exiting the elevator, were the most captivating eyes I have ever known or imagined. I was too blinded by her resonance to notice her features, her clothing, her gait. All I noticed were those smiling eyes looking at me, penetrating my masks, summoning heart, soul and essence to the forefront. They knew me, I knew them. God at first sight.

This is *you*.

And then she was gone, totally gone. I stood up and looked about, but her smiling eyes were nowhere to be seen. I steadied myself, lost in a sea of feeling.

The door opened, and the previous class emptied out. I waited a few minutes before entering, just in case she made another appearance. *Where are you, smiling eyes? Bring me back to life.* No such luck. She was gonzo. I entered the class and sat down among the circle of desks.

An annoyingly calm Buddhist monk walked in and sat down. After an agitating meditation, he began discussing abstinence and the disease of desire. All the while, I ached for Smiling Eyes to walk through that door. Fuck abstinence.

Twenty minutes in, the door opened. Smiling Eyes entered. I watched her walk across the room, as though the eye of God was clearing a path between our hearts. As she walked, my experience of the whole room changed form. Everything slowed down; everything transmuted into something more beautiful. She sat down on the opposite side of the circle, almost directly in front of me. She didn't look up for a few minutes. I tried to look away but failed miserably. Some loves pull you close over time. This one had me by the heart-string instantly.

I watched her gently rubbing a small blue stone. She touched it the way one touches something precious to them. I also noticed scribbles, some kind of writing, on both her hands. She appeared to be uncomfortable, almost as though she was steeling herself, preparing for a great challenge. In the background, the monk was talking about the principles of non-attachment: "Nothing to grasp…" Such irony!

Then she looked up starkly, and her smiling eyes looked right at me, into me, through me. My soul stepped up to meet its other half. The world around us fell away. All heaven broke loose. Such grace.

The non-attachment chatter faded into the background, as we stared into each other's eyes for what seemed like forever. Whose eyes gaze out at me? Whose eyes do I view you with? Are these two souls or one? Intertwined with the divine, we deepened into pools of time-less knowing. It was both the longest and shortest fifteen minutes of my life. Our first undress rehearsal.

The class went on break. I avoided her. I felt entirely disoriented—quaking, rumbling, heaving. My inner tectonic plates had shifted. It was one of those experiences that up-frames everything before it. What I thought of as vastness was revealed in its smallness. What I once called color was exposed in its drabness. I had just landed on an entirely new planet.

At the same time, it frightened me. My feet had grown wings, but I didn't know how to fly. What mad magic had I stumbled upon? Drugs in my lunch bowl? No, I hadn't eaten lunch today.

Back in class, I felt my fear-body pushing up against me. Little tremors of excitement signaled great awakening, but there was a deeper level of anxiety churning below the surface. When I finally looked her way, I saw that she was squirming, too.

The class ended. She quickly got up to leave. I thought to leave her be, but my inner warrior commanded, "*Go, get her before she is gone forever.*" I got up, knocking my empty notebook on the floor. When I finally found my way into the hall, I saw her stepping into the eleva-tor. I raced across the corridor to stop it, pushing the door open at the last moment. I entered and stood right beside her. I turned to speak, but she touched my lips and gently whispered, "No words, there can be no words now." Touched by God(dess) for the first time, I fell quiet.

We got off the elevator in tandem, exiting the building into a large, open field. We walked for many minutes, in seeming silence. She was right. Words were unnecessary. Our hearts, they spoke.

When we reached the road, she turned and looked at me, her hand lightly touching my arm. She stayed like that for some time, tenderly stroking my wrist as if remembering something she had lost. Then she reached up and whimsically pulled my hat up and away from my face, gazing warmly into my eyes for yet another eternity.

And then it was enough. She didn't need to say it. It was time for her to go. I thought to kiss her, but, as if she was reading my thoughts, she touched my lips again and quietly said, "Not yet." I reached up to touch her face, but she shook her head 'no.' It wasn't unkind, it was simply clear. And then she turned and crossed the road without looking back. I thought to follow, but a quieter voice inside told me not to. I kept watching her until she vanished off in the distance.

## Deep Shit Love

I walked, then ran, back to my hotel room, completely oblivious to everything and everyone I passed on the way.

I lay down on my bed, anxiously feeling into an unfamiliar landscape. It was as though my inner world was re-organizing, adjusting to a radical shift in resonance. Stretched miles beyond my comfort zone, I searched inside for something to calm me. But there was no peace to be found. None at all. I lay awake until dusk met dawn, feeling into waves of emotion that transcended the familiar. Sometimes you meet someone whose light is so bright that you immediately realize how dim you have been. What a thing—to be catapulted to wonder simply by being in the presence of another. What a thing.

I got out of bed at 7 a.m. to look for her on the streets of Boulder. Wild-eyed and alight, I walked the town all morning, searching for a heart I felt I had known forever. I looked in the direction she had walked yesterday. I scanned coffeehouse tables, grocery store checkouts, bookstores. Surely she needs to read love poetry on this morning of all mornings!

At lunch, I perched myself on a tree beside Naropa University and lay in wait like a lonely dove, anticipating the return of his long-lost love-mate. Late afternoon, I walked back into town to look for her again. I searched well past dark without any luck.

On the way back to the hotel, I was overcome by dread. *What if I never see her again? Why didn't I ask her name? Why didn't I get her num-*

*ber? Why didn't I SPEAK to her, for heaven's sake? What was I thinking?*

I fell into an exhausted sleep—searching for your beloved is a tiring process. The next day, I woke up early and headed to the conference headquarters. Maybe they could tell me something. Maybe someone knew her? I walked into the main office, ready to lay down my charms in service of love. There was no one in the office other than a middle-aged woman with a particularly rigid quality.

"You may think this is a little crazy, but I fell in love, like deep shit love, with a fellow student the other day, and now I can't find her."

"How long you known her for?"

"Just an instant. She had blond hair, and smiling eyes."

"Ain't love, buddy—just infatuation."

This wasn't going to be easy. "What about love at first sight?"

"Crashes and burns."

"Always?"

"Guaranteed. You can take that advice all the way to the bank."

I went quiet. Love's battlefields are everywhere.

"Oh, and get a pre-nup signed, so they don't rob you blind."

"Yes, good advice."

I wasn't sure if I should hug this wounded woman or let her vent. Goodness, how do you describe God at first sight to someone utterly blinded by pain? I opted to let her vent. When she was done, we got back to the business at hand.

"So what is it you want from me? You think I can help you find her?"

"Yah, something like that," I said tentatively.

"All student information is confidential."

"Well, how about if I told you which class she…"

She cut me off, "Don't matter, I can't tell you her name."

I thought fast, or so I thought, "Are you a romantic at heart?"

"Not anymore," she snapped, forcefully slamming her book shut.

"Well if I could just talk to that previously romantic part of you for a moment. Maybe you could send an email to everyone who was in the class and provide my contact info?"

She just stared at me, like I was an idiot, "No can do, buddy. You're on your own."

"Yah, I know. How about if I give you a grand?"

"I'll pretend you didn't say that. What's your name?"

"Jehoshaphat... no, just call me madman, and leave it at that."

I left the building and sat down beside the river. Closing my eyes to meditate, seeking the inner peace that had eluded me for days. No such luck. I was too agitated, like I had been stopped right in the middle of lovemaking—though this cut much deeper. I tried to sidestep the feelings, but there was no way to float this love on a leaf down the river. It wanted to be embraced wholly, holy, soul-y. I had to keep looking.

I walked Boulder for hours, looking for her in the oddest of places. I thought I saw her at least six times, but never once in fact. Midday, I bumped into someone I had met at the conference. He thought he knew her—her name was Margot? He gave me the number of someone who knew Margot. I called her. Wrong woman. I felt like some two-bit detective, chasing down empty leads. But I couldn't stop looking, not with my heart so freshly opened.

I returned to the hotel room, discouraged and confused. Why would God grant me a glimpse of grace, only to yank it away before it could be savored? How does this serve my spiritual path? What cosmic clown busted this move?

I fell asleep briefly, until the phone rang. I reached for it, irrationally imagining it was her. It was Daniel, confirming that he was going to pick me up at Toronto's Pearson Airport the day after next. It was good to hear a grounding voice, the voice of reason: "Take it for what it was, a nice opening experience. If she was available, she wouldn't have left like that. More women will come. They always do. See you in a few."

I was actually comforted by his perspective, if only for a moment. Maybe this is how it works, we get little glimpses of God(dess) before she is fully revealed? We see her eyes, then her toes, then her belly, then her breasts, and then she arrives in complete form, but only when we are ready to embrace her. Perhaps I wasn't as ready as I imagined. Is anyone?

### Graffiti Mountain

I got up the next morning overcome with sadness. I decided to head for the Flatirons. Perhaps getting a little higher in altitude would shift my perspective.

Taking a cab to the edge of town, I asked the driver to let me out near a trailhead. After chastising me for not wearing hiking boots, she pulled up in front of a narrow path beside a small creek. "This is my favorite hike, stay to the left till the dip, then walk straight up. It's not for the faint of heart, but it's well worth the climb," she said with a detectable glint in her eye. Then she handed me her business card, "Just in case you get lonely later," smiled and drove slowly away.

Faint of heart? Was my heart faint? What was this messenger trying to tell me? I entered the trailhead. A few feet in, I spotted a handwritten sign hanging from a tree, marked "Insatiable Point." Does the universe not have a fine sense of humor?

As I hiked the trail, my pessimism deepened, darkened. I looked inside for an affirmation to support me, but there were none to be found. Where is my daily affirmation book when I need it?

I sat down by a river to gather myself. On one level, it all seemed so surreal. Gone in a heartbeat, she didn't even leave her name. Yet, on another level, it was as real as real gets. I had been with many women, and never experienced a knowing like this before. It superseded all evidence, all that could be seen, yet it felt entirely true. A new earth, one with its heart wide open.

As I stared at my solitary reflection in the water, tears formed in my eyes. Like a wild beast of prey who had forever hunted the impossible, I looked disturbed and disheveled. Was this my karmic plight, to wander this planet alone? Strung between the mantras of wishful thinking and surrender, I wondered: Do you wish for it so hard that it comes true, or do you just let it go and leave the universe to its own devices?

Again, yet again, how do we breathe love into reality?

I got back on the trail, determined to lighten my mood. I had looked hard and wide for her, and she was nowhere to be found. I got to the dip, and made the turn upward, climbing the mountain itself. The path was slippery from a rare night's rain, and it took all my focus to keep from falling. Mindfully, with measured steps, I made my way toward the peak of Insatiable Point. Halfway up, I felt something hit my arm. I looked down—a bird had shat on my shirt sleeve. Nice—a message from above?

When I arrived at the peak a few hours later, I lay down on Mother Earth to catch my breath. It had taken all my energy to get here, but my perspective had expanded. I got up and walked toward the edge of the cliff, looking out toward Boulder. A lone hawk circled just above, sketching his legacy in the sky.

I closed my eyes to meditate, but I couldn't get my mind off my unnamed beloved. The more I emptied my thoughts, the more her presence filled my innerspace. Breath within breath, my consciousness kept returning to those memories of connection. However fleeting, it had filled my cup of wonder. And I liked mine full.

After only a few minutes, my consciousness shifted towards a quiet scratching sound, perhaps a small animal burrowing in the dirt. I opened my eyes and the scratching suddenly stopped. I looked out over the valley. The hawk was now circling closer. I closed my eyes again. The sound returned, this time louder, nearer.

I stood up and moved toward it. It was coming from another rock formation, some fifty feet away. When I got to the edge, I looked down and saw nothing but large rocks. I started to climb down, carefully scaling the craggy edges. The noise was closer now. I soon spotted a small opening between two large boulders. The boulders were touching at the points, and there was a small crawlspace at the base. I found my way through it, and sat down on a large, flat rock on the other side. The scratching stopped.

After a few moments, I saw something move below. I lay down on my belly on the rock edge and looked down.

Just below me, standing on another flat rock, was she, the nameless *she* of my heart. At the peak of Insatiable Point, no less. She was standing back on the rock with something in her hand, staring intently at the cliff face before her. For a moment she vanished and the scratching returned. Then she came back into view and it stopped. Again and again, she vanished, then returned. What the fuck?

I thought to climb down to her, but waited and watched. As I watched, I noticed vivid changes to my inner landscape. A tornado was spinning in my diaphragm, a swirl of excitement and apprehension that shook me to the core. I was compelled to run toward and away from her in equal measure. My heart fluttered, my breath shallowed. Could I take all this in?

I heard a little voice inside whispering sweet somethings in my inner ear: *Go to her, go to her.* I ignored it, preferring the safety of voyeurism to the perils of real contact. But then I realized that it had been many minutes since I had last seen her. And there were no more scratching sounds. Flash of panic—oh no, not again! Hurriedly, I got up and scrambled down the rocks to where she had been standing. Sadly, she was gone, no doubt scampering down the steep trail off to the left.

Or did I make the whole thing up?

I looked at the cliff face. Everywhere, there was chalked graffiti scrawled on the rocks. Have I found a mad one? I looked closer:

Truth eyes

REAL-EYES

REALIZE,

ReMeMbRanCe

mUm

accept the invitation.

Right in the middle of the largest stone facing me were the words:

When two hearts beat in the same direction,
all gaps narrow.

She had clearly been working the language, because she had crossed out other possible endings: "the bridge appears," "the distance narrows," and something I couldn't quite read. I picked up a small piece of chalk from the ground, rubbed out her second sentence, and added my own ending. Finally, we were conversing again:

When two hearts beat in the same direction,
the meeting point is God

Then I scurried down the trail to find her. I moved quickly, falling twice on my ass in the steep sections. Reaching the bottom of the hill, I picked up the pace, jumping tree roots and fallen trees with reckless, heartfelt abandon. The sun was bright in the forest, patchy rays of light that made it difficult to gauge exactly where I was stepping. But I was on some kind of a mission. Mission Impossible?

### The Enchanted Forest

I stopped to catch my breath. In one way, I felt exhilarated. It was as though my body had sprouted wings of hope. At the same time, I berated myself. Here I was, chasing after love like an abandoned child. My childhood all over again. Does it have to be this difficult?

I got up to run the trail, but decided against it. I heard the gurgling sounds of the river, and cut through the forest toward it. I wasn't sure why, I just had to reach that river. I began to run again, this time at a more measured clip. A deer crossed just ahead of me, causing me to stumble. Walking, I soon located a clear trail to the river.

I saw her standing quietly by the river's edge. A cosmic missile to my heart.

I stared at her for a few moments, watching her watch the river float by. It was beautiful, a timeless perfect painting, almost too pristine to touch. And then I moved up beside her, gazing at our shared reflection in the river. She didn't move. Funny, I didn't look so wild with her standing beside me. Now and then the rippling waters distorted our images, making it difficult to distinguish where she ended and I began.

"What took you so long?" she suddenly asked.

"Got stuck in traffic. Wait, you knew I was coming?"

"You would make a bad stalker. Sooo obvious."

"You saw me? But then why did you leave?"

Softly smiling, she replied, "I don't like to be stalked. I like to be *met*."

"I met you the other day."

After a few moments, she turned to me and replied, "Too soon…"

I saw her physically for the first time: high cheekbones, wavy blond hair, and bright green eyes that sparkled of whimsy and wonder. She had an adorably cleft chin, light freckles on her cheeks and small crow's feet around her eyes, just like mine. She was small in stature—perhaps 5'2"—but with a powerful, dignified presence that made her seem taller. She looked wholesome and pure, but there was an edge to her too. I imagined her 23 years old, at most.

"Do you always write on rocks?" I asked.

"Often. I like to talk to nature. It listens."

"Isn't chalk bad for the environment?"

"Smart-ass, I use eco-friendly chalk. But what do you *really* want to know?"

"Really want to know?" I echoed.

"Below the smart retorts, how do you *really* want to relate with me right now?"

I was taken aback. She was calling me to a place below my defenses. Too soon.

"It's getting dark, shall we head back?" I suggested.

Sensing my discomfort, she let me off the hook. "Yes, let's go."

I followed her as she moved through the forest like a lithe and graceful animal. She walked close to the ground, avoiding trees and boulders, skirting the main trail. I could barely keep up. After only a few minutes, we cleared the forest and stepped on the main road. I reached for my cell phone to call a taxi, but she motioned me to put the phone away. "Let's walk, okay?" she said.

I walked beside her in silence. She walked lighter now, almost whimsically, bouncing a little off the ground. As we got closer to town, I was overcome by the surest sense of familiarity. *My God, I know this being, I know this essence.* And then it went deeper, as her arm against mine excavated our shared lineage: *Did I not tell you to turn left at the enchanted forest all those lifetimes ago? Why did you turn right? I've been wandering this world looking for you ever since.* I felt a deep relief, as though lifetimes of isolation had finally come to an end.

I wish I could say that it all seemed fantastical. But it wasn't like that at all. I had just entered an unmistakably deepened reality, one where the terms of engagement are beyond the grasp of the rational mind—one where the soul's journey is paramount, where essence isn't a concept but a felt experience.

And all of that from a thirty minute walk.

We arrived in town and sat down in a small park. With our toes in a creek, we shared some of the details of our lives. Her name was Sarah Lynn Harding. She was actually 26—ten years younger than me. Born in Rensselaer, Indiana, she moved with her parents to Boulder at the age of 2. The adopted only child of a welder and a tailor, her Dad had actually helped to construct the Morrow Point Dam, in Colorado.

A poetry major as an undergraduate, Sarah made her living as an aide in a nursing home with the elderly, until she could figure out her ultimate career path. She lived with her parents in their mountain home with two golden retrievers, Smokey and Bear. Her Catholic parents went to church every Sunday. She seldom went with them, preferring nature as her place of worship.

Not surprisingly, we loved and recited some of the same Rumi and Kabir poems. We were entranced by the same kinds of music: kirtan, devotional chants, rhythm and blues. We both loved impressionistic water colors and the surrealistic magic of Salvador Dali. We shared a love of camping and hiking. We even shared a passion for handicapping thoroughbred horse races, a hobby our fathers had both introduced us to. And it was so much more than that. Cut from the same soul cloth, our connection felt both transpersonal and deeply personal at the same time. We danced to the same heartbeat in the seen and unseen realms.

"Ten years difference, that's significant," I said, suddenly concerned she would find me too old.

"Stage not age, Lowen," she said matter-of-factly.

"But I'm at a different stage."

"Maybe... or maybe you're just delusional."

I laughed. "Why did you say 'too soon' about our first meeting?"

"Because we weren't ready."

"How do you know that?"

"Because I had something to clear first. And I felt you... I *feel* you."

"Am I ready now?"

"You'd better be, because I am, and I asked for this."

"I asked for it too. On my knees, in the forest, last year."

"Me too. On my knees, in the forest, last year."

"I saw this coming from a thousand miles away."

"Yes, *we* did."

Deep shit love.

We both reached in for a hug at the same time, melting into each other with great tenderness. Although silent, I could almost hear our souls conversing in the deep within.

After some time, Sarah got up and asked if I was free tomorrow. I answered yes, completely forgetting my flight home.

"Meet me here at 11 in the morning. I have somewhere to take you."

"Take me, you have already taken me," I mumbled.

"Corny, dude. Let's stay away from corny."

Not a chance.

Then she jumped up like a sprite and bounded down the trail lickety-split. As her image faded into dark, I was sure I heard a loud scream of delight. Was it coming from her... from me... or from God himself? Distinctions were becoming difficult to make.

Walking back to the hotel, I felt anxiety and ecstasy dancing through me in equal measure. As my joy increased, my fear intensified. Perhaps this is always the way it is when we have something precious to lose? The precarious nature of life reveals itself, reminding us to hold our treasures safe.

# 3
—

# Hearticulations

I got up after another sleepless night and postponed my flight to the next day. No choice. I walked down the path to our meeting point at exactly 11 a.m. She wasn't there. I panicked, remembering that I still didn't have any real information about her—no phone, no email, nothing. I started pacing, anxiously looking for her in every direction.

Suddenly, I heard a giggle emanating from above. I looked up to see Sarah sitting on a high branch of a large tree, her back pushed up against the thick trunk. Her smiling eyes immediately calmed me. She scaled down like a tree-climbing Olympian, a blue piece of chalk in her right hand.

"Talking to the trees again?" I remarked, in my usual sarcastic style.

"No, the chalk is for later. Let's go," she said, slightly annoyed. "My car is close by."

As we drove away from Boulder in her circa 1967 VW Beetle, I experienced yet another déjà vu, as though we had stumbled into the pre-written movie of our lives. I sat beside her in silence, completely sated. In her presence, the psychic locomotive slowed to a crawl, as a unified consciousness filled the space. The petty details fell away, the essentials emerged. Sarah was a mouthful, a handful, a dram of sweet metaphors. I already loved her completely.

## Rivers of Essence

We soon arrived at a place called Rocky Mountain National Park.

When we got out of the car, she headed straight for the brush, yet again. I followed her, scurrying tentatively over fallen trees and rough ground. There was no visible trail, but it didn't seem to matter. She knew where we were headed.

After a half hour, we opened to a wondrous valley. At its heart was a lively river, sparkling and churning between two rock formations. Spidery rock climbers scaled the jagged mountain across the way. After a few moments, she took off her shoes and ran down the hill toward the river. I took my shoes off and clumsily raced after her. She was fast, a spry little wood nymph with winged feet. Whenever I got close, she darted off in another direction, laughing joyfully. Just before the river, I caught up with her and we found our way to a large rock at the river's edge.

Sarah spoke: "This has always been a precious place for me. I come here to remember. I never came here with anyone. Until now." I looked into her eyes, not knowing quite what to say. I was never at a loss for words when I was talking about nothing, but heart-talk was an entirely different thing. I had yet to establish the resonance and groove.

The river raced by, as the sun's rays bounced off the water. I moved in to kiss her. Our lips brushed. She pulled back, tilting her head to the left. Then she furrowed her brow and looked square on into me, as though to say, "This moment should not be taken lightly. This little kiss is a BIG step."

"You know we don't need that. We're already there," she said.

"Need what?"

"The physical."

"But..."

"Desire gets in the way."

"But what about healthy desire?"

She was quiet for a moment, and then asked, "Does it ever stay healthy?" like someone whose youthfulness belied her wisdom.

I stepped back and looked right at her. With one gaze into her eyes, all words fell away. And it didn't matter at all. In this place of hearticulation, there was no need for words. This love spoke a language all its own, a grammarless lexicon of longing and union. Who needs syllables when you can hear each other's souls?

I moved toward her again. This time she met me. We stayed with our lips locked for minutes, plummeting deeper and deeper into love with every breath. Entranced by her divinity, my breath fell into alignment with hers, bridging our hearts across the dimensions. Profound love sensations coursed through me, stroking my armored heart back to life. I opened my eyes, and I saw that her eyes were opened too. It was the nature of this love to want to be seen.

This love didn't just transcend the details, it transformed them. The rock we stood on became an eternal bridge, erected for she and I alone, ushering us deeper into wonder with every kiss. The cold water that splashed against our ankles, the rivers of essence. The hands that touched my face with tenderness, the hands of divinity. The more time we spent together, the holier the world became. We had opened the door to a sacred universe. I felt both impenetrable and entirely exposed at the same time. Yet another undress rehearsal.

In the no-blink of an eye, I got it. Enlightenment isn't a head trip—it's a heart trip. Gusts of God blowing through the portal of the heart. We may want to enlighten through the safety of the mind, but the God-self lives in vulnerable places. As we dunked our hearts in the rivers of essence, everything became God. And God became everything. Holy moly!

After what felt like an eternity, we started to walk the trails. I looked at my watch. We had only been by the river for 30 minutes. So strange. Time lasts forever when you are actually in the moment.

"How do we hold this safe, Lowen?" Sarah wondered aloud.

The question struck me.

"What do you mean?" I inquired tentatively.

"Just being with you is enough. I feel so close to you already. Maybe if we keep it simple, we will avoid the upsets."

"But how do we keep it sim…"

Before I could finish my sentence, a red cardinal flew right past us, perilously close to Sarah's face.

Sarah became excited. Her eyes lit up like a child who had seen something beautiful for the first time. "Do you know what a cardinal represents, Lowen? They represent transformation. Pa used to study the birds. Red cardinals are a fiery symbol of change. Seeing them is a strong sign. One came close to me the day we met, too."

I couldn't help but wonder if it was the same one I saw.

She bounced like a tigger down the trail, before getting serious again.

"Perhaps we keep things chaste. Avoid the sexuality. Just being together is everything, yes?"

"Are you not attracted to me?" asked my ego.

She stopped dead in her tracks and turned to face me.

"My essence, my body want you fully, but this connection feels so pure. I just don't know if spirituality and sexuality can mix without getting spoiled. Maybe the saints are right."

I wanted to protest, but said nothing. Not because I didn't have an argument for her—I mean, surely sexuality can be a spiritual experience—but because a part of me resonated with her words. I could feel tremendous energy in the sexual field between us—expansive, but potentially explosive—so bloody hot to the touch. Too hot to the touch? The connection felt like a precious jewel. How to protect it from itself?

"Let's lie down on the ground, okay?" she suggested.

I nodded yes, as she steered us towards a small clearing between two large trees.

We lay down beside one another on a patch of long grass. Sarah wrapped her body around mine, her legs entwining mine like two trees with a unified root. We fell fast asleep on the valley floor, merging our energies with Mother Earth. Our first sleep together.

After a few hours, I was startled awake by strange, foreboding dreams. Sarah was sitting beside me, staring at me intently. I got the feeling she had been staring at me for some time. It was getting dark in the forest.

"You okay?" she asked.

"Wild dreams."

"Yah, me too. We bring up everything in each other."

"How do you mean?"

"I mean: the brighter the love, the darker the shadow."

"You *love*... me?"

She looked away, quietly speaking, "It seems too obvious for words."

Obvious or not, it felt good to hear it.

"Let's head out before it's too dark. I don't want you to get lost in the bush, city boy," she said with a mischievous smile.

As we drove back to Boulder, I heard from a whole boardroom of inner cynics. My defenses were much too sturdily constructed to evaporate this quickly. My rational self dropped down from the clouds to remind me that I don't actually know this woman: *This is way the hell out there, Lowen. You just met her—you need to get to know someone before you love them.*

I also heard from my warrior self, stoking my fear of failure with visions of career sabotage: *This connection threatens everything you have built. You need focus to build your practice. You need to hold yourself together. Don't let this derail your ambitions.*

My inner humorist had the final word, reminding me that the only way to see God at first sight was to be born in heaven. *God at first sight? You must be on LSD!*

Maybe I was—Love's Supreme Drug.

The cynics went quiet the moment I looked over at her. A tear tumbled softly down her cheek. I didn't need to ask why she was crying. I knew. Tears of joy. I reached over and stole her tear, putting it to my lips.

We stopped at a red light. She turned to look at me, eyes tender and moist. "I'm scared too," she said. The light turned green.

When we got back to Boulder, she pulled up in front of my hotel to drop me off.

"I'm leaving tomorrow. Will you come up?" I asked.

"I need to do a few things. Can I come back in an hour?"

"Of course, room 718."

I kissed her softly on the lips and got out of the car. She drove away right after I closed the car door, again triggering my fear that I would never see her again.

When I got to the room, the phone was ringing. It was Daniel, calling to make sure I was still alive. After hearing my voice, he inquired into my well-being, "You alright? You sound strange… not like you?"

His point was well taken. *Who am I* took on a whole different meaning in the heart of this love. Which *me* is real—the localized consciousness I have habitually called home, or the vaster terrain I was called to in her divine presence?

Our conversation ended with his version of wisdom: "Stay strong. She's just one chick, after all." As much as I wanted to whack him, a small part of me appreciated the reminder from the brotherhood. I had a feeling I would need to lean into him in the coming months.

## Touching the G(od) Spot

There was a knock on my door a few hours later. I opened the door and Sarah was standing there with a small bag in her hands.

"I brought my pj's, Lowen. Let's have a sleepover."

She threw the bag on the bed, and reached over to hug me. I stepped back from her, momentarily afraid to connect. She looked at me, puzzled. I quickly moved back in for the hug.

We soon found ourselves lying on the bed, facing one another with our eyes wide open. We lay there for hours, soul-gazing to our heart's content. Goodness Goddess, where have you been all my life? Where have you not been all my life? Were you not always right here, awaiting our cosmic re-embrace?

Late into the night, she asked me to touch her body. I felt suddenly shy, reluctant to see her. I stood up and turned off the light. She understood. This was the nature of the process: revealings, resistance, deeper revealings. I guess we still needed to keep something hidden.

I walked to the bottom of the bed, and undressed her with a tenderness I had never experienced with a woman. I didn't care at all about my own pleasure this night. I wanted only to worship this divinity. With great reverence, I began to touch her whole body. My usually selfish hands became tools of devotion, praying at the temple of her. The smell of her body comforted and ignited me—heaven scent. My fingertips became highly charged love-lights, hungrily searching for dark, hidden wonders to infuse with light. We fell asleep around sunrise, after many hours touching the G-od spot. I had no idea my hands could love another that deeply.

When Sarah woke me the next morning at 10, I realized I had missed my flight home. And I didn't care at all. I just felt ecstatic. A bridge of light was forming between our souls, as though a cadre of invisible angels were weaving it while we slept. Clearly, I had taken a different kind of flight home.

After we dressed to go, we lay back down on the bed one more time. I felt a strong desire to make love to her, but it almost felt redundant. It was amazing to me how intimate we were together, even with our clothes on.

She drove me to Denver airport to catch a later flight. On the way, a bright red family van pulled sharply in front of us, causing her to swerve to avoid hitting them. Their Ontario license plate read *Heart Unity*. We laughed. Where were we... Serendipity Central?

When we arrived at the airport, Sarah handed me a large hawk feather she had picked up on our first walk together, "To fly our hearts home to each other." I left the car pulsating with hope.

# 4

## The Yoniverse of Meaning

Even before my plane landed in Toronto, I could feel the world closing in on me. It's one thing to feel ecstatic on vacation in the mountains of Colorado, quite another to sustain it in the heart of an over-stimulated urban life. To drive the point home, the taxi I rode in from the airport had a fender bender with a garbage truck on the way into the city. Back to reality.

After two days at home, I was overcome with confusion. Immediately upon my return, I began an intense two week jury trial and found it incredibly difficult to keep my heart open in such an armored, hostile environment. If I was going to be an edgy warrior in the courtroom, I had to emotionally shut down some part of myself. If my opponent sensed even the slightest vulnerability in me, he pounced. In a way, it was like a war between worlds: the harsh world where most of humanity still lives, and the heartfelt world that awaits us. How to bridge the gap? Had I opened the heart-gate too early?

And, of course, it was more than the outer world alone. It was my inner world as well. My habitual range of emotion was much tighter at the seams than this startling love experience. Although I had laid the groundwork for deeper opening in my therapy, it was quite another thing to do it in real life. I understood the machinations of the marketplace, but love's mysteries were beyond my comprehension. I knew virtually nothing about soul-sourced intimacy.

As I moved through my days, I found myself retreating deeper into my shell, even wondering aloud to Daniel if I had simply lost my mind in Colorado. He was sure that I had. It all felt strangely unreal, even otherworldly. Like landing on a planet devoid of gravity. Where the hell is the ground?

At the same time, one serendipitous act after another eroded my resistance. When I pulled out of my driveway in a hurry one morning, a VW minivan with a Colorado license plate just missed hitting me. What's with this strange car-ma? And while sitting in my backyard, a red cardinal flew over and dropped a feather not six inches from my feet. Often I would think of Sarah and our favorite driving songs in Colorado would sing to me from the radio, sometimes two in succession.

I didn't have the audacity to think that all these reminders were intended for me. But… *were they*? Is there a complex universal framework that invites those who are opening to love to open further? Is it possible that our connection was being orchestrated by a Universal Broadcasting System with benevolent intentions? If so, where was this orchestration leading us?

I avoided Sarah's calls for a few days, until one afternoon she caught me at the office. Shit! I tried to keep it superficial, but she would have none of that.

"Where have you fled to, Lowen?" she asked directly.

I deflected, "Nowhere, just trying to get through my days."

"I can't feel you. Please speak from your heart…"

"Not sure where I left it, to be honest."

Long pause.

"You left your heart with me. I'm carrying it for us," she said softly.

Arrow to the heart. Shit.

She insisted on staying on the phone with me in silence until she could feel me. It worked—I slowly began to feel me, too. And then I could feel her. We were back on holy ground.

When I got home that day, I received a card from her with her words written in that familiar scrawl. Divine Timing…

When like the sudden wind
on the ocean,
the tides of life washed me ashore—

*you collected my heart among the remnants,*
*then breathed deeply*
*into all my quiet dreams.*

On the back, where one writes their return address, she had scrawled:

*You are my home. I am homeless in your absence.*

Say no more. Deep shit love. Try as I might, there was no turning back. Onward and upwards.

### Mount Hurricane

We planned a five-day camping trip in the Adirondack Mountains in New York State a few weeks later. Sarah would fly to New York and rent a car. I would drive down from Toronto.

On the way to meeting her, I was overwhelmed with fear. Same bullshit again. So frightened, like being called to a vast canvas with tiny brushes. My breath shallowed and my shoulders rose as though in response to an imminent threat. Is love a threat? At the same time, a wave of optimism was shaking me loose from the inside out. I was about to see her again, my beloved, and the thought made me tremble deliriously. It was all there, terror and enchantment and delight.

I pulled up to the meeting spot, a parking area at the base of Mount Hurricane near Lake Placid. Just after I got out of the car, she arrived. When I saw her, I stopped live in my tracks, quickened within, frozen in timeless. Instead of getting out of her rental car, she just sat there in her seat, staring deeply into my eyes. Penetrating me to the core. Again, yet again, the minutiae fell away, as our souls bridged across dimensions. Forged in ecstasy, there was only this wholeness, this majesty, this infusion of love breath.

When she at last got out of the car, she raced toward me and jumped into my arms, joyous and alight. She climbed onto my shoulders, facing me with her legs wrapped around my shoulders. I could smell the sweet fragrance of her yoni (Sacred Sanskrit term for 'vagina'), as it pushed up against me. I wanted to bury myself in it, to taste her from the inside out. Jumping down to the ground, she pulled me towards the forest, "Make love to me *now*, Lowen Cooper!"

I ran with her into the woods, down a small hill to a little thicket hidden from view. She leaned against a shaded tree and beckoned me close with her smiling eyes. As she undressed completely, I took my shirt off. We began to kiss ferociously, and I pushed up against her, lost in our shared resonance. But when she reached for my hardness, I pulled away, suddenly self-conscious—looking for a way out? She coaxed me back, kissing my chest, working her way down my stomach with her sweet kisses. And then I turned right off, losing my sexual charge. Still she kept kissing me, until I said the wrong thing.

"Suck my cock, baby..." I moaned.

Suddenly, the energy shifted and she stood back up and glared at me:

"Is that what I am to you, Lowen? Some cock-sucking baby? Is that your default position when love scares you—porn talk?"

"Yes, I suppose it is," I responded, embarrassed. "Sorry, I didn't mean that. Not sure what to say. I don't understand all of what I am feeling."

Loving Sarah really was like learning a new language, one I couldn't easily download into my archaic warrior system. I could persuasively articulate any concept, but to express my true feelings was an entirely different matter. When it became uncomfortable, I reflexively turned back to my caveman dictionary.

We dressed and walked back to the car in silence. After gathering our camping gear, we began to hike the trail. Not a single word was spoken for almost two hours, as we climbed Mount Hurricane in an uncomfortable silence.

When we reached the top, Sarah lay down on the ground and began to sob. Her body convulsed, like she was exorcising a long-embodied demon. I got down on the ground to hold her, but she put up her hand to boundary me. Backing off, I granted her the space she asked for.

After she calmed down, she quietly shared her piece, "I'm sorry, I have no compassion for that. I hate to be objectified, to be turned into a play thing. Especially by you." A final tear fell onto her cheek.

"I am so sorry, I'm just scared. I don't have a template for this. This love is beyond imagining."

"Yes, it is. Let's just be with that Lowen," she softly replied.

We pitched the tent and then sat together silently on the cliff edge. The sun was going down, its light softening to meet the darkness. Although it was quiet, I heard everything—our mutual heartbeat, my love-quickened breath, a symphony of ecstatic rhythms gliding through the air. This is what God must sound like.

In her presence, everything that happened before in my life seemed up-framed, held in a whole new context. My painful childhood, my foolish mistakes, my chaotic relationships, my many detours, all seemed like perfect teachings. Even my prior commitment to non-commitment was validated. I really did have preparatory commitments to honor: clearing the emotional debris that interfered with my capacity to partner, building the internal girders required to sustain a genuine commitment. Before I could really take someone inside, I had to carve a space for her, a canyon for her river of love to run through. It was all ready-making for this moment.

It was getting cold on the mountain. We crawled into the tent and tried to sleep. Impossible. There was too much longing. Although we needed to slow the physicality down, we couldn't contain the urge to meld. We got lost in a soothing cuddle-fest, holding one another breathily close, shaping against each other, trying to find the form that best reflected our love.

Cascading into oneness, our sexuality ignited. Sarah reached for my genitals, and I reached for hers. My heart opened wider, as I readied to penetrate her for the first time in this lifetime.

And then, suddenly, arose waves of terror, doom, a fear of death—if I crossed this line. Not physical death, but the death of the separate self. I wasn't ready. Poised before the temple door, I shrunk back.

This time, she was compassionate, holding me close, looking deeply into my eyes. I felt so seen, like she was seeing straight through my armor to the essential being quivering beneath. After some time, she closed her eyes and smiled. Then she opened her eyes and looked right at me again. And then, she closed them yet again, smiling.

"What are you doing, Sarah?"

"It's something I like to do with you, sweetness. I sync with your eyes then close my own to feel the radiance."

Ahhhhh.

Lying in her arms, I felt into my warrior resistance. I could feel him breathing down my neck, determined to keep me separate. For the first time in this incarnation, he wanted me flaccid. Better limp than vulnerable. In every way, this love was a threat to everything that held me safe on this planet. It demanded surrender and boundarylessness, when it had been vigilance and rigidity that had kept me alive. I had no template to stand in this heart-fire.

It is such an odd thing to embody armor and longing at the same time. On the outer plane, my musculature reflected my unyielding nature, but down below, a river of longing was pushing up against it, slowly softening its edges. Because this armor was fueled by so much more than conditioned masculinity—calcified from the hardened tears of a mad childhood—it was much more difficult to soften. I could feel myself shedding one thin layer of armor at a time, but would I get there in this lifetime? Could I truly bare myself before my beloved, or was half-hearted intimacy my best shot?

I awoke at dawn to a now familiar scratching sound. Sarah must be writing. Stumbling out of the tent, I wandered over to the cliff edge. Down a few dozen feet she stood, naked, writing on the cliff wall. It was like looking at the maker and his finest creation at the same time. The maker has the sweetest lower back curve. She looked up at me, smiling eyes in all their glory. I climbed down to join her. I turned to the cliff wall. The stone was covered in writing—she was on fire this morning.

I reached for the chalk. She put her hand up to stop me, "Write naked, or get your own chalk, city boy." Hippies! I shyly undressed, and she handed me a piece of chalk. Like two excited children, we turned to the wall and wrote together to our soul's content.

When we were done, we sat down and welcomed the day. I longed to touch her, but there was no need—I was already touching her. Reaching deep into her. And she into me. We sat in silence, enchanted by our shared divinity.

Sarah got up and climbed a tree at the cliff edge. Crawling out on the thickest branch, a naked purring lioness, she hung herself upside-down. A new yoga asana: Upside-down tree pose? It was a perfect reflection of my current experience. Everything I had identified as reality was being turned upside-down. Or was it now right-side up?

## OGDO

Raindrops started to fall. We packed up the tent, and began the hike back down the mountain. As we hiked the trails, prior incarnations rose into view, reminding us of the magic and the madness that is our story. Hand in hand, heart in heart, we were called back in time, excavating our shared karmic lineage from the cells of our being—the enlivened beginnings, the seamless mergings, the harsh fall-aways. There was no question—this was not our first lifetime together. Our souls had danced together before.

As we moved through the days, we continued to deepen our recognition of one another. We were together for the first time in this lifetime, and yet we both somehow knew that this moment would come all along. We shared a quiet sense of each other that transcended language. In looking at one another, we gazed at our own reflection. Whatever the manifest differences, they were transient, temporal, surface. At the place of essence, no difference.

It is such a profound relief when great love comes your way after years, lifetimes, without it. In Sarah's presence, prior connections were revealed for what they were—necessary rungs on the ladder of wholeness, leading to the true destination. Every prior involvement could now be seen in its futility, in its sobering limitations. At some level, in all the various stages of my development, I was always weaving a nest for this love. All those times I had projected love onto strangers, chased them down on the street to say "hello," left notes on their bikes, were revealed for what they were—a search for what I had lost so very long ago. It was always a quest for Sarah. And now, as my heart opened, her spirit re-entered, returning us to our rightful inheritance. The One-nest. Our eternal stomping ground.

At the same time, an air of danger enshrouded us. I didn't know if it was mine, ours, or humanity's, but it was palpable. I felt it very strongly one morning while we were washing each other in the shower. It was only a quick flash, but there was an instant when I thought I saw the path ahead of us. I saw a merging so remarkable that it opened a portal to an entirely different level of consciousness. And I saw a darkness looming within and beyond it, as though foreshadowing its impossibility. Was this love-dance all pre-encoded, both the meeting and the farewell, the hello and the goodbye? Or was my childhood trauma again projecting its worst imaginings?

That afternoon, our light shone through. We were sitting at the back of a quaint French restaurant, waiting to order dessert after a wonderful Pain Perdu lunch. Sarah was sharing stories from her adventurous early life in the Flatirons. I was listening closely, but even more, enjoying her endearing idiosyncrasies: the freckles that sprinkled her nose like a constellation of stars, the sparkle in her eyes when she spoke about her chess champion grandfather, the excited tenor in her voice when she shared her great love for poetry.

From the outside, it looked like any mundane moment in a life. A simple meal, a series of stories, a moment's pause from the midday heat. But it wasn't. Because we weren't alone. God was sitting with us at the table, communing with us, encompassing us in his resplendent glow. I could feel him close at heart, like a friend who never leaves, a devoted guide who ferries us from one incarnation to another, ushering us along love's corridors. I was under no delusion that he appeared for us, and us alone. God is always at the table. It is the love that reveals him.

Sarah noticed something, too. "Do you feel something near us?" she asked.

"Yes, God is here," I replied matter-of-factly.

"Oh God, you are delusional," she replied, just as matter-of-factly.

"Yes, but..."

She scrunched her nose with delight. "I have a new nickname for you. Your nickname is now OGDO."

"How do you spell that?" I asked.

"O-G-D-O, and do you want to know what it stands for?"

"Not sure that I do."

"Well, it stands for, are you ready... Oh Great Deluded One," she said with a cackle, clearly pleased with her linguistic ingenuity.

"You're not going to write that on a wall are you?"

She smiled softly, and reached for my hand.

"Yes, but... you are right. God *is* here, OGDO. For reals."

My turn to deflect, "Shall we order him dessert?" I asked with a smile.

"I'm sure he has already eaten."

"Angel food cake?"

"Cute. No, I see him as more of a Crème Brulee type."

"Yes, that feels right. It has that heavenly quality."

That heavenly quality. When two hearts touch, the heavens open.

We ordered a Crème Brulee for God and his two love-struck devotees. Before it arrived, Sarah leaned over and whispered in my ear, "IU, OGDO."

"IU, Sarah?"

"Yes, I love you implies a gap. There isn't one, OGDO. IU..."

After dessert arrived, Sarah motioned for me to take the first bite. I did, and she leaned in to kiss my Brulee soaked lips, "Mmmmmm, actually I think OGDO means O' Great Delicious One. That's you. Creamy and perfect." It was all I could do to contain my impulse to jump on top of her. Instead, we settled in for a long delicious kiss, the kind that even public kissers would find embarrassingly steamy.

## A Truly Happy Ending

That evening, the soulevator finally arrived back at the ground floor. We were walking back to our motel, when I noticed Sarah drifting away. Ever-vigilant, I asked her what was wrong.

"Nothing wrong, I'm just worried," she replied, her lower lip quivering.

"Worried, why, my dear?" I inquired gently.

"This love. I hope that I can hold it safe."

I was too caught up in the love swirl to fully grok the meaning of this, but I knew enough to ask, "Why do you doubt it?"

"I feel like I lose myself in you. Am I strong enough for that? Not sure sometimes."

"But you don't need to be strong alone. We find our strength together."

"Yes, but I just feel so young."

Her voice became softer, slightly trembling, "...and this love feels so old."

Then she broke away from me, cutting down an alley as though fleeing a crime scene. I followed her until she suddenly stopped and turned to face me, staring at me with frightened eyes. I asked her to tell me what she was feeling. She glared in silence. The silence catapulted me into a terror of my own: can we die this fast? She pulled a piece of chalk from her bag, and wrote this on the alley wall:

How to hold love safe?

She reached over to hug me and we cried together for a very long time. Sobbing, heaving, we released eons of emotional holdings. How could we hold this many tears? And whose tears were these anyway? Clearly, we had entered a new dimension, one that did not subscribe to traditional emotional parameters and relational expectations; one so energetically charged that it would demand everything of us. Like artistic expression, it was ecstatic, chaotic, and ever-morphing. There was no question. We were in for a challenging creative process. But there was nowhere else I would rather be.

When we awoke in the morning, the heaviness was gone. Sarah was lying beside me, staring at me in that way she did when she had been looking at me for hours. I jumped on in, gazing into her eyes, traveling back and forth on our bridge across forever. She moved a little closer and began to stroke my face with her hand. Oh, how I loved those long, nimble fingers. Then she reached down and stroked my chest, lighting my heart aflame. The fire spread to my loins, where an erection of eager proportions rose into view. This erection wasn't like my usual hard-ons, inspired by external stimuli. This one was ignited from the inside out. A heart-on.

I lay back on the bed and she gave me a long and beautiful heart-job, touching me with the perfect balance of tenderness and tension, repeatedly bringing me close to the peak, before backing me off for another ascent. My face remained buried under her still arm throughout, happily smelling her sweaty perfection. Then, when the moment was just right, my throbbing essence erupted into rapture. I had never experienced such a sacred, triumphant release. The heart-genital highway was finally open for travel! A truly happy ending.

Before parting, we took our final shower together. Sarah got out early to call her family, while I let the water run over my head, drowning my imminent sorrow. How to return to the armored world after another taste of eternity?

As we made the long drive back to my car, it felt like a funeral procession, morbid and haunting. How do you part from your own heart without dying?

We pulled into the lot and sat in silence. I clutched on to her hand for a very long time. We got out of the car to hug goodbye. Hugging wasn't enough. We walked down the hill to the same thicket where we first began our trip together. This time it was different. So much had transpired in these past days together. We were now being nourished from the same root.

She leaned up against a wide oak tree while we kissed ferociously. Kissing wasn't enough. I needed to imbibe her fully, so her honeyed life force could sustain me during our time apart. I lowered her pants and began to worship her with my tongue. This wasn't oral sex as I had known it. Sparks of aliveness ignited inside me as my heart opened wider with every taste. She was the perfect elicksir for my love-starved soul.

In the heart of the worship, I had a profound realization. As my lips merged with hers, I felt the presence of the Godself rising up to meet me. Outside the portal of connection, I couldn't quite see it. But here, in the moistical membrane of co-creation, he was heartfully revealed. God wasn't up there, on a pogo stick to the stars. God was right here, in the heart of the yoniverse. Here was the proof that God exists. Here was the treasure I had sought. The yoniverse of meaning was before me.

# 5

—

# Growing Edge

Driving home, I felt like an escorted soul, cradled in the safe arms of Providence. With my third eye opened wide I saw the divine mother revealing her splendor everywhere. I looked to my left and saw a field of brilliantly pink, effulgent flowers, opening their sweetness to the world. Through the open car window, a soft heavenly fragrance greeted me. Up ahead, a sparklingly radiant sky. To the right, a flowing river of wonder. All of it here to show me, in vivid color, the intimate, sensual universe waiting on the other side of perfect love. I would never have noticed in my usual *here now*. Love's immaculate perception.

When I arrived home, I took a long nap. I wanted to dream Sarah back into my arms. After I woke up, I unpacked my bag. There, between two smelly t-shirts, was a small pink envelope with OGDO on it. In it, she had written only this:

*You are me inside I am you.*

A few days later, I retreated again. Like a turtle, I needed to go inside and integrate this startling heart opening before I could step out still further. Each time we met, I experienced a radical dissolution of my usual framework of perception. As I shed one self-sense, another way of being stepped up to take its place. It was like I was dissolving and re-forming at the same time.

Who was this man, now?

And, now…?

At the end of the work week, I turned off my phone and drove to the forest for the weekend. I needed some alone time to reconnect with my center. While hiking in the woods, my cynicism took over again. I thought of the geographical distance, the religious differences, the age gap, our shared tendency towards solitude. Surely there was too much against us?

It was all I could do to resist my desire to take the first off-ramp. The monkey mind clicked into gear: *Do I really need partnership? Who says we need a partner to be whole? Isn't wholeness found within?* On and on it chattered, comparing path choices. Truth be told, I was frightened beyond measure. The connection beckoned me toward a formlessness beyond my reckoning. Yet the unknown had always led to disappointment. How to trust the mystery when it has never proven kind or generous? Why surrender to emptiness when it has always been consistently painful?

At the same time, I was tired of looking at my isolated reflection in the mirror, tired of being alone in pictures, tired of walking alone in the forest, tired of the isolated lair of the lone wolf warrior. How many lives had my warrior soul sat alone at the riverbank? How many centuries had I avoided the path of the heart? How many lifetimes had I put self-protection ahead of soul-connection? In my efforts to avoid humanity, I had surely averted my own humanness.

Now felt like time. I had journeyed intensively on my own. I had worked hard on myself for years. And I knew, whether my fear-body liked it or not, that there were aspects of myself, hidden treasures, that could only be brought forth through a depthful relationship with another. I think they call this "the growing edge." But was this blade too sharp?

Just before coming home, I walked back to the rambling brook to meditate on the connection. Sitting beside the sacred place where I had first asked for this love, I wondered: *Had love really hunted me down, or was I just a wishful thinker? Maybe I truly was the great deluded one?*

Still not much of a meditator, I was distracted by a high-pitched chirping sound that wouldn't let up. I looked up and only a few feet from me was a bright red male cardinal sitting on a cedar branch singing his body electric, eyeing my bag of trail mix with fervent desire. He kept chirping his mantra, as though communicating an imperative message. A birdsong with my name on it?

What's with the fucking cardinals?

## Meta-dating

Before returning to my apartment, I went to meet Daniel for Dim Sum in Chinatown. We have a long standing tradition of discussing life over dumplings and noodles. To get a sense of Daniel, imagine a stocky panda bear. Now add a pair of very thick glasses—thick like the bottom of a pop bottle. Now redden his hair, and brush some of it forward. Now add a kippah (a Jewish skullcap), and a small gold stud to his left ear and make him unstoppably cuddly. Oh, and magnetic blue eyes. That's Daniel.

When I got there, his head was buried in yet another Eastern spirituality book.

"Good to see you Danny," I said as I kissed his forehead and sat down in front of him. "How are you?"

Without looking up, he replied, "Neither good nor bad—just here."

"Oh good, detaching from your wound-body again, are you?" I replied sarcastically.

He put the book off to the side and looked me square in the face. "It's better than activating it, my friend. Much much better."

The showdown had begun.

I replied sharply, "It's always active, my friend. Transcending it doesn't make it go away. Doesn't heal it either. Just comes back later and bites you in the ass."

When I first met Daniel in law school, he was a passionate love seeker. If he wasn't in a relationship with someone he called "the one," he was sure he had just spotted her. And then he met Hannah—a woman that he loved so deeply he would have given his life for her. Two orthodox Jews madly in love, we were sure they would get married and raise a beautiful family. But then she left him on his 26th birthday to "explore other possibilities." Three weeks later, she died in a scuba diving accident in Belize. Perhaps to manage the pain, perhaps to find an answer, he became a spiritual seeker, focusing on various Eastern perspectives. Lately, his focus was on detaching from emotional pain. He was desperate to find the moment, while sidestepping his unresolved wounds.

"Non-duality requires a more expanded consciousness, Lowen. Less ego more…"

I cut him off, "No, not less ego, Daniel. Less unhealthy ego. Listen, you can't call it a unified field of awareness if you remove everything uncomfortable from the moment: the ego, your body, your unresolved pain, your personal identifications. That's not expanded consciousness, buddy. That's dissociation."

"Quite a soliloquy, but let's look at the facts. You spent the last few days tormented by your latest love relationship, right? I spent the last month unperturbed by anything."

"Like a robot."

Clearly agitated, he shot back, "You are pissing me off."

"Wound-body awakens. That was quick!" I replied.

He went quiet and took his glasses off to clean them—a habit that signaled he was feeling uncomfortable. This dialogue was hitting a nerve.

"Just let her go. It's too intense. What's the point? You're just gonna crash and burn," he said with great certainty.

We sat and slurped our noodles in silence for some time. Although he was annoying me, I also felt grateful for his impeccably timed message. In a way, he was the perfect reflection at the right time, representing the part of me that wanted to detach from Sarah; that wanted to find nirvana without risking loss; that wanted to find my answers in concepts rather than feelings. He was the wounded part of me that was still chirping in my inner ear, trying to convince me to give up on love as path. He was the isolationist part that wanted to make God a fleshless head trip. It was good to see myself from the outside.

I thought of Sarah in those last moments just before we parted in the mountains. The way the sun danced on her face, the way her smiling eyes sparkled, the softness of her hand in mine. Only once in an eternity does God launch this kind of heart rocket. How could I turn away?

I suddenly felt compassion for my friend, struggling as he was to find his faith in love after such a tremendous loss.

"Right now you can't relate but you will again, Danny," I said softly.

He replied, much less confident in his position, "I get there meditating."

"Yah, me too," I replied. "Meta-dating, there's just something about the effect of two destined hearts merging that deepens the meditation experience."

He quickly responded, "It's destined to fail," with a shaky voice, failing miserably at sounding firm.

I wanted to challenge him again, but I looked up and noticed a tear in his eye. There was suddenly nothing to debate. He was doing his best to manage his pain. I was doing my best to believe in love. To each their journey.

When I got home, there were flowers waiting at my door from Sarah. In the heart of the most radiant sunflowers I have ever seen, was another card. This one said it all:

```
     Love of my life, I remember us.
  We fell once then climbed a mighty summit.
   Clinging together, our hearts sharing a
    new pulse, our seams woven and knitted
   closely, we tumbled together down a grassy
         hill, staining our hearts with
           one another's love pledges.


    I remember you. I loved you a thousand
   times before—your sweet fire still burns
  inside my breast. I'll love you a thousand
        times more. Eternity prompts me
          to join your love with mine.
```

Like a hot arrow to the heart, I was immediately felled. Rendered completely vulnerable, open and raw. If I had any remaining doubts, they were instantly erased. No sense resisting reality. She is my calling.

# 6

—

# V-Passiona Meditation

Sarah wanted us to go on another trip together. From a practical perspective, it was entirely inconvenient. She had the perfect working life: three weeks on, and one week off. But I didn't. I had a locked-in litigation practice, with endless details and obligations. And I was already behind on my work.

Nonetheless, I had no choice but to go. I rearranged a series of appointments, passed a drunk driving trial to an associate, and somehow made it happen. For this moment at least, my soul was calling the shots.

Two weeks later, we met at the Ascension Institute, a holistic retreat center in New York's Adirondack Mountains for a 3-day Vipassana meditation workshop.

Or so we thought.

### No-Entry Trauma

Sarah was late. Instead of waiting for her, I went for a long walk around the grounds, finally landing at the beach where a small gathering of drummers and dancers were jamming in the sun. They had just ended an African music workshop and were joyfully charged. So much fluidity and freedom in their energy, in their movements, in their eyes. Much to my surprise, my body began to move effortlessly. At first I danced alone under a large maple tree, and then found myself drawn into the circle as their infectious warmth pulled me closer. I had always felt uncomfortable dancing in public, but today I danced without self-consciousness.

And then I felt her. I didn't see her, but I felt her. My spirit soared with excitement. I kept dancing, as the drummers intensified their beat. Soon the beach was filled with dancing fools everywhere. I moved into the center of the crowd, lost in a swirl of hips and toes. And then, I felt her right behind me. I turned, and there she was—her vibrant green eyes looking right through me, her sun-freckled face crunched into a warm, playful smile. We stared at each other for some time, as the world around us fell away. With our eyes in perma-lock, we merged with the divine, yet again. Soul-gazing, the *real* contact lens.

She reached for me, pulling me close. Her body felt delicate against my firm frame, as love shaped our forms into one, lost in our own private soul-o dance. We danced like we had danced together forever, tripping the love fantastic. I soon became the center that she orbited, turning her about like a whirling dervish. Every time she passed my left ear, she would whisper 'I love you.' *I love you*, spin, *I love you*, spin, *I love you*... I was dizzy with delight.

After hours of celebration, the drummers ran out of steam. Good thing, I was parched. After getting some coconut water at the café, Sarah took my hand and led me into the nearby forest. As we walked, our experience of love blossomed outward. I had often wondered how a single human heart could hold great love—it is so tiny, and love so vast. The answer is simple: it doesn't. It spills over. It becomes the everything.

That night, we had a beautiful, quiet dinner at the café: organic salad, angel hair pasta, soul-gazing for dessert. As we often did when we shared food, we nestled together on the same side of the table. As we ate, I had visions of us as parents, raising two raucous children, living in a small mountain home, simple and happy. I also saw us working together one day, teaching a new paradigm of relationship consciousness to a starving world. These visions felt deeply resonant, like strands of knowing encoded in my DNA. We were exactly where we were supposed to be.

After dinner, we went outside and sat at the edge of the lake, brightly lit by the full moon. I could feel my anxiety building as the pristine evening set the stage for intimacy.

Returning to the cabin, we undressed. As we began to heartily explore one another, I became intensely excited. Her body ignited my longing like nothing before: the exquisite curve of her ample breasts, her soft luscious lips, her mystery canyon with all its tender blessings.

At the same time, I was still sexually reluctant. I could touch her forever, but when it came to intercourse, I couldn't bring my heart and genitals together. Every time I came close, I hastily retreated. Amour or armor? I kept choosing the latter. Merging with her felt like a huge step, an irreversible transition from *me*-consciousness to *we*-consciousness. It was crossing a huge threshold. There would really be no turning back.

After a few moments of foreplay, I lost my sexual charge entirely. Damn warrior—he just couldn't surrender. And then I went reactive. I got out of the bed and cross-examined her about a woman she had dated years before: "Are you sure you don't prefer women to men? How do I know you won't leave me for a woman? Would you prefer it if I had a pussy?" Typical man covering up his feelings of inadequacy by taking it out on the woman he loves. But she wasn't biting. After answering the first wave of questions, she just looked at me, softly, and said, "You can't hide from us forever, Lowen Cooper. It's just a matter of time." Damn woman!

Frustrated and embarrassed, I grabbed a blanket and pillow from the closet and made myself uncomfortable on the cabin floor. Sarah fell fast asleep on the bed, while I lay awake until dawn, interfacing with my demons.

### A Root Awakening

When I woke up, Sarah was gone but there was a carefully prepared fruit and yogurt breakfast waiting for me on the bed. And a little note, hand written on a small piece of white cedar:

I want to hold your heart.
Heart it over.

53

My schmaltzy wordsmith.

We spent the day apart. Sarah went to the meditation workshop, while I hung out in the forest, negotiating with my fear. We already knew that real closeness wasn't my strong suit. Lost in the morass of primal triggers, it was all I could do to stay in the room. Yet I wanted to open, I *really* did. I wanted to taste this love whole. But how to unravel these imprints embedded in my psyche? Trapped between a cock and a heart place, I didn't know how to bridge them.

There are two forms of courage in this world. One demands that we jump into action with our armor on. The other demands that we strip ourselves bare naked and surrender. I was an expert at the wrong form. I had always assumed that courage on the battlefield was the greatest achievement. Until now.

That night, we went to a concert in the main hall. A troupe of monks were sounding with beautiful Tibetan healing bowls. As I listened, I felt a strong vibration moving through me. I felt space opening up inside, as though the sonic waves were chiseling away at my emotional blocks. I also felt its opposite—the fearful, shrinking small-self expert at sabotage, clinging to what it knows.

Sarah leaned toward me, insisting on connecting deeper. Go(o)d timing. We fell quiet and gazed into each other's eyes for a long time, while the chant built to an ecstatic frenzy around us. Goodness Goddess, whose eyes are these, anyway? My mind tap turned off. I felt myself slowly submitting. My heart opened wider. Our love was a truth serum that had to be drunk.

A few minutes later, she tussled my hair and whispered in my ear, "I'm going to the meditation Sanctuary. Come if you want, or I'll meet you back at the room later." I could see her hard nipples pressed up against her blouse. She kissed me with a fierce tenderness and left.

Right after she was gone, I heard a quiet voice inside say:

*You're either in, or you're out. No more stories, no more sidestepping, escape hatches, veiled retreats. You're either in, or you're out.*

My inner warrior was actually challenging me to choose a path.

Hercules or *Heartcules?* Goliath, or *Go-lie-with?* Who you gonna be, tough guy?

A few minutes later, I made the long walk up the hill to the meditation temple in the dark. I didn't want to be without her. The stars were bright tonight, lighting my way, the perfect flashlight to my beloved. As I set foot on the cedar deck, I stopped for a moment to listen to the water trickling into the deck pond. Such a peaceful invitation to soften.

I left my shoes beside the door and entered. Inside, there were dozens of empty meditation back-jacks organized in rows. Sarah wasn't here yet. I sat on a back-jack in the back row and closed my eyes to meditate. My breath deepened, as I searched for a mantra to center me. After a few minutes of jittery contemplation, I heard the door creak open. The room came alive. Sarah had entered. Rain began to pound on the temple roof.

I tried to meditate, but it felt avoidant, preposterous, unnecessary. The proverbial leaves kept floating back into consciousness with her juicy body on them. Who needs mantra when God is already in the room? There was only one mantra I wanted and her name was Sarah. Detachment was one path home. Selective attachment was another.

After some time, she coughed and my longing rose to the rafters of consciousness. Be still, my surging heart. I opened my eyes, and saw her sitting two rows ahead of me, back-jack reversed, staring deeply into me with her smiling eyes aflame. We looked into each other's eyes for yet another eternity as shards of love-light merged into the perfect mirror in our shared heart. At each stage of in-to-me-see, new universes rose into view, as though birthed into being by our love alone. The next undress rehearsal. How many more until we were truly bare?

I felt my soul yearning to merge with her, stretching at the seams. The yearning first took root in my heart—a heart-on of momentous dimensions—and then spilled over to my genitals. Soon enough, my desire flooded me and demanded expression. It wasn't enough to heart-gaze with my beloved. I had to merge with this Goddass, or risk internal dam-nation. Block it, or express it. It was time to express it.

Without any effort at containment, I hurtled over the back-jacks and pounced on top of her. In a soulbeat, we were undressed and writhing madly on the temple floor. The Buddha was aghast, as we attached, desired and clung our way to God. The rain intensified, and flashes of well-timed lightning lit up the temple—her temple, too. It was *all* a temple now.

I surrendered to a sexuality that was different than anything before. Suddenly my genitals were a pipeline to divinity, my whole body a conduit to the cosmos. My usual lovemaking had no place here. Love was the turn-on, at last! There was so much love that I had to cry, moistening our sex with tears of gratitude. Oh the heart, the heart.

As we moved together, we became a divine invocation to the Godself, a prayerful homage to the love-soaked wellspring that sources the all. Had a team of monks stormed in on us, we would surely not have noticed them. Tonight, lovemaking was the loom that wove our spirits into one. With every rhythmic thrust, we smashed through the veneer between our hearts and the universal heart. We moved together until there was no felt distinction between our bodies. Her pleasure was my pleasure, my arms hers, her breasts mine. We became one unified body-being, crossing the gender bridge with every breath. I was touching she who was me who was God. This was *our* body.

At some point, I felt a need to speak the love poem that was us, but my mouth was busily lost in hers. The writer within made his way down to my root chakra and I began to write my love inside her, dipping my pen-is in her liquid well of wonder, inking heartspeak all over her inner walls… *Beloved, Grateful, IU.* I felt my hips take to the task, a true poetry in motion, spelling out this love with perfect penmanship. She received my poem with a heaving hunger, her love walls tightening their grasp, then loosening at just the right moments, as though our love sonnet had been pre-choreographed by the divine. This was the highest form of expression—God's cosmic heart graffiti. I wrote one love poem after another inside her, until I had nothing left to say. After a wondrous orgasm, we fell deep asleep on the temple floor.

We got up with the sunrise, stirred to awaken by the sacred chiming of monk's bells outside. We looked at each other aghast and scrambled to put our clothes back on. Just as we opened the temple door, a group of resident monks entered the Sanctuary for their morning prayers. Divine Timing. Sarah and I smiled at them, and they smiled at us, as we walked past. I could have sworn the head monk gave me a knowing nod. Everyone prays in their own sweet way.

We found our way back to the cabin. Before falling back to sleep, we wove yet another tapestry of love. With hearts weaving and hips heaving, the soulfire ignited the heartfire ignited the rootfire time and time again. It was like we were co-creating a new form of meditation, one where our impassioned lovemaking was a portal to everything divine: *V-passiona* meditation.

Afterwards we lay startled, awe-struck. We could only say "perfect," because it truly was. Holding Sarah's hand was like holding God in the palm of my hand. It was wordless, but it said everything perfectly. Even if we wanted to move, where would we go? We were already everywhere. It was as true a thing as I could ever imagine.

One person will come to divinity while sitting alone in a temple. Another will find it in the arms of his beloved, lying side by side, hand in hand, in a little cabin in the woods. Grateful and Gracious—in the arms of God.

## IU

I left the room before Sarah woke up, wandering the grounds with my heart on my sleeve, her spirit held close. I felt like a remarkably different person from the one who had walked alone the day before. The conditioned male warrior who had ruled my consciousness was nowhere to be found, melted into oneness by love's transformative medicine. The change was manifest throughout my body. There was a liquidity to my movements, a beautifully bearable lightness of being. Oh my, armor weighs so much more than magic.

What a journey this had been already. Within seconds of our first sighting, I had entered a startlingly new landscape, a karmic boot camp of such fervor and ferocity that I could not help but be transformed. By the time we spent our first full day together, I had already changed forms countless times over, shaped and re-shaped in love's cosmic kiln. And now, in the heart of our first complete lovemaking,

I was catapulted to yet another dimension, one where unseen universes rose into view, revealing their sacred fruits. It was as if we had entered a great temple together, with our intimacy as the master key. Now I knew how to answer when asked what my favorite sexual position is: LOVE is my favorite sexual position.

Most startling was the quietude of my mind. Love had put my big brain to sleep and revealed its true purpose as servant to the great master: the love-oxygenated heart. What a realization. The way to calm the monkey mind is to open the human heart. I had spent so much time looking for peace outside of my own heart, but it wasn't out there. It was within the heart itself, with love as the magic codebreaker. How very simple it actually is—open the gateway to the heart and peace enters.

As I wandered, I marveled at how genderless I felt, almost as though I had entered a gender-inclusive or trans-gender dimension. Together, our energies had bridged us into something higher, more whole, holier. Although it was sexual union that took us there, the chemistry wasn't gender sourced, nor was the state we entered gender identified. What got us there was the merging of our twin souls along the heart-genital highway. They wanted only one thing: to merge with their other half.

It struck me that those who condemn another's sexual orientation merely reveal the absence of depthfulness in their own sexual lives. Because when you have had the highest form of sexual experience—one that is soul-sourced and heart-driven—you immediately recognize that gender is entirely irrelevant. The soul doesn't care about body parts. It simply loves who it loves.

Through the eyes of essence, I saw gender for what it is: a way station on the karmic quest for wholeness. Perhaps this is what it means to be trans-gender, in the ultimate sense? You identify with gender until you are ready to transcend it. When you enter great love's door, you enter an entirely different dimension. The ultimate form is polyphrenic, an inclusive embracing of all archetypes and energies. The perfectly blended juice of divinity. Drink from love and see as God sees.

I floated back to the cabin to find Sarah. Opening the door, I saw her lying there, eyes wide open. Her hair was lovemaking messy, her juicy left breast deliciously exposed. I entered and lay down beside her, hungry to merge. But as I reached my hand over to hold hers, she pulled it back sharply and turned her head away.

"You okay?" I asked.

Silence.

"Did something happen?"

Silence.

"Sarah…"

She softly replied, "Scared, Lowen."

"What of?"

Turning to face me, she said, "Too many doors feel open. I don't feel safe. I don't feel like myself. How can we live this open in this world?"

"With our hands together." I reached to hold her hand again. It was freezing cold.

"I don't trust you," she said, turning away again.

"Why?" I patiently replied.

"Because you have been with so many women."

"You have been with more men."

"It's different."

"How so?"

"I loved all those men. You didn't love all those women."

Now I was pissed off. As if!

"And that's supposed to make me feel safer. You loved over 30 men by the time you were 26!" I shot back.

She leapt out from under the blanket and stormed out of the room rapid-fire, but not before expressing a clearly articulated "Fuck-you!"

Woah, that was fast, bipolar, startling. After such intimate merging, how could this happen? Holy shit! Must be the way a duck feels when it is shot from the sky. I lay there, sweating in the noonday heat, burning with confusion. My heart felt pierced, overcome with blindness after a morning of deep seeing. Is this the nature of great spiritual openings? They are followed by harsh closings? You soar together on the wings of a love, only to plummet to earth in shards moments later? Is that the deal—ecstatic sky, or thorny earth? Where's the dependable middle ground?

I remembered Sarah's own words, "The brighter the love, the darker the shadow." Is this why great love never lasts? It brings our unhealed wounds so blisteringly to the surface that we can no longer see one another clearly? I had managed to keep my abandonment wound in check for months, but now hers had erupted to the surface to awaken mine. Perhaps a love that stirs—but doesn't shake—is all we humans can sustain at this stage of our evolution? How to swim this deep without getting caught in our own nets?

I left the cabin to look for her, but I couldn't find her anywhere. Since searching for her was only exacerbating my abandonment triggers, I went down to the beach to do some yoga.

While I stretched and opened, I felt the wound arise with ferocity. As always, a combination of terror and nausea overcame me, but this was even more intense. I felt a burn unlike any other I had known, the fear of being abandoned by the beloved herself. The ultimate exile. I lay down in child's pose in search of comfort.

As the sun was going down, I walked back to the cabin to look for her. Empty. After a few minutes trying to get comfortable, I heard the key turn. I felt afraid: *Please no more fighting. Please no war.* Sarah entered, eyes softened by tears, yet none the worse for wear. I opened my mouth to speak, but she touched her finger to my lips, "Ssssshh, my love. Not now. It's okay." Clearly, she had worked something through. She reached over and ran her hands through my hair, melting me into submission.

She stopped to undress, slowly, while gazing into my eyes. Fully naked, she climbed atop me, straddling my chin with her hips. The river was already flowing, drip-dropping its delicious love juice onto my waiting lips. I again became the river mouth, hungrily receiving her offering in the harbors of my heart. There really is no taste like the taste of the beloved.

Then she reached for my penis and I retracted. Our conflict was still with me—I couldn't surrender to her touch that fast. Some of us can't give when we feel emotionally unsafe. Others can't receive. I couldn't receive. She looked me in the eyes, but I couldn't hold the heart gate open.

I closed my eyes and went back to my default warrior position, imagining her an object to fuck. I began to talk dirty in an effort to get excited, but she refused to join me. She moved to the other side of the bed, leaving me alone with my heartless hard-on. When I eventually reached for her, she made a hissing cat sound. Message easy to decipher: *stay over there!*

What a dichotomy this love was. Love so powerful that it could reveal another universe. Love so fragile that it could turn to stone in a heartbeat.

When I woke up in the morning, she had already left for home. Only two things remained to remind me—a little bouquet of wildflowers, and a word graffitied on my right foot:

$$|\mathcal{u}$$

Not sure how she managed to do that without my waking up, but it didn't soothe me. Not even close. After such a heavenly encounter, she hadn't even said goodbye! Ouch.

I reluctantly got out of the bed to pack my things. It was time to go home. On the way to the parking lot, I stopped in at the Meditation Sanctuary for a few moments of contemplation before driving the seven hours back to Toronto. Bad move. Flashbacks to our lovemaking mixed terribly with last night's memories. I felt both elated and ruptured at the same time. It was deeply confusing.

When I got to the parking lot, I saw her. She was standing against her rental car talking to someone sitting on the ground. I walked a little closer and saw a rough-and-tumble tow truck dude putting on her spare tire. She had a flat. Strange, the car hadn't been used and the tire was perfect when I checked it the day before. Clearly someone, somewhere, wanted us to part on loving terms.

We walked to the edge of the lot to say goodbye. The world was in technicolor again as I held her close to me. She looked up at me with a wide smile as I kissed her face delicately, feeling her soft breath against my cheek. We said nothing at all, as our souls spoke their regret and healed the rupture. When her car was ready, she kissed me once more on the lips with an almost unbearable tenderness and drove away. I felt myself unbuckle inside. Sometimes silence really is the perfect way to say farewell.

# 7

___

# Breaks and Mends

Soon after returning home, I became melancholic. As I went about my daily business, everything felt inconsequential, microscopic in meaning by contrast to love's expansive openings. Even my habitual friendships seemed uninteresting and pointless. Earth and sky are such different vibrations. How to reconcile them? I had gone to some other place and didn't want to come back. How to return to a worldly consciousness after being shown the euphoria that lies beyond the daily grind? How to get it up for the mundane after getting down with the beloved?

Sarah was my only hope.

One afternoon, I received an email from her that charmed me silly:

```
You are my beloved and I want to come home.
      There you may snore next to me.
       I miss that lovely racket.
```

It's no easy feat to find a woman who actually misses your snoring. Sweet. I called her and we made a plan for her to come to Toronto early the following month. Knowing I would see her bolstered my spirits.

Before she arrived, I dedicated myself to fixing up the apartment I lived in. Just before returning to law school, I had moved to a quirky, one bedroom apartment in Kensington Market, one of downtown Toronto's oldest communities. The Market is an edgy part of the city where butchers, head shops and used clothiers sell their wares in a kind of timeless bubble. When you walk down Baldwin Street, you are at once overwhelmed by the smell of fish, coffee and ganga, while a fascinating, ethnically diverse collection of people walk, bike and skateboard about. Long established as a mecca for creativity, the place is like a human art gallery, where every person that passes by is a living portrait. It's alive!

The apartment itself was on two floors of a century-old Victorian home. The entrance was in the back, with another unit in the front of the property. My place was the oddest mix of archaic and modern, with a forty-year-old fridge and a small boarded-up milk door for the good ole milkman to place bottles on the kitchen counter, sharing space with a newly installed bidet (AKA plant holder) and remote control vertical blinds. The bedroom, kitchen and a sunken living room were on the main floor. Upstairs, there were only two rooms: a spacious bathroom, and an angle-roofed sunroom that looked out over a tree-lined back alley. This apartment had stories to tell. Soon it would have more.

I walked on air all month, creating a nest for my soulmate. Then, the week before she came, I fell into a panic. Something about bringing her into my home felt perilous. To this point, we had only ever met when I was on vacation. But now I would be bringing her right into the heart of my daily life. I was already having a hard enough time merging these worlds. How to assimilate our relationship, too? What if she couldn't accept 'city-boy Lowen'? And what about 'lawyer Lowen'? I mean, I look pretty good in a suit, but what if her love for me gets lost in urban translation? And those heavenly realms, would they have a safe place to land, here in downtown Toronto?

### A Tour of the Yoniverse

She came to stay with me in Toronto for ten days. As soon as she stepped into the apartment, we were drenched in intimacy. We spent almost two full days in bed, lovemaking between naps, nap-making between loves. All my resistance was gone, as my desire to deepen this union took flight. As we intensified our lovemaking, we rose up and beyond this earthly realm, floating to heaven and beyond on our love-loomed magic carpet. Who needs earth when you have the whole universe?

In this divinity, I also lost my trepidation about a woman's yoni. Where before it was a complex foreign object that scared me off, it was now a wondrous invitation to commune with the creator. As I worshiped, I plunged deeper and deeper into the mysteries of the divine. It was a tour of the yoniverse from the bottom up, a wake-down call of the highest order. As I explored her inner world, I again remembered the power of this sacred place, a knowing all-too-easily forgotten in my objectification phases. Is this not God's love canal, the tunnel from possibility to humanifestation? How easily we forget the place where life began, the first wonder of the world. How easily we turn the sacred yoni into a sacrilegious plaything. It was clear as a stream: if a man can't honor the yoni, how can he honor his own, precious birth? If we can't value the feminine, how can we value life?

As the portal to divinity opened wider, my lens on God's gender transformed. I had grown up with my God as a man. But there (S)he was, lying open before me, fully revealed as the Divine Feminine, in all her receptive glory. For this moment at least, God was Sarah, and Sarah was God. My tongue darted in and out of the temple door, hungrily ingesting the (w)hole of creation. Like a soul who had finally met his maker, I was down on my knees praying for more.

When the moment was ripe, I would enter her temple with my sacred shaft aflame, merging my love with its fleshy reflection. As I plunged deeper and deeper into Goddess, her mysteries rose into view, revealing the splendors that await us when we can finally cum clean with the divine. When we climaxed, it was like a colossal galactic explosion. On our bodyship to the stars, we had pierced the veil of separateness that blinds earthlings to their intertwined destiny. Liquid God meets Liquid God—the real milky way.

Of course, we could also drop down and enjoy some raw sex now and then. Not straight to heaven, no significant God sightings, but always held within the context of deep love. With our soul connection as our sacred container, pure physicality was like a wild-eyed free-for-all, a frenzied Sufi dance where both of us were whirled into wonder.

After a three day sexathon, I left Sarah at home and went to work. Although I called throughout the day, she didn't answer. On the way home, I picked up sushi in the market—Unagi this and Unagi that. Sarah loved slippery eels. Unagi was weird, but I loved her anyway. When I got home, I called out her name. Not home. I changed into my casual clothes, grabbed my mountain bike and rode around the market streets looking for her. No luck.

When I arrived home again, I went upstairs to the sunroom and noticed a photo album on the floor opened to a picture of my law school graduation. In it, I was standing beside my date, Karen, who had a particularly proud expression on her face. I wondered whether Sarah had felt jealous and stormed out of the apartment.

I lay down on the couch to wait for her, finally falling asleep around midnight. A few hours later, I was woken up by the door opening. I opened my eyes and saw Sarah come into the house with something in her hand. As she drew closer, I noticed that it was a bottle of vodka.

"Booze?" I asked.

"Good eye, Ogdo. I thought I would bring you some."

She sounded a little off.

"I didn't know you liked booze," I said. "You're not drunk, are you?"

"Up to me... you don't own me," she shot back.

I tried to stay calm, "No I don't, you're right. But I do love you."

"If you love someone, let them go. If they never come back, they were yours... Oh fuck, you know what I mean." She was sharply interrupted by the bottle breaking on the kitchen floor, as it fell from her hand.

She stormed upstairs. The door to the bathroom closed. I heard the shower turn on and imagined Sarah stumbling into it. I felt fearful—*war again?*—but I couldn't leave it like that. I went upstairs to join her. As I approached the bathroom, I heard her sobbing through the door. Entering, I took off my clothes. She was sitting on the tub floor crying, while the water fell directly on her head. It was oddly beautiful.

I got into the tub and sat in front of her, my legs intertwined with hers. I reached over and softly rubbed her neck and shoulders, steam swirling around us. There was nothing to say. Soon my own tears began to fall too. I wasn't even sure where they were coming from. A moment of empathy? A shared healing? We stayed like that until the water became cool.

After we got out, I dried her off and carried her in my arms to the sunroom futon. I had never felt her this delicate. She seemed defeated, like a fallen soldier, or a fragile bird with broken wings. Placing her under the white duvet, I stroked her head until she fell fast asleep. Such a majestic sight, even in a room drenched in darkness.

Concerned I would wake her if I crawled in beside her, I went back downstairs and fell asleep on the couch. A few hours later, I was awakened by the sound of Sarah bounding down the stairs. I opened my eyes and peered at her. She had a crazed look in her eyes and was moving toward me aggressively. Clearly, she wasn't defeated. Who was this madwoman?

"I saw that woman in the grad picture. You look like you're fucking married. Are you married, Lowen?" she irrationally inquired.

She moved to within a few inches of me, booze still heavy on her breath.

"Yah, to a madwoman from Colorado."

"It's not funny," she said, with a nasty edge.

No, it wasn't funny. It wasn't funny at all. Her tone was like a dagger piercing my broken-open heart. A little to the left and I staggered. A little to the right and I staggered more. With all the vulnerability that had opened up between us, I was a sitting duck for her fearful projections.

For the next two hours, she grilled me about my relationship history.

"How many women have you looked in the eyes during sex?"

"How many women have you lied to?"

"Who did you love more than me?"

"How long till you leave me?"

"Who else have you fucked on that ragged couch?"

Whatever tenderness I had seen in her had been replaced by a powerhouse prosecutor determined to prove her case. Of course, every word of it was irrational. Not only was it irrelevant where I had been before, all those old patterns had already melted in the face of this love. Unfortunately, telling her this just made it worse. The more intensely I protested, the more certain she became I was lying. That's what you call a lose-lose proposition.

Early in the morning, she ran out of vitriol and stumbled upstairs. I fell back to sleep and had the first of what would become a recurring nightmare about us. The details were seldom the same, but the symbology always pointed in the same direction. This version featured a knight crossing a watery battlefield with the severed head of a woman in his hand. The head was Sarah's.

Although it was easy to imagine that the dream was reflecting this morning's conflict, I had the oddest feeling this had really happened in a prior lifetime. Lying on the couch torn asunder by an all-night trigger-fest, I couldn't help but wonder: Is this the lifetime that I repay my karmic debt?

### Love and French Fries

When I finally left for the office late in the morning, I was in such a haze that I forgot my socks. I realized I was barefoot in my loafers about halfway to the subway and stopped in at a dollar store in Chinatown to buy a pair.

Sitting down on a bench to put them on, I noticed a tall homeless man rifling through a nearby garbage can. I had seen this guy before. He looked like he had just woken up from a month-long sleep in a park, except his clothes were expensive and perfectly pressed: a Harris Tweed blazer under a full-length charcoal gray duster, a loose-fitting purple tie, and a pair of designer jeans. On the other hand, he was wearing hightop black basketball shoes with a cracked pocket watch hanging from his belt loop. I imagine the duster was there to protect his fancy wear, kind of like the way my grandmother used to cover her couches in plastic so they would last for all eternity.

He seemed to notice me noticing him.

"How you dudin'?" he asked.

*How you dudin'?* I rolled my eyes, and then realized he was serious.

"How my dudin'? I dudin' shitty, if you really want to know," I snapped.

"Love troubles?"

"Yah, how did you know that?" I wondered aloud.

"You forgot your socks—usually means love troubles," he replied matter-of-factly.

"Or homelessness."

"You don't look homeless, man," he shot back.

I felt like an asshole, "Sorry, I didn't mean that the way it came out."

He kept rifling through the garbage, pulling things out and setting them on a pushcart on the side of the road. "I know. It's okay. Love can make us mean, especially if it's real. You know what they say..."

I cut the wise hobo off, "No, what do they say?"

"The higher the mountain, the deeper the valley. If it's real love it's gonna bring all the pain behind it to the surface. If you really love each other, it's got to get ugly."

"Right, right. The brighter the love, the darker the shadow." Sounded familiar.

He nodded yes, then reached into a paper bag he had pulled out of the garbage and offered me a french fry.

I flinched. "No thanks... too early for french fries. But thanks for the words of wisdom."

"Anytime, kid. They call me Dude."

I got up and walked the rest of the way to the office, all the while thinking about love and soggy french fries. Was this Dude-guy right about love? Does it have to get ugly if it gets beautiful? *Does it?*

## The Glory Cave

That evening, Sarah and I had a beautiful dinner and walk through the market. It was like nothing had happened. We held hands on the steps of the old synagogue for hours, then fell gently asleep in each other's arms on the sunroom futon.

A few days later, on a rainy Saturday, we took a drive to one of my favorite places in the world: Goshen Provincial Park. About an hour north of Toronto, the park has a pristine, otherworldly quality. Limestone cliffs and cozy caves meet waterfalls and ancient potholes in a cornucopia of mystical delight.

The day was so perfectly complete that words were unnecessary. As we wandered the park, we took the soulevator up another level as the boundary between us further disintegrated. Initially alone, then co-independent, and now soul-united, we walked through the forest like a one bodied minotaur o' love. There was no distinction between us and the outer world. The forest laughed. We were the laughing forest. Intertwined branches rooted in divinity.

That's the thing about great love. It elevates everything around it. You walk through a forest together and it becomes a great temple. You eat a meal together and you sit at God's banquet table. You merge your bodies and all heaven breaks loose. That's why we can't stop singing about love. Every verse is a cry for wholeness.

We splashed and kissed our way to the edge of the river, where we began to climb, stepping gingerly on the rocks, looking for a hidden treasure to explore. At precisely the same moment, we spotted a small triangular cave opening, peeking out from behind dense brush. A cave after our own heart. It appeared as though someone had tried to cloak it deliberately.

"Someone doesn't want this cave to be found, baby," Sarah said.

"Makes me more curious... I'll go in, first," I confidently replied.

Removing the brush, I got down on my knees, while Sarah reminded me to be careful: "Ogdo, remember—you're an intellectual. You don't do caves."

I ignored the smart ass and crawled in, quickly reaching the back of the space. It was a small cave, no more than five feet deep, with very little headroom. If we were going to share it, we would have to get close. I reached for her hand and she crawled in to join me.

With the brush cleared, the cave was just bright enough for us to see one another. Sarah wrapped her legs around mine as we looked into each other's eyes. Marveling at her radiance—a glory glory hallelujah that never failed to sing me home—my heart quickened. She looked so pure in the softly muted light, like a timeless garden of wonder, wet with rain. My love was blossoming in her garden.

The rain soon intensified outside, and we began kissing furiously. The energy quickly accelerated as Sarah reached down and unzipped me, taking my ready penis and sliding it inside her while she contorted in the strangest of positions. The ground was cold, but our bodies were hot, as we made love like twisted pretzels on the cave floor. It was steamy wild—a perfect end to a perfect adventure.

We drove home in a peaceful silence. I am convinced that if we have even one perfect day in our life, we can endure almost anything that follows.

The next morning we began to fight again. It started with one of her pet peeves—I left the bedroom without kissing her good morning—and then escalated. When she didn't respond to a simple question, my abandonment issues spiked into awareness. When I sloppily mentioned a woman from my past, her betrayal issues were ignited. By nightfall, Sarah had retreated to the sunroom futon, and I was sleeping on the couch.

Clearly the homeless Dude was right. We didn't fight because we didn't love one another. Quite the opposite, in fact. We fought because the purity of the connection was excavating love's shadows. We were in the heart of essence, and every painful association with vulnerability rose into view. Here, in the heart of the everything, *everything* was being revealed.

We spent the entire weekend alternating between lovemaking and jealousy triggers. And sometimes both at the same time. A wave of lust intermingled with anger as we made love with a ferocity I have never known. After each merging, I had to lie down for a few hours to recover. It was a beautiful release, but the underlying tensions were growing in intensity.

A few days before Sarah was supposed to leave, she caught me off guard. I walked into the sunroom, where she was leaving food on the window ledge for her favorite black squirrel, one she called 'Little Friend,' when she asked to go.

"I need to go home now, Lowen."

"But why?" I inquired. "We have two more days."

She just sat there, cold and detached.

After a long period of silence, she turned my way, although she didn't quite look into my eyes when she spoke. "I feel ferocious, like a wolf. Our love is turning me into a beast. I don't know how else to protect myself. I have never been this jealous and triggered in a relationship. I don't know where any of this stuff is coming from."

"Why do you have to protect yourself?" I asked.

Silence again.

She turned onto her side on the futon, curling up in fetal position. I could see a tear gathering at the edge of her eye, not quite ready to fall. She was resisting showing her vulnerability. And then, in a soft young voice I had not heard before, she spoke her truth of the moment: "I guess I never had this much to lose."

Amazing how we push away what we most want to hold close. Humans.

### Role Reversal

We fell asleep until Sarah's cries woke us up. She was sweating profusely and mumbling in tongues. I was afraid to wake her, but I was more afraid not to. I got down on the floor and called out her name. No response. I reached for her and she reached back, clinging to me with all her might. Her eyes opened. She began to sob deeply for some time before falling quiet in my arms.

"What was the nightmare about, baby?" I asked.

"A man... a man he came into my room..." she gasped, "And raped me."

"Where? At home in Colorado? Here?" I inquired.

She sat up and looked at me, perplexed.

"No, it wasn't now." She closed her eyes. "It was from another era altogether. But it felt so real, like I had been catapulted back in time. But he was... I mean... it was so strange. The oddest thing was that I didn't experience it as though it was happening to me. I felt like I was living out someone else's nightmare. I was in someone else's body, and I was witnessing her at the same time."

She reached for me again, nuzzling her tear-streaked face into my chest.

"Did you cry for help?" I asked.

"Yes, I did, or she did, but no sound came out. Voiceless, powerless."

We already knew that this love was stirring the ghosts from the past. But which lifetime? And *whose* past? Can a love be so powerful that it brings up collective pain memories? Can great love uncover others' ghosts as well? Or had I simply fallen in love with a tortured soul?

That afternoon, we went out for lunch with my parents. Despite years of conflict, they had managed to find a way to stay together. My theory is that they had worn each other out so much, neither one had the energy to leave. Their theory is that life is shit no matter what you do, so there's no sense leaving one path for another.

Excited to finally meet my family, Sarah had arranged the occasion a few days earlier. Yet apart from a few pleasantries, she said nothing at all at the table. My father tried to engage her with stories about his childhood in Montreal, but she didn't stir. Eventually, the meal turned into a dialogue between my parents about the bugs taking over the rosebush they had planted. On the drive home, more silence. That evening, she didn't so much as look my way. My heart, it ached. I felt like I had been ripped away from the source-spring. Why was I exiled, again?

It was as though our roles had been recast overnight. I was now the frustrated woman yearning for contact, and she the armored man. Now it was *her* turn to decide. Defend against this great love, or surrender to its depths? Goliath or *Go-lie-with?* Hercules or *Heartcules?* What choice would *her* soul make?

The next morning she woke up at dawn sprinkled with wonder. My heart filled with optimism. Whatever she needed to work through had cleared. The house was again alive with whimsy, filled with energy, as she danced around the living room to kirtan and hip-hop, playfully sexy in one of my baby blue button-down shirts. Something about that hot little ass popping out from below my suit shirt got my sexual juices flowing, something fierce. She made me a delicious breakfast—steel cut oatmeal and a blueberry papaya fruit salad— while I snapped pictures of her with my cell phone. What a beauty!

We had planned a picnic on Toronto Island, but I prayed for rain so

I could stay inside and ravenously devour her before her night flight. As we walked into the bedroom to get dressed, the storm began. God is good! Into the bed we went. Time to get wet.

I spent hours savoring every part of Sarah's body. It was all I could do to avoid her yoni, but I didn't want to discriminate. I wanted to know every room in the temple equally. I moved my hands and lips over every contour and curve, absorbed and tasted every texture, learning her like a beautiful new foreign language. Past, present and future all merged into a single tense as I discovered a grammar my heart could finally understand. At one point, I spent half an hour just kissing her armpit. Not just any armpit, but God's ticklish hiding place. And then the small pink birthmark on the back of her neck. When you love someone fully, you are always kissing the divine.

As I worshiped, I had visions of us flood through me: canoeing together down a marshy river, sitting side by side in an old-time prairie schoolhouse, lying beside each other on a desolate beach. I didn't know where these visions were coming from, but it seemed impossible to imagine a lifetime without this woman in it. And one persistent future vision: Sarah with a baby born of this love, fast asleep in her arms.

Later in the day, my tongue led the way down her body, lingering at her nipples, sliding over her soft belly, circling her belly button, and finally plunging into her moist and ready love-cave, taking this tour of the yoniverse to a whole new level. As the rain splashed against the bedroom window, I too got wet, soaked to the bone by sweet yoni rain. What an immature man calls a hot pussy, an awakening man calls God in liquid drag. The more I ingested, the more I awakened to source. God is a dish best served juicy.

When we finally stopped, we realized Sarah had almost missed her flight. We packed and dressed hastily, while I inwardly prayed for a traffic jam. With the salty smell of sex all over us, we raced to the airport, arriving just in time. She kissed me quickly and darted out of the car.

When I returned home, I found this little bit of farewell prose chalked on the bathroom wall by my complicated beloved:

We break
we break and mend
we flow
against the surf
we fold
we bend and twist
we splay
we break again-
and again, we mend.

Just as long as we mend, I can bear most anything.

# 8

—

# Fly Away Home

I got undressed and sat down in the tub, letting the water fall on my head as I contemplated the week that had passed.

*Who was this man, now?*

Not anyone I had known before.

This love was working me hard, kneading me, transforming my consciousness with a kind of merciless persistence. There is no question—love is a sculptor that molds you from the inside out. With your heart as its clay, it reaches deep inside you and reshapes your inner world. One form, then another, then another, until the earthen form you once identified as "self" has grown resplendent wings of light. Even my body felt different every day—softer, more pliable, more truly naked, more *seen*. Our undress rehearsals were revealing more and more.

### The Museum-mobile

I spent the next few days overcome by a deep desire to marry Sarah. On one level, I recognized that it made no sense. We had only known one another for a few months, and we were becoming increasingly combative. Yet, on a level beneath that, it made all the sense in the world. Though we had only known each other for a few months, we had known each other forever. After too many lifetimes apart, I wanted to carve our union in stone. This was no love affair. This was a life affair—one lifetime after another, after another.

Validating my certainty were a myriad of soulendipitous moments. A brown female cardinal seemed to have become permanently affixed to my backyard apple tree, as if waiting for her mate. Feathers landed at my feet on city streets. A neighborhood child kept chalking the word "L O V E" on the sidewalk in front of my house. Nowhere else, only my house. And not just any child, but a young girl that looked remarkably similar to Sarah as a youngster. The universe was busy with us.

I flew to Colorado two weekends later to be with her. We considered going camping in the Flatirons but decided to make it real by bringing me into the house she shared with her parents. She had been folded into my daily life—now it was time for me to join hers.

Even before I landed in Denver, I could feel her near. When I entered the baggage area, Sarah raced to me with tears in her eyes. She was wearing the same skirt she had worn for one of our first meetings—but now I knew what treasures lay below it. I lifted her high in the sky, as she playfully spread her arms like wings in flight, smiling eyes abright. What an eyesoar! After she landed, we stared into each other's eyes until there was only one suitcase left on the baggage carousel—mine. As we left the airport, all I could think about was the treasure hunt I wanted to go on when we got back to her house.

For the first time in my life, I felt absolutely sure why I was here. I was here to love and marry this woman. And when the time was right, our love would spill over into the creation of new life. Little souls would be born. It just had to be.

We drove to her mountain home in her dirty, fascinating car. Her car was a kind of museum of her life, replete with artifacts from her childhood, keepsakes from her nature digs and walks, along with a wardrobe of clothes for quick changes. I called it the museum-mobile. A tiny childhood doll hung from the rear-view mirror, with the letters LF written on it. "LF?" I asked.

"Lightnin' Foot—Dad's nickname for me. Because I would vanish so quickly." The car smelled like cedar, no doubt from the strips of cedar bark strewn all over the front dash with poems written on them.

She was a true eco-poet, driving a filthy VW Beetle into eternity.

From the moment we arrived at her family home, I knew that I was actualizing a soul-scripture written before I was born. Absolutely everything was familiar. The old gray country house, those two retrievers, that long winding, snake-like drive up the dirt road—they were all part of the karmic blueprint. As if I needed any more evidence that love is an encoded path, I had seen this coming from a lifetime away.

As we stepped foot on the big ole porch, out stepped Jessie—Sarah's mother—a tall, heavy-set woman with a wonderfully kind smile. Her face told me two things in an instant—that she had known tremendous suffering, and that she had chosen to keep smiling anyway. She was like a warm billowing cloud of kindness. She hugged me like she had known me forever, kissing my cheeks and thanking me profusely for coming all the way from Canada. Then she sat me down on an oak rocking chair on the porch and told me to not move until she returned. A few moments later, she came out the front door with a plate of cinnamon bread big enough to feed a small troop of boy scouts. A mama after my own heart. I tuned out the rest of the world and ate to my belly's content.

After being licked profusely by both dogs, Smoky and Bear, an old black pickup rolled up the driveway, sputtering to a stop right before the porch. Out came a bald, edgy man, wearing worn-out overalls, with a bright white goatee and combat scars all over his neck and arms. One of his hands was missing two fingers. This guy had been to hell and back. I instantly knew who he was: Sarah's father Norman, a decorated WWII combat veteran. He was about twenty years older than Jessie, a seventy-five-year-old man with the vitality of a youngster.

As soon as his feet touched the ground, he jumped up on the porch heading my way. I chuckled to myself as I imagined him coming through the incarnation portal with his guns blazing. Not sure the gate-keepers would have had the courage to take them from him on the pass through. When he reached me, he picked me up from my chair like a twig and gave me the biggest bear hug I ever did see. It was both welcoming and terrifying at the same time.

"The man who conquered Lightnin' Foot... that ain't no easy feat. Glad to finally meet you, Lowen," he said with pointed intensity and a big smile on his face.

"Good to meet you too, sir," I politely replied.

"Don't sir me, kid. Just call me Norman. We're family now. Ma, when's supper? I worked up a serious appetite fixin' Pete Shepherd's barn door."

I'm always more comfortable with people who call it supper.

Sarah called out from inside the house, "It's now, Dad. Outside, or in?"

"IN!" he shouted back, grabbing my arm and pulling me inside the house.

Before we ate, Sarah took me on a quick tour. We began with the upstairs, which could only be reached by walking through the kitchen. On the way up the stairs, I paused to look at a series of old family photos. Like me, Sarah was an only child. She was adopted by Jessie and Norman when she was six days old, because they were unable to have children. Most of the pictures were of her growing up, and almost always, there was an animal with her. Dogs, cats, horses and—in one unforgettable picture—a small brown bear.

"A bear?"

"Dad liked to bear-wrestle."

"I bet he did," I replied with a chuckle.

At the top of the stairs, we stepped right into Sarah's bedroom. Above the bed was the same Albert Bierstadt picture that I had on my bedroom wall, along with a series of beautiful photos Sarah had taken on her nature walks. Beside the bed, there was only a small armoire and a rocker near the window. It was like a simple Amish room.

"Is this where we're sleeping?" I asked.

"This is where I'm sleeping. You're sleeping in the living room. Ma and Pa are old-fashioned," she said with a twinkle in her eye. I could tell she had great respect for her parents' values, even if she didn't share them.

I sat down to one of the finest home-cooked meals I have ever eaten: pork chili, elk burgers, mashed potatoes, corn on the cob and something dangerously fantastic called buttermilk pie for dessert. I probably gained fifteen pounds, and it was entirely worth it.

While eating, I listened to effusive stories about Sarah's childhood from both parents—her brilliant academic achievements, her tendency to sneakily return the fish to the lake on family boating trips, the pig she saved from a neighbor's barn fire when she was only six years old. Every story they told, they gushed with pride. She was clearly the apple of their eyes. At the same time, something else hung in the air. I couldn't quite identify it, but there was a Pandora's box in this family, one their intense positivity couldn't quite disguise. This little house had seen plenty of pain. I could almost hear its silent screams.

After dinner I went for a walk with Norman down the mountain road. He seemed determined to let me in on a few of the family's secrets. After minimal small talk, he cut to the chase. "I called her Lightnin' Foot because she was feisty and fast as a little one. At any sign of trouble, she would sprint away, faster than lightnin'. You met her feisty side yet, Lowen?"

"Yes, a little," I laughed, nervously.

"Well, you gonna meet more of it. She love you a lot. That means it's gonna be a war."

Oh God, not this advice again.

"The key is staying on the battlefield till she knows she can trust you, however long that takes," he said with warrior conviction.

I felt like I should salute. "Does it have to be a battleground, sir?"

"Stop with the sir, boy, and yes, it do. Real love is ferocious."

"It can't be kind and gentle?"

"Sure it can, but only some of the time. We Hardings are spitfires. We don't go down without a fight."

How fascinating was this as a matter of karma. I had fallen in love with the daughter of a warrior. Try as I might to shed my own, a warrior consciousness was never too far from my path.

### The Tree Fort

That night, Sarah and I went for a drive in the country. On the way back, she pulled over the museum-mobile and kissed me. She smiled softly and said, "IU, Ogdo, IU," with her heart shining through her face. Then she opened the car door and got out, calling to me, "Come on, I have something to show you."

I got out of the car and followed her as she entered the pathless forest. God forbid she should use a trailhead!

After a few minutes, she stopped in front of a tall limber pine tree that was partially pushed up against a cliff edge. It had a stout trunk that must have been twelve to fifteen feet in circumference. Taking my hand, she brought me around to the back of the tree. I could make out a tiny opening at the base of the trunk, just large enough for a small person to fit into.

"This is where I would live when they were fighting," she said softly.

"Live? You would live *in* here?" I asked, flabbergasted.

"Yep, I would bring my blankets, pillow and food, and hide here until it was safe. Sometimes I would stay out here near a week."

I felt heartbroken imagining her out here, cold and alone, as a little one.

"How bad was the fighting?"

"Bad enough that they didn't always notice I was missing. And bad enough that the police had a special jail cell with Dad's name on it. Dad has a soft heart, but he has PTSD from his time in the war. Nobody understood that back then. They would let him out in the day to weld, and then Ma would have to drive him back to his cell at night."

And I thought I had it hard.

She turned to kiss me, and then took out her penknife and flashlight and climbed on in. She actually still fit.

"Gonna slay a dragon with that penknife?" I asked, in an avoidant attempt at lightening the mood. Why do we always have to lighten up uncomfortable truths?

"No silly, something much sweeter. I loved it here. The trees were my friends. They shaded me from the madness of the world. Come, look inside..."

I went around and stuck my head into the hole. Sarah turned on her flashlight. Inside there was a small space with a flat area to lie on. I could imagine a little Sarah sleeping in here, undisturbed by humanity.

"Look, Lowen," she said as she pointed at one of the inner trunk walls. Carved into the wood were the letters…

$$S.H.$$
$$+$$

"I carved those there when I was eight years old, my very first nature writing. I knew that one day I would meet my soulmate… and finish it." With that, she reached for her pen knife and carved my initials:

$$S.H.$$
$$+$$
$$L.C.$$

"There, finished," she said, before reaching over and kissing me tenderly. I had never been kissed inside a tree before. Well, I wasn't entirely in a tree, but my lips were. We kissed like that for some time, before the darkness slowly crept in. It was time to go back.

On the walk back to the car, I couldn't get her story off my mind. "You really were hiding in the woods at eight years old, sweetness?"

"Earlier, actually, it began around five."

"Wow, you saw so much madness so early."

"Yah, but think of the benefits… " she said pointedly.

"The benefits?"

"Yah. I learned how to find the light in the strangest of places."

Her smiling eyes lit up, and she turned to face me. "Loving Ogdo is evidence of that." It took me a moment to realize she was ribbing me. By the time I caught on, she was already sprinting towards the car. I tried to chase her through the woods, but my little tree nymph had lightnin' in her feet.

When we got back to the house, her parents were sitting in their matching recliners watching an old musical on their rabbit-eared television. Sarah and I went into the kitchen and played checkers for hours. Now and then, Ma would get up and pass me nibbles of buttermilk pie. I don't remember ever feeling more comfortably at home anywhere.

### Fifty Million Shades of God

Sarah and I set out for a day hike the next morning. Little did I know, she had a picnic planned. Little did she know, I had something planned, too.

About a half-hour in, we heard the sound of barking dogs coming our way. Turning around, I saw Smoky and Bear racing up the hill like they had just seen a ghost.

"They always wait till I am long gone, before they race after me," Sarah said as she crouched down on one knee to greet them.

"Can't say I blame them. Your absence does leave a mighty big hole," I said while fending off Bear's face licks.

We continued our hike, now as a family of four.

As we stepped into the forest at the end of the road, our souls deepened in intimate conversation. They had been talking for months, but we had only scratched the surface of our lexicon of soul-speak. Something about the forest always called us deeper.

We moved crisply among the blue spruce and cedar, hiking to the beat of our own unique drummer. As we walked, there was this unforgettable moment when I felt myself die to everything inside me that was not love. I just died to it. I was watching Sarah walking ahead of me when my love for her exploded into eternity, fervently consuming all that was unlike itself. Leaving a tranquil sea of love, everywhere.

In a heartbeat, I entered an experience of vulnerability so startlingly naked, so absolutely present, that I knew I would never be the same. I had never before felt so transparent, so fully open. My heart was so wide open that the whole world fit inside it. The whole bloody world. I felt the love, the joy, the sorrow of humanity pouring through the gateway. No filters—I felt it all.

There was no question in my mind. This state of complete and utter love is our collective birthright, the state we are born to inhabit, the way of being that is eagerly awaiting humanity at the end of a long, perilous journey. We either walk toward love as a way of being, or we walk away from it. There are only two directions. This decision shapes our life and our world.

After about an hour, we stopped near a small creek to rest. Sarah stepped in gingerly, leaning down to splash water on her face and upper body. "Freezing!" she cried, while motioning me to come in and join her. I hated cold water, but how could I resist those warm, inviting eyes?

I stepped into the rocky creek, working my way over to her cautiously. Smoky and Bear soon followed, splashing and drinking like mad monkeys. When I reached her, I leaned in for a kiss. Not just any kiss, but a kiss of particular tenderness. If my soul had lips, this is how it would kiss.

I opened my eyes to look at her as we kissed. Her eyes were open, too. Eye-to-Eye, and I-to-I, one universe after another rose into view, each one more vivid and expansive than the last. What felt like unity consciousness at one stage of opening was revealed as a mere fragment of possibility in another. Then to my wonderment, I had the distinct sense that our love was not simply revealing a new cosmos—it was actually helping create one. Our love was more than a portal *into*, it was also a weaver *of* new galaxies, a crafter of new possibilities, a brilliant artist with an expansive and limitless imagination. Fifty million shades of God.

Whether we chose or were chosen, Sarah and I were clearly blessed to walk this path. We were carriers of a divine seedling of possibility, two adventurers who had been granted a glimpse of the new earth that awaits humanity. Not a planet riddled with affectless detachers—masters of self-avoidance masquerading as realized masters—but one characterized by heartfelt connection as the path home. This was a relational dance, not the solo performance perfected by the isolationist masculine. Not one limited to the vertical Kingdom of God, but also the horizontal Queendom of Goddess, a receptive and heartfelt temple of delight that only opens its gates to us when our minds are asleep and our hearts wide open.

In just a few moments with Sarah, I encountered a much more relational, inclusive God than I had ever experienced in isolation. Clearly, there can be no God without Goddess. Can't have one, without the (M)other. God meets Goddess meets Human Being.

I had to wonder, *what if LOVE—not mindfulness, not detachment, not disciplined focus, not perfected asanas—is truly the great door opener? What if relationship is the primary mode of transport on the royal road to divinity? What if our experience of God is actually more complete when we co-create her together, when She arises alight and enheartened on the wings of our love? What if we are here together not only to keep each other company, but to show each other God? And even more startling, what if God actually IS relationship, in all its myriad forms?* Such imaginings!

At the same time, I also glimpsed the weight of the challenge. As I looked deeply into Sarah's eyes, I saw both the power and the fragility of this degree of vulnerability. The consciousness I accessed alone may not open as many gateways, but it felt easier to sustain than a relational weave. It was already so challenging to navigate my own consciousness, so how to navigate the vaster co-creative consciousness generated by our love?

I couldn't help but wonder whether relational ascension has to be mirrored by cultural ascension before it can be sustained as a way of being. If the world around us is still egocentric and toxic, can this kind of relationship survive? Where's the model for how to move through the torrent of triggers and arrive safely on the other side? The state we were co-creating was so subtle, so tenuous, and so entirely out of step with the more pragmatic vibration of the world. Did we need training in vulnerability before we could plumb its depths? If so, had we met too early in our individual development? Or was this happening exactly as it was supposed to?

With great intensity, Smoky and Bear busted through my thoughtful reflections with a flurry of barks. A hare had caught their attention on the opposite shore, and they ran at it full throttle. They jumped out of the river and into the forest at almost the same moment, hunting bunny like we hunted love. We quickly lost sight of them, though their barks continued to echo through the valley. Sarah began walking her way back to the river's edge.

"Shouldn't we wait for them, baby?" I asked, concerned they would get lost in the wild.

Laughing heartily at my urban naivete, she replied, "No need for that, sweetness. They can smell us just as well as they can smell bunny. Let's get back on the trail. I want to take you somewhere."

## A Picnic with a View

We walked for some time. Sarah stayed just a little ahead, giving me the perfect view of her perfect backside. Once an ass man, always an ass man. I admired her from every angle, but this one was particularly luscious.

Every now and then, Smoky and Bear darted onto the trail at breakneck speed, crisscrossing back and forth in front of us before sprinting back into the woods. They felt like our dogged guardians, touching base to be sure we were okay before racing back to scout the periphery.

As we worked our way to the top of a mountain, the trail grew steeper. Sarah moved up it with skillful ease—she obviously had been here many times before. After a particularly rocky ledge, we arrived at the summit. I longed to lie down and catch my breath, but Sarah motioned me to follow her down a small rock face.

"We're almost there, city boy," she said with a teasing smile, "just a few more steps."

I carefully followed my mountain goat beloved down a steep path between the rocks until we landed at a spacious clearing on the mountain's edge. I turned to look out over the most beautiful valley I had ever seen. Magnificent Colorado! When I turned back around, Sarah had disappeared. I looked up. Nothing. I looked down. Nothing. Mountain goat nowhere to be found.

Then I heard a giggle from the rock face. Moving toward it, I found her lying on the ground in the shadow of a giant boulder. The boulder leaned against the cliff face in such a way there was a space beneath it. Clearly Sarah had been here—the underside was covered in her writings, including a few sentences with my name in them. She noticed me noticing them.

"I come up here to visit with you."

"I'm honored."

"Other than inside your heart, this is my favorite place in the world, Lowen. I come here to get away from everything."

"How many hiding places do you have?" I asked.

"Many, but this was more than a hiding place. It was my sanctuary. This is where I would come to regain my faith when the world closed in on me. Look up..."

I looked up and saw exactly what she meant. There was a hole at the top of the boulder where the sun shone through. But it didn't just shine through in a single linear ray. It fragmented into a beautiful colorful prism. I felt like I was looking at a crystalline reflection of our connection. One wave of ecstasy after another, each with its own distinct luminosity, like a multifaceted diamond.

When I looked back down, Sarah was again nowhere to be seen. Lightnin' Foot had vanished. I peeked my head outside and saw where she had gone. A red flannel blanket lay on the ground at the edge of the clearing. On top of it were two cardboard plates and three open containers filled with leftovers from last night's dinner. She had prepared the perfect picnic—a picnic with a view.

### Happy Birthday

While eating, I was again overcome with the knowing that all my life struggles were intended for this reason: to live in the richness of loving her. She was the culmination of millions of steps my soul had taken to arrive at love's door. I closed my eyes and imagined us old and gray, eating coconut ice cream and drinking sweet chai by the light of the silvery moon.

I knew it was time.

I reached into my bag, and pulled out my surprise. Then I got nervous and put it back in. Scared shitless, I began talking about trivial things before catching myself and going quiet. It's never rude to interrupt your false self. I wanted to be genuine, but I was afraid. My toes were tapping wildly.

I closed my eyes and centered myself before reaching for the surprise yet again. While Sarah was looking out over the valley, I placed a small red box with a gold bow in front of her.

When she turned back around, her smiling eyes exploded with delight.

"What's this, Ogdo?"

"It's my way of saying sorry for missing your birthday," I replied.

"My birthday?" she said, perplexed.

"Yah, all twenty-six of them."

I reached down to pick up the box, holding it in the air between our close faces, smiling at her. Sarah looked confused, but curious. Then I opened the box slowly...

"And it's also my way of saying that I want to be there for the rest of them—for all your birthdays to come."

I pulled the ring out of the box. It was a simple ring, one that called to me from the back of an antique jewelry store in Kensington Market. It wasn't large, nor pretentious, but it was truly our ring—two small diamond hearts woven together as one. It had always made sense to me: the deeper the love, the more subtle its presentation.

I leaned forward with the intention of getting down on my knees to formally propose, but my speech evaporated into nothingness. I became a gushing pool of adoration. Sarah's eyes flooded with tears. There was nothing to say that wasn't already said.

Then we gazed into each other's eyes for as long as our hearts could bare. Our gaze said it all—the bridge exit was closed. There was no going back. Then her eyes smiled and she reached for the ring, seamlessly sliding it onto her ring finger. A perfect fit. When the real one comes, you don't have to think about commitment. It just *is*.

Although we had only known each other for a few months in this incarnation, we had known each other forever. After too many lifetimes apart, we couldn't wait a moment longer to seal our union.

Right after the ring went on, Smoky and Bear began to bark down at us from the summit. Were they getting nervous up there all alone, or did they know we just got engaged? Sarah and I packed up the picnic and readied to go. Just before leaving, Sarah pulled out a piece of chalk and turned to face the boulder. She began to write...

When two hearts beat in the same direction

before handing me the chalk.

I turned to face the boulder and wrote:

They become one.

We climbed down the mountain in silence. When we reached the blue spruce forest, Sarah began playing with the ring on her finger. She seemed to have something to say.

"I love the ring, Ogdo. I love it. But we don't really need this, you know? I mean, we're beyond the worldly idea of marriage. We already got married somewhere else. The place where it really counts."

"Yes, but don't we meet here, too? Can't we span both places... ALL places?" I inquired. Then I was struck by a flicker of worry. "You're not having second thoughts are you?" I reluctantly asked.

At that, she stopped dead in her tracks and turned to face me.

"Never," she said as she reached for my hands. "I just don't want us to forget where we meet when we bring our love into this world."

I understood. She didn't want the world to corrupt our love. She didn't want us to forget the source. She didn't want our ageless love to be confined by a social institution. She didn't want us to forget the place where we truly meet. I shared her concerns.

"We won't. We will always meet there," I said with a certainty that belied my uncertainty.

We fell back into silence and walked the rest of the way hand in hand, our hearts interlaced like the two diamonds. Only the dogs spoke, celebrating our engagement with their triumphant barks.

# 9
---

# Dark Night of the Soulmate

Sarah and I agreed to move in together later that autumn, making our home in my apartment in Toronto. She was initially hesitant—her unstable early life made moving a shaky proposition. Finally she succumbed to my constant assurances. Then, not thirty minutes after she gave notice at the nursing home where she worked, she got into a fender bender with a car with an Ontario license plate. Not just any car, but the same make and color that I drove. Cosmic collision.

In my part of the world, the black squirrel she had befriended on her first visit kept peering into my bedroom window, tapping on the window early in the morning, as if looking for his friend, Sarah. Crazy squirrel—was he nuts... or seeking nuts... or both? Also, the female cardinal that was affixed to the tree had finally met her fiery red mate. And feathers kept landing on the ground in front of me at the oddest of moments, often when I was thinking of Sarah.

It would have seemed strange if we hadn't passed this strangeness marker long ago. By now we were officially intimate with soulendipity. It was the way this love-train rolled.

While waiting for her, I prepared the nest. A nurturing part of me that I didn't know I had suddenly kicked in. I remembered everything she loved—sea salt chocolate, beeswax candles, organic bath oils and sandalwood incense—and made sure I had plenty in stock. I repainted the bedroom the fuchsia color she loved. I created space in my armoire for her wardrobe. And, to the great chagrin of my inner frat boy with his proclivity for objectifying, I took down my favorite naked heartthrob poster and threw my lesbian porn collection in the garbage. Oh he whined, and whined...

In the meantime, time stretched and twisted me miserable. I experienced an agony I had never known in another's absence, as my soul cried out for its source-spring. So eager was I to feel her near that I sometimes imagined her delicious scent wafting through the house. Be still, my yearning heart.

The day before her arrival, I couldn't sit still from excitement, so I went outside and walked for hours. This wasn't the same city I remembered from my bleak childhood. Through enheartened eyes, Toronto felt like a living response to my state of being, with its city lights clearer and more vibrant, the people more smiley and connective, even the traffic lights seemed stuck on green. My heart was in a state of 'go.' Everywhere I went, I was met with a wave of goodness. I was truly happy, like an artist who had finally come home to his canvas after decades of wandering.

That same night, I had a disturbing dream. I dreamed that I was a marine on a battleship in World War II. I had fallen in love with a nurse, who was tending to a bandage wrapped around one of my legs when the ship was hit by a torpedo. Everything went dark, and suddenly she was gone. I looked for her everywhere, all the while enraged at God for giving a gift and taking it back so quickly. A past life glimpse, or simply a reflection of my great fear of abandonment?

I woke up feeling discouraged. If love is so hard to hold onto in our dreamscapes, how difficult might it be in the light of day? My faith was restored when I opened an email from Sarah. My Rocky Mountain poet was at it again, reopening my heart with her entrancing prose:

```
Last night I dreamed you were with me.
You saw my body age and I became con-
cerned about ailing. Then I looked and
your face was gentle, still, even as I
grew older. You spoke to me, like al-
ways, so reassuring. There is beauty
```

```
outside of beauty and there is hope
        within hopelessness.
```

Her words quelled my fears.

### *One Ring Circus*

Sarah moved to Toronto to a cosmic drum roll. When I arrived to pick her up at the airport, I remained out of sight. I brought a small bouquet of sunflowers and a portable stereo with me, which I placed against a pillar just outside the baggage claim exit. As my beloved stepped into the main lobby, I played one of our favorite love-songs. Luckily no security guards were close at hand, just enchantment wafting through the air. I hid behind the pillar, as she intuitively walked in the direction of the music. When she came close, I stepped out from behind the pillar, and we began our life together with the sweetest embrace and a chorus of kisses.

When I picked up her bag to carry it to the car, I noticed she had chalked all over one side of it, "When two hearts beat in the same direction, they merge in Toronto." I roared with laughter. For her, *everything* was a notebook. Then she noticed I was wearing a t-shirt I had made for the occasion—one with I♡U hand-written on the chest. And just to intensify the corniness factor (since the universe knew how much she appreciated corniness!) a beautiful East Indian boy appeared out of the blue as we were leaving the airport. Not more than seven years old, he circled around us, pointing, laughing and shouting out, "Shiva Shakti, Shiva Shakti!" Then he would circle back around and say it again with a big smile on his face. Did Providence send us a pint-sized welcoming committee?

Our first month together was lovely. Our private language burst at the seams. On the days when I didn't have to work, we went on one Toronto adventure after another: cycling through the Rosedale ravines, walking on Cherry Beach, doing Vinyasa at Kathryn Beet's amazing Yogaspace studio, exploring Toronto Island, kissing madly at the top of the CN Tower while Asian tourists surreptitiously snapped our picture. We went to Woodbine racetrack twice and won. We dressed like gangsta and chalked graffiti on alley walls. We made a lot of delicious love at God's banquet table.

One morning, we decided to get a kitten. Sarah needed an animal in the house to feel at home. After all, she was a country girl. Moments later, we saw an ad on a pole for free kittens. When we arrived, we spotted her instantly—a spirited cinnamon colored Persian with a furry white chest. We knew she was our cat. First lil member of the family. That afternoon, we sat in the car and pondered her name. It only took a moment—Lightnin. Dad's name for Sarah. It had to be.

It was quite a thing to be engaged to my beloved. I felt elated, proud, certain of our shared destiny. We made wedding plans, then kept changing them as better ideas rose forth. At first, a wedding on the peak of Whistler Mountain. Scrap that, a wedding on a beach in the Turks and Caicos Islands. No, better yet, a quiet ceremony at Toronto's Old City Hall, just like my parents had. Oh God, no! And then my favorite, an all-weekend camping wedding in Boulder's Foothills, the source of our first divine encounter, with all our friends and relatives dancing in the moonlight.

Sadly, our little glimpse of heaven was soon interrupted. One night, we were lying down on the couch when Sarah quickly jumped to her feet. "Did you tell Emily about the engagement?" she pointedly asked. Emily was the last woman that I dated before Sarah.

"I didn't even think about it, baby," I replied. "I haven't spoken to her for over a year. Why does it matter?"

"Why does it matter? Are you fucking kidding me?" she shrieked as she stormed up the stairs. Before she got to the top, she turned around and came flying back down with the ring in her hand. With a nasty glare she flung the ring directly at me. It landed hard on the rug near my feet. Ouch. Has my lover been momentarily possessed?

Sarah stormed into the sunroom while I lay on the couch with the ring by my side. I felt heartbroken, utterly crushed. How could she tear off the ring so easily? Imagine if we had something real to fight about. What would she throw at me then?

When I awoke in the morning, the ring was gone. I went upstairs and opened the door. Sarah was fast asleep, the ring on its usual finger. I crawled in beside her and she turned over to kiss me. We made soft, perfect love as the sun rose. We were getting used to this dance. Open, retreat to defenses, surrender yet again, re-open...

Of course, the ring and ex-girlfriend were not the issue. Fear was. Fear of being left, fear of being seen, fear of being betrayed by the love that lived between us. Our ever-deepening love was excavating more and more unresolved baggage from its storage sheds. Just when I thought it was safe, a new load arrived. And each one seemed heavier and more dangerous than the one before. Would there ever be an end?

Jealousy issues were only the tip of the painberg. Next up on the fight card were Sarah's engulfment triggers. As it turned out, she could only stay close for so long before feeling imprisoned. Right after we melted into togetherness, she needed to create distance. And when she retreated, it would trigger my abandonment issues and I would try, feverishly, to pull her toward me. Then she would dig in her heels even more, demanding more space and distance. "You can't pin me down, Ogdo." Who wanted to pin her down? I only wanted to love her. Soon we were unconsciously reenacting what we lived as children, a power struggle between a young girl afraid of being trapped inside her conflictual home, and a young boy afraid of being abandoned by his mother.

To make matters worse, I was having a difficult time living in two worlds simultaneously. It was one thing to readjust to the density of the courtroom after little trips with Sarah, quite another while living consistently together. Perhaps if the practice of law was my highest calling, there would have been no dissonance between the vibration of my working life and my love connection. But grinding it out all day in the courtroom, then being vulnerable with Sarah, felt bipolar. Take mask off, put mask on, take mask off, put...

Sarah's fear of engulfment soon shifted into a fear of being ignored—the test of attunement. If I didn't pay perfect attention to her every word, she went silent. If I didn't remember to call when I was leaving work, grenades were launched. When I forgot to bring her chocolates after work one evening, bombs fell. It was impossible to win. If I attuned too much, she felt smothered and ran. If I gave her space, she felt I was neglecting her.

If this had been an ordinary love, I would have been out of there at the first sign of nasty. Now and then I could spot my inner runner putting on his sneakers and readying to sprint. Yet I was determined to keep my heart open. I had been brought to my knees by this mesmerizing love and it felt sacrilegious to run away. In the same way as Sarah held the space patiently when I was resistant, I was determined to do the same with her.

It was clear we had fully entered the next phase of our love relationship. This is where the transcendent, mystical threads must integrate with the nitty-gritty of human patterning in the friction of daily life. A messy business.

Intensifying the tensions was Sarah's difficulty communicating what was happening for her in direct terms. Perhaps she was too lost in the triggers. Or perhaps she couldn't discern the source of her reactivity. Whatever it was, her challenge with speaking directly from her heart was only deepening the rifts.

But one day I came home from work and there was a letter chalked on the bathroom wall:

> Ogdo, I have never been this reactive.
> Are these reactions even mine?
> I don't know whose heart I am protecting
> because my heart wants only to love you.
> Whose table are we sitting at?
> Whose battles are we fighting?
> Whose story are we telling?

Indeed—whose story was this?

### Woundmates

Sarah insisted on going back to her family home for a week to center herself and reconnect with her roots. Intellectually I knew a little space was healthy, but I was too lost in my abandonment triggers to appreciate it. I spent two hours at the airport sobbing my guts out like a baby and protesting her departure. It was all she could do to get on the plane.

On the way back from the airport, red-eyed and snotty, I saw Dude walking down my street. Attired in his usual duster and fancy wear, he was pushing one of his carts, this one filled with sparkly purple boxes and bags. I pulled up just ahead of him and parked, then got out of the car and walked toward him.

"How you dudin'? Shit! You look beat up," he said.

"Feels like it, yah."

He laughed in his uniquely crazy, wild way, "Love Wars, coming soon to a theater near you."

How did this guy know I was at war? Was I at war?

We began to walk. It felt good to be with Dude. "You ever known great love, Dude?"

"Now and Zen," he replied.

"What does that mean?" I inquired.

He stopped dead in his tracks, as though he was recalling something profound. Then, he quietly mumbled, "If only I knew then what I don't know now."

We kept walking.

"It's like we are riding this glorious kundalini wave, one that just builds and builds... until some old bullshit gets in the way. Do you know what I mean? Do you know about kundalini, Dude?"

"Yup, I dated her."

I rolled my eyes.

"Seriously, I dated a woman named Kundalini when I visited BC. I hitchhiked across the country knowing I would meet a fantastic woman at the other end. Met her on Vancouver Island when I was surfing Tofino. She was all Goddess all the time."

"Was it super charged sexually?"

"Never had sex with her. Just looked into each other's eyes a lot and went for ice cream."

He stopped to adjust the pushcart, and then started to walk again.

"Where on earth do all the triggers come from, Dude? Are they just ours from this life, or another life, or could they even be other people's stuff? Are they unresolved…"

Before I could finish, he cut me off, "Stop thinking so much. Excessive analysis perpetuates emotional paralysis. Don't worry about where things come from. You can't figure out the heart with the mind. You can only understand the heart with the heart. Surrender, man, surrender."

I thought I had.

"But be sure you aren't woundmates," Dude added.

"Woundmates?"

"Yah, you know, like scar-crossed lovers. Sometimes the passion comes from real love, but not always. Sometimes it's cause two people got their wires all mixed up. It's their wounds way of getting the best of them."

"That's not us. We may be scar-crossed lovers, but our stars align."

We walked in silence for a few moments. I let Dude's ideas mill around in my mind. *Woundmates.* Could that be us? Finally, I asked, "How can you tell the difference, Dude?"

"That's the great challenge, my friend. It can be real tricky. Lots of toxic connections masquerade as something special, when they are just destructive battlegrounds. When nightmares may come! Trouble with a capital T! No growth there. Run for your life."

His answer didn't help.

When we got to the front of my house, I hesitated, feeling almost guilty for taking this homeless man's advice and then going inside. He sensed it. "Don't worry about me. I don't want that. I got exactly what I want." Before I could ask, he crossed the street with his pushcart in front of him and kept walking.

I spent the next week swinging between getting lost in my growing law practice and wanting to shoot myself. Despite my agitation, I continued to stay open, holding to the love. This is the choiceless nature of great love. Once you pass the point of no-exit, you have no other option but to see it all the way through.

Sarah and I spoke every day while she was gone. It was tense at first, but the energy softened a little each time we connected. Visiting her family and eating Ma's home cooking was just what the soul doctor ordered.

## *An Egg and a Hard Place*

When I picked her up at Toronto's Pearson Airport, her heart was right back on her sleeve. At the same time, something was different in the energy between us. It was like a new understanding had been birthed, as though we had accepted that we were on an extraordinary human adventure where the normal rules didn't apply. Bonded in ecstasy and grief, we walked hand in hand through the airport like two fallen warriors who had fought epic battles and risen from the ashes. Whether we could sustain the ascension was another matter altogether.

When we arrived back at the house that afternoon, we made exquisite love. We moved as love moved us, beyond and within breath, (he)artfully merging from one fluid form to another. Our lovemaking became a perfectly choreographed dance of sacred imagination, moving seamlessly across the cosmic dance floor, tripping the heart fantastic. It had no beginning, no end, no point of departure. Lost in timelessness, the weaver and the weave were now indistinguishable. Isn't love the ultimate choreographer?

In a way, we weren't actually making love. We were love, opening to more and more of itself. We didn't need to read about tantra, intend it, work at it. We were tantra. Not just some narrowly construed, sexualized version of it, but the breathy, hearty, rhythmic wholenest. It was clear: When you add soul to sex, it's not sex anymore. It's God.

At the same time, I had to wonder: What happened to all the issues that triggered us before she went home to visit her parents? Were they worked through on some unspoken level, or would they return later with even more ferocity? Were these tests we had passed, or harbingers of greater difficulty ahead? Is the answer focusing on the issues, or is the answer to just focus on the love until the issues melt before it?

I woke up overcome with love. It spilled over the banks of my consciousness, oxygenated my cells, perfumed my world. My beloved Sarah was overcome as well. For days, she danced with Lightnin, and chalked love poems all over the walls of the house.

One evening, I came back from work to find this bit of lovely pinned on the coffee table:

*I woke up with you on my mind and in my heart.*
*Someday I will take all your sweetness and my affections,*
*Our kisses and my soft caresses,*
*Then stitch them together to make a blanket*
*to keep us warm forever.*

Then I made a mistake. At least, in her eyes I did. After making heavenly love one morning, I told Sarah that I wanted to have a baby with her. There was just so much love—her and I alone could not contain it. I needed somewhere to put it. I wanted us to replicate our love in flesh form. I had flashes of a true love child with her softly freckled nose and my wild black hair. Gushing with love, I began talking about the wee ones we would have, as though it was destined.

Wrong move.

Sarah went from raw pulsating orgasmic receptivity to hardened armor in about 1.5 seconds. I had never seen anything like it. From soul-mate to woundmate in one fell swoop. Clearly I had hit the mother-load of nerves. She didn't talk to me all day despite my best efforts. I had no real understanding of what had happened.

The next morning, she woke me up to tell me what had triggered her.

"I don't want children, Lowen, never have," she said with certainty.

"But how can this love not create life, Sar? It feels so natural to want a child with you."

"For you. For me, what's natural is to love you. Our love creates life with every breath. That's perfectly enough."

I delved deeper: "But where does the resistance come from? Is it early life issues? Did all that family madness make you cynical about bringing children into the world?"

She got quiet for a few minutes.

"No, it's just a knowing—it's not resistance. Don't psychologize everything. I just have always known it isn't part of my future."

"And our love connection hasn't changed that even a little?"

She looked away for a moment before turning back and looking me straight in the eye, "No, Ogdo, it hasn't."

Ouch.

Not what I wanted to hear, but I got it. It simply wasn't part of her path. How to argue with that?

I argued with her all morning. Having a baby was always essential to me: the holy deal-breaker. I had such a deep certainty that this was an inevitable part of my life journey. At one point, I had actually collected items for my first child—Guatemalan sweaters, little wool hats, little toys, adorable T-shirts. I even contemplated starting a bank account for my child's future. How could I give that up?

When arguing got me nowhere—she was both defiant and clear— I went for a long morning walk through the freshly fallen leaves. The melancholy of autumn intensified the feelings. Caught between an egg and a hard place, I asked myself if I could replace my baby-making dream with another. At this point, it felt impossible. I expected a woman who loved me to want to create life with me. Isn't that how it goes? My traditional sense of attachment couldn't see through to another way of loving, one that's satisfied with the perfection of the moment without agenda. I had no idea how to let love lead me in its own direction.

And not to entirely pathologize my wanting. There was a more symbolic meaning to it as well. My yearning was a reflection of the fertility of the connection itself, one where our souls had been impregnated with each other's love. Where before my capacity to love was embryonic, now our twin souls were being birthed inside of me, cocreators dancing in possibility and burgeoning with life. Even in our darkest, most conflicted places, there was an abundance of fecundity in the field between us. Our shared aliveness was spilling over at the seams. How to let that die?

### Twin Blames

The baby debate reopened the door to Sarah's engulfment issues. Triggered by the fear that she would have no way out, she began pushing me away, leaving for hours at a time, picking little fights, talking about going home again. Again, I resisted my tendency to go to war. I continued to hold to the love, to see the fights as false fronts, to keep my focus on the connection beneath, to keep my heart open.

But my patience only stoked her. After a few reactive days, she went after my abandonment wound in the most ruthless way: poly-amory. The path of multiple lovers. Her defenses knew exactly where to twist the knife. She began talking about her desire to bring other people into the relationship—not as lasting connections, but as "adventurous explorations."

"I think it would be good for us to open up our relationship to other people," she suggested. "How do you feel about polyamory, baby?"

I didn't like where this was going. Not one bit.

"Great, at certain stages of relationship exploration, but not something that interests me with you."

"It doesn't have to be men. I would be okay with a woman in our bed."

"I'm fully satisfied as things are. Why do you need this?" I inquired. She continued to instigate, "Because I love you. I want to share you with others."

"As if! You're just afraid. You're looking for another escape hatch."

She came right back, "Not afraid at all. I just want to live."

"Oh, we're living."

She added fuel to her argument by dressing it in reason: we would still remain "primary partners" but share ourselves with peripheral connections. On a rational level, I didn't believe she had any real interest in this, but who was rational at a time like this? With our hearts maximally opened and our fears ignited, reactivity was now running the show.

I had some experience with the poly path. There was a time when I hooked up with a small gaggle of poly tantricas in my explorative years. I became intimately involved with two of them, sometimes both in the bed at the same time. We jumped from one pleasure to another, bliss-tripping as far as it would take us. It didn't take us very far. Before I knew it, we were caught in a web of jealousy and reactivity, one where the childhood trauma that fueled our non-attachment philosophy had come back to haunt us. Although joyous on the outside, we were actually bubbling cauldrons of unresolved feeling in the deep within. No fun at all.

One day I came home and Sarah was sitting with a young Spanish man in the living room. He was on the chair, she was relaxing on the couch. She had told me that she was going to try to make new friends in Toronto, so I didn't suspect anything inappropriate. After simple introductions, I went upstairs to shower and change. When I came back downstairs, he was now sitting at the other end of the couch looking oddly smitten. After a few uncomfortable moments, he quickly hurried out of the house.

Then I lost it, just as her unconscious wanted me to lose it. Provoked by a week of jealousy triggers, I began to fight back. Although standing my ground restored my dignity, it made things worse between us. The more I fought back, the further she went in her efforts to trigger me. At one point, she picked up the phone to call an ex-boyfriend "just to see how he was doing." After a few sleepless nights, her timing was impeccable. I picked up the phone and smashed it against the wall, giving her the excuse she needed to plan another trip back to her family home a few weeks later. Lost in the thickets of early transference, we needed a forest fire to clear the field.

The blame-athon had begun. We spent the next few weeks blaming each other for everything that triggered us. When she wasn't blaming me for pushing her on baby-making, I was blaming her for deliberately igniting my jealousy triggers. Sarah walked softly, but carried a big shtick. And so did I. She became very judgmental and mean-spirited. And so did I. Having grown up in a shaming family, it wasn't difficult for me to enter that consciousness. I knew how to defend, knew how to deflect, and knew how to attack.

*War. Oh, no, not war again.*

One night I lay alone on the couch, flashbacking to childhood. It had been a long time since I had felt this close to war, and the early memories were brewing. Waves of nausea overwhelmed me as I remembered some of the battles I had with my mother, particularly those from early childhood—the screaming, the hitting, the shaking, the hiding in her walk-in closet, where she would be least likely to look for me. So much hostility per square meter in that tiny house of hate. Although I consciously recognized I wasn't there anymore, these grueling claustrophobic battles with Sarah were feeling eerily similar.

In one sense, our conflicts often seemed to emanate directly from our souls. Two warrior souls, longing for and resisting their merger in equal measure. At other times, it all felt entirely avoidant, like we were bypassing our vulnerability with war games. And at other times, I was sure the pain of the collective unconscious was rising up to obstruct us. We were like receptacles, choicelessly channeling the world's trauma. We felt our connection to the universe in the ecstasy, so why not in the suffering, too? I had to wonder, again and again, can anyone hold this degree of love safe before the collective unconscious has itself healed? Although it seemed enmeshed in personal triggers, it also seemed to be linked to something much broader.

Yet, what was so fascinating about this dynamic was that nothing ever touched the love at the core. This wasn't a question of moving in with someone, then finding out that you never really knew them. No matter what darkness emerged, it never diminished the love. It never hampered the longing. It never made her look any less beautiful to me. It was more a question of the love shining its light on everything not love, again and again…

And often the veil would lift all on its own, with the shadows seamlessly turning to light. One day, in the middle of the most intense arguing, I was overcome by a feeling of tremendous vastness. It was like the Divine had entered the room, instantly deepening the vibration. Sarah was lying naked on the couch and I just couldn't stop loving her. Everything else fell away. That delicate corner where her upper and lower lips met, that one stray hair that always tickled her nose, the soft pubic mound that hinted at the temple below. My eyes teared up as I watched God's chest rise and fall. How can the world hold such grace?

Before the battles could turn uglier, we decided she should follow through with her plans to go home for a visit. When I was driving her to the airport, she couldn't stop crying. I asked her why she was sobbing so deeply. She wouldn't answer. Her silence was deafening. When we arrived at the terminal, she gave me a peck on the cheek and quickly left the car.

I came back to an empty house, filled with grief. Before going to bed, I discovered her latest graffiti on the shower wall:

*Stay true to us.*

What choice did I have?

# 10

# Hol(e)y Ship

I lay down to nap, but I was too rattled. It confused me to no end how this depth of love could arise with so much hostility in its wake. It didn't take a genius to make the connection between my triggers and my early life experiences, but sometimes the pain felt so foreign to me, like we had walked right into someone else's nightmare. Had we? Where exactly is the line between one love story and another?

Despite the challenges, I had gone too far from shore to turn back now. My love for her filled the spinnaker of my heart, carrying me from placid sea to raging torrent, then back again. Even if I wanted to turn back, where would I go? She was both my ocean and the ship I traveled on. I had to stay the course.

We spoke on the phone, but there was a tension that just wouldn't dissipate. I did everything I could to wrestle it to the ground, but it just hung there, like an ominous cloud that won't move until it rains. If ever we needed the support of someone who had walked this love-path before, it was now.

On the way back from work one day, I saw Dude sitting at an outdoor café, sipping a tall dark one. He motioned me to come over. "Sit down, man. How you dudin'? You need to take a load off your mind."

"Got that right," I replied, sitting myself down across from him.

"Why so sullen? Lover got your tongue?"

"Kind of. She left for another break. Too many fights."

"Got to clear the runway or the plane can't land. You guys want to take off or land?"

I ordered a beer from the waiter and sat quietly for a few minutes pondering his strange question. "We both asked for this love," I said at last. "The universe delivered. I just don't understand why it has to be so painful."

Dude didn't waste any time replying. "The ladder to heaven is made from broken rungs. You got that? Let me spell it out for you. T-H-E-L-A-D-D..."

I cut him off, "I can spell!"

"The universe delivers what people need to grow, man. It don't care what you ask for. Maybe it brought you together to teach you something. Maybe you already got the gift."

"It's not feeling like much of a gift."

"Look! Love is lawless, unruly, chaotic, radical. It ain't subtle and smooth. It can't be tamed or controlled. Forget about it! It's a cosmic tornado that sucks you up and drops you to the ground when it's done with you. Nothing will ever be the same. N-O-T-H-I-N-G. If you can't handle heights, you won't last a minute."

Then he noisily slurped down his beer and continued, "Look kid, I'm gonna tell you again. The higher the mountain, the deeper the valley. How many metaphors do you need before you get it?"

He dug for his pocket watch, then quickly got up to go. "I forgot, I got to rock. I'm late for the three o'clock doughnut bake. I like my Powdered Cinnamon warm."

Before he got to the other side of Baldwin Street, he turned my way to give me one more Dude-bit of sagely advice, "Keep the faith, and the faith will keep you." Then he picked up his pace, and raced off in the direction of deep-fried wheat.

When he had faded from view, I noticed he had left his $15 bar bill behind. Seems a reasonable price to pay for such a cornycopia of wisdom.

I finished my beer and walked home with a sudden shot of optimism. Something about Dude's presence always lightened my mood. Maybe it wasn't as bad as I imagined. Maybe Sarah and I were doing exactly what Providence intended—opening, retreating and consolidating growth, then expanding outward yet again... into defenses, below defenses, into defenses, below defenses. Each opening guided by grace, each closing prevented from permanence by Providence. Reminding us with the feel of our Persian cat against our ankle, or a feather falling from the sky at an opportune moment, that we were only to separate for a brief moment before returning to each other for another try.

Maybe.

## The Colorado Monologues

Sleepless in Toronto, I flew down to see her in Colorado the next weekend. When I arrived at the baggage claim, Sarah raced across the floor and jumped into my arms, inadvertently knocking my carry-on and its contents to the ground. We both got down on our knees to gather everything up, entirely unaware of the world around us. When everything was put back in place, we remained on the ground and soul-gazed, again turning an airport into our own personal love nest.

As we vacated our separateness, up came the songs of prior unions, bridged to deeper callings and eternal rhythms. Crisp and clear, the music was unmistakable. Beyond our localized perceptions was something far vaster—a co-created symphony, rising to a crescendo on the wings of our love. The song of Us.

There really is no feeling like reconnecting with a soul you have known since time immemorial. Not only does it bridge you to one another, it grounds you deeper into your own karmic legacy. Suddenly the worries of the day aren't quite as pointed, as the cozy blanket of shared lineage warms your heart, reminding you that you have both been here before and that you will surely be here again. In the eyes of the beloved is the evidence that life truly does go on. Soulmates both call us back in time and prepare the nest for the lives to come.

As we drove back to Sarah's family home in the museum-mobile, we didn't speak at all. Although silent, I could hear our souls dialoguing, speaking their truths in the deep within:

*I'm afraid.*
*Me, too.*
*I don't know how to keep us in the light.*

*Nor do I.*
*I'm still hopeful.*
Pause.
*Yes, me too.*
Pause.
*I'm afraid.*
*I am, too.*
*You are my everything.*
*That's why this is so frightening.*
*It's so much to hold.*
*Yes.*
*Will we get through this?*
*I don't know.*


We were shaking inside, we were.

Before going to the house, we went for a walk in the woods. The lively perfumed forest had lost its scent as winter crept in to steal the sweetness. It was the beginning of the dying, before the first snowfall. After a few minutes, we came to the edge of a powerful rushing river. Too cold to sit, we crouched down beside it and simultaneously began to cry. The river received our tears, as the residue from our conflicts emptied out and merged with nature. It was a beautiful release.

I couldn't help but remember the first time we sat at a river's edge together. It was only a few months ago in real time, but it felt like a century had passed between us. Time is an entirely different experience in the land of the beloved. A minute lasts a day, a day lasts a month, a month lasts an eternity. We had already scaled the heights of divinity and crash-landed on a bed of childhood memories. Where would we travel next?

We went back to the house in time for dinner. Jessie and Norman were sitting in the living room waiting for us. It felt so comforting to see them—a couple that had been through the love wars and survived intact. After a solid man-hug from Norman, we went into the dining room to eat. After weeks of tension, it felt wonderful to be with my beloved and her family. Such fullness of being, as her beautiful parents shared their own stories of connection and overcoming. Smoky and Bear kept playing with my feet like no time had passed, and the buttermilk pie!—there really is nothing like buttermilk pie to soothe the savage beast. All the while, Sarah and I shared seductive glimpses across the table. We were hungry for each other, too.

After dinner, we went into her bedroom to have a dialogue. The room was in a chaotic state, with plates of old food and unwashed clothes laying all over the floor and armoire. So different from the pristine Amish room I had seen on my first visit. Even the vertical blinds were topsy-turvy, with one side higher than the other. It looked like a cyclone had hit it. Or, a challenging relationship.

I sat down on the old rocker at the bottom of the bed, while Sarah plunked herself down at the head of the bed. Open on the bed were two well-worn photo albums. Sarah picked one up and began to talk. At first tentative, she became more energized as she spoke, rapidly laying down her theories about what was blocking our path: the positioning of the planets, our Vedic chart misalignment, the problem of timing. She spoke straight through for almost an hour, before lying down on the bed and going quiet.

I couldn't hear a word of it. It wasn't that I didn't care what she was feeling. I just couldn't feel *her*. It all felt conceptual and avoidant, like she was deliberately bypassing her vulnerability. I knew it was in there somewhere, but I couldn't feel it.

When she was done, she asked me if I understood. I lied, "It all makes perfect sense." I didn't want to make matters worse. Then she asked me to express my truth. So I did, with equally ungrounded banter, evading my vulnerability.

When I was done, I asked her if she had anything to say. She said, "No, it all makes perfect sense." I knew she hadn't heard a word.

Too confused or too afraid, we could neither speak nor hear our truths when our pain was active. It was as though we had left our bodies at the same moment, shadow-jumping away from the wound-body because it felt too large to confront. It's astonishing how effective we humans are at ignoring the push to consciousness when it's staring us straight in the inner eye.

After we were both done, I lay down on the bed beside her. We kissed tentatively with our eyes open. Then Sarah turned the other way, and I spooned her, nestling my face in her hair. Her smell began to intoxicate me, reminding me of the delights of her flesh. Oh, how I longed to make love with her again.

Perhaps the turning away helped her to feel safe, because now she spoke more clearly from her heart. "You're just so controlling, Lowen. I feel suffocated."

I replied softly, "How do I suffocate you? I feel like I give you all kinds of space."

"I'm independent. I have to make my own choices, for myself. Pa always said that about me. You don't understand where I come from. No one can choose my path."

"But what do I try to control?"

"I'm wild, Ogdo—wild as the wind. I always will be."

As if to emphasize her words, the wind banged the blinds against the bedpost. The natural world clearly agreed with her. Point taken.

After a long pause, she spoke again. "Our love forces me to belong to something, but I don't belong to anything, only nature. And nature is wild. It can't be tamed. You can't tame us."

Us? Did she get engaged to the trees? Talk about playing it safe. Marry the forest, and other than the occasional thunderstorm you won't get upset. For a moment, I felt tempted to psychoanalyze her fear of belonging, but I caught myself. It would only create more friction and, truth be told, who even knows where these patterns come from? Maybe it's not a play-it-safe pattern sourced in childhood trauma. Maybe it's a soul path? Maybe it's not a willful child clinging to her independence. Maybe her path really was that of the wild and free. I had learned from my own life that what is neurotic through one lens is expansive through another. And what is one person's relationship prison is another person's liberation from loneliness. Maybe she was right—I was trying to hold a bird in my hand.

Out of respect for her parents, I left her room early in the morning to sleep on the couch in the living room. But I couldn't sleep at all, choosing instead to perch myself on the kitchen windowsill, waiting for the sun to emerge through the darkness. I nestled into my confusion for hours, scouring my inner world for a reference point that would help me traverse this complicated terrain. None were to be found. Clues everywhere, yes, but nothing that felt like a clear path to walk.

As the sky slowly brightened, two birds began flying past the window. One was a black raven, thick and ominous. Glaringly obvious against the brightness of the full moon, it kept swooping down erratically from above before rising above the tree-line. The other was a sparkling red and yellow Western Tanager, gliding peacefully back and forth between two pine trees right in front of the window. The symbology was painfully obvious. We had two paths before us: dark and foreboding, or sparkly and smooth. Pick your flight.

We spent the next two days fighting about everything and nothing. It's astonishing how much energy young lovers have for needless conflict. I went down on my knees countless times and asked God, "Why? Why bring this ecstatic nightmare into my life? Why open my heart so wide to another, then make it so painfully difficult to sustain? Why?"

We had been gifted with something so wondrous, but we couldn't hold it safe alone. In uncharted territory, in a culture more concerned with ego than essence, we were adrift alone on this raucous river. Our ship was riddled with holes from our past, everyone's past, and we had no idea how to patch them. And even worse, we mistook each other for the pirate ship itself. How to stay afloat and ride this hol(e)y ship?

# 11

## Scar-crossed Lovers

Sarah returned to our home in Toronto the following week. Before she arrived, we agreed to a period of celibacy. No kissing. No fondling. No lovemaking. Just presence.

This agreement seemed to defuse the tensions between us. We moved through our days softly, quietly lying in each other's arms whenever we could, enjoying the simplest moments without complication. Like it was in the beginning, we made love without making love. And there was chocolate, lots of it.

Each morning, I would wake up to prose written on the sunroom wall. It was like Sarah was channeling Anais Nin, her writing was that beautiful. I was blessed to be the recipient of her outpourings:

> I woke before the dawning morning to sit
> and watch the stars for a while.
> I thought about how some of them out there are binary,
> two that share a common motion.
> Then I remembered,
> you are the poem in my soul singing softly to me.
> You were in my heart
> the very moment my soul was conceived.

Enhancing the softening was a natural shift toward silence. We said little in our time together, choosing, instead, to speak with our presence. We intuitively knew that ceasing talking was the way we could hear each other again. And it was there in the silence that the love portal again opened widest. Of course, the bond had never been the words. It was always the breath in between them.

I was finally at peace after weeks of conflict and confusion. It seemed we had passed our tests. We had surmounted some seemingly unsurmountable challenges. Our love was the healing balm for my lost soul, its home away from no-home, the all-encompassing heart embrace that every soul longs for. Even a moment here was enough to ignite optimism in the most wayward of hearts. It was like I had traveled this planet homeless for 2,000 lifetimes, and now it was time to come home.

In the heart of the peace, Sarah's writing flowed and flowered, and often right on my body. I would wake up to "I ♡" written on my penis, "Home is where the Lowen is" written on my belly, "Home" fingered in red paint on my forehead. Such delicious madness.

The walls of the apartment—inside, and on the stucco around the front door—were also recipients of her graffiti-fest. One night, I came back from buying her churros in the market to find a short Rumi poem written in fluorescent green chalk on the front door:

> Lovers of God,
> sometimes a door opens,
> and a human being becomes
> a way for grace to come through.

When grace walked through that door with churros in hand, grace met him on the other side with the sweetest hug ever. Not sure if it was the churros or the man she wanted more, but I wasn't complaining either way.

Later that night, Sarah woke me up with sweet kisses. She had said so little all week, but words were now effusively bubbling to the surface. "Love just ain't enough word for us, Ogdo," she said with the adorable country twang that made me crazy happy.

Rolling over to face her, I quickly replied, "No, it's much too limiting," in the hope that I could now go back to sleep.

She wasn't finished yet: "How do we live in this world with this much ecstasy? Where do we put it, Ogdo?"

"Isn't it enough just to feel it?"

Sarah nodded her head, then digressed, "I kind of want some co-conut ice cream." Then she smiled, "Wait, I already had too much pleasure this week." And then she got serious again, "Yah, well, no, it feels too big, like it needs to be channeled into something else?"

I knew not to mention babies. "Maybe we need to help the love-starved, convert the energy of our connection into optimism for those who have given up on love?"

She went quiet for some time. "Not sure, but it feels like it's not just about us. We are supposed to do something with this gift."

The conversation ended our week of perfect celibacy. Our call to bond was again too strong to contain, as our love sought its favorite forum for expression. This began a deepening exploration of our love in sensual form.

We made love for hours each evening without fail. As we grew more intimate, my body continually changed its way of relating to her. My hands, in particular, became even more subtly attuned, as though the love between us had transformed them from the rough hands of a miner to the (he)artful hands of a sculptor. It's amazing how opening the heart renders the entire body an instrument of the divine.

My genitals became more devotional as well, moving my Godrod in and out of her like a salty prayer for love. It takes more than just a loving connection between two people to create a sacred sexuality. We must also see the genitals at their highest—as reflections of the God-self, as devotees to our purest imaginings. The lustful self sees flesh, but the sacred self sees God.

Then something beautiful happened. Feeling safe with each other opened us to a new level of vulnerability and self-revealing. When-ever I moved inside of her, we looked deep into each other's eyes, holding the gaze all the way to climax, merging our essence above and below. At the same time, we surrendered to whatever emotions came up, inviting and allowing each other to feel it all.

It was all about allowing. Sometimes we simply smiled all the way to orgasm—but more often than not, it was tears that emerged—tears of joy, tears of sorrow, tears of no fears. It was a deep and thorough cleansing, the kind of healing that can only happen when you are truly seen by your beloved. There was no judgment, no resistance, no effort at distraction. We would cry and cum until sleep overtook us.

### Attached at the Waste

We may have leaped in too far. As we continued to deepen our intimacy, more than healing emerged from our vulnerability. Soon enough, darker shades of feeling again arose from the embers. As we connected more meaningfully, our intimacy became like a depth charge, digging deeper and deeper into our fear-body, like a shovel determined to excavate untold sufferings from their internal burial grounds. Goodness, there is so much pain. Is there ever an end? Yes, the higher the mountain, the deeper the valley. Oh, Dude, here we go again!

And it wasn't only our pain. To be sure, we both had negative associations with vulnerability, but it felt like it went much deeper than that. Every time Sarah and I opened our unfiltered hearts to the next level of vulnerability, we touched the pain of the world a little bit more. When you travel along the heart-genital highway at this level of intensity, you can't help but bring the collective code of all humanity along for the ride. And that necessarily includes much of the unresolved anger and toxicity humanity carries. It's all there, awaiting its moment of liberation.

Nightmares soon ruled our sleep. Many of them felt like symbolic replications of tumultuous past lives. One of the core, oft-repeated themes was gender and control, as though we were still working through unresolved issues with each other. Is that why we were brought together in this lifetime? To soften those edges and finally meet on equal footing? Was her inner tigress a carry-forward from our history, to finally bring our union into balance? Was my unwillingness to be subdued a perpetuation of my controlling karmic legacy? Can relationship challenges actually be understood this way?

As the reactivity between us became increasingly ugly, we made a conscious decision to slow down the physical intimacy, again. But it was too late. The tsunami of toxicity was already in motion and gaining momentum. We jumped in right where we last ended our conflicts, as Sarah began attacking my relationship history, looking for signs of betrayal. She stormed out of the house three times in one evening because I refused to name all the partners I had been with. Why did she need names? How was that going to resolve the fucking jealousy wound?

Then it was my turn. Overcome with feelings of insecurity, I began to cross-examine her.

And then there was more, the deep dark more. Finally, after her persistent probing, I snapped. One Saturday evening, I went on the offensive and sought out ways to hurt her back. Instead of refusing to answer her questions, I told her everything she wanted to know. Every sexual detail, every experience of love, every heart I broke. All of it. She asked for it, so I delivered.

I ruthlessly rehashed and exaggerated my objectifying years. All the women I won over with my charms, seeing them as prized objects to be claimed. After a childhood with no control, I loved the control I had over a woman in bed. Their moans were badges of egoic glory, spurring me on to greater acts of supremacy. I told her how I dated as many women as I could, quantifying my bounty like a hunter counts skins. And the revealing that triggered her the most: the ridiculously cocky pride I took in the earrings that they left behind, gathering them like prizes on top of my bookcase.

Then I took her on a full-blown excursion into my law school years, when I was still carrying a motherload of childhood anger. I told her about Suri's gorgeous breasts, Bobbi's hungry mouth and Elsa's love of anal. I even told her about Beth, a hot yogini who showed me the wonders of a perfect blow job while I drove us through the streets of Buffalo, New York.

As I was rehashing, I heard my deeper knowing telling me to shut the fuck up. But the boxing gloves were off and I couldn't stop. I was driven past the point of return. I actually wanted to hurt her.

And then she returned the favor by sharing everything I didn't want to hear. I heard about Reggie's massive penis, Marco's bluer-than-blue eyes, and Phillip's love songs. I even got to hear about the wonders of oral with Pamela, her doppelganger lesbian lover. You'd think we'd have the good sense to take some space, but we couldn't. We were attached at the waste, determined to wound what we most loved in the world. From beloved to be-hated in one breath.

After we were done, we retreated to separate rooms to suffer in silence. As I lay there, I recognized a startling dichotomy alive within me. I didn't know how to understand it, but there was a wide chasm between my karmic age and my emotional maturity. Simply put, I was an old soul with a baby psyche. This was also true for Sarah. She had such a great depth of being, coexisting within a vast array of primal triggers. How very strange to be so remarkably mature and so deeply regressed at the same time. How do we understand this? How do these two opposite spectrums of consciousness reside within the same being? And can someone build a stable relationship with another before they have brought these discordant aspects into alignment?

As things spiraled out of control, I suggested that we go into therapy to see if it would help. Sarah was reluctant but willing to try one session. I booked a two-hour session with a well-regarded Jungian psychologist who specialized in couples work. I had two friends who had worked with him successfully, and one of his books was a key healing tool on my own journey.

Initially hesitant, we got rolling fairly quickly and shared everything with him—the ecstatic, the reactive, the downright nasty. Without trying to control or define our experience, the Doctor asked brilliant questions. Near the end of the session, he offered the most intelligent diagnosis I have ever heard a therapist utter: "I'm not sure I can help you. To be sure, psycho-emotional issues are all over your relationship, but I agree, you have entered a terrain that transcends conventional therapeutic models and techniques. I call it 'the outer reaches.' Spiritual maturation is your only hope. If you use this connection to grow you, you have a chance. But if you don't, it will fall apart."

And so it was. This love was either a call to wholeness, or a call to fragmentation. There was no middle ground. We either went all the way to God, or crashed in pieces down below. What we most needed was to let this love grow us strong enough to handle it. But where to get the strength to remain in the fire in the meantime?

One thing had become clear among the confusion—great love takes no prisoners. Die to its expansive ferocity, or die within your resistance. Let love's embrace burn you whole, or become karmic ash in love's cosmic kiln. Sometimes there really are only two choices. When the heart door opens, jump on IN.

## River of Wounds

After two days of silence, Sarah took it all to the next level. As I was waking up, I heard her in the sunroom talking and laughing on her phone, a conversation that continued for some time. Then she came out of the room and walked into the bedroom where I was doing some sun salutations on my yoga mat. Her ring was off her finger.

"Do you know who I was talking to, Ogdo?" she asked with a slightly mischievous expression on her face.

"How would I know?" I responded nervously.

"My ex. He wants to go on a camping trip to see if we can find some closure."

Her ex—Chang—was a Tae Kwan Do Master she dated a few years earlier—she had left him because he was too cold and aggressive. He wasn't someone she had ever expressed a need to find closure with.

Then she took it one step further.

"He is going to be in Collingwood for a few weeks. Says he knows a nice resort area in the Blue Mountain region. Have you been there, hun? It's not too far from here, is it?"

Now, I am not a violent man, but this little game held the potential to change that. I felt my frustration building. The brat in me wanted to kick the brat in her right back across the US border.

Everyone has their favorite weapon. Betrayal was Sarah's. Aside from the question of whether betrayal was intrinsic to our shared soul history, she had betrayed and been betrayed many times in this life-time. It was a core theme in her life. Plus, she knew my issues from the inside out. She understood there was no better way to push me away than to plant the seed of betrayal.

I responded, as she knew I would respond—by acting out. I yelled, I cried, I turned into a blithering idiot. I even threw a stapler against the newly painted bedroom wall, knocking over a lamp in the process.

"You aren't stable enough for me, Lowen," she said calmly. "You scare me."

Rage building. OMG! The perfect set-up! I was the unstable one? Eegods! She had insidiously woven the path of excuse she unconsciously needed to retreat from this terrifyingly profound connection. Suddenly I saw a young teenage girl standing in front of me playing silly love games. *Who was this woman?*

My worst nightmare was upon me.

And then all of the triggers flooded in at one time. It was like a great cosmic sewage dam had been broken through, spilling its refuse everywhere. The conflicts intensified. I fused. She refused. She was on the run, and I couldn't stop chasing. Our rushing river of wounds was alive and there seemed no way to contain it.

In the heart of the madness, our sexual relationship stopped altogether. This time it wasn't a conscious choice. The river was both dammed—and damned—and I could no longer open to her in that way. A line had been crossed. Our perfectly aligned stars had fallen from the sky—we were now scar-crossed lovers. Souls in anguish, we created the monsters we most feared, one projection at a time.

One afternoon, I found myself crying at the back of the courtroom while we were on recess. A tidal wave of torment overcame me as I tried to make sense of this relationship. If this love was revealing anything, it was that finding your beloved doesn't mean finding perpetual bliss. If it does, then it's probably love sailing at half-mast. If a love is that deep, it is a portal to the everything, shredding through the masks and disguises that separate us from reality, excavating shadow and light from their hiding places. The glory and the gory rise in unison, calling us to the sky and the earth in one instant. Real soulmates are actually wholemates, penetrating the everything on the wings of their love. What a magic, tragic carpet ride.

Overcome with frustration, I was riddled with hopelessness. The connection was like a portal into all that is real and connected, and yet we could not protect it. We were simply not conscious or healthy enough, or not individuated enough, or we have landed on a pathway that humanity itself was not ready to embrace. How to be wholemates if you can't even live in the same fucking house?

When I got home that day, she was gone. And so was all her stuff.

There is no sound like the silence after your beloved flees. I suppose I should have been relieved that the little brat had left, but no such luck. I fell to the floor in a crumpled heap of anguish. Though I cried from a real place, I couldn't escape the idea that all of these challenges were superfluous, as though there was some transcendent truth that superseded the silly details; as though we were just distracting from the heart of the matter, back and forth, to and fro, opening and retreating, loving and testing. Or was I just deluded, *after all*?

I lay on the carpet all night, chilled to the bone. Had I not known better, I would have thought I'd contracted a virus. But it was far worse than that—a heart attack, a heart-ache of twin-flame proportions.

What do you do when your heart walks out the door?

Brace yourself.

# 12

## Karmageddon

I stumbled up with the sun to get ready for court. If ever there was a day to ask for an adjournment, it was today. But I had no shot at it—broken-heartedness doesn't mean shit to a trial judge. The harshness of the world doesn't end when we are torn to shreds.

I stayed in the shower for a long time, hiding from the world, riddled with confusion: How could she do this to us? Who trashes this kind of a gift? The whole world longs for even a moment of great love. What fool runs from it?

Baffled, I lay down in the tub, letting the steaming hot water crash down on my exhausted body. I wanted to curse her, but I was too tender to hate. My heart was blown wide open. It would take something much worse to shut it down. But what to do with this open heart now? Should I surrender to her choice, or chase her down?

On the way out of the house, I came upon a scene in the lane between my house and the neighbors. Violet, the elderly Jamaican lady who lived next door, was kneeling at the foot of a dead squirrel with two of the neighborhood kids. I shuddered, concerned it was Little Friend, the squirrel that Sarah used to feed. Until I got up close—this one was much younger.

"Saw it fall from your roof this morning when I was hanging the laundry," Violet recounted, her voice crackling with upset.

"So strange. Squirrels almost never fall from heights," I said, uncomfortably aware of the synchronicity between Sarah's departure and the squirrel's untimely exit.

"God works in mysterious ways, Lowen. A few nights ago a bird hit my bedroom window and died. Been in this house for 47 years and never saw that happen once."

I didn't dare to ask if the bird was a red cardinal.

I had to wonder—is this the way the universe works? When a connection is moving in a deeply true direction, everything around it blossoms with life. When it goes down a dark road, does the discord get reflected in the outer world as well? Or was my pained mind simply drawing conclusions that reflected its current despair?

I looked up and saw another squirrel peering down from the roof, staring at the events below. If I wasn't mistaken, she looked upset by the loss of her beloved. Or was I projecting again?

On the drive to the court, I called Sarah's cell phone incessantly. Her phone was off. When I got to the courthouse, I sat on the front steps and attempted to gather myself for the ending of a trial. *Turn heart off, Turn mind on, Turn heart off, Turn mind on.*

It was my turn to address the jury in a complex fraud case. My client, an elderly Italian man, was accused of misrepresenting the books and stealing recipes from his long time business partner. They owned a chain of popular bakeries, and my client was allegedly selling the recipes to their competition in exchange for retirement property in Panama. The irony wasn't lost on me, as I too felt like a kind of fraud, one who was being unmasked for his foolishness before the universal courtroom. Luckily, I had written the jury address before Sarah took off. If I had to ad lib, I would have only spewed nonsense.

At the first recess, I tried calling Sarah again. No luck. Then I called her parents' home. No answer and no machine. Hillbillies!

The trial ended at noon with an acquittal, thankfully. And now my real trial began. No distractions now, only the searing pain of loss.

Before I went back to my empty home, I met Daniel for a taco lunch. Probably the wrong move, since Sarah and I had kissed over many tacos at the same restaurant. In the line to order, I kept flashbacking to the last time we were here, when we shared a chorizo and drank the perfect margarita. To make matters worse, I directed Daniel to the table we had eaten at. Because that's what you do when you are sad about love—you dig the knife in even deeper. What the fuck?!

Daniel had just completed a ten day Vipassana retreat in the Berkshires and was calm as a cucumber. I was already annoyed before he opened his mouth.

"This is the first time I've spoken in ten days," he said. "I even drove back from the retreat in silence."

"Wow, you didn't talk to yourself all the way back from Massachusetts?" I asked sarcastically. "That's quite an achievement. Good thing there are self-serve gas stations. How was your workshop?"

"I got so hungry there, I ate like a horse. But I stayed disciplined with my practice. But first, how are you feeling today? I read your text. Why did she leave?" he asked with great compassion.

I didn't have an answer, not even a pretend one. With tears welling in my eyes, I turned my attention to my tacos, and spent the rest of the meal in silence with my dear old friend.

## *Fall from Grace*

After Daniel and I parted, I got back to compulsively calling Sarah. Still no luck. Or, perhaps much luck. Was there really anything to say right now? Too sad to sit still, I decided to leave my car parked in the city hall underground lot and walk home.

As I walked, I felt into my interior landscape, ravaged by weeks of conflict and confusion. Great love was invigorating, but it was also exhausting. I would have expected this degree of depletion from military training, not from a love relationship. I wanted to find some respite, but the questions wouldn't stop: *How does one prepare for great love? Is there a recipe, a formula, a path to follow through the gnarly forest? Must we work on ourselves first, or does the real work begin after the love arrives? Must we create certain conditions to attract it, or does it come of its own accord? Does it choose us, or do we choose it? And how on earth do we protect it? What kind of girders do we need to keep it solid? And how do we develop them if we are lost in our triggers?*

I was entirely unsure what to do next. I could hear a rational voice telling me not to chase her, but that voice was overshadowed by a far more powerful inner voice calling me toward her. I could even hear Sarah's soul calling out to mine, asking me not to give up. Wherever she was in physical form, her spirit was hovering near, attempting to communicate.

That's the thing about soulmates. They don't stop dialoguing when they are physically apart. They simply turn on the soulular phone and communicate in the deep within.

After turning onto Augusta Avenue, I saw Dude sitting in Bellevue Square, the concrete park at the south end of the market. He was eating a churro dripping with caramel sauce. Dude loved his pastries. I reached into my pocket and handed him a tissue. He took it and wiped the sauce from his beard. We made small talk—rare for us—before he went in for the kill.

"You look like shit again. She gone?"

"What are you, a frickin' detective? How the fuck do you know everything?"

"Not complicated. It's written all over your face. Plus you're carrying a big wad of tissues in your pocket. Men don't carry tissues unless they're having love troubles."

That's probably true.

Before I could say anything more, an elderly black man called out Dude's name from across the square. "You're up, Dude!" he shouted, pointing to one of the outdoor chess tables at the edge of the park. Sitting on one side was a young girl, clearly waiting for her chance to checkmate the Dude.

Then Dude got up and walked toward the garbage can at the end of the bench. He was just about to throw the last bit of churro out, when he remembered his manners. "I got to go. This kid keeps beating me, but I feel lucky tonight. Do you want the rest of the churro?"

"No, thanks Dude. I prefer my churros whole," I said with unnecessary attitude.

Sweet man ignored me. "Whatever happens, keep your heart open. If not, it will all have been wasted."

*Wasn't it already wasted?* I wondered.

He tossed the rest of the churro into the garbage and went off to play chess.

By the time I arrived home, I felt oddly calm, in that exhausted state where everything slows down. I lay down on the couch where we had so often made love and continued to dialogue with Sarah's essence. Trapped between a rock and a heart place, she couldn't disentangle from me, but she couldn't hold this love safe either. Equally fearful and full of longing, she was searching hard for an answer. But was there an answer to be found? Or was it simply a choice to be made? The choice to love bravely, even amid the most ferocious patterns and triggers. Essence to essence, we hearticulated some more:

*I can't give up on us.*
*I can't either... but I have to.*
*There is no have to.*
*There is, Lowen. I need to be free of this prison.*
*How can love be a prison?*
*When it locks us in with our pain.*
*Shit.*
*I can't find the key.*
*Shit.*

I got up to call her on the real phone. But it was still off. The pain intensified. *Come on, Sarah, answer the fucking phone.* I wandered around the house, looking for signs of her. I needed something to fill this desolate void. I went into the sunroom where she loved to rest. There was a small card with writing on it edging out from under the pillow. Reluctantly, fearful of more pain, I reached for it. In her familiar scrawl, this time in black crayon, was another variation on our favorite love graffiti. This one stung:

When two hearts beat
in the same direction,
they go to war.

Ouch! This is what you leave me? Fuck you!

I went down onto the futon in child's pose. Anything to feel safe. After some time, I turned over onto my back. When I opened my eyes, I was struck by a picture of Sarah I had taped to the ceiling. It was one of the first pictures we took, kissing in the forest in Colorado. Our eyes were open, sparkling with delight. *Oh Sarah, Oh God.* In a way, nothing had changed since that moment. Nothing ever could. I unbuttoned my shirt and placed the picture on my chest, facing my heart. Closing my eyes and remembering her body, her smiling eyes, those light wet kisses. Come home, my true love, come home and kiss me.

I reached down to masturbate, but my heart wasn't in it. Pleasure wasn't currently on the menu. I lay there, agitated, trying my best to keep the inner wolves at bay. But they wouldn't have it. They were all out of their cages, prowling for prey. After a few hours, I managed to fall asleep, until I was awakened by a strangely comforting dream. This one touched deep.

I dreamed of my Auntie Dora, my mother's sister. She had died some time ago, but sometimes appeared in my dreamscapes. In this dream, she was walking beside me on a forest trail, holding my hand. I kept asking her questions, but she remained silent, focused on the path ahead. At some point, I tried to free my hand and cut off the path. She grabbed on tighter. I turned to look her way, and she stopped and looked right at me. "Now is not the time to let go, Lowen. I'll be keeping you close for a time."

I woke up with a jolt at exactly 7 a.m.—sweating and startled. I reached for the phone to call Sarah again.

At last, I heard the other line pick up—someone fumbling.

"Sarah," I exhaled.

"uh-lo," said the breathy, sleepy voice.

A man's voice.

I had no idea who he was but I knew what had happened. I hung up the phone and vomited all over the futon.

And then, I vomited again.

There are no words for that fall from grace.

No words.

# 13

## Care(less) of the Soul

Spiraling into a vortex of black, the lights went off everywhere. *Oh my Goddess, Where do I go from here?* Breathless and bloodied, I lay down on the floor, desperate for support. My own inner floor had collapsed, like the chain snapping on an elevator. With no warning— plummeting DOWN. Please, God, give me something solid.

I heard my soul pleading with hers: *Sarah, oh Sarah- how could you do this? What kind of madness is this? No, just tell me it's not true. OH SHIT, it is true, isn't it? How many lifetimes till we get this right?*

I couldn't sit with the feelings. Too damn intense. I got up and paced. I opened the fridge a hundred times. I opened every self-help book I owned, looking for some stupid spiritual aphorism to tide me over. I walked around the house like a lost puppy, searching for com- fort anywhere. There was none to be found. I picked up the phone to call someone but I was too embarrassed to share. I turned every pic- ture of Sarah upside-down. I was turned upside-down.

I could feel my heart turning against itself, blaming me for every- thing. Suddenly it was all my fault: *You horny shit. You should have kept it celibate. You caused this catastrophe. Why can't you keep your cock in your pants? The writing was on the wall, fool!*

Oh shit, her writing was still on the wall. I grabbed some pushpins and bed sheets and covered them up.

It felt easier to blame myself than to blame it on Sarah. If it was her fault, there was no turning back. If it was my fault, there was still a chance of redemption. All I had to do was behave differently and there would be a different outcome. Delusional thinking is of great value in times of tremendous suffering. It can be the only thing that keeps us alive.

I fled the house to go for a run, but I was too mangled to get very far. Actually, it was more than mangled. It was a fucking heart holocaust. A karmic misappropriation of funds that left me spiritually bankrupt. I lumbered into the back alley, and fell down to one knee, in submission to God. Then I threw up again. Tears mixed with vomit as I lay down on the mucky ground and dialogued with the universe, or its satanic rep, seeking salvation: *Come on, Universe. This is a fucking joke, right? This didn't really happen, did it? There is a way through this, isn't there? Or maybe it's a great blessing? Rumi was right, wasn't he? "Don't grieve for what doesn't come. Some things that don't happen keep disasters from happening." Is this what he meant? That if we had stayed together, something worse would happen later? But what could be worse than this? This IS the fucking disaster!*

I went back home and threw up again. Then I darted into the garage in a blaze of madness and grabbed a can of black spray paint. If the writing is on the wall, let's remove the writing from the wall. *Fucking graffiti.* I went upstairs to the sunroom and got to it. As I sprayed, I inwardly cursed the words she had written.

I woke before the dawning morning to sit
and watch the stars for a while.
Liar!
I thought about how some of them out there are binary,
two that share a common motion.
Bullshit!
Then I remembered,
you are the poem in my soul singing softly to me.
You were in my heart
the very moment my soul was conceived.
And then I fucking betrayed you!!!

After I had darkened every bit of graffiti I could find, I crumpled into a heap of exhaustion on the bedroom floor, the walls now as black as my soul. I fell dead asleep, empty paint can by my side.

## *When Nightmares May Come*

I awoke before dawn, overcome with tremendous anxiety. I quickly dressed and fled the house, desperately needing to move. As I walked, my self-hatred turned to hardcore rage. I wanted to call her out on the bitch that lived inside of her: *You little bitch, you fucking hypocrite, you gamesy vixen. You invited me to this open-heart party, then ate me alive.* "Be true to us, Lowen! Please be true to us!" *As if! What a fucking joke. What a deadly projection.*

I had visions of flying down to Boulder and punching the dude out. But how could I blame him? She was the cheater, after all. It could have been anyone.

*Fuck that little shit—I'll punch him out anyway.*

The sun was starting to peek through, as I stormed through the market. I stopped at all the locations we frequented, trying to make sense of it all. Not a chance. Maybe there was some higher perspective, but I couldn't see it. Instead, I sat in front of our favorite coffeehouse and tormented myself with beautiful memories. Oh the knife, it twisted.

There was one memory in particular that kept at me. It was a Sunday morning after a full night of exquisite lovemaking. I was sitting in the café window watching the market wake up when Sarah bounced in and playfully sat on my lap, also facing the street. Whenever I turned my head, she turned her head too and laughed, "We are a four armed Cyclops, Ogdo. One eye is all we need." It was the sweetest thing. We drank chai and watched the world go by as one.

The fond memories ended there. By lunch, I mustered up the willpower to walk home, all the while tormented with visions of Sarah fucking some other man. One question kept eating at me: *Did she fuck him with the ring on? Did she fuck him with the ring on? Did she fuck with him with the ring on?*

With more triggers than a firing range, I lay on my couch in the most intense pain I had ever experienced. If ever there was a time I needed my emotional armor, it was now. All opened up with no place to go, I was stripped entirely bare—unclothed, undisguised, skinned alive. Spasms of agony ripped through me as I searched my consciousness for a mechanism, any mechanism, to numb this pain. But after months of opening, my habitual defenses were long gone. I was heart wide open when this bomb dropped, and my armor too far from the battlefield to serve me. I should have taken her threats of polyamory more seriously.

Was the whole universe laughing at me? It sure felt like it. I had been seduced, widowed, cheated by love itself! I had been so sure of us, and so dismissive of other connections. Meanwhile people in more 'practical' relationships were falling asleep together night after night, and I was lying alone on my couch, with Lightnin and her fur balls at my side. And I had named her Lightnin—an eternal reminder of Sarah's fleeing feet! Idiot!

But why? Why would the universe bring this love my way, only to crush me into bits? For what possible purpose? Was this my penance for objectifying so many women and breaking so many hearts? For breaking hers in the last life? Whose black magic worked this deal?

Who was this man, *now*?

### Hello Abandonment, My Old Friend

Completely incapacitated, I stayed on my couch for days. I called into the office to tell them that I was too sick to work. By the pathetic sound of my voice, there was no disputing it. While lying there, I found myself looking for Sarah's spirit to dialogue with, but I could no longer make the connection. The soulular phone line was out of order. The betrayal had seen to that. Now there was an irreparable cut in the cord between our hearts.

Great love is powerful like an ocean and fragile like a reed.

Then she called. At first I could barely hear her, she spoke so softly. In a little girl's voice that I had only heard once before, she whispered, "I can't do it, Lowen. I can't handle this depth of connection. It's too much for me. I was the deluded one, not you. I'm too afraid. I'm so, so sorry. This is just too hard." The primal self had spoken.

"But why *that* way? You know my wounds."

Then her voice changed and I heard a stranger, armored and aloof. "I think that must be why. I don't know. He meant nothing to me. I had just met him. It was a suicidal act. I just had to kill it. I can't hold this much love in my heart."

"I held it," I whispered.

For a moment, I felt her soften. We both fell quiet.

Then my ego stormed in, "And why the fuck was he answering your cell phone?"

"I asked him to. I'm so sorry."

Then the words stopped again. We sat in silence for a long time, feeling into the love below the tension, not quite able to hang up. It was as though there were two entirely different entities taking up space inside us at the same time: the soul's boundless love and the psyche's limiting beliefs. How to bring them together?

We stayed on the phone for the whole evening, wordless but deeply present. Both trying to take this in. Trying to fathom the un-fathomable. Could this really be THE END? In the meantime, Light-nin tried to jump on me every few minutes, as though inviting us to remember our love. After midnight, my heavy eyes closing, I told her I had to go, but she wasn't ready. Neither was I. We fell asleep on our separate couches, phones in hand, momentarily suspending the real-ity of what had happened.

I woke up to a dial tone before the sun came up. I lay there shiver-ing in the dark, as the warmth from our phone sharings faded away. I tried to hold on, but reality wouldn't be denied. Soon the pain from the betrayal rose right back into awareness, and I found myself again enraged. It was just too much to bear—the stark void of her absence, this brutal ending. I railed out loud: *How can you abandon this gift? People long for love their whole lives and never find it. Not even a single day of it. And you just walk away without a fight? Cowardice! Do you even have the right to refuse this gift? This shared destiny? Do you?*

In the same way as she couldn't hold the love, I couldn't hold the hurt. This love had introduced me to an entirely different universe. How could I abandon its possibilities?

I fell asleep again before being awakened in a cold clammy sweat. It was a familiar nightmare—all too familiar. I was sitting outside an ex-lovers apartment waiting for her to leave for work in the morning. Fully lodged in my rejection triggers, I was desperate to talk to her, desperate for any form of contact. I woke up, as I always did after dreams like this, just before seeing her. Eternal frustration.

Throughout my relationship history, this recurring nightmare had always signaled that my abandonment wound was crossing a threshold into madness. My first girlfriend Naomi was the original revealer. When separating from Naomi activated this wound, it went so earth-shatteringly deep that it was all I could do to stay alive until the pain passed. Completely overcome by heart-ripping anxiety, I couldn't find my footing anywhere. Time and time again, I plummeted painfully alone into a primal abyss.

And here I was, back again. Hello abandonment, my old friend.

How to stay true to the feelings about Sarah's absence without slipping into a primal woundhole? It didn't seem possible. Please Goddess, hold me safe.

That night, I frenetically wrote Sarah a 12-page email, pleading with her to come into therapy with me, to talk things through, to heal. She wrote back without speaking to my request. "Off to Boulder for yoga teacher's training. Things must be as they are." Must they?

I had to take action.

The next morning, I borrowed Daniel's credit card—this relationship had cost me in more ways than one—and booked a weekend flight to Denver. Madness, yes, but I had no choice. I was too tortured to sit still. I emailed her to let her know, and she replied, "DON'T COME." That's all I got. Certain that it was my job to fight for our little piece of God, I packed my bags, as the stampeding hooves of unrequited longing trampled my spirit whole.

## Trigger Unhappy

As I flew down to Denver, I couldn't help but notice how frozen I was emotionally. I could feel the pain surging through my body, but I couldn't release it. The river was all dammed up again, confused as to its direction, shocked by the rupture to its integrity.

I rented a car in Denver, and drove toward Boulder. Somehow I ended up outside Rocky Mountain National Park first—the home of our first kiss. I didn't dare enter, remaining instead in my car outside the entrance, frozen by the searing pain of memories. While I was waiting, an industrious cardinal zipped in and out of view, as though to remind me that our dance wasn't yet complete.

When I finally got to my hotel—the same one I had stayed in when we first met—I fell fast asleep until morning. During the night, I had one abandonment dream after another, always involving Sarah and another man. You would think that our healthy defenses would take over in a situation like this, keeping our pain at bay. But it doesn't work that way. The wounds call out to each other, feeding off the weakness in their host. I awoke in another cold sweat, trigger unhappy, waiting for the next bomb to drop. A woundathon had formally taken root.

I went to get a coffee. Agitated, I dropped out of the line before ordering. I didn't need a coffee. I needed a hug. I needed Sarah.

I went for a walk downtown. *Boulder, shit. Here you are again. The place where it all began. You annoying new age pseudo nirvana. I hate you. I* pondered my next move. *Now what? You've chased her to Colorado. What you gonna do now, kidnap her?*

A wave of nausea hit me. *What am I going to accomplish here? Can we go back in time even if we want to? Can a profound love relationship re-enter heaven after it has plummeted to the depths of hell? Aren't I just delaying the inevitable?*

I called her cell—immediately to voicemail. Probably fucking a stranger again. More triggers fired in me. The voice of reason interjected: *Go home! Are you not meant for better than this? Stop giving your power away to this ungrateful runner. Just leave.*

Not a chance. The wound insisted I find her to heal it. I held onto the belief—delusional or rooted in the bigger picture—that I had to fight for this love. I wanted to be heroic in its name. God had gone to a lot of trouble to bring our souls together. Surely there was a greater reason than separating? How can I give up without a fight?

I would soon wish I had.

## Zombie Beloved

The yoga training was being held at a small Vinyasa studio in downtown Boulder. I walked over and sat on the steps outside, somehow imagining that Sarah would serendipitously appear as she had many times before. My inner world was a jagged wreck, my heart racing, my stomach queasy, my thoughts a mixture of madness and longing. I kept attempting to recreate the inner peace that love brings, but it was long gone.

After an hour I lost my patience and went inside the building. No one was around. Just a large poster of a chubby Indian guru with an oddly inauthentic smile and dozens of shoes on the ground beneath it. I stopped to stare at the guru, wondering if he had some piece of ancient-wisdom for me. He stared at me in a stony silence. Oh no, not another soul-gazer! I was tempted to rip the picture from the wall but decided to leave him be. Karma would teach him about soul-gazing with strangers.

Chant music melodiously drifted down the stairs from above. I felt entranced, as I involuntarily climbed the stairs toward it. When I reached the top, I noticed a door open at the far end of the hallway.

I gathered myself outside the room. I knew she was in there—I could feel her. When I was ready, I peeked my head inside and spotted her almost instantly. She was right in front of me, dressed in the yoga pants I had bought her, facing to the left in a twist. My heart burst with joy. Then she twisted to her right and I noticed that there was no ring on her finger. My heart sank back into my chest. I stepped back into the hallway.

*And what did you expect, Lowen? Do you really want me to wear the ring now, after everything? Would that really work for you? How much more pain do you need?*

More. Still more.

I went back outside and sat on the steps waiting for the class to end. After an hour, the door to the building opened and dozens of sweaty yoginis poured out. Sarah wasn't one of them. I waited a few more minutes, then went inside the building. There she sat, alone on the couch, staring off into space. I was pretty sure she saw me, but she continued to stare off to the side of the room. Was this high school? After a few minutes, she slipped on her shoes and walked around me toward the door.

"Sar...," I pleaded.

Halfway out the door, she replied, "I told you not to come. It's all been said."

Who was this woman? She didn't even sound like the same person. Glazed over, heartless eyes. She was like a zombie. I raced out the door and chased her down the street.

"It's all been said?... ALL of it?... That's it?"

She kept walking fast and furious, while I struggled to keep pace. I kept at her with desperate words and pleas, but she ignored every one of them.

Just as I was about to grab her arm and stop her, a woman stepped out from a small café in front of us, and called, "Sarah, we're in here. They're waiting for you to order."

Sarah stepped in. I kept walking. Clearly I wasn't invited for lunch.

I stopped around the next corner and sat down on a city bench. A muttering, homeless man wandered by with a grocery store cart filled with beer bottles. *Where is Dude when I need him? And who the hell is that woman standing in as Sarah? How can someone be so evolved on so many levels, yet be a reactive infant on so many others? Wait, am I talking about her or me? What the fuck is going on here?*

### Insatiable No-Point

I felt crazy enough to do something stupid—stupider than flying to Boulder to stalk my beloved. Instead, I made a wiser decision. I walked to the cab stand across the street.

"Take me to the entrance of Insatiable Point," I said to the Indian man leaning against his taxi. Funny, he looked an awful lot like the guru in the poster.

After fifteen minutes half-listening to his diatribe about US immigration, he pulled up to the trail.

"Come back in two hours, okay?"

"Yes, Sir, I will," he obediently replied, like a devotee to the cause.

I had only been here once, but the trail felt so familiar, like I had walked it forever. With great determination, I walked toward the river where we had first seen our shared reflection. As I walked, everything felt gray and tiresome. I was back on the miserable earth, as I once knew it. And it fucking sucked. I wasn't sure I wanted to live here anymore.

I soon found the riverbank. Our riverbank. Rivers had always been a comfort to us. But what God giveth, God can taketh away. I looked out over the water, and now saw nothing but peril. Where before there had been a river of essence, I now saw a freezing cold torrent that would swallow me whole if given the chance. It really is amazing how hopeless everything looks when our heart is closed.

Ouch.

I sat down at the river's edge. Closing my eyes, wandering inside, remembering many of the steps we had taken between then and now. So many dance steps, so many ballrooms.

I kept returning to a particular memory for comfort. It was the moment we first kissed in Rocky Mountain Park. I had kissed dozens of women, but this was my first *real* kiss. I felt like I had died and gone to earth: the real earth, the loving earth that is our birthright. The afterglow of that moment warmed my frozen core. And somehow, I sensed it always would. It was the kind of timeless memory that could not be impacted by changes to the flesh, nor undermined by the conflicts between us. Is it possible to embed a memory so deeply that it becomes eternally etched in soulstone?

After some time, I began to shiver. After all, it was winter in Boulder. I left the river of haunting memories and walked hurriedly back to the trailhead where my devoted Indian cabbie was waiting to return me to town. The universe does send us support at the most difficult moments, if only we can lift our head out of our stuff and notice.

I went back to the hotel, too exhausted for words. Back in the room, I fell into a dead sleep. I was soon woken up by the ringing phone. It was Daniel, "Bro, come home. She doesn't want to see you right now. Seriously, you've got people here that love you. Don't give your power away. Now get your ass home." I slammed down the phone in denial. Drifting back to sleep, another abandonment nightmare soon woke me up. Sarah hungrily indulging in an animalistic ménage a trois with a woman and a strange man. I switched on the television to distract me. Scanning the movie network, I ordered a romance film, because I just had to suffer some more. After tormenting myself for ninety minutes, I drifted off before being awakened by another nightmare—again with Sarah. In this one, I was chasing her down an icy Toronto street. I shot up in bed, seized by the desperate need to find her.

Nightmares do come true.

## This is Not Yoga

I bolted awake the moment the sun peered in, and threw on the same crinkled clothes I had been wearing for two days. I left the hotel and made way for the yoga studio in a frenzy. I couldn't leave it like this. I had to connect with her! We just had to!

Isn't it amazing how often in life we feel so sure that we are going to miss the key moment if we don't act now? And isn't it equally as amazing how often those moments prove not to be key at all?

This was one of those moments.

I arrived and went straight upstairs. The door to the studio was closed. As I opened it, I spotted Sarah near the front of the room. The whole class was lying peacefully in savasana, corpse pose. Poor sops. Most of their eyes opened as they turned their heads to see a wildman stepping over them on the way to his zombie beloved. I was clearly insane—it's a miracle I didn't crush heads.

When I got to her, I sat down on my knees beside her and reached for her face. She turned away, again cold as ice. Now even more triggered, I leaned in to kiss her cheek. When she didn't respond, I began to speak: "I love you so much, Sar. I can't live without you. How do we fix this?"

She turned to look at me with vacant eyes. "We don't, Ogdo. We move on." Then, with a voice that sounded momentarily familiar, she softly mumbled, "You look gaunt. You need to eat."

Before I could respond, the yoga teacher interrupted us by chanting "Ohm," signaling the end of the class. The whole group chimed in with her, and then quickly got on their feet to leave. This seemed to turn Sarah cold again, as she also got on her feet and walked toward the door.

I got up and followed her, but the teacher blocked my path. She had a large purple water bottle in her hands with the word "Chakra" written on it in neon lettering. I wasn't sure whether to Namaste, or jump through the window in embarrassment.

"Yoga is about union. This is not yoga. Stop chasing her. She clearly doesn't want to be caught," she said in perfect yoga-teacher speak, with a credibility that stopped me dead in my tracks. She wasn't nasty, she was just clear. In an unexpected way, I actually appreciated her groundedness. With only a few words, she had given me the gift of boundaries.

Without even looking for Sarah, I left the building and walked back to my hotel. It was time to leave Boulder, before I did any more damage. Not just to the union, or whatever was left of it, but to my own self-concept as well. It's enough to be abandoned by your beloved—it is quite another thing to abandon your dignity. Pride does indeed goeth before a fall.

I immediately checked out of the hotel and went standby at Denver airport. I was calm until I got on the plane, where I fell apart again. Resolved to accept the ending, there was no way to stay calm—I was a blithering, sniveling mess. Sarah didn't fool me either with her routine. My zombie beloved was a cold mess, but a mess nonetheless. For someone as warm as her to turn that hard meant she was out of control, grabbing onto any mechanism she could find to hold her head above water. We were both in the same capsized boat, too drunk on pain to pull each other to safety.

Sarah would often say, "We are explorers. We are exploring the outer reaches of the love universe." As I flew back to Canada, I wondered, had we reached the outer edges of this exploration? Or, does love continue to expand our consciousness, even after our beloved is gone?

What is this love, *now?*

# 14

## Broken Closed

Once I stepped off the plane, my determination to detach began to wilt. It was one thing to say goodbye in her presence, quite another to accept goodbye in her absence. Waves of darkness began closing in around me. Stripped of the magical shroud of enchantment worn by lovers, I came crashing back to earth as I had known it. The world felt like an empty, meaningless place.

That night, I lay awake in a burning pool of anguish, as reality had its harsh way with me. There is no doubt that the soul and the body are inextricably linked. I tremored and shook all night, as my body registered the ending of my once-in-a-lifetime soul love. It was as though a cosmic umbilical cord had been severed, one that had been nourishing our twin-ship for all eternity. I woke up in the morning untethered and adrift in an ocean of despair. Now what? *Where do I go after God?* Clearly I had made the greatest mistake a warrior can ever make. I had let my shield down so low that I couldn't raise it back up to protect me.

### Truth Time

I felt deformed in her absence, stumbling through my days in a bloodied haze. The depth of pain was beyond imagining, as a soulnami of suffering flooded my consciousness without respite. Everything, everywhere, hurt. Instead of fighting my way to the surface, I soon found myself resigned to my own demise. It felt better to let myself die than live with this loss. My lifeline had already been severed.

I began to look for ways to anesthetize myself. In support of my efforts, Daniel did what male best friends do. He brought me self-altering substances—pot and whiskey in generous doses. Sadly, pot and whiskey together make strange grief-fellows, taking me further into the angst.

In the hope of numbing me further, Daniel began bringing his spiritual books with him every time he popped in with the drugs. Sensing that my suffering might create an opening to his ideas, he would sit and read to me. He called it "Truth Time." At first the timing was perfect.

Before we got to it, he would lead me on a mindfulness meditation. I closed my eyes and focused on my pained breath. Then he would invite me to watch my feelings float down the river: "Don't identify with them, just watch them leave the screen." And it would work. The more I watched them float, the further I got from my torment. And sometimes more than feelings floated away. Sometimes I imagined Sarah floating away, getting smaller in the distance.

Then he would read to me, slowly, with equanimity, in the calm, measured tenor of non-duality teachers. For a number of nights it was the perfect antidote for my tortured heart. I would close my eyes, slow and deepen my breath, and savor the fleeting feeling of calm. It became the one thing I looked forward to at the end of most days, a momentary spell of relief from my chronic state of torment.

One evening, something shifted while he was reading two excerpts from Eckhart Tolle's *The Power of Now*:

> *The pain-body may seem to you like a dangerous monster that you cannot bear to look at, but I assure you that it is an insubstantial phantom that cannot prevail against the power of your presence.*

> *...the pain-body doesn't want you to observe it directly and see it for what it is. The moment you observe it, feel its energy field within you, and take your attention into it, the identification is broken. A higher dimension of consciousness has come in. I call it presence. You are now the witness or the watcher of the pain-body. This means that it cannot use*

*you anymore by pretending to be you, and it can no longer replenish itself through you. You have found your own in-nermost strength. You have accessed the Power of Now.*

While he was reading it, an unexpected wave of pleasureful memories flowed through me. The depth of longing, our first exquisite lovemaking in the temple, the hand-holding walks in the forest, the cuddling on the futon in the mornings, that night when we danced by the firelight on Toronto Island, the vastness of our soulscape. The memories began to melt me open. I could feel my body feeling again, remembering what it was to *live*. It became clear: this witnessing technique was not for me. It brought temporary respite—in moments of great distress, at times when a vaster perspective is essential—but at this point, I felt like I was just locking myself inside with my own pain-body 'monster.' I was paying cerebral attention to my wounds without actually transforming them. And closing off the pain-body 'monster' with witnessing techniques also meant closing off the joy body, the memories of delight—you can't sever one without the other. As a well-practiced head-tripper, I knew that game well—hiding from feelings in a witnessing consciousness and calling the resulting pseu-do-equanimity 'healthy' and 'enlightened.' Was it, or was it simply another way to bypass challenging feelings?

Suddenly, I began to revolt against Daniel's messages. Although I liked the 'idea' of witnessing and observing my pain, I didn't like the non-feeling of it. I didn't do all this work in my life to heal and open my heart, only to close it down the moment suffering entered my life. What was the real drug—the pot we were smoking, or the philoso-phies Daniel was articulating? Watch your feelings float down the riv-er—is it that simple? Presence happens when you witness your pain-ful emotions? Huh? But how can I be in the moment if I disconnect from my feelings? How can I be present if I haven't worked through the unresolved pain-body? What linear, patriarchal, head-trippy ver-sion of the *moment* is that? Won't those feelings impede my presence? Won't they come back to haunt me? Are they really monstrous, or is there something fundamentally human at the heart of them? Don't you have to move through a deepening feeling process before you can come to a genuine feeling of peace? And isn't healing and resolution essential to my expansion? How will I grow and mature if I don't work through the pain-body material?

Yes, I did want some relief from the pain—but not at the expense of fully and deeply living. As pained as I was, some part of me still wanted presence to be a whole being experience. I still wanted to be here for all of it.

After we smoked another joint and drank a little more whiskey, Daniel began to read from the book of his new favorite spiritual teacher—American born Hindu-wannabe Krishna Roy McMaster. His book *Transcending the Hurt Locker* was a best-seller among those who had given up on therapeutic process. I knew McMaster from my seeking days, when I sat before him for a long weekend while he spewed the oddest concoction of positive thinking affirmations, Sanskrit pseudo-wisdoms, and strangely disorienting disembodiment teachings, while incessantly sipping a drink he called "Wisdom Juice" from an oak barrel with a crazy straw shaped like the Elephant God Ganesh. I hadn't realized how much he pissed me off back then, but today, it all came clear.

As Daniel read, my mind drifted into the most vivid daydream, one where my contempt for ungrounded spiritualities had an opportunity to be expressed in all its savagery.

In it, *McMaster was sitting in my living room doing one of his teaching-monologues, in his irritatingly calm know-it-all voice, waving his hands around while sipping from Ganesh. Suddenly, I lost my no-mind and lunged across the room, knocking him to the ground with one push, spilling his wisdom juice all over the floor. Then I got down on top of him and smacked him hard on the side of his face: "How does your no-body feel now, transcendent one? Shall we witness it from afar? Where's your monkey mind when you need it?" With him crumpled up on the ground, his elephant head straw lying on the hardwood beside him, my rage turned nastier, "Why do you look so shaken, you fuckin' new age twinky? It's all a crazy illusion, isn't it? Where's your compassion for my anger?" He got up, and bolted for the front door, but I beat his no-body to it, standing firmly against it. Apparently, I had more of an issue with spiritual bypassing than I realized. Confronted with a ticking time bomb, he wisely turned around and raced to the back door, scooping his Ganesh straw up off the floor as he fled. I went out after him, determined to finish my monologue: "How does 'All One' feel now, great Mixmaster? What—you haven't forgiven me, yet? Non-attach, non-attach!!? That was then, THIS IS NOW!"*

After revisiting and refining my fantasy a few times, I began to laugh, interfering with my best friend's reading. "What... what's so funny?" he asked in the most serious of tones.

I opened my eyes and looked at him fondly. "Nothing, dear friend, nothing. This just isn't working for me." And then I asked him to take his drugs and books and go.

How ironic, McMaster the Master Detacher had driven me back to the world of feeling.

### The Blame Train

Moments after he left, I wished he would return. I missed my no-pain body! Without detachment practices as a buffer, I was back to nonstop misery with no relief... shit! There was a kind of madness circulating inside, a dark and torturous mix of rage and heartbreak that felt too powerful to feel, and too powerful not to. How do you get the strength to grieve when your heart, the very source of your strength, is torn asunder?

I needed a sabbatical from work. The next morning, I contacted two of my colleagues to take over my practice until I was ready to return. I had two trials coming up—a theft and a sexual assault, and I was in no condition to take them on. The thought of doing the sexual assault was particularly upsetting. After all, Sarah had used sex to assault me. Criminal law was getting too close to home.

My pain deteriorated into an overwhelming sense of confusion as the reality strengthened its grip. In only a few short months, I had gone from armored warrior to receptive lover, from deep isolation to profound connection, from soulmate to sole-fool.

I grappled for optimism, a forward-moving philosophy, anything to keep me afloat. Perhaps this is the way it has to be as a matter of evolutionary stages. Perhaps the soul can't go from the mundane to a fully actualized soulmate experience this quickly. Perhaps the process demands an opening that can't be fully actualized, a karmic taste test before the next level of cosmic penetration. Perhaps I was being prepared for an even greater love along the path.

There was only one problem with this theory. There wasn't going to be any greater love—not likely! More likely, I was just fucked with by the universe. But why? *Why?*

Perhaps the greatest source of confusion was how to re-establish my sense of separate self. In merging with Sarah, I had experienced a genuine dissolution of my individual self. Love had reached inside of me and reshaped me in its relational image. I felt such peace in that, as though I had returned to my wholeness, my true essence, after lifetimes alone. But how, now, was I to understand myself? I wasn't a man, as I had understood manliness, and I wasn't a separate self any longer. I wasn't Lowen, alone—and yet I was. How, now, was I to return to an integrated form? To know myself as something separate from that merging? To know where I end and the other begins? I was like a baby learning how to walk, except this time I was stepping out with busted feet.

And it was about more than just my merging with Sarah. It was also about my relationship with the universe. In her divine presence, the gateway to unity had swung wide open, bridging my consciousness, my very identity, with an entirely different universe of meaning. Fueled by our love, I had entered a vaster, richer terrain—one that upframed the banality of daily life and reflected the divine possibilities at the heart of every birth. But now what? I was sitting at the precipice of the universe, all opened up with no place to go. How do you readjust to earthly life after a tour of the cosmos? How could I sustain this awareness without her? Where do you go from God?

Perhaps this is why it's so very difficult to lose a soulmate. You don't just lose your companion. You don't just lose your friend. You don't just lose your lover. You lose your portal to divinity. You lose your gateway to God. You lose the whole bloody universe.

My confusion soon turned to anger. At first it was directed at Sarah. I wrote one unsent letter after another expressing my disdain for her behavior: "How could you desacralize us in that way? How could you refuse God's invitation?" I hit the futon with a baseball bat, cursing her with furious abandon. I drove the highways late at night, screaming at her at the top of my lungs. But none of it changed anything. After every release, I would come back to the same feeling—love. She was still my heart's beloved. She was still lodged in my cells. It just felt so sad to be without her.

I needed a much bigger target. I soon turned my attention to God, the orchestrator of this heartless horror. I sat down one night and put my anger to words:

Dear God,
Why the hell did you create this,
you motherfucker!
Fuck you.
Why ignite Providence to open my heart if you
knew I would suffer?
Why take me on a magic carpet ride only to pull
the carpet out from under me?
Why? Why? Why? Why?
Surely you knew it was impossible. Surely you saw
this coming from a thousand galaxies away!
You brought me a love beyond my wildest
imaginings. For what purpose if we couldn't be
together?
Why make me whole and then rip me to shreds?
Why this cruel joke?
APOLOGIZE! APOLOGIZE!
Finally I have the willingness to open, and my
beloved is an escapist!
What an insidious set up.
You sadistic shit.
I hate you God.

Like a man made mad by rejection, I printed the letter and taped it face up on my skylight so that God would be sure to read it. Fucker, I want answers!

Before I went to bed that night, I wrote "fuck you!" on Sarah's favorite mirror, using the cherry blossom lipstick she left behind. Clearly I wasn't ready to look inside for the answers. I needed to be a victim just a little while longer.

## Armor Up!

The next morning, Sarah called. Had she felt me looking back at us in the rear-view mirror? Was she also looking back through hers? She was sobbing terribly. Soon I was too. The loss of the beloved cuts the deepest vein.

"I don't know if I can live without you, Ogdo. I feel so lost. All my old ways of bouncing back are failing me."

"Yah, mine too. It's a whole different planet. We're not the same people now."

"No, we aren't. What do we do about it?" she asked, almost hysterical.

"We work on it," I replied. "Work on what's obstructing us."

"No, Ogdo. I don't want to work on it. I just want to love you."

"Then come back here and love me," I urged, forgetting we already tried that.

She said nothing for a long time. Then, very quietly, she spoke, "I can't. I know I can't do this. I can't work on this. I don't want to open those doors again."

I spent the next two hours trying to convince her to make a commitment to couples counseling. She refused. I re-fused. It got me nowhere. Just as it had gotten any woman who ever tried to persuade me to join them in therapy nowhere, until I was ready.

Whatever assumptions I had made about gender availability were officially turned upside-down with Sarah. No matter what anyone tells you, the flight from love is not gender specific. It's not always the men who won't do the work. Fear is fear. Sometimes the woman is the one sprinting away when the truth hits the fan. Great love is the great equalizer. Its terrors don't discriminate between the genders. It frightens most everyone who walks through its all-consuming door.

After we got off the phone, I went upstairs and punched the futon hard. Fuck feeling again! Where's my no-pain body? I yelled at God

145

again. What the fuck! !*#&&%^&*%#*!! I so wished I could fall out of love. Just for a day, an hour, even a minute, give me a momentary respite from this longing. It's so much easier to let go when the love connection is of a practical nature. When it stops serving its purpose, we stop longing for it. It's damn near impossible to let go when the love is emanating from the soul, because it never stops calling to us. Damn!

Isn't there a pre-nup we can sign against pain?

The darkness deepened as the pain of loss moved through my inner world like a devilish fog. Soon every crevice was filled with doom, as I couldn't begin to imagine anything worth living for. It was my childhood all over again, only this time I really was homeless: my home had up and left me. For weeks I went through the motions everywhere, barely managing to deal with the practical world before collapsing into heartache in the evening. It had taken all my courage to surrender to the unknown, and now my worst fears were realized. No realms made any sense to me now—not the exhilarating love universe I had entered, nor the pragmatic world I had abandoned. And the unknown was a storehouse of suffering.

I embarked on a self-numbing rampage. First, I raced back to my law practice, largely in an effort to close off my heart. It worked. Soon the armor began to form around my vulnerability. I witnessed it while it was happening—the return of my hyper-vigilance, the re-emergence of my pseudo-machismo, and the shallowing of my breath in an effort to dampen the pain. A return to the invulnerable form that had protected me as a traumatized child. Back then, closing my heart may very well have meant the difference between life and death. This moment felt no different.

At the same time, I went right back to my head-tripping ways. It seemed to be a synonymous process—turn off the heart and turn on the monkey mind. With an obstructed energetic flow in the body itself, the energy has nowhere to go but up. I found myself trying to figure out Sarah's actions with conceptual, repetitive thinking. Not how I *felt* about what happened, but what did I *think* about what happened? A losing proposition—the path of the egghead.

Then, I turned to food. No better way to stuff down grief! Over the next months, I sought out one culinary comfort after another in a desperate quest for relief. I began with sweets—ice cream and chocolate—and then graduated to heavy and depleting foods—pasta and fried chicken wings—in a relentless effort to keep myself so tired that I couldn't feel a thing. The more pain I felt, the more food I ate, until I had gained nearly twenty pounds in ten weeks. It was ugly. My buttons were popping. Now I too was a cold mess.

I was willfully determined to neglect my body, depriving it of anything that would nurture the flow of feeling. I stopped walking. I stopped getting massage. I unconsciously blocked every pathway of release, ensuring there was no fluidity anywhere in my body. With the river all dammed up, very few feelings got to the surface. It's amazing how many systems need to cooperate in order to shut down our feelings and close the heart. You have to shallow the breath, tighten the musculature, cerebralize the moment, and bury your emotions. It's like a perverse game of twister, contorting your entire being away from the heart. It takes a lot of energy to deaden our aliveness.

My law practice was the sole beneficiary of my armored consciousness. Moving again like a lone wolf warrior, I won one trial after another, kicking the prosecution's butt hard. Where before my heart wasn't in it, now my heart *was* a (not-so) lean, mean fighting machine. If I couldn't succeed at love, I was going to succeed at something.

It is one of the great ironies of our Western survivalist culture. If you turn off your heart, you become a success. If you open it, you get eaten alive. Nowhere is this madness better reflected than in the legal system. It's like the entire system is built on a plate of man armor. You want to win? Crush your own vulnerability, and then you can crush any opponent.

But there was a chink in my armor. A small one, where the light shone through. When I would get home from the office—usually around 1 a.m.—I would go into the sunroom. I would reach into a box I kept near the futon and pull out a special group of pictures I had taken. Sarah with our lil kitten lying on her chest. Sarah lying naked on the couch with a playfully seductive smile. Sarah relaxing in the bathtub, eyes closed dreamily. I loved these pictures so. Then I would put them around the futon, in a very methodical manner, before crawling under the blanket to go to sleep. This ritual soothed me—I felt as though her spirit was protecting me—and sleep often came easy.

In the morning, I would wake up with the alarm, soon after sunrise. Quite often, Little Friend would appear on the outside window ledge looking for Sarah to feed him. I wasn't planning on feeding him nuts, so he would linger, staring at me, trying to win my affection. I would stare right back at him for a long time, practicing my soul-gazing with a rodent. There was a way in which I felt like she was with me, when he was at that window. She lived on in the heart of his longing, just as she lived on in the heart of mine.

Once he gave up, I would get up, lovingly place her pictures in the box, and leave the sunroom. After closing the door behind me, I would grab a small chair and place it against the door. It was a little red chair that Sarah had loved to sit in when she was sketching. Until that chair was against the door, I couldn't begin my day. After it was against the door, I felt ready to put on my shield and take on the world. Where before the whole universe was our temple, now it was all contained to one small room. And I was devoted to keeping that room safe.

# 15

## The Bleak Between

The isolation of my daily life became unbearable. Whenever I wasn't working, I was alone in the house with Lightnin, too embarrassed and immobilized to connect with humanity.

Early one Saturday morning, I went looking around for Dude—my pushcart guru. Perhaps he could light a fire under my hopelessness. I found him sitting outside of me and Sarah's favorite coffeehouse with a large hand-written sign at his side:

> **1 WISDOM for $1,**
> **or 5 WISDOMS for 1 MEAL**
> **(you can defer some of the wisdoms**
> **but not the meal).**

As usual, he was dressed in a quirky spread that only Dude could pull off: a blue velvet blazer, a red Hawaiian shirt, a pair of patched up khakis and what appeared to be 1950's bowling shoes.

A young woman with spacey eyes and a yoga bag strapped around her shoulder was just finishing with him. She was crying as she got up to leave. Dude looked at her square-on and said, "And, remember, Skye, transcend nothing, include everything. You won't find it up there. You can only find it down here," pointing to the ground. "Thanks, Dude," she said before bouncing down the street, feet not quite on the ground.

I sat down beside him on the sidewalk.

"How you dudin'?" he asked.

"Horrible. You?"

"Dudin' perfect. How can I help you? Love again?"

"Yah, love again… and again."

"She left *again*?"

"Gone like the wind, Dude. She's just gone."

"No way to get her back?"

"Not likely. She's not ready."

He paused for a while and then looked me in the eye. "Then you are blessed by her absence. Can't make someone ready to walk a path they aren't ready for. Just don't work."

"Sometimes people push each other along…"

"No, they got to want it. Listen buddy, if one person doesn't want the relationship, then it's simply not a fit. No sense trying to figure out why they don't want it. No sense blaming it on their commitment issues. No sense waiting around for them to realize they wanted it after all. Because it doesn't matter why they don't want it. What matters is that you are met heart-on by a fully engaged partner. If they don't want it, then you don't want it, because you don't want to be with someone who isn't there for it fully. That's the thing about love relationship— it's an agreement that has to be signed by both souls. If one doesn't sign, then nothing has been lost. If it's not a fit for them, it's not a fit for you either."

"But Dude, she DID want the relationship! She asked for it, and her soul signed on the dotted line! She can't just break our contract!"

"Sure she can. Maybe she just signed on for the short term, not the long haul. Look, she's got free choice. Maybe she needs to do this stage alone. Fact is, it doesn't matter how much two people love one another if they're developmentally incompatible, or if they don't have a shared willingness to become conscious. That's why we call it a relationship and not a *loveship*. Love alone isn't enough. If you want it to last, you have to relate to each other in ways that keep the ship afloat."

"That's profound. You just make that whole thing up?"

"Nah, long ago. I say all of that to about a dozen people a day, all of them in tough relationships, usually women."

We sat in silence for a few minutes while a series of fire engines raced by.

"I keep asking God to help me understand..." I said, breaking the silence.

"God!" He started to chuckle. "Don't be looking that far away for the answers. The only one who knows why it happened is you. You brought her into your life. Stop looking for answers outside yourself. Don't ask God, BE GOD. You're the sculptor of your own reality—don't hand your tools to anyone else. Even the Big G!"

"The universe had something to do with it, didn't it?"

"Sure, but you were the originator of this. Yah, I know tragic things happen, but most of the time there's gold in the dross. You know what that means? It means there is a kernel of glory in there somewhere. You just got to go down into the mine and find it."

"I don't want to. I want to close down."

We sat in silence for a few minutes, before Dude spoke again.

"Look, bud, you can close down, that's your right. But—just so ya know—if you close down, you miss the opportunity. The gift didn't die when she left. It's still in front of you. She was just the wrapping paper. Don't you get it—she wasn't the gift. If you stay with the feelings, you'll find out the real reason the love came to you. Maybe it wasn't for you to be together. Maybe it was for another reason, Bud."

I tried to imagine "another reason" for Sarah. A greater reason than loving her? This didn't make sense.

Annoyed at his certainty, I got up to leave when his hand shot up to stop me. He was mumbling to himself and counting on his fingers.

"Loveship, sculptor, wrapping paper... three wisdoms. Hey, you owe me three bucks!"

"You mean you have like a rolodex of wisdoms that you tell everyone?"

"No, I'm not a computer—I shape my expression to my client's needs. I'm an attuned Dude. I really listen. But I need to eat, you know," he said with a kind of wounded defensiveness.

"Sorry, Dude. I really do appreciate your wisdom." I dropped five bucks in his bowl and walked inside to get my morning latte.

## *Open Bless-A-Me*

When I stepped inside the coffeehouse, I did the oddest thing. I ordered Sarah a latte too—her favorite kind, pumpkin spice. I knew it was insane, but I needed to pretend she was here. When the drinks were ready, I brought them to the same table we used to sit at.

I closed my eyes and imagined her near. I remembered the smiling eyes that would drink me in, as I drank my latte. She loved to watch me, when she thought I didn't know. Most of the time I did know, but I pretended I didn't because it gave her so much pleasure to stare in secret.

I opened my eyes and looked over at her latte. It hadn't even dropped an inch—surprise, surprise. I drank mine and emptied hers on Baldwin Street. I needed to walk today.

I wandered for hours, all over the city: places we had been, places I had wanted to take her. I talked to God under my breath, waiting for an answer. (S)he was silent, again. Perhaps Dude was right and I alone held the answers. Perhaps.

I kept seeing women who looked like Sarah. They got out of cars, raced by on their bikes, talked to their boyfriends on street corners. She was everywhere, and nowhere at all. How could there be so many Sarahs?

After a quick smoothie at our favorite juice bar, I walked down to the harbor and sat on a bench overlooking Lake Ontario. My body of wounds was activated again, nattering at me with tireless intensity. Again, I juggled two narratives simultaneously. My inner lover insisted that I hold to the opening I had courageously chosen all those months ago. And my inner warrior cajoled me to return to the ways of the unawakened man. In fact, he berated me for staying so long in the pain, "What kind of man needs this? Who is this bitch to get all this power? Enough already—you're a broken record. Move on." Such polarized views. Was there no middle ground? Was there no way to bridge the sturdy masculinity I embodied before her, with the more enheartened version we explored together?

I reached for my cell phone, eager to call her. I dialed her number time and again, hanging up on her voicemail every time it came on. I didn't want to hear her voice recording and come into stinging reality. I factually knew she was gone—*that* much I had integrated. But there were deeper levels of acceptance I just couldn't assimilate. I still needed to pretend there was someone waiting for me on the other end of the phone.

I walked back to the market hopelessly confused. I didn't know how to live in this world any longer. I had climbed heart mountain and landed, face first, on a rusty spike. The contrast between the wondrous world that love reveals, and the materialistic world below, was almost too much to bear. When you love as God loves, all life forms appear beautiful. When you fall from grace, you can't help but wonder why he ever bothered creating them. Would I ever smile again?

I got my answer around the next corner. As I turned into the market, I saw Dude sitting against his pushcart in front of the taco place. He was sipping a beer and taking in some sun. I put $20 in his bowl and sat down beside him.

"Not needing any wisdom. Just want to sit here," I said. Nothing comforted me more than Dude right now.

After a few minutes, he reached inside a small knapsack and took out a nail file. He began filing his fingernails slowly, methodically, like he was engaged in a meditative practice.

"Look at my last finger," he said, holding up a finger with a long, rough nail.

"Okay, I see it."

"That's like the soul when we begin this incarnation."

"The soul is a fungal fingernail?"

He guffawed at my sarcasm. "It's not fungal, it's just dirty. Look, the point is that life is the nail file. It wears the nail down until all that's left is the true essence."

I rolled my eyes. "But why do some nails get rougher over time?"

"Those people didn't live their real lives. They didn't learn the lessons that smooth the soul. They hid from reality."

The guy was a walking metaphor. I didn't know what to do with him. "You mean smooth the fingernail, don't you? Have you taken this theory to the beauty salon to see what they say?"

He didn't answer, filing his nails mindfully.

"Not judging you at all Dude, but how come you live on the street? Why homeless? You could get social assistance and get a place, or… "

"For the same reason you couldn't land that divine love in this here world. The more open something is, the more difficulty it has with society. Society was built on a foundation of fear, not authenticity. I get too numb when I join the world. I lose my openness, my access to the divine." Then, pointing to the world around him, he added, "This way, I'm always part of it."

He did seem more alive than the rest of us. "Okay, I get it."

"And I ain't homeless—I'm *houseless*. The bunch of you are the ones without a home. You got a house, but you ain't got no home. You can't be at home on this planet if you're not at peace in your own skin. That's where our real home is."

Soul-food for thought. And he was right. Right now I felt like one of those people: housed, but homeless.

"Any last thoughts on my heartbreak?" I asked as I stood up to leave.

"Yes… Open Bless-a-me."

"Open Bless-a-me? You mean Open Sesame!"

"No, silly. Open Bless-a-me. Say that whenever you feel your heart closing. Open bless-a-me! No sense asking the universe to bless you if you aren't blessing yourself. It all starts with you."

I thanked him and started walking. When I got halfway down the street, I heard him yell to me at the top of his lungs, "OPEN BLESS-A-MEEEEEE!" I looked back and he was waving to me with a big fat smile on his beautiful face. It was contagious. For the first time in weeks, I actually found myself smiling, too. Twenty bucks for a heart-job, well worth it. My pushcart guru of the heart.

### Blink of an Eye

The following weekend, I found a love note in the house written by Sarah. Hidden under a plate in the kitchen cupboard, it just about made me insane:

Though the sea rushes forth
washing away sands before,
still clinging to you
I am breathless
While misty shadows
dance upon the shore
still watching for you
I wait,
restless.

I was instantly catapulted to a deeper level of self-avoidance. The ground had just begun to feel a little solid again, but this was too much pain for me to hold. Was this the way it was going to be for the rest of my life: two steps forward, two steps back?

For the next few weeks, I dropped in at the neighborhood bar every night after work. True to my Jewish roots, I would drink one glass of beer before getting tipsy and stopping. After I stumbled home, I immediately checked the phone to see if she called. Of course, I knew she hadn't. Of course.

I began to have sexual dreams about other women. Some of the women were unknown to me, whereas others were women I had shared intimacy with before. The dreams grew more and more intense, sometimes waking me up in the middle of the night. I couldn't help but wonder if my inner world was trying to lead me away from Sarah.

I decided to go on some dates. I didn't feel ready for intimacy, but I wondered if the presence of other women would revive my optimism. She had fucked God-knows-who since, surely I could have a meal with another woman. I hadn't so much as sat across a table from one in the better part of a year.

I wasn't ready. All I did was project Sarah onto every woman I ate with. I couldn't even hear what they had to say. I just kept looking for Sarah. One woman had her sharp wit, another her nose, and one even had her Cheshire cat grin. The illusion of soulmate in volume form. If only I could mix them all together, my beloved Sarah would jump out of the blender!

I longed for the days when I could have sex for the sake of pleasure. But I was ruined to fucking for fucking's sake. I wasn't that guy anymore. The most I could do was cuddle with Danielle, a beautiful Ashtanga yoga teacher whose natural scent reminded me of Sarah's. I would lay behind her with my eyes closed, momentarily imagining Sarah. Then I would try to touch her hair like I touched Sarah's, and my hands would lock up. I could fool my mind, but I couldn't fool my body. It knew who it loved.

My body began to reflect my self-avoidance. Blessed for many years with no physical problems, I became a regular visitor to the doctor. I got strep throat twice in one month. I suffered from constipation for the first time in my life. And I developed a rash on my lower back that wouldn't respond to conventional or alternative treatments. Clearly, unresolved heartbreak finds a way to express itself.

Interestingly, the more intensely I disconnected from my heart, the more serendipity occurred to remind me. Where before I saw serendipity as yet another indication of divine intervention, I was now inclined to see it as the work of the devil. Clearly I had pissed off someone in charge. How else could I understand their determined efforts to keep me connected to the impossible?

I continued to rail at God and the universe. This time, not in the form of a letter. That was too quiet. Instead I bellowed. Loudly. One snowy night, my anger built to a crescendo that bordered on madness. I got into my car and began racing down the highway, the harsh hail pelting on the windshield, howling at God or his devilish stand-in: *"I want a fucking apology, you bastard!"* I accelerated as I howled, my words getting louder with every quickening mile. "DID YOU HEAR ME? I said I want a fucking apology! WHERE THE FUCK IS IT? I didn't have a hard enough early life—you thought I needed more pain? For what bloody purpose? Apologize! Apologize! Send me a sign of your fucking remorse!"

Suddenly the car hit an icy patch on the highway and I lost control. In the heart of my fear, my anger at God fell silent, transformed into prayer in the blink of an eye. The car swerved into the shoulder and then spun right around, now facing oncoming traffic. Luckily, there wasn't any.

Was God the enemy, after all?

## A Thousand Sexy Imposters

Although I could easily rage, I seemed to have lost the ability to cry. I couldn't get below the anger and sink into the crippling pain of loss. It was too tender, too haunting, too permanent. I preferred the habitual comforts of drama to the nakedness of raw, stinging grief.

And then a blessing walked through the door. An old girlfriend contacted me after many years. Tracy was someone I always enjoyed spending time with. There was no profound attraction, but there was a real sense of acceptance between us.

She knew that Sarah and I had parted, so she offered to come over to cook me dinner. When she arrived, she hugged me warmly, just as she always had.

"You look worn. You've been to hell and back. Let me feed you." She brought me to the couch, covered me with a blanket, and made us the best mango salmon dinner imaginable. It felt good to have a woman in my space, particularly one who wasn't fazed by my dirty dishes and unkempt appearance.

After we ate, she curled up beside me on the couch to cuddle. It felt perfectly comfortable, as my sense of isolation evaporated in her arms. And, much to my surprise, I began to feel sexual charge, something I hadn't felt in months. We kissed and built energy in front of the fire for hours. It was very sweet.

She took my hand and led me up the stairs to the bedroom. The room was dark, and we both undressed before jumping under the covers. The kissing intensified as we touched each other's bodies. I so needed to feel pleasure again. I worked my way down to her yoni, my mouth eager to taste her. And then I froze, as the contrast between the love I felt for Sarah and the way I felt about Tracy became too much to bear. I was overcome with memories of Sarah—on her back, in the shower, moving perfectly beneath me on a resplendent wave of love. She was so close, I could almost taste her.

I rested my head on Tracy's belly, and sobbed like a baby for hours. Kind soul that she was, she comforted me until I fell asleep.

It was clear—there is no better way to summon the pain of loss than trying to sleep with someone that you don't love, too soon after losing the one that you do. I was almost better off alone than risking the reminder of what had been lost. It was proving to be one of life's greatest challenges to go from intimacy with my beloved to intimacy with a mere mortal. Of course, the beloved is surely mortal, but the contrast between soul-sourced intimacy and attraction-driven intimacy was startling after I had touched God with love's fingers. My sexual body had become indistinguishable from the divine and longed to remain united. Separating them again felt like a kind of suicide, a desecration of my innermost holiness. Better to have the memory of one beloved, than the presence of a thousand sexy imposters.

## Dudin' Fantastic

I woke up the next morning feeling lighter and more open. Months of frozen pain had melted and moved through me, momentarily deepening my presence. I felt a sliver of readiness to understand what I had been through. Sarah and I had been adventurers, traveling the yoniverse on our magic carpet. Now a new adventure had begun—the journey of making sense of it all.

Where to begin? I sensed that Dude was right. There was gold in the heart of the dross. But how to uncover it?

My mind took over. I spent weeks contemplating and analyzing the relationship with Sarah, with no clarity. Frustrated, I found myself turning to positive thinking techniques, Krishna McMaster style. And, for a brief time, they were super effective. I suddenly felt grateful for the experience, certain I had forgiven Sarah, convinced I had transformed my suffering into understanding.

Then, Dude caught me. He spotted me sitting at a table in the window of my favorite Thai restaurant, happily slurping down my favorite dish—a yummy bowl of Pad Woon Sen. In he came, dressed in the baggiest overalls I had ever seen with a silky red turtleneck beneath. What a character.

Dude looked hungry. I motioned for him to sit down.

"How you dudin'?" he asked.

"Dudin' fantastic, Dude. Feeling a lot better."

"You are, are you?" he asked, like a guy who knew something I didn't.

"Yah, I'm feeling grateful for all that was."

"And the love?"

"I'm grateful for the love, even though it didn't last. I'm just lucky to have experienced such love in this lifetime."

"Really? That was a quick healing for such a great loss."

"I'm a fast healer when I put my mind to it."

"Oh ya. Good ole' mind. That'll do it, eh? And what does your heart have to say about that?"

"My heart... my heart says: it's all good. The love, the pain, the loss—all good, all God. No difference," I quickly replied.

He was annoying me. I motioned for the waitress to come over. She took Dude's order. While we were waiting for it to arrive, Dude started in on me, "You're lying to yourself, buddy."

"It's okay, Dude, you don't have to dish out any wisdom tonight. I'm happy to feed you for free."

"Oh, thank you, but you see, I can tell... I see it all the time... premature healing. It will leave you the worst kind of broken. Broken with a bullshit smile on your face."

Irritated, I sat in silence for some time, hoping he would get the message.

"Better hurt than hardened, kid. Look, you can't heal if you don't go deep into the pain."

"I know, man, I went in fucking deep..."

"Oh yah... how fucking deep did you go?"

"I grieved hard. Really, really hard," I insisted.

"Did you almost die?"

"No, of course not."

"Then you didn't grieve hard enough."

Shit. Who needs a therapist when you have Dude?

Then he looked straight at me and said with firmness, "You have to truly grieve her. Then, you have to let her go."

"I have. I know she's not coming back."

"Knowing it and letting go are entirely different things. Look, repressed emotions are unactualized spiritual lessons. You have to go all the way through the emotional stages before you can see the gift. Going halfway leaves you halfway between the worlds. That's a shitty place to be. What people don't realize is that there's no difference between their emotional and their spiritual life." He pointed to the world around us and said, "This is all the school of heart knocks. The deeper you go, the more you grow."

Oh no, not more metaphors. But I sensed he was right.

Ugh, Dude.

"Okay, but how do I keep from getting trapped there and never graduating?"

"Look, I told you before—you can't heal your heart with your mind. You can only heal your heart with your heart. You got to go all the way through the process. Feel the heartbreak and the anger; feel all of your feelings to their very core."

"For how long?"

"As long as it takes. The feelings will only hurt until they convert into the lessons at their heart. Feel them until you can feel them no more."

He was silent for a moment, before speaking up again. "And that also means don't be doing that artificial forgiveness trip people do. You can't forgive her this fast! Most people just fool themselves into thinking they have forgiven when all they have done is tucked their feelings away. Covered them over. Forgiveness is over-rated, bud. Healing first, forgiveness later! And don't be doing that bullshit spiritual story re-frame either: the *'it's all good, it's all God'* bullshit. I tried that for years—it doesn't work. This is not just *some* story that you can re-write whenever it feels uncomfortable. This is your life, man!"

The waitress brought over his noodles and he slurped them down rapidly. Dude really was hungry.

"Slow day on the street. Thanks for feeding me," he said as he got up to leave.

"My pleasure. Thanks for bringing me back to earth," I sighed in resignation.

"Sure. It's better down here."

I wasn't so sure.

# 16

## Dead Path

Maybe Dude was right. Maybe I hadn't truly grieved her absence. I knew I hadn't truly let her go. But how does one let go of their beloved? How does one extricate themselves from their very breath? Where does one live after their soul-home has been demolished? How does one return to aloneness after swimming in the sea of oneness? How many more fucking metaphors for the same tortured memories?

Oh Sarah.

I wish I could say that this was a co-dependency issue, but it was so much more than that. It was entirely existential. Reality had taken on a whole new meaning in the heart of this love experience. Where to find meaning now? If my life's purpose isn't to love my beloved, then why on earth am I here?

Bewildered, I went back into my head to find my answers. No luck. Dude was right again: excessive analysis perpetuates emotional paralysis. I briefly returned to therapy. No luck there, either. I just talked around the issues. I created space in my work week to process the feelings, but found it difficult to go deep in my daily life. My trial law practice was growing fast and it was increasingly more difficult to extricate myself from the masks that I wore in the courtroom. Vulnerability and armor make strange bedfellows. And perhaps most difficult of all was trying to let go of Sarah in the apartment we had shared. The scent of my lost beloved was everywhere.

And then she called one day at the beginning of spring. It had been a long time since I had last heard from her.

"I want to say goodbye, Lowen."

"You already did, loud and clear. Where you going now?" I asked, afraid to hear her answer.

"I'm just taking the car. Gonna drive to Austin, Texas, to start over," she said softly, as though some part of her knew it was avoidant.

"You could drive to Canada..." I said, immediately hooked back into my longing.

"No, honey, I can't. I need to start over..."

"You're just running..."

She hung up the phone.

Lightnin' Foot in action. Fuck.

I fell to the couch in an excruciating mess, lying there for hours in my tiresome hopelessness. Lightnin came over to comfort me and just made it worse. The last thing I needed was a reminder of Sarah. There was something about this hang up that felt almost worse than the betrayal. As soon as I heard the dial tone, I knew she wasn't coming back. My delusions and fantasies were exposed. This was the real deal. There was nowhere to go from here. This was a dead path.

I could hear myself say it, again and again...

*This is a dead path. This is a dead path. This is a dead path.*

As I said it with more conviction—for the first time, I began to believe it.

### Shame Shackles

When I got back on my feet, I plunged to a place so dark, so barren, that I began to consider suicide as a means of escape. The hope of death felt better than the death of hope. Perhaps the way out of this crushing darkness is absolute darkness, itself.

Oddly metabolized grief became my earnest companion as I fumbled through my days pained and confused. When I wasn't working, I was back to hiding in the house, reluctant to connect with a world that had nothing to offer me. I lay there on the couch, spun out on my victimhood, waiting for the cosmic guillotine to sever me whole. I hated everything, most of all myself.

One day, the pain leeched out in the heart of a trial. I was defending a man charged with sexual improprieties, when I broke from tradition and attacked his female accuser on the witness stand. Until now, I had become known for my subtle cross-examinations in sexual assault trials. But not today. This time I wanted blood—Sarah's blood.

"And your history didn't include seducing men as an act of revenge?"

"I don't know what you're talking about."

"That's not the feeling I get from you. You feel like a woman who knows how to get what you want with your body," I snarled accusingly.

I went after the witness all afternoon—so nasty that the trial judge had to rein me in on numerous occasions. And then we lost the trial, a trial I could easily have won. Sarah had defeated me yet again.

That night, the intensity of my desperation escalated. On the way back from court, I stopped in at a bar I used to go to when I was in law school. I got a table in the corner and ordered some gin. After about an hour, I became uproariously drunk, almost to the point of collapse. Fuck love—booze was my path home.

I left the bar and took a taxi to Lake Ontario. I needed something vast to swallow my pain. I stumbled along the boardwalk until dizziness landed me on my ass on the beach. I surrendered to it, lying down on my back looking up. The night was dark and ominous, as heavy clouds cloaked the full moon. I scanned the entire sky for a little bit of light, but none could be found. Closing my eyes, looking inside, no light there either. Something worse than madness—complete and utter existential hopelessness. A soular eclipse of the heart.

It had all come down to one fundamental question: *What is life without love?*

Before her, I could ride on the hope that one day it would come. After her, there was nothing left to hope for. No light of understanding, no reason to believe, nothing. I had tasted the sweet fruits of divinity and then was cruelly banished from the garden. Perhaps my parents were right all along—I'm not welcome on mother earth.

I fell asleep on the beach and awoke to the glaring sun. For a moment I was disoriented and confused. My darkened soul didn't know what to do with the light. I walked up to Lakeshore Blvd., and waited an hour for a taxi to take me back to my crypt. When we arrived, I realized I had neither money, nor keys. They must have fallen out of my pocket onto the beach. I woke my neighbor at 7:30 to borrow the $25 I needed to avoid a criminal charge. After the driver left, I broke in through my back door. Sleep came easily, until the abandonment wound woke me up with a screeching howl. Again, you would think that our worst wounds would go to sleep along with us, especially when we are most overcome with hopelessness. But not a chance. The little bastards never miss a pity party.

The nightmare related to my mother. I was catapulted back in time to an early childhood episode that never left me, often returning to haunt me during difficult times. I was five years old and my mother was standing at the foot of my childhood bed, reminding me I was unworthy: "You worthless little brat. You'll never amount to anything. Me and your Father wanted a daughter—not you! You were just a mistake!" I heard her shrill voice cutting through me, determinedly imprinting her shaming mantras in my cells. I lay there, frozen in time, unable to defend myself, taking in her demeaning message as true. She was my mother after all.

Given the weight of my shame shackles, it's little wonder I had spent so much time alone in my life. Imprisoned by self-hatred, the bad boy's sentence was to wander the cosmos alone, forever prohibited from connecting to anything nourishing outside himself. A separate universe felt both safer and the limit of his entitlement.

I then began a campaign of self-hatred that lasted for months. I had never cared for serious drugs, but they now became my bypass of choice, as I finally took the cocaine plunge. If I couldn't find ecstasy with a woman, I was going to find it with a substance. I snorted some every evening with my tacos and spent weekends lying on my couch in yet another ecstatic nightmare. Why do we turn against ourselves when we most need to give ourselves comfort? What will it take before we learn how to hold ourselves in our own arms?

One night, it all came to a head, as I found myself struggling to breathe in the middle of the night. When I finally got to my feet to call an ambulance, I threw up all over the bed. And the floor. And the hallway that led to the bathroom. On my way through the door, I looked up to see Sarah staring down at me from the ceiling. How did she get up there?

I couldn't make it to the toilet, preferring to make the tiles my home instead. I lay on the cold floor, looking up at my beloved, speaking to her in tongues. Now and then I threw up still more, before returning to my disoriented soliloquy.

After running out of steam, I fell asleep on the floor. When my eyes reopened, half my face crusted in vomit, I looked back up at the ceiling. Sarah was gone. Staring at the empty ceiling, I felt into the pain that enveloped my heart. It was like an unending tsunami, a torrent of torment that transcends time. *Oh Goddess. You have left so much pain in your oceanic wake. Do you know? Really, was there no other way? Harshly severed from the breastmilk of eternity, what on this earth will nourish me now?*

Lying there, I knew I had shifted from self-distraction to self-destruction. I was now in a full-blown life-and-death struggle. I was intimately aware of the decision before me: close down and die, or open up and live. If I continued to avoid my pain, it would surely kill me, one way or the other. As desperate as I was to not feel the pain, I wanted to die just a little less. I somehow knew that dying in this condition would ultimately provide no relief anyway—my soul would wander heaven's corridors for all eternity, searching for Sarah. I had to find a way to stay here.

It was time for something to change.

Do, or die.

# 17

---

# The Trembling Hand of God

The next morning, I made a spontaneous decision to go away. I couldn't shift this self-destructive pattern in this house of pain. I telephoned my colleague and begged him to manage my cases for the next two weeks. Exhausted by my shenanigans, he agreed, in exchange for a promise to resolve this situation once and for all. I went online and hunted for a healing center far from home. Scanning through dozens, I kept coming back to Rockwood Hot Springs, a clothing optional retreat center near Sedona, Arizona. I had been there once before for an empowerment weekend and had the strangest, strongest feeling there was something waiting there for me. If anyone needed to bare his naked truth, it was me.

I flew to Phoenix the following Friday. As the rental car snaked through the mountains that surrounded Sedona, I experienced tremendous inner conflict. I felt the kind of pressure that builds inside when the soul is longing to expand. I also felt its antithesis, the ever present small-self, clinging yet again to its fear-based lens. It wasn't going to be easy to die to this dream.

Pitching my tent up in the hills, I spent the rest of the evening soaking in the Rockwood healing pool with all the other naked seekers. The call to detach rose with a vengeance, inviting me to race back to my warrior urban life... RIGHT NOW. In my imaginings, I left the pool and drove straight to Phoenix airport a hundred times. Yet there was a deeper call, a subtle hint of knowing, that kept me there.

As the water swirled, I imagined my heart floating away from me on a small leaf that kept cycling past. I could reach out and bring it back, or I could let it travel a little further until it was gone. It was entirely up to me. How deeply I live is always up to me. For the longest time, I recognized that opening to Sarah was the most significant event in my life. And it was. Until now. Now, the tide had turned. Now the most significant moment was deciding whether I would turn away from the loss, or turn towards it. Return to hardened warrior, or become a tenderling warrior, once and for all.

I reached for the leaf and held it gently against my chest.

The next morning, I awoke with the sun and went to yoga class. I had learned from long experience that the deepest opening happened in those asanas I most resisted: shoulder stand, bridge pose, the dreaded pigeon. And so I devoted my practice to those poses, staying in the fire for as long as I could bear. It may have been the most excruciating class I had ever done, but it set the stage for the depthful excavations to come.

After class, I went to the massage office to book my bodywork regimen for the week. While I was waiting to book, an elderly practitioner entered the office. As she browsed her appointment schedule, I was utterly struck by her glowing demeanor and translucent blue eyes. I also couldn't help but notice that her left hand and leg shook. She clearly had cerebral palsy, but she didn't emit an energy of being disabled. This was a powerful woman, full of ability. I was mesmerized. And there was something else, something I couldn't put my finger on. Something about her crone spirit called to me.

I began my healing cycle with a water massage that afternoon. Naked and surrendered, I was held, moved and massaged by a female practitioner in the heart of the healing pool. As she moved me, I sank into a softly primal state, one that touched into the first layers of unhealed pain from Sarah. Although it wasn't ready to move, this grief was no longer frozen. It was now warm to the touch, beginning to thaw, coming back to life.

That evening I took my healing to the next level during a deep tissue massage. As the practitioner kneaded into those deep hidden trenches, dark memories rose into consciousness. Waves of hot pain rose into awareness along with them. I stayed with it for as long as I could, before backing off. Then the practitioner went in deeper, and I opened a little more before retreating yet again. At the very end of this session, I cried for the first time in months, since that night with Tracy. But this wasn't an outpouring—it was a quiet sprinkling of tears. Perhaps even more real, as I was beginning to open to the tender sensitivities of feeling once again. The dam was finally sprouting a leak.

In the middle of the night, I had a horrifyingly vivid nightmare. I was locked in a small crawl space, unable to reach the latch that would set me free. I kept adjusting my body to reach it, but I always fell a few inches short. Inside the space was a small child's pillow and a red skirt, not unlike the skirt that Sarah used to love. I was using the skirt as a blanket. There was very little oxygen in the space, and I had the perception that the narrow walls were slowly closing in on me.

I woke up startled, gasping for air. The dream was the perfect metaphor for my inner world—still attached to Sarah, all bottled up with no place to go, closing in on itself. Reaching for the tent zipper, I lowered it, urgently gulping air. I couldn't get enough. The last time I was in this tent was with Sarah—scrunched up together in one sleeping bag, we made love on a farmer's field in the middle of the night. Closing my eyes and remembering, I reached down to masturbate. As I approached climax, I stopped dead, sharply overcome with pain. I couldn't fool myself—there was no joy, here, now. Instead of ejaculating, I spurted tears, remembering the love, remembering the heartbreak, remembering. My bottled-up inner world had reached its limit. It wanted out.

### Wisdom Keeper

Come morning, I went for breakfast in the Rockwood Café. I enjoyed the tastiest eggs benedict ever created, and then threw them up ten minutes later. Clearly my body had release on its mind. On the way out of the bathroom, I literally bumped into the crone practitioner as she walked past. Again, I was captivated by a radiance that shown through her wrinkled skin. Her transparent eyes had a glint of other worlds—something beyond, yet mixed with deep earthly wisdom.

"Sorry, I wasn't looking."

"I knew I would see you again," she replied.

"I didn't even know you had seen me the once."

"Oh, I did," she said with certainty. "Come for a treatment this morning. You're ready."

I'm ready? Ready for what? "What kind of work do you do?" I inquired.

"My own form of somatic energy work, but don't worry about that. I have an opening at 11 a.m. Come to my hut." Somehow I trusted her and agreed.

"I'll get the details at the booking office, then?"

"No need to book—this one's a gift, dear one. My hut is about 500 yards up the path, right between the white building and guest cottages. I am Miriam."

Just before 11, I walked up the path to meet her. I walked slowly, not particularly eager to arrive. Nauseous and sleepy, I wanted to crawl back in my tent and sleep the day away. When I came down the last hill, I saw her there, sitting outside a small cabin smoking a clove-scented cigarette. This calmed me—she was human, after all.

She motioned me inside. "Lie down on the table. I'll be in soon. Start on your back," she said with a firm, clear voice.

I opened the door to a stark room with a massage table right in the center, covered in an old flannel sheet. It looked just like the flannel sheets my grandmother used to hang out over the apartment balcony to dry. At one end of the table was a worn out stool that had clearly done its time. And there was nothing else.

I climbed up on the table, and immediately felt like crying. I wasn't sure why, but something in this stark room called to me. I contained my tears, though not easily. A large wave of grief was pushing up against me. It was just a matter of time before another break in the dam.

The door opened and Miriam entered the room. She uttered what I thought was a Native American chant, and placed a small cloth over my eyes. I could smell sage burning close by.

After a period of silence, I heard her sit down on the stool at the end of the table. She placed her trembling hand on my left foot and held it there for a long time. The vibrations emanating from her hands were like powerful sonic waves. Then she placed that same hand on my knees. Then my stomach. And then at various points all over my body.

Everywhere she touched, I felt a strong kinetic charge. Waves of energy pulsated through my body, expanding my awareness. Her potent touch was ushering me into another energetic dimension. It was unlike anything I had felt before. I was entirely within my body, yet hovering above it at the same time. Her seemingly disabled hand was like a depth charge for divinity. It was that powerful.

As her hand continued to work its magic, I flooded with memories of Sarah. Not any memories, but only those too painful to experience alone. It was as if her hand was a kind of magnet bringing distinctly unresolved material to the surface. And soon enough, I couldn't feel her hand at all, although I knew it was there.

Within the memories were streams of feeling, ready to be moved. I surrendered fully, gyrating my lower body and discharging its tensions like my life depended on it. In truth, it did. I soon lost all self-consciousness, as sounds and words flew out of my mouth. I knew not what I said, until I heard myself scream, "Sarahhhh!"

I spiraled back into the room, suddenly aware of the practitioner's presence. Both of her hands were on my forehead. And she soon began to speak:

"It's all over your energy. You had a remarkable love, one that few souls ever know. It was a glimpse into what will one day be possible for humankind. She came to show you, and you to show her. That is a great blessing. Few ever see where humanity is heading, the galaxies that await. They imagine they will expand through their minds. *Few really understand that the portal is each other.*"

I began to sob. She was saying everything I intuitively knew to be true. She was seeing where we had been. How could she know?

She got up and moved again, this time placing her hands right over my heart.

"Let it move through you. It wasn't a loss. It was a gift."

What? Did she read my diary? Was this Dude's karmic doppelganger?

"How do you know this?" I asked.

"Because I had a similar experience. My energy was locked the same way as yours is. You feel exactly the way I did. And I too had no idea what to do with the disappointment. There are endless books on meditation as the golden road, but few on love. Repressing the memories is often the first step, but it can't work. You're not able to close your heart like before. You're not the same person anymore."

I began to cry. "No, I'm not."

With that, I heard the door creaking open. "Please wait outside, Kim. I'm sorry, the next client is here."

At that, I removed the cloth from my eyes and got up off the table. As I was walking to the door, one more pressing question entered my thought-stream.

"Sometimes I feel crazy being this dramatic about a love that only lasted a few months and..."

She interrupted me. "Nothing crazy about it. You don't measure love like that. You measure it by its effects. It doesn't matter how long it lasted. It's how much it grows you that matters."

As I walked back to the tent, I measured this love in growth. It was lifetimes of growth, all within a few months. And I was momentarily grateful for all of it, even the hardships at the end. My gratitude included this remarkable healer woman who had just helped me to unearth another layer of wound-body from its hiding place. What a Godsend! If she could turn her seeming affliction into a gift, surely I could turn one relationship ending into a blessing, too?

### Heart Wash

My gratitude soon faded. It was too early for gratitude in my attitude. There was work to be done. That afternoon, I walked to the meditation hut at the tip of Rockwood Mountain to sit in peace. I positioned myself on the well-worn cushion, eyes closed, mindfully witnessing my feelings. But there was no peace to be found, as memories of Sarah again flooded the banks of the river. And the pain again rose with them, more determined than ever to be felt. No, this was not a time to witness my emotions. This was a time to get lost in them.

I suddenly flew down the hill at breakheart speed, sending a flock of wild turkeys scurrying off the path to safety. They could spot a madman when they saw one. Feelings moved through me, yearning for release. At the bottom of the hill, I spotted someone coming up the trail toward me. I darted into the forest, eager to be alone with my burgeoning emotions. When I ran out of breath, I lay down on the warm earth amid a small thicket of cypress trees. The earth felt so inviting, like a lover's embrace, pulling me down, down, down into the depths of feeling.

When my breath returned, I began to roll around on the ground, expressing my body alive. As my body opened, deep waves of longing moved through me. I longed to touch Sarah again. I longed to feel myself move inside her. I longed for one more smell of her underarms. Just one more whiff of her breath. Just one more morning kiss.

And then I began to shake madly. I writhed and wept, as the pain moved through me and merged with the world. The universe would have to hold it now. I lay there for hours, breaking at the edges, surrendering to a loss that was far beyond my comprehension. Deep heart-wrenching belly cries filled the forest as the maimed wildebeest that was me grieved the death of its beloved.

And then the anger. I smashed the ground, roaring at God: "I want one more smile, you fucker! One more kiss! One more walk! Just one more, you motherfucker!" I let myself go to the edge of my hatred, cursing the creator with all my puny might. "Why don't you tell us WHY? WHY love must end. WHY it can't be sustained. WHY everything wondrous turns to dust. WHY? Show yourself, you lazy, silent, fucking conman! Come down from your cowardly perch and GIVE ME ANSWERS." I was ready to face the maker, if (s)he dared. No answers. Typical.

My attention turned to Sarah. I picked up a large tree branch and imagined it her head. I smashed the ground with it, pummeling her cowardice into submission: "IU my ass! If you can love like that, you can fight for it. What kind of justice is this—I am left on the runway with your baggage while you fly away from reality! Fuck you."

And then I said it, what I had protected her spirit from hearing since that horrifying moment: "You are a fucking user! You are the worst kind of user—you use others to carry your pain. It's easier than facing your own demons, isn't it! Hook them in when things are easy and fun and then when things become difficult—smash them to bits when they are most vulnerable. Coward! Just open your heart, Ogdo, I have something to give you—MY OWN SUFFERING. MY OWN BETRAYAL HISTORY. MY OWN ABANDONMENT WOUND! Well, you can have it back! It ain't mine! Find another host! How dare you use me to hide from your shit! How dare you defile us like that! Own your own fucking pain Sarah, OWN IT!"

My raging escalated into a full body tantrum, breath and limbs moving together in an oddly choreographed cry for freedom. I felt like an archaic warrior, drenched in warpaint, determined to release everything that didn't serve. I stayed with the release well beyond exhaustion.

When I was finally done, my hands were shaking and bruised. And there was a small dent in the dirt, just large enough to hold the hate. It wasn't my hate anymore.

On wobbly legs, I found my way down to the healing pool to soften my edges. I dunked my head in the warm water, longing to hide from the next stage in the unraveling process. Anger was easy—what was next wasn't. If I wanted to let Sarah go, I had to take my grief to another level. I had to feel us die.

That night, I went to the kirtan chant in the temple. Kirtan had always been a powerful linkage for Sarah and I—the ancient rhythms bringing us right into the heart of feeling. I hadn't listened to any since she left. At first I kept my breath shallow and chanted without feeling. But the reverberation of my own voice shook my heartstrings loose, and another flood of grief emerged. Afterwards, I went back into the healing pool and let my tears fall freely. As I cried, I felt momentarily liberated. Crying released the sweeter man who lived inside. Yes—sensitivity isn't a sign of weakness. It's a sign of life.

I spent the next few days opening to deepening levels of soulbreak. I found just the right tree way up in the hills and sat against it for hours. It was a tree Sarah would have loved, gnarled leafless branches and hauntingly stoic. Warm tears poured down from me like spring rain. I felt like I would die time and again, then dug down for even more pain. I wanted to empty it all. I wanted to breathe fresh air.

In the heart of my release, I couldn't help but marvel at the courage it took to surrender to this depth of pain. Suddenly I was struck by a new appreciation for the feminine, particularly the many women I had known who had kept their hearts open amid great disappointment and loss. They now seemed extraordinarily courageous to me. They had felt it, they had grieved it, and they had risen again with their hearts open and bare. Through my armored masculine lens, they had often appeared fragile and foolhardy, wasting their precious time on frivolous emotions. But as I lay in a pool of heartache, they were revealed as great warriors. How often they had suffered on life's battlefields without losing faith. The Divine Feminine: Warrioress of the heart!

After three days of heart-washing, my body was emptied of tension. Now I understood what depression is: frozen feeling. By stoking the heartfire, I had thawed myself out. With my tears emptied, I had released much of the pain from our past.

But I had not said goodbye. I had not let Sarah go.

## Letting G(r)o(w)

That night, I went to the weekly community dance. It was pure Rockwood style—semi-naked people, conscious movement, freedom of expression. Self-conscious at first, I began to spin, like a determined dervish, whirling away from the familiar, spinning to God-knows-where. I got lost in the spin, doing what I had seldom ever done—fully trusting the unknown. My spin transformed into a wild dance, a cathartic quest for a place I had yet to live. I got spun by the universe for hours, surrendering to the involuntary, swept away.

The following morning, I went in for the next wave of the healing journey. Waking up early, I raced up the hill to the mountain trails. Something was stirring inside me, and movement was the way to bring it through. I ran and ran until I could run no more.

Drained of all resistance, I returned to the meditation hut to gather myself. I lay on my back and felt deep into my heart. It ached. It knew it was time to let us die. But... to what? The love? The dream? The galaxies we had created together? How do you let go of the beloved? Crack open your ribs, reach for your heart, cut it in two? No need, she had already done that. So what then?

I lay there imagining a farewell. It's so hard to say goodbye when they've already gone. To let her go, I needed to trust there was something else to hold onto. Not a woman. But a benevolent universe. I needed to feel the universe holding me again. And yet, I was no longer sure such a universe existed. I had felt it while in the cradle of love... but now... what? The only thing I had ever been able to count on was the warrior within me, but, after all the changes I had been through, I couldn't go back to him again, without destroying who I was now. Who is that again?

I drifted off to sleep and had another familiar nightmare. My girlfriend was in a room with another man—the door was locked, and the windows were too high to look through. No way in. Same old tormenting narrative. I woke up in a cold sweat, reminded yet again that letting go of Sarah meant coming face to face with my own abandonment issues. No wonder I resisted.

I descended into a deepening sense of loneliness. On the other side of letting Sarah go was an unbearable void. I could feel it there, calling out to me—an abyss with my tarnished name on it. In many ways, Sarah had been the perfect balm for my lifelong loneliness. Letting her go meant embodying the emptiness again, but now with more scar-tissue as evidence that aloneness was my destiny.

I needed something to hang on to to, something to shepherd me through. I went back into the woods and wrapped my arms around a sturdy oak tree root, clinging to it for dear life. With mother earth to root me, I went deeper into the letting go.

When I felt ready, I moved off the root and rolled around spasmodically on the forest floor. Like a snake, I slithered from tree to tree, fully letting go of one tree, and then clutching on the next. As I moved in deeply primal ways, I felt my body merge into the natural world. I felt myself resist. Letting go is a process, but it's also a choice. Then, taking a deep breath, I dove deeper into the pain, summoning the letting-go from the marrow of my being. It was time to embody the farewell, just as I had embodied the hello. With mother-earth to root me, the pain washed over me in waves, as a swell of goodbyes flooded my consciousness. I vomited twice, as my body released the dream. One last "fuck you" to God, and then I heard myself say aloud: "She isn't coming back. She isn't coming back. She isn't coming back."

*She isn't coming back.*

*She isn't coming back.*

After two hours on the forest floor, I finally believed me.

*She really wasn't coming back.*

I got up off the earth as the sun was setting and walked down the mountain in peace. It wasn't a once-and-for-all process, but I had made real progress. I longed to hold her hand for all eternity, but recognized within the pocket of my deeper knowing that eternity would have to begin in the next lifetime. We had walked as far as we could go in this one.

That night, I went for my final treatment in the healing pool. As I was being moved delicately through the water, I saw Sarah's face in my heart's eye. Soft tears fell as I surrendered to the grace of loving her. Although the loss hurt terribly, it also hurt beautifully. Hanging on had shielded me from my pain, but it had also severed me from the satisfaction that came with having loved so abundantly. With no attachment to a shared future, perhaps I could love her now without expectation. Perhaps.

Afterwards, I soaked into the wee hours of the morning. The pool emptied, until it was just me. Me and God. And, we weren't enemies, after all. She had risen into view in my ecstasy, and now she had risen into view in my suffering. And it was finally crystal clear that she hadn't inflicted this pain on me. It wasn't God's choice, God's doing. She had graciously handed us the opportunity of a lifetime. What we did with it was in our hands alone.

## Path Show-er

The next morning, I woke up feeling a newfound sense of serenity. Something sweet had come through the darkness. My struggles felt like blessings that had birthed a kinder, gentler order. But I still wasn't clear: what was the gift? What was the *GIFT*?

My gaze had shifted from the blame-filled outer world of aggressors and wrongdoers to the inner world of self-responsibility. Blaming God had tied me to a victim consciousness, but I didn't want to be a victim. I wanted to become a victor. I was ready to ask the real questions: Why did *I* bring these circumstances into my life? Why did *I* attract a soulmate who would crush me? What was at the heart of this journey of the heart?

I went for a long ponderous walk, looking for answers. None were found. I headed toward the river and sat on a large rock in the center. I looked down into the water, searching for clarity like a miner searches for gold. I imagined myself with a sieve in my hands, separating the gold from the dross. But what was the gold? What was the dross? And what was the alchemical process that would convert my dross into gold? I asked myself—is it the suffering that refines the gold? If so, is that the gift of suffering?

While looking at my own reflection in the river, my mind wandered back to the moment when I first encountered Sarah by the river near Boulder. Such a glory-filled moment. I had appeared behind her, and we had simultaneously stared at our shared reflection in the water. In that moment, I tasted my first experience of wholeness. I was made whole by her presence and by the love we shared.

Yet, from that moment forward, my wholeness was dependent on something outside myself. In truth, I had never fully experienced wholeness on my own. Was that the gift of this love? To point me back in my own direction? Is that what it takes for many of us to realize that we had it all along? The savage dismantling of our illusions of completion with another? Was that the crushing gift of this love?

When I returned to the village, I went directly to the massage office to book a session with Miriam. I needed to be in the presence of one who understood. Divine timing—she just had a cancellation. It was meant to be.

When I arrived at her cabin, she was outside smoking a cigarette again. I knew the drill. I went inside and lay down on the table. Many minutes later, she entered. This time, she started on my crown. Her hands were on fire. I loved those trembling hands—they were tentacles of divinity. This was a woman who had taken her affliction and converted it into love. Soulrebral Palsy—the trembling hands of God.

I closed my eyes and surrendered to her knowing. After she uttered some Sanskrit mantras, she went completely silent. Within seconds, I felt myself moving—not on the table, but through a brightly lit energetic portal. The pace accelerated, and I crossed into a valley at the end of a hollow tunnel. The space I entered was brilliantly fragrant, with a luminous sky, like the Northern Lights. There I was—both my self, and a consciousness witnessing me. And both the experiencer and the witnesser had the most profound sense of completeness.

After removing her hands from my body, she began to speak. "You have to become the love and pass it on."

"What does that mean?" I asked.

"You have to become the love you experienced. You have to embody that expanded heart consciousness, and bring it to the world. That's how you keep the love alive."

"Like, become whole without her?"

"Yes, but its more than that. You become the love, and then you share it with the world. You are a carrier now. You have seen something magnificent. You are called to bring it to humanity. You just have to discover the form that works for you."

"You mean find the gift, right?"

"Partly, Lowen, but it's more than that. You actually *become* the gift. It continues to live on through you, even in her absence. You become whole when you find a way to express that in your life."

"But we failed..."

"Failed! How can love ever fail? If you can be in heartbreak, and keep your heart totally open, you are living so very close to God. Love is the great door opener. It opens our guarded hearts, grants us a glimpse of another universe, leaves us with a taste of the divine. Love doesn't fail us—it's our expectations that fail us. We expect it to last when it came for a different reason altogether."

I lay there for a few more minutes, trying to fully download her meaning.

"What happened to your great love?"

"She's in Bali."

"Are you still connected to her?"

"Connected at heart—forever. Connected in this body, in this life... no. We chose goodbye."

"I'm sorry."

"Oh Goodness, don't be. The gift is unwrapped, and I am blessed. It's easy to confuse those who show us a path with the path itself. But they are just path-showers, that's all. They show us a path we couldn't see on our own. Once you see the path, it is for you to continue walking. Once you understand that, you will stop suffering."

With that, she got up from her stool and left the space. After a few more minutes, I stumbled outside to say goodbye. She was nowhere to be seen. Somehow that was perfect.

# 18

---

# Premature Emancipation

I spent my last few days at Rockwood feeling light as a feather. I had undergone a remarkable transition in only two weeks. It felt as though everything had momentarily transformed into the light at its source. Was this the gift of Sarah fully unwrapped?

The positive feelings continued after I arrived back in Toronto, like the universe had burst my pain balloon in one fell swoop. I felt free of suffering, free of confusion, free of longing. If nothing else, I had left my closed heart in Arizona. It was all good.

With a tremendous outburst of energy, I poured my focus into new beginnings. Over the course of the next month, I threw out half of my belongings, bought new bedroom and living room furniture, and repainted the entire apartment—even Sarah's remaining graffiti remnants.

When the house was complete, I channeled my boundless energy into transforming my law practice. Through this more enheartened lens, traditional litigation felt too harsh and incongruent. It was a ruthless game, and I was determined to enhance the world in a real way. With the support of a friend with a bustling mediation practice, I began to weave mediation and alternative dispute resolution into my legal practice. In a matter of months, I was doing very few criminal trials and finding greater purpose in my work for the first time. The gift of Sarah was beginning to take form.

By the following spring, I felt ready to bring my hopeful energy into my relationship life. I began dating Janice, a beautiful nurse with a kind heart. I really enjoyed her company but I felt repelled whenever we got intimate. Being naked with her felt like a radical fall from grace. Thud! I *wanted* to want her, but I just didn't want her. Good woman, wrong soul. Oh no, not this again.

The same situation occurred with two more women. Good company, attraction, definitely a basis to explore further. And then the disconnect every time we approached intimacy. With one of them, Renee, I actually had intercourse, of sorts. She was fully present, but I was nowhere to be found. While I was inside her, I was overcome with images of Sarah lying beneath me. I closed my eyes to imagine her, but Renee didn't cooperate. She kept shrieking as I was thrusting, an ear-piercing reminder that that she wasn't my beloved. After she left the house that night, I drank a bottle of Amaretto to help me forget—and I hate Amaretto.

After this experience, I fell into a quiet depression. It was not dark and hopeless like before—I truly had released an iceberg of pain at Rockwood—but it was much more confusing. Before, I knew why I was depressed—I hadn't even begun to process the pain of loss. But now... why? I had moved a weight of darkness out of me in Arizona. Everything in my life was forward-moving. I felt ready to begin again. Why so sad?

I looked for Dude to help me, but he was nowhere to be found. In fact, I hadn't seen him in months. *Where have you gone, my houseless mystic?*

I was again riddled with questions. Is it natural to jump back and forth between darkness and light, shackles and liberation, after a beloved is gone? Is this part of the healing and integration process? Is it possible to release the pain once and for all, or does it keep returning, like a wave that cycles back to shore? Does one ever come into balance after a loss like this?

The lingering heaviness persisted for months. Despite my claims that it was all good, it clearly wasn't. Premature emancipation, all over again. Yet, this time there was a new sliver of understanding. It was beginning to dawn on me that this was the nature of the growth process. Once one plateau is reached, another calls to us, inviting us to do the necessary work to arrive there. If we honor the invitation, we expand toward a greater peace. If we ignore it, we become depressed from resisting our own expansion. Part of being truly on your path is being available to grow to the next level.

I was becoming stagnant at this level of healing. I felt the nudge from within—it was time to grow forward. I knew intuitively there was more. And I realized I could use some support in getting there. But how? I wasn't sure in what form the support would arrive. But I was ready to receive it.

## Sally

I woke up one Sunday morning agitated after dreaming about Sarah. She was walking just ahead of me on a familiar Toronto thoroughfare: Harbord Street in the student Annex. Every time I got close to her, she would magically land steps ahead. In dreams as in life, I always seemed to be a step behind the beloved.

I rose from bed, and made my way for the Annex. I didn't imagine Sarah would be there, but perhaps something else was. As I turned onto Harbord from Spadina Avenue, I spotted a woman sitting on the steps of an old Brownstone about a block away. From a distance, she could easily have been Sarah. Same wavy blond hair, same style of dress, same small frame. Same feeling as my dream.

I picked up my pace, determined to see her up close. I intuitively knew she wasn't Sarah, but I wanted 30 seconds of fantasy. When I got there, I saw a beautiful young woman, probably around 20, talking on her cell phone, getting up to leave. She smiled at me as she passed by, in that kindly way that a young woman smiles at an older man who could easily be her father. Humbled yet again.

I looked up at the building. It had a series of brass name plates fastened to the wall. I walked up the steps to take a closer look. My eyes fixed on one of them: "Dr. Sally Lesser, Humanistic Psychologist." An electrical current surged through my body. I had the strangest feeling that I had to call this woman. Following that impulse, I booked an appointment with her for the very next day.

When I walked into Sally's eclectic office for the first time, I immediately felt a sense of home. She came out and greeted me, and looked so familiar, like a long lost member of my family. Or, maybe this is what it feels like to reunite with soul-family. A tall, slender, brown-haired woman in her late 50's, she looked entirely conservative, with the exception of funky purple-framed glasses. A very warm and grounded person, it was immediately obvious that she had a keen and depthful intelligence.

I sat down across from her in a cozy leather chair, in her colorful little office—a fascinating mix of East Indian, Egyptian and New Mexican decor.

"Tell me what brings you here..." Sally invited.

Without hesitation, I began outpouring... just about everything. I didn't hold back. I simply couldn't. A built up reservoir of expression was being released.

Throughout my sharing, Sally's gaze did not waver. I felt her truly with me. Her unwavering presence invited me to keep speaking, and revealing, layer upon layer. It was the first time I truly got to tell my story without inhibition. A warm relief flooded my body. Deep exhale.

When I was done, she said with confidence, "I know exactly what you're speaking of."

"You really do, don't you?"

"Yes, although not firsthand. This is a special and sacred subject that has always engaged my interest. And I have worked with rare couples who have encountered this experience. I even wrote my master's thesis on this subject. It was best explained in the writings of a woman named Jeanne Achterberg. She gave these types of unions a name: *Uncommon Bonds*. They are way-showers for the evolution of consciousness."

I let the words seep in. Uncommon Bonds.

Sally went over to her book-shelf, handing me a copy of an article written by Jeanne. "Here take a look..."

I scanned the article and immediately my eyes fell on a few sentences:

*The unions have what appear to be transcendent or transpersonal elements. The relationships appear to have been destined and are frequently described as resulting from grace.*

I felt a stirring in my soul.

Then my eyes fell again:

*Parapsychological, or paranormal events—synchronistic occurrences and nonlocal communications—that defy known laws of time and space are often present.*

And then, dropping in for more:

*The bondeds described having recognized one another as cut from the same cloth or as having occupied the same body in a previous life; they felt they were distantly related or were one soul residing in two bodies.*

With that, my teardrops sprinkled the page.

"Bring that home with you," she said. "Read it and absorb it. And let's explore more next session."

As I walked home, I felt like I was holding a sacred text in my hand. This was no ordinary writing. It was a transmission from beyond. And so was Sally—I had clearly come to the right place.

Instead of going straight home, I wandered over to Bellwoods Park and propped myself against a tree. I knew I would need some support, as I drank this in.

I couldn't stop reading, ravenously consuming—it was water to my thirsting soul.

*Any soul work is likely to be arduous, complex, and accompanied by many 'dark nights' as well as, often, incredible bliss during the course of the transformative process.*

Suddenly the pieces of the puzzle began to gracefully fit together. I wasn't insane. This wasn't some outlandish phenomena. There was a reality to this. It was like I had discovered the master key.

I went in for another drink:

*Sexuality is clearly a spiritual practice for them...*

A sea of memories emerged of me and Sarah together, touching the divine through our body temples: the first time I touched her G(od) spot, my first exquisite taste of the yoniverse with her back pressed against an oak tree, our first cosmic penetration in the meditation sanctuary, the unseen galaxies we co-created while lovemaking in my Toronto apartment. And one memory in particular—that very first kiss in Rocky Mountain Park—when we dunked our hearts in the rivers of essence and everything became God. God has such soft wet lips.

I sat against the tree and read the same pages over and over again, as the cosmic tumblers clicked into alignment, finally making sense of my experience, deepening my understanding of the paths Sarah and I had walked. Finally I felt *seen*. Jeanne's description presented the form of the relationship in such perfect detail. Now it all made sense: the soul's familiarity, the sexuality portal, the relentless synchronicities, the transpersonal energy, the ecstasy and despair, the sigh of relief as if coming home after decades of wandering. It was us. It was comforting to know that we were not the first people to walk this way.

As the days passed, I felt myself encircled in a glow of new understanding. Everything was up-framed into its true context. I could now begin to see the once-elusive backdrop that held our bond. It was peeking through in all its splendor. No wonder I had felt perpetually unsettled. I had no framework of understanding to explain what I had experienced.

In the weeks to come, I allowed this new understanding to integrate and weave into my cells, reshaping me, just as the love had. The only gap in my understanding was the knowing of WHY it came. Uncommon, to be sure, but why did we summon this bond into our lives? Why manifest something so impossible? What was the point of such a profound relationship, if not to grow old together? How did such a sacred connection lose its way? And still the lingering question: *what was the gift?*

## The Integration

I began dialoguing very deeply with Sally, bringing to her what I assimilated throughout the week, in my readings, and in my deepening heart-explorations. She had no answer to my key questions—they were for me to answer—but she did know how to support my process. From her studies, she was able to acknowledge that these connections do tend to fall apart, particularly if at least one of the individuals isn't egoically strong enough to handle the intense merging of their soul with another. In her words, "strongest me, strongest we." A healthy, sturdy ego to come home to is essential to sustaining the bond, particularly when the shadow emerges. Without it, there is a tendency to push the bond away until it can be developed.

"Could this be why she fled?" I wondered.

"Yes, it's likely a part of it. She was only 26. Evolving beyond the familiar into a higher way of being is a great challenge for anyone, even more so when two people attempt it when they are younger. Does that feel resonant?"

"Yah, kind of like dying to an old paradigm and being born to a new one..."

She quickly added, "Yes, and without any terms of reference or teachers to guide them."

"Oh yes, you can say that again. I remember during some of our intensely rocky patches—I wished we had someone to shepherd us over the terrain. Someone who had been there before."

"Yes, something like a 'Love Elder'," Sally laughed. "Well..." she continued, more serious, "Love Elders are out there. Not many, at this stage of development, but some. As more people awaken to love as a spiritual path, more Love Elders will spring forth. And, people like you are also clearing the way for those who are just beginning their conscious relationship journey."

I sat with that for some time, reflecting on Love Elders, and remembering my own challenges with opening to this new way of being, and, even more so, the challenge of figuring out how to process the ending.

I continued the dialogue mid-thought: "...perhaps that is also why closure has been difficult."

"Tell me what you mean..." she invited.

"Well, I felt like all my traditional ideas of healing and resolution got thrown out the window here. Some healing was possible, but it wasn't a simple process of healing and letting go. It was much more complicated than that."

"Because you were attached on a soul level?"

"Yes, for sure—the world definitely made no sense in her absence, but not just because of that..."

I went quiet again, knowing I was coming close to understanding something essential. And then it came. "It's like this. The love didn't just touch my soul. It transformed it. It polished it, worked it, kneaded it, kind of like clay. The love itself was the sculptor. And when she fled, my sculpture ruptured, cracked, parts fell off. I was in between forms, in a way. It's hard to heal something that doesn't even know what it is anymore. It's like trying to heal a disease when you don't know where the host is. It was like I was 'Soulshaping.' Does that make any sense?"

"Yes, it does, and even if you were feeling solidly rooted in the next 'soulshape,'" she echoed. "The soul doesn't heal like the psyche. It requires different understandings, different techniques, a timeline all its own. Transformed in the unseen realms, it has to heal there too, in ways that us humans haven't even begun to grok."

What a remarkable gift to be able to have such a transparent and elevated conversation with another human being. Bit by bit, the pieces were coming together.

In a key subsequent session, Sally initiated a conversation about the heightened nature of uncommon bonds. I would soon realize why.

"These connections are often reported initially as ecstatic in nature, a kind of sky experience where the lovers' feet seldom touch Mother Earth. Not to pathologize them, but just to acknowledge that higher

187

level connections have a tendency to catapult one's consciousness up, up and away from the earth plane, one breath closer to heaven."

"Yes, that was entirely my experience."

"Of course, they usually come crashing back to earth. As one aspect of the lovers' consciousness reaches for the heavens, another element inevitably seeks the stability of Mother Earth. If both lovers are grounded in their consciousness, they can manage the landing while holding the connection safe. But if one or both lovers are even somewhat ungrounded, they tend to come crashing back to earth, shattering the relational cord on the way down. It's like landing without a parachute—a soft landing isn't possible. This isn't a personal failure. That they were able to enter the portal at all is a triumphant act of tremendous courage. The inability to remain there is a reflection of the distance the culture has yet to travel before it can hold divine life safe. It's a delicate and subtle art to integrate and interweave both realms—earth and sky—one that few people can sustain. Most of us don't have the developmental girders. It takes a solid and sound maturity— psychologically, spiritually and within their personalities—to hold an uncommon bond together over the long haul."

I knew where she was guiding me. She was guiding me to look more deeply at my own immaturity and ungroundedness. Then she said it, "While you may have been slightly more mature than Sarah when you both met, I'm not convinced that the relationship would have ended any differently if she hadn't fled it. I wonder if you wouldn't have eventually left because of your own earthly issues. Is it possible that neither of you had the developmental girders in place to sustain this relationship at that stage of your lives?"

It was an annoyingly good question, one that challenged my belief that I was the capable one in the connection. That I would never run or flee. That I would never reject such a gift. Maybe I would, or maybe I wouldn't, but it's true that the connection never felt safe enough for my own engulfment issues to emerge. I was too busy chasing Sarah to imagine running in the other direction. What would *have* happened had she stopped running? Would I have put on my sneakers and made for the next off-ramp?

Sally continued, "If this therapy is going to serve you, we have to do more than just help you to contextualize where you have been... we also have to prepare you for the next soulmate that walks through your door. Whether she actually arrives in tangible form, or not. What has to mature and solidify so that you—not Sarah, not some other person—but YOU can hold love safe? What has to happen so that you can hold sky and earth in your consciousness at one time?"

After some resistance, I began to focus our session work on my own ungroundedness. Yes, it was fundamental to the heightened nature of the experience, but I knew there was more to it than that. Born into that chaotic family dynamic, my imprinting played a role as well. It wasn't obvious when interfacing with my willful personality, but a part of my consciousness did always want to get out of here. I was aware of my tendency to jump to the ecstatic sky at a moment's notice, without first ensuring that the foundation was solid. I even felt it in the way I walked, particularly when life became difficult—quick on my feet, not lingering on Mother Earth for any longer than I had to. Almost like a bird that's ready to take flight at any moment. Not unlike Sarah, my migrating beloved. For both of us, it felt safer up there.

And for those who knew me well, there were many signs of a similar immaturity on the earth plane. Those signs included financial irresponsibility, unreliability with friends and family, and a certain youthfulness akin to Peter Pan. There was a part of me that wanted to delay adulthood for as long as possible.

With this awareness, Sally encouraged me to work deeply on the physical plane to ground and integrate the higher planes of consciousness that I had traversed. I wasn't a bird, after all. We devoted many sessions to simply grounding my feet: rubbing them into the earth, digging my soles into golf balls, and learning how to stand my ground firmly and unwaveringly. As she knew it would, this work brought me deeper into many uncomfortable elements of reality, including a giant vat of unreleased primal pain that I had never accessed in my previous healing work. My body was like a museum, filled with toxic artifacts from childhood. It was early stuff, too early for words, but the body knew. With her support, I worked those holdings, healing more of the early life material that had catapulted me away from the earth.

One of my clearest realizations was related to my own isolation, which seemed to live at the heart of my depression. When Sarah arrived, my faith in the universe was restored after decades, lifetimes, of aloneness. It wasn't just a homecoming between our two souls, it was also a restoration of my faith in humanity and a benevolent universe. Finally, I could exist in relation to something outside myself and not get disappointed. Finally, someone up there was watching over me. Finally, my entire existence was infused with purpose.

When she left, I not only lost my love, I lost my faith in God. If my beloved couldn't hold me safe, there was nothing and no one that could. I was right back in my locked childhood cage, alone and unprotected, while the universe poked sticks at me between the bars. My isolation had returned, with a fierce vengeance. Finding Sally seemed to be a sign from the universe that I really wasn't alone—the universe had brought me someone who could help free me from my cage.

As our work together deepened, I became certain that this healing phase was not solely about my personal healing. I wasn't just crying for me. This ocean of tears was too vast for one soul alone. I was also crying for Sarah, and the entire collective. In the same way as we had entered the collective heart when we fell in love, we had also entered the collective wound. In the same way as our ecstatic moments had elevated the collective vibration, these moments of release contributed to its healing. I cried for my loss, her loss, your loss—all those moments when all of us had longed for love, retreated from love, lost love before it could be fully lived. Oh my God, there is so much unfulfilled love on this troubled planet. Doors that opened and closed before their time. All the salt in the oceans must come from the unshed tears of humanity. When will we learn to honor love when it comes?

As I worked both intensively with Sally and independently, over a two year period, the healing work integrated within me, inspiring change on many different levels. Perhaps most significantly, I grew to feel more mortal, more capable of holding the space for all elements of reality at once. Instead of looking for heaven up there alone, I was better able to search for it down here in the nuances of daily life. And I also developed the capacity to hold both at once: light and shadow, shopping list and unity consciousness, fresh mangoes and stale bread. It was all God, even the dust that fell off my awakening heart. In a way, I had gifted the earth back to myself—finally, after many decades of internal rootlessness. Dude was right—it doesn't mean anything to have a house, if you don't feel at home in your own skin.

Surprisingly, I also felt my heart opening to the idea of another relationship. What would the universe bring my way? Or rather, what would I walk my way into next?

## *Lover's Leap*

Almost four years to the day of our first meeting, I felt ready to move to the next stage of letting go. I woke up early that Saturday morning and gathered my things for a trip to the Elora Gorge, a natural wonder a few hours outside of Toronto. I now understood what happens when we say goodbye too soon. It comes back to haunt us. So I waited until I felt truly prepared internally. Today was that day.

I picked Elora because it had a particular symbolism for the relationship. We had gone there once and made love by the side of the Grand River, at a time of the year when no one with good sense would take their clothes off. But we did, and the heat from our bodies turned the chill of autumn into summer's fiery furnace.

After reaching an exquisite climax together on the riverbank, we climbed back up to the trail above. On the hike back to the car, we spotted an overhang called Lover's Leap. At the end of it, there was a plaque with a story on it. The story goes that a heartbroken Aboriginal Princess had jumped to her death here after receiving news that her beloved had died on the battlefield. After reading the plaque, we sat down on the ground beneath it and prayed for their spirits.

I wanted to let go here.

I drove to Elora, and parked in front of Café Creperie, the wonderful restaurant that we had eaten at after our riverside adventure that afternoon. I went inside and wandered over to the same table we had sat at, and ordered the same crepe we had shared. I was testing myself. Was I ready to let go? Although I felt quietly sentimental, I also felt an unusual sort of peace. It was clear—that was *that* crepe, and this was *this* crepe, and there was no crepe in between. It was a new day.

After a wonderful conversation with the owner about love and life, I made my way to the river. When I found a quiet spot, I reached into my wallet and took out my favorite picture of Sarah. It was a shot of her sitting in a grassy field at the Ascension Institute in New York. It was a beautiful picture she had taken with one hand, while her other hand rested gently on my face. I had always refused to remove this photo from my wallet, no matter what went on between us, including the past years of our torrential separation.

It was time.

I reached down and placed the photo on a small angular rock in front of me. After several minutes, water began to gather under the picture. I watched the photo rise until it began to merge with the current. It was just about to be carried away... when I snapped it up.

I lifted it away from the water and looked at it one last time. The final reach-for. Such a beautiful picture. Such a magnificent love, perhaps too magnificent to hold on to. I lifted the picture to my lips and kissed it softly. As I gently held the photo, it seemed so impossible, so complicated, to even imagine letting go. After all, our souls were involved—how could we truly let go? As I released the photo, it dawned on me—it wasn't a letting go. It was a letting through. Letting the pain through the holes it left behind so it could find its ultimate destination. I wasn't letting go of the love. I was only letting go of the dream of being together. I watched the current carry the picture away. My tears splashed on the rock below, joining the journey home.

Everything was still. Sweet surrender.

As I made the climb back up the cliff, I had no illusions about my process. It was a pivotal moment, to be sure, and one with great symbolic meaning, but I now understood that dramatic moments are not the end of the story. The most lasting transformation happens in the subtleties, in those private moments of acceptance when the bond loosens its grip and the heart readies itself for new possibilities. One soul step at a time.

And perhaps there is never an end to a love story. Once the gateway has opened between two souls, it never fully closes, even if they imagine themselves separate.

# 19

## Truth-Aches

I entered into a place of real contentment in my own skin. Not ecstatically happy like I was with Sarah, but a different kind—the kind of happiness that comes after a long and arduous journey. I was now at peace with path for only the second time in my life, and the first time alone. I enjoyed my soulitude not like a lonely man, but like a man who had seen something extraordinary and would never be the same.

Intrinsic to my peacefulness was an integration of my warrior consciousness. I moved through the world in a more balanced way: a conscious in-coupling of anima and animus, a tenderling warrior who had finally found his balance. The pendulum had landed in the middle. Perhaps this was the real reason Sarah had come into my life—to soften my hard edges, to teach me how to live in my heart before, during and after incredible heartbreak. To become a true warrior of the heart.

### The Coin Roller

Quite often, I would go and sit with Dude. Just sit and have a drink. Nothing dramatic, the simple enjoyment of one another's company. I wasn't looking for answers, and he wasn't giving them—at least, not without payment. Then one morning he surprised me with some free wisdom. The timing was perfect.

"You've worked hard on yourself. Now you need to find someone to love. You're all opened up with no place to go. You're overworked and underlaid," he said firmly.

I protested: "I give my love to my clients and my friends."

"Not enough. You're a lover. That's your path. And, you should be more afraid of avoiding your path than walking it. Time to get back on the love train, bud."

Oh God, the cliché machine had returned.

"It's fine, Dude. Really. I'm finally doing good. No need to go looking for love. No need to fix what ain't broken."

He paused for a moment, allowing his next bit of wisdom to surface.

"You know, Detachment is the mantra of the walking wounded. The new cage movement can be very persuasive, but don't believe them. They are locked inside their own avoidance. Detachment is a tool—it's not a life."

There it was.

"I'm not detached. I have an involved life," I said with a tinge of defensiveness.

Then he got to the real point: "You're much more interesting when you have a lover."

"You saying I'm boring now?"

He shrugged his shoulders knowingly, while reaching for his coffee cup. "Not boring, just sleepy."

"Maybe I'm getting caught up on lost sleep."

"Maybe you're in a solitary confinement of your own making," he said firmly.

After a long silence, I spoke the truth: "It's not easy to love again after… that."

"It's time, Junior. How long's it been since you had a girl? Like five years, right?"

I nodded my head yes.

"There are many forms of love. Try on another for size," he said, getting up to leave. "That was free of charge. Now get prowling."

Halfway across the street, he turned back and called out, "Don't end up like me, Lowen, alone with a pushcart as your companion."

Ugh. Maybe Dude was right.

It had actually been more than six years since Sarah, and three years since my last attempt at intimacy. Which wasn't real intimacy at all—only a half-cocked attempt. I didn't want to make the mistake of giving up on love altogether.

After seeing Dude, I went for lunch with my Bubbi—my feisty 84-year-old Jewish grandmother. She rolled my coins for me, a job she relished. When they were all rolled up, we would spend the money on lunch. She loved doing it so much that I secretly bought rolled change at the bank, unwrapped it, and threw it in the bottle so she would have a full load to work with.

Once she got rolling, she wouldn't stop until it was all done. She was ninety pounds of coin-rolling might. She would call me through-out the rolling process, often filling my answering machine with the ongoing totals: "Lowen, we're up to five bucks. Will call back soon." "Honey, I hit the jackpot—we're at twenty bucks and still climbing." "Lo Lo! I just hit a C-note!" It was the most annoyingly cute thing ever.

On this glorious autumn afternoon, I was instructed to pick her up at her apartment so we could go to the bank to convert the rolls into bills. She didn't like leaving them in her apartment, certain that the great robber in the sky knew she had thirty bucks in nickels in her cedar chest. After the bank, we drove to our favorite Jewish Deli. It was one of my favorite rituals—baked whitefish and bagels with Bubbi.

Her and my long-deceased grandfather had loved one another since the first moment they saw each other, walking up Bathurst Street in Toronto on the way to synagogue. They were married for 56 years and had never stopped loving each other through wars, poverty and disease.

They had also never stopped loving me. They were the ones to shower me with the unconditional love I had never found anywhere else. Throughout my life, they had lavished me with praise and en-couragement, serving as a perpetual refuge from my parental battle-ground. Shelter was there whenever I needed it, and it came with back tickles, warm food and unwavering acceptance. Oh, and five bucks every now and then from Zeyda, my grandfather. "Every kid needs a fin in his pocket. No kid should walk around penniless." They were a blessing.

On this day, Bubbi was on a mission, even before the whitefish got to the table.

"I'm worried about you, Lo Lo."

"Why, Bubbi? All is well."

"You've been alone too long. It's not natural."

What, were her and Dude on the same cosmic tag team?

"I know, but it's not that simple. I can't go back to regular love."

How do you explain an uncommon bond to your Jewish grandmother? Through her practical eyes, if a couple didn't stay together through thick and thin, there was never a bond at all.

"Who said anything about regular love? How about a wonderful love, with great-grandchildren even," she said with a little smile.

"I feel at peace on my own, Bubbi."

"I am happy to hear that—Zeyda would be pleased—but I don't see why you can't go to some dances, and see if something good comes your way."

"Dances? No one goes to dances at the Jewish Y anymore, Bubbi."

"Doesn't matter where, go find her on that computer phone if you want. Tilly's daughter met her husband on a computer. You know what the Rabbi always says..."

"No Bubbi, I don't go to synagogue—what does he say?"

"It's a woman Rabbi, but that's not the point, Lo Lo. She says 'The sun shines on those who keep the faith.'"

"That's pure schmaltz. And I have faith, I just don't want to settle for less."

"Who's talking about settling? Not trying to meet someone, that's settling, sweetheart. You need someone to take care of you. You want to be all alone when you're old?"

Oy gevalt! Old style scare tactics.

The Bubbi wanted more than lunch today. She wanted great-grandkids and my happiness, and she was willing to use any technique she could find. Even old style scare tactics!

They worked.

## Back on the Love Train

And so, I began to date. And date. I went at it hard, with mixed results. I dated one woman who was super solid. But she had no emotional fluidity. Then I had two dates with the opposite—a woman who was open but lacking in boundaries. Next I spent a weekend with a nurturer—she gave and gave and never talked about herself. And then a youthful, beautifully bodied yoga teacher, who lacked the richness of character that comes with age. One way or the other, I didn't find what I was looking for. Oh by the way, what was I looking for?

All the while, reminders of my former beloved were back on the radar screen, after a long dry spell: Colorado license plates, cardinals and hawks, a man running down my street yelling for his daughter Sarah, and her graffiti scrawl When two hearts beat in the same direction coming through the sunroom wall, no matter how many times I repainted it.

Dear Universe, isn't it time for another channel?

And then I met someone. At a library cafeteria, no less. And her name was Miriam, just like the crone at Rockwood. I liked that.

I met her over lunch. She was sitting across from me at a large communal table and I felt an immediate resonance. I shared my orange jello with her. She shared her cherry. And we talked until the cafeteria emptied.

She had soft, chin length dark hair, deep brown eyes, and particularly pink cheeks—a round face full of kindness.

We quickly formed a lovely relationship. A single mother and busy medical doctor, Miriam's mature nature spoke to me. Before the birth of her daughter, she had devoted herself to philanthropic work—serving as a doctor in war-torn and third world countries—and it had taken her beyond the realm of petty self-involvement. There were no games, no mixed messages, no manipulations. She was deeply present during our time together. A devout student of conscious relationship, she was earnest in her efforts to process the few issues that came up in the connection. And she loved to laugh, dance and make love.

The timing was perfect. If she had come any earlier, I wouldn't have even noticed her. I needed the time that I took to heal. After all, love needs an entry point. If our emotional body is all blocked up with unresolved issues, there's no way in. The more we empty the vessel before it comes, the more space love has to flourish. Healing our hearts gives love a place to land.

When we were together, I felt satisfied and nourished, like I had just eaten my favorite home-cooked meal. I loved being part of her family—her daughter, Chloe, was 9 years old and a spunky firecracker of delight—and I loved making her part of mine. There was nothing to fear, nothing to flee, and no need to distract. The memory of my shaky union with Sarah faded as I finally stood on solid relational ground.

Miriam was 52 when we met, older than me by nearly nine years. Where before I had never imagined myself with an older woman, it now deeply filled me. I had grown tired of perfect younger bodies. They had no story to tell. And I had grown tired of being alone when in company. My story wanted to be met by another story. Miriam and I had a storybook beginning. Not a fairy tale, but a true-to-life story—raw and real, in all its beautiful imperfections.

In the heart of this solidity, my rapid-fire way of being slowed down even more. I began to appreciate the subtleties of daily life: the way the light changed as the day passed, the way it feels to actually taste your food, the poignancy that lives at the heart of stillness, the healing capacity of a simple touch. Miriam was teaching me that it can be truly safe to be vulnerable in connection. And that it was possible to be deeply connected and still have identifiable boundaries, rather than being completely and inextricably subsumed by the flames of love.

Perhaps most importantly, she taught me it was possible to heal our wounds in a relationship, not by using conflict and intensity as the excavator of the wounds, but by being with someone whose kindness gently invites the wounds to the surface to be healed. Miriam's unconditionally loving nature was the perfect healing balm for the wild man that still lived somewhere inside me.

This was so radically different from the fiery intensity I had known with Sarah, the heated word wars and the ruthless attacks, going hand-in-hand with the leaps into God-consciousness. I had also witnessed other couples too, who thrived off intentionally triggering each other under the guise of spiritual development—trying to heal the fire by recreating the fire, as many trauma survivors do. They believed that they need the triggers in order to bring their unresolved wounds and patterns to the surface. For them, their tumultuous connection is the primary way they become conscious of their issues. This is one kind of conscious relationship.

Because of Miriam, I came to prefer another kind of relationship: one where the connection is so stable and loving that your armor melts into sweetness. In the heart of that opening, your wounds and issues feel safe to reveal themselves. Not perpetually triggered by your partner, not re-traumatized by the connection, not lost on that slippery slope between forward moving trigger-fests and co-dependent woundmating—but invited into healing by their loving presence.

For now, this was my kind of conscious relationship.

### The Call of the Be-loved

Then, something shifted.

After four wonderful years together, my heart began to feel called away. At first the message was difficult to decipher—a subtle form with no discernible texture, an inexplicable loss of attunement, a microscopic agitation, a little voice speaking in tongues. Then it became clear. What began as an amorphous 'truth-ache' became impossible to ignore—the call of the beloved, yet again. I felt it in my yearning hands, as they longed to touch another as I had touched Sarah. I felt it in my searching eyes, as they scanned for the beloved in the trees, in the sky, in the market. And I most strongly felt it in the night, when the unseen world peeked through with intimate dreams of Sarah, waking me up beside Miriam—aroused and confused. Was I smitten with a ghost?

I tried to resist, but I yearned for the experience of unity I had tasted with Sarah. It was everything any traditional therapist would have warned against—the illusion of wholeness with another, the addiction to ecstasy—but the longing took root, haunting me without remorse, refusing to budge. Had I buried this longing all this time, or was Miriam another step of preparation, readying me for the next beloved?

Whatever it was, I wanted it back. I wanted it in my arms. I wanted it in my bed. I longed to be catapulted to higher consciousness in the presence of a beloved. For some time, I tried to create it in my relationship with Miriam, but that wasn't our way. We got along beautifully, but we just didn't have that kind of soul-synergy together. She was chicken soup for the soul—grounding and nourishing on many levels—but she wasn't my soulmate. We had chemistry, but we didn't have karmastry. I wanted both.

And then my confusion became a full-fledged existential crisis. Those deeply rooted questions again rose to the surface, questions I thought I had long resolved. What path am I here to walk? What kind of love relationship reflects my destiny? Who am I, really? *Who is this man, now?*

It is an odd thing to be so loved by someone sitting right in front of you, while your heart is with a ghost. Even stranger, to know that the ghost is never coming back, but that her essence lives on, enlivening your spirit, reminding you from your tomb of shared memories that there is more to love than what you have settled for.

In truth, I adored Miriam. It wasn't just a practical thing, a security thing, a healing thing. It was a love relationship, one with tremendous care, warmth and affection. I was woven into her life, she was woven into mine, and Chloe and I had grown very close. Very few individuals would have walked away from this nourishing relationship, but very few had experienced an uncommon bond. Very few had gone straight to the heart of God with a simple glance. A whole different playing field.

I soon lived a tormented life, weighing the paths like a butcher weighs chickens. Which path has more meat on it? Which path will leave me hungry? I was now 47 years old—wasn't I too old to start over again? And for what? The remote possibility that another great love would come my way? Or, the promise of a lifetime spent miserably alone? Truth-aches tossed and turned me, refusing to let me suppress the yearning, demanding that I end the relationship. What kind of fool walks away from the healthiest relationship he has ever had?

This one.

*In With the True*

One day, I had gone as far down the torment path as I could bear. I had tried to put the beloved away, but you can't tuck the divine away. Once you see that startling glimpse of God in human form, it can never be forgotten. I loved Miriam so, but the connection didn't bring me home. It was like we both loved God, but they were two different versions. Remaining together was not the highest for both of us. She deserved a man who was completely satisfied with her. I deserved a life that reflected my deepest yearning. Every person has the one thing they cannot live without if they are to feel complete. The beloved was my wholly grail, my yoniverse of meaning. It didn't mean that I would find my ultimate love in this lifetime, but it did mean that I would rather die looking than resign myself to a half path. Better to have yearned and lost than to have stopped yearning altogether. Better to live alone and die true to path.

Many of us know the moment when a love connection is over, but few of us stop then. I'm not talking about reactive endings. I am talking about the deep intuitive knowing that it's time to move on. Yet we are either too afraid, or too stubborn, or too concerned about the other's feelings to make our move. But it's perilous to delay, both because we suffer in the wrong connection and because we hold two souls back from finding the next step on their individual paths. Whether there's another love waiting around the next corner, or whether it's simply time to be alone, no one benefits by staying in an outgrown union. We have to notice the moment of ending and take it to heart. Everyone's expansion depends on it.

I called Miriam and asked her to meet me for lunch. She was excited, as I hadn't taken her out in months. I met her at the hospital and we drove to our favorite restaurant.

Somewhere between the appetizer and the entree, I told her the truth.

I saw her lower lip quiver. She looked down. Then she looked up at me, eyes glistening with tears. "I was expecting this," she said in a whisper.

"You were?" This surprised me.

She nodded. "I knew I wasn't your final destination. I was a stepping stone along the way. I have just loved being with you. Every moment."

"And I have loved being with you," I said tenderly.

Struck by a wave of emotion, she said, "Are you sure? Is there any way we could work on it?"

I knew in my heart that the decision had been made. My hunger for expansion took precedence over my hunger for security. With a tear falling down my face, I shook my head.

She nodded in acceptance.

As we drove back to the hospital, waves of emotion shook through both of us. It was not easy to leave a relationship, especially one that had served as such a nest. "Come here..." I said. I held her in my arms, stroking her hair, feeling both of our chests rise and fall in quiet sobs.

After a long moment of holding each other, she looked at me, eyes filled with tears and pure sincerity, and said, "I honor your courage. Please find what you are seeking."

"Thank you for the many gifts you have given me, darling," I replied. "You were truly a blessing in my life."

And she was. What a beautiful, selfless woman. I had been transformed by her presence. She had taught me that love could be immeasurably kind, without a hint of war, anywhere.

I drove back toward home, heart aching with sadness. Suddenly the reality hit me. I was alone again. A lone wolf warrior. Voices of uncertainty rose to taunt me: *How could you leave her, schmuck? Now what? Living your life and growing old—all alone? When you have such a solid love in your life? Run back to her! You can still catch her—don't let another one go!*

I pulled over to the side of the road. I could still turn around and go back to her. I did love her.

Shakily, I drove forward. Past the voices of doubt and remorse. Past the aching heart. Past the fear of aloneness, again.

Shakily, but steadily, I walked... into what... I did not know.

Out with the old, in with the true.

# 20

# Love It Forward

Ispent a few months quietly grieving and processing the end of my relationship with Miriam. Reflecting on the blessings, ready-making for whatever would come my way next. And then I began to date. Again. Lots of lovely souls, but no beloved.

Then, one stormy night, the winds of change struck. I had a profoundly vivid dream. It was more of a life-changing event, manifest in dream form. The kind of dream you can't possibly ignore except at your own peril.

In the dream, I was sitting in the sunroom of my apartment writing. The room had become a wild creative space. There were love words and phrases written all over the walls. The branches from Sarah's favorite tree had broken through the window and were stretched out all over the ceiling. The squirrels were inside the room, running to and fro. I was naked and tearful and happy as a lark. It was a kind of chaotic magnificence.

Suddenly I spotted Sarah's familiar hand-writing. In big red letters across the side wall was a phrase that I had never heard before: LOVE IT FORWARD. The words reminded me of the words the crone had spoken to me, when she had told me to become the gift and bring it to the world.

I woke up the next morning completely clarified about the next step of my journey. I was going to write a love story about Sarah and I. All that love needed some place to go. This was the way I was going to gift back to the universe for blessing me with a taste of ecstasy.

This was the way I would convert our suffering into gold. This was my offering to the beloved. Perhaps we couldn't make it all the way through the passage, but we could surely help others to walk a little further together.

Perhaps, even, that's why it came our way.

## Cave of Remembered Dreams

That morning, I drove to Goshen Provincial Park. I found my way to the tiny cave we had discovered that magical afternoon on our walk through the forest. The place we had made crunched up love, merging with each other like horny little pretzels. I crawled inside it, and remembered the dream that was our love, the greatest gift this soul had ever received.

I closed my eyes and meditated on my intention to put our uncommon bond to words. My whole body relaxed and softened. Yes, this felt true to path.

When I was ready, I said aloud:

*We will live on. In our breath, in our hearts, and in the words I write, I will love us forward.*

The cave echoed back my benevolent intentions. Then I scrawled the words LOVE IT FORWARD on the cave wall with chalk and left.

I would return here many times in the writing process. To remember my pledge. To remember what is never truly lost. To commune with the beloved in the cave of remembered dreams.

# 21

## Spiritual Graffiti

Before beginning to write, I created space for it. I committed to only the most essential social interactions and events, removing everything else from my schedule. I cut my legal mediation practice down to three successive days a week, leaving me Thursday to Sunday to write freely. Although the idea excited me, I really had no idea how, or what, I was going to write. I had been a capable academic writer in law school, but I had little experience with writing from the heart. It was like stepping into completely new territory, yet again.

Finally, after a week of preparation, I was ready to begin. Or so I imagined. I unplugged the phone and went to my writing desk in the sunroom, doughnut and coffee in hand. Five minutes later, I spilled the coffee all over the keyboard and had to spend three hours shopping for a new one. When I got home, it was time for lunch. Writers need energy! After a thick and creamy pasta dish, I lay down for a power nap, waking up close to five in the afternoon, almost four hours later. Time for dinner!

Someone wasn't ready.

After another day of glutenous distractions, I finally made my way back to the computer on Saturday. It was a crisp autumn morning, reminiscent of the first day Sarah came to live with me. I opened a word document, and was immediately swept up in a sea of memories. Closing my eyes, remembering that beautifully hopeful moment when we brought her luggage into this room and ended up twirling in rapture on the carpeted floor. "Shagging on the shag," we used to say. Every time I touched her, her eyes smiled like the first time I saw them, inviting me deeper into her valley of delight. I remembered how her eyes beamed on me the rest of the day, watching my every move like a tracker in the wild.

I opened my eyes and stared at the screen. It stared back at me. Neither blinked. I felt the temptation to leave, but willed myself to stay. After an hour and a half, I began to write words, but nothing that felt true. My mind kept returning to that lovely afternoon. The day we had begun our lives—*together*.

I returned the next day. Same thing happened. I sat there all morning, Lightnin cat by my side, writing little more than gibberish. She purred now and then, as though to inspire me, but it had little impact. I wrote a few words, and then my mind wandered back to joyous experiences Sarah and I had shared. I tried to write something wise and insightful, but there was no juice. It all felt purely conceptual. I was dry-docked.

Perhaps I wasn't cut out to be a writer, after all.

## Words from the Alley Wall

In the middle of the afternoon, I got up and went for a walk around the market. I saw Dude, but I avoided him, preferring to seek my own counsel this day. I went North on Augusta and crossed College Street, not consciously aware of where I was going, but getting the quixotic sense that I was headed somewhere in particular.

I turned left on Harbord Street and crossed Bathurst Street—my grandparents' childhood stomping grounds—and took a right at the first alley. Oh, now I knew where I was headed. Of course, how could I forget? I walked another 150 yards and stopped to face the back of an old Theater. There, on its back wall, were the words Sarah had painted on our six-month anniversary, ten years ago. If you didn't know what they were, you couldn't possibly have made them out, but I remembered.

I leaned against the garage nearby, and stared at Sarah's heart-speak. I wasn't so much interested in her ironic words as I was in their faded, weather condition. As though to emphasize the passage of time, there was bright writing all over the wall, reflections of the newest generation of graffitists. Oh God, was it that long ago?

> O, river of love,
> streaming out from my soul...
> How can I ever swim back to before?

And then the outpouring of tears. *Yes, Lowen, she is gone. It was more than a decade ago. For all you know, she married a mountain man and has a gaggle of children. For all you know, she's dead. Get Real!*

My tears continued to fall. A bottomless well. Goodness, where do they hide?

Hours later, I walked back home in a somber stupor. What was I thinking? That I could write her back to life? That I could just write the happy moments? It doesn't work that way. If I was going to write our love story, I had to tell the truth. I had to include the death of our union, too.

Once inside the house, I made myself a warm cup of chai and went right back to the computer. It was staring at me, just like before, awaiting my inspiration. Divine inspiration, anything, take me, I'm ready! Then I realized—something wasn't right.

I got up from the desk and grabbed a marker from the windowsill. I turned to face the wall—the wall Sarah had written on time and time again. Staring at the blank canvas, remembering.

Suddenly, I reached up and wrote the words she had written on the alley wall:

> O, river of love,
> streaming out from my soul...
> How can I ever swim back to before?

And, like a call-and-response, I answered:

> My river of love,
> We can't swim back to before.
> Broken waves we are to the very end,
> yet the seas can't hold all we've perfected.

I stepped back and stared at what I just wrote. Wow. As I gazed at the words, I felt something building inside me, a voice of my own demanding expression. I reached over to the wall and began to write some more. At first the words came through me tentatively, uncertain of their worth. Then quite suddenly a wellspring of realizations began to flow. The first sentences came out raw and chaotic, but gradually the words became more seamless, almost like they were pre-written in the manuscript of my being. Soon my first full paragraph was born:

> It seems counter-intuitive to romantics and those who feel ready to partner when someone walks away from a beautiful love connection. But some people can only handle a half-love because whole love shines a light on their dark places. Real intimacy requires real presence, and if someone isn't ready to be truly here on an individual level, they will find it very difficult to manage all the triggers that come up when real love comes. Only a small few can hold the gate open when profound love enters.
> A blessed and courageous few.

Then another wave of expression came through me, and I wrote it on the wall. And then I began scribbling on the blank wall like a madman, barely fast enough to keep up with the flow of expression. One paragraph after another moved through me without cessation. A floodgate had been opened.

After a while, my hand began to ache. I stepped back and stared at the wall in awe, wondering where this fluidity of expression had come from. Is this what I had been crafting all these years in the quiet recesses of my being? Before I could answer, I was seized again, surrendering to another wave of words in pre-encoded form. The writer had been released from his cage.

And, apparently, he was a Graffitist too.

## The Wholly Holy

Soon, writing became an all-encompassing spiritual practice, one I could not live without. I woke up every morning like a man on a mission. The passion to write was so alive that I couldn't just limit it to my home. Even during my work day, words poured out of me, demanding immediate expression. I wrote them on scrap paper, left them on my home answering machine, and emailed them to myself so I didn't forget. Even when I came home after an intense trial, I was propelled back to the wall to write deep into the night. As my colorful dream had predicted, the walls of the sunroom were soon covered in love-writings, as I let the creative process turn my idea of feng shui upside-down. I was becoming Sarah, or so it seemed.

Interestingly, there was only one thing that turned the expressive channel off: fantastical visions of Sarah and I together. Whenever I imagined us still united, the words would dry right up. I simply couldn't write from the fantasy of Sarah's presence. I could only write from the reality of her absence. Clearly, my writing voice was present—and presence—centered, directly linked to my own truth, to my own inquiry, to my profound interest in understanding love and the true-to-life road we had traveled. But not to keeping the dream alive.

Where before I had imagined I would write a love story, what was actually coming through me was a blend of story and insights into relationship as a spiritual path.

One night I sat on the porch thinking about ways to measure love. Although I had been with Sarah for the blink of an eye, I was remarkably transformed. I recalled speaking to the crone about this at Rockwood—wondering if I was crazy for feeling so different after such a brief spell of love. And she said with clarity: you don't measure love by how long it lasts.

How do you measure love, then?

My being responded, and I went to the kitchen wall and wrote:

You don't measure love in time.
You measure love in transformation.

Sometimes the longest connections
yield very little growth,
while the briefest of encounters change everything.
The heart doesn't wear a watch—it's timeless.
It doesn't care how long you know someone.
It doesn't care if you had a 40 year anniversary,
if there is no juice in the connection.
What the heart cares about is resonance.
Resonance that opens it,
Resonance that enlivens it,
Resonance that calls it home.
And when it finds it, the transformation begins...

That night, I was startled awake. But this time it wasn't a night-mare. It was more like a vision, visceral and palpable—as if it were truly happening to me. This one had an ethereal quality to it. I was floating through a timeless space with another genderless form. The space was constantly changing color, as we passed through one portal after another, holding each other close, intertwined with the divine. We were beyond the identifications, the battles, the confusions, the learnings of human form. And we were deeply, completely in love. Not just with each other, but with the space between. With the portals of possibility that awaited us. Love relationship may have been our first step in, but we were now well beyond it—inhaling God, exhal-ing love everywhere we looked. It was like a vision of possibility for humankind. The wholly holy.

I woke up overwhelmed with optimism for our humanity.

### The Great Bazaar

Sometimes, I went to sit with Dude, to discuss my insights. We had graduated from the relationship of teacher-student, as I grew to carry my end of the dialogue well. It was rare to find a man who wanted to talk about something other than automobiles and competitive sports, so I was grateful for our rich conversations. Yet in our conversations, I noticed how he would seldom share details about his personal love history. His great wisdom must have been lodged in life experiences, but he didn't share them. One day I prodded him a bit.

"C'mon Dude," I urged, "Tell me something about your personal love story."

Silence.

I persisted, "Come on, Dude, you can't hide from me... fess up."

"Not now, now I am more interested in getting that taco you promised me."

"Okay, Dude, taco it is. If I get you two, will you share a little of your own story?"

"Better you get me just the one."

Then, as the perfect deflection, he got up from the curb, reached into his crumpled suit jacket, and pulled out a small hardcover book of Rumi poetry. Entirely weather-worn, with dozens of ripped pages, it looked like it was hundreds of years old—a book from the hands of Rumi himself. How long had he carried this book? He opened it, and began to read aloud, speaking the poems with such panache and familiarity that you had to wonder if he had actually written them in another life.

Soon the whole sidewalk was filled with passersby who stopped dead in their tracks to hear Rumi brought back to life. Was this Toronto's Kensington Market, or Turkey's Great Bazaar? It was such a startling, spontaneous event, one you would seldom ever see in a modern city, one that called the spirit back in time. He read for almost an hour. At the end, a throng of dozens clapped and demanded an encore. He pulled the book back out of his jacket, and read something that spoke directly to my heart:

> Without You in me how could I bear one moment
> This grief of living without You?
> And these tears—aren't they You rising in me
> To flood me ruthlessly toward Your hidden arms?

Thereafter, half the crowd left, while the rest of us got into a lively discussion about the nature of love. Some argued that great love is destined before we are born, others contended that it was all left to chance. A couple at the front held each other and cried, admitting to the crowd that they had just broken up over lunch and didn't even know why. Two women from the crowd came over and comforted them, placing their hands on their backs. Even a Kensington beat cop stopped and chimed in, sharing his belief that love is a hopeless catastrophe. I looked over at Dude, and saw a tear falling from his eye. He looked like he was missing someone—Shams perhaps?

Beaming with warmth, I went back home and wall-wrote with Lightnin by my side, delighted to know I wasn't the only one trying to make sense of love's perplexities. I mean, it's not like we're going to figure it out without each other, are we? I picked up my marker, and wrote my own version of Rumi:

> Great love is the great cosmic kiln
> where souls are set ablaze
> until they finally surrender to God.
> Remain open in the heart of that inferno,
> and your separateness
> will melt into wonder.

### To Each Their Path

I awoke the next morning with a new inquiry burning inside: Is love partnership for everyone? Is it essential to a life well lived, or is that just a cultural myth? Was the love I experienced with Sarah something that was designed for everyone? Or did each have their own path to God? Is there even an ultimate path, or is life just a patchwork of arbitrary happenings?

On a spiritual level, I was truly at peace with my journey, my choices, my high standards: Live Beloved, or die! Maybe I was single, but it was different now. When you have loved as God loves, you no longer yearn for companionship in the same way. You no longer feel isolated when you walk alone. Because you have been penetrated by divinity. Because you have been transformed beyond yourself. Because you walk in shared shoes. Because you always feel the beloved close at heart.

Yet sometimes, I did feel tinges of doubt and fear creep back in. After all, there was still the practical world to consider. I was middle-aged and still single... was this my destiny? To grow old alone? To cuddle up to my eco-pillow? To drive myself to the hospital when I got sick? Had I forgotten my basic needs in my quest for everything beloved? What about companionship, dear man? What about a hand to hold on a cold winter's night?

Holding my inquiries close at heart, I went walking. I soon saw Dude leaning against a head shop taking the sun. I opted to run into him—been a long time since I had been fed a Dudism.

"So Dude, I got a question for you... Is partnership for everyone? I mean, it's clearly not in this chaotic world we live in, but in a healthier world, would most of us be in conscious relationship? Is it necessary as part of a complete life?"

His answer was unusually brief: "To each their path."

Then he crossed the street and walked in the other direction. Clearly I had touched a nerve again. Love is such a difficult subject for so many of us.

I picked up some churros and sat on the curb and ate them. Dude was right: to each their path. For some of us, a relationship isn't particularly relevant to our journey in this incarnation. That's not to say we can live without relationship altogether, but only to say that intimate love relationship isn't everyone's portal to God. Love connection is only one way home.

I went home and scrawled the following on my writing wall. The wall was already filling up, becoming a kaleidoscope of soulspeak.

I have heard so many theories on the question of whether we are complete on our own, or only complete if we are with another. Because of all the pressure to be partnered, so many people walk around feeling badly if they are on their own, and many others stay where they don't belong for fear that they will be seen as a failure outside of relationship. All of this misses the point. What is most important is that each of us lives a life that is true to path,

whatever that means to us. For some, their sacred
purpose is inextricably linked to love relationship.
It is there that they excavate and humanifest
their deepest meaning. Yet others are called in
a different direction and find their purpose in
their creative life, in their work, in their individual
spiritual practice. Everyone's soul-scriptures are
unique to their own journey. The important thing in
life is not whether we find the "one" but whether we
find the path.

And then I began to cry as I felt into the implications of what I had just expressed. In one way, it was beautifully uplifting. There was hope for all of us, even if we never found a life partner. We were all here for a reason—we just had to find ours.

But in another way, I sensed that I had just penned a reflection of my true destiny: perpetual singlehood. There wasn't going to be another beloved. My path lay elsewhere.

# 22

# Forgivings

As I went deeper into the story, it became clear that the writing of the book was inseparable from my own healing and growth journey. In order to find words for love's stages, I had to become an inner detective, unearthing and sifting through more of my own unsolved mysteries. The levels had no end.

Although there was always more to discover, I was also pleased to recognize how far I had come on my journey. Those of us who are doing consciousness work are often so preoccupied with healing and expansion that we fail to notice how far we have traveled. As I worked the wall, I was in quiet awe of the wellspring of insight I was discovering within. Not simply about relationship, but also about one's individual path. Little had I known that while focused for years on the rigors of my inner work and the pain of our separation, subtle wisdom was ripening in the recesses of my being. The fruits of my soul's labor.

To support my creative process, I became a regular meditator, something I had often shunned on my journey. Sometimes I would go back to the cave of remembered dreams, meditating on the memories of our time together. I would linger with a singular memory for hours, plumbing its depths for subtler insight and clarity. The deeper I went, the more insight I brought to bear on the writing of the book. Each memory was a microcosm that I could never grow tired of exploring—even a decade later. And I imagined I would feel the same way, until my very last breath.

One day I came back home and wrote:

You can connect from all kinds of places—energetic harmony, sexual alchemy, intellectual alignment—but they won't sustain love over a lifetime. You need a thread that goes deeper, that moves below and beyond the shifting sands of compatibility. That thread is *fascination*—a genuine fascination with someone's inner world, with the way they organize reality, with the way they hearticulate their feelings, with the unfathomable and bottomless depths of their being. To hear their soul cry out to you again and again, and to never lose interest in what it is trying to convey. If there is that, then there will still be love when the body sickens, when the sexuality fades, when the perfection projection is long shattered. If there is that, you will swim in love's waters until the very last breath.

I thought back to Sarah, the way I was continually captivated, surprised, fascinated with her—from our very first meeting. From the moment we looked into each other's eyes, and that bridge formed between our hearts. There was nothing I could do to create or will that into being. It was God's gift. From the very beginning, ever-present.

I scribbled:

It goes to show you.
You can look for relationship
but you can't look for love.
Love finds you when it's ready.

## Expectations

While attempting to ground my inquiry in real life, I spent a fair amount of time with a number of couples I knew. I dialogued with

216

them about their relationships, inquiring into their challenges, their breakthroughs, the nature of their love. They were all remarkable, in their own way. Every relationship was a world unto itself. They touched me with their determination, and with their commitment to love as spiritual practice.

One night, after a long dinner with two couples I loved, I came home inspired to pour on my bedroom wall...

> However love arrives at your door, it is always a brave path. It is like taking a long walk in a deep dark forest and never quite knowing where your soul will land. It isn't for the faint of heart, nor is it ever to be taken lightly. Real love is heartcore. You have to be tenacious. You have to be innovative. You have to be willing to drop to your knees time and again before its wisdom. And you have to forge the tools you will need from your own imaginings, as very few who have walked the path before can describe the terrain. Most fell into quicksand soon after the romantic phase ended.
> Relationship is always a spiritual practice, even when we imagine it otherwise.

Not only is it a spiritual practice, it is the most delicate kind. I thought back to Sarah, and how much skill it would have taken to navigate our challenges, our patterns, to keep us woven together. A masterful trade indeed:

> It is ironic that the greater the love, the more fragile the patchwork that holds it together. You can pull on practical love weaves and they just get stronger. But soul love tapestries are more fragile. Holding them together requires great imagination and a willingness to mend the seams time and time again. And regular needles won't do the job. You need special tools to reconnect indistinguishable

threads of the same heart weave. It's not a trade
for the faint of soul.

But what a beautiful heartloom awaits those who
can remain devoted to their co-creation.

The next morning, I tried to excavate more gems from my inner treasure chest, but something was in the way. It is amazing how ever-deepening one's emotional process can be when it comes to great love. You heal one layer and feel free, before the next layer appears, sometimes years later, demanding your attention. Here she was again.

I got in the car and drove to Elora. When I arrived, I went back to the river where I had released our beautiful picture. There was something there for me, something I needed to see. I could feel it in my bones. I sat by the river edge, remembering us. As the river raced by, my memories raced past, bringing me closer to an awareness that I had long resisted. The word "expectations" kept rising up to the surface. There was something in that word that wanted to be unlocked and confronted. I suddenly remembered the crone's words: *"Love doesn't fail us—it's our expectations that fail us."*

I stayed there for hours, trying to get below the word to see how it interfaced with my journey.

Nothing came clear.

Late in the afternoon, I walked back up the cliff to go home. On the trail, a young couple walked past me, completely oblivious to my presence, laughing and holding hands. The woman looked to be in her mid-twenties, the man about ten years older. They could have been the same ages as Sarah and I when we first connected.

I felt emotional as they passed, not so much envious but more curious about how they would hold their love together. I turned back around to walk behind them for a few minutes, not too close but near enough to feel their vibration. A sweetness filled my being.

After a few minutes, I came to the sign for Lover's Leap, the place Sarah and I had prayed after reading that plaque—the pain of true love lost. I turned off and walked to the ledge, gazing at the river below. Is this the last thing the Aboriginal Princess saw before she jumped? Was the sun this magnificent on that fateful day?

What about me? What had I expected? What had Sarah expected? How did our expectations influence the outcome? What can any of us expect from great love in an unawakened world?

I sat down on the rock edge, and closed my eyes. I could feel myself resisting something, something I had been hiding from for years. It was time to uncover that missing piece.

I imagined myself as she, the Aboriginal Princess, standing on the cliff edge, riddled with so much pain from the loss of the beloved that death seemed comforting. I imagined myself flying through the air, seeking salvation on the rocks below. I felt my heart quicken, as though I was there then, a woman eager to join her beloved in their eternal tomb.

I flashbacked to a moment soon after Sarah and I first met. We were walking beside Boulder Creek, at one with everything. I looked over at her, and saw this beautiful girl, more beautiful than anyone I had ever seen, but so young by contrast to the aged quality of our love. And I, of course, was not much older. For a split second, I heard myself say inside, with clarity, *"This can't work yet."* Then I immediately put the thought away, covering over the tiny voice of knowing. I didn't want to hear it—my expectations were too overpowering.

### Pictures of Possibility

This memory was the tipping point in my awareness. I was instantly catapulted back in time, not in a sentimental way, but in a way that was uncomfortably self-admitting. I closed my eyes and watched the film that was our relationship through different eyes—the eyes of someone whose own expectations had played a role in pushing the connection away. Perhaps if I had backed off and expected nothing, we would have remained connected until the time was truly right.

I remembered how impatient I had been with Sarah's emotional immaturity, as though impatience could catapult her to the next stage of readiness. I remembered how strongly I insisted she move in with me, even when it was clear that she had some hesitations. I also remembered how urgent my energy was around marriage and babies, somehow overlooking that she had to want this too. Goodness me, if the love was eternal, why was I in such a rush?

I retreated from writing and spent the next days inquiring into my motivations. There were obvious influences—cultural conditioning, my egoic need to be a husband and father by a certain age, the desire to give my Bubbi something to be happy about, a fear of abandonment that kept me grasping. But it went much deeper.

At the heart of my push was my lack of faith in happiness. I somehow didn't believe we had much time. We had to be together, to get married, to create life *now*, with urgency, before something or someone tried to take it all away. Weathered soul that I was, I had so little faith in a love that grew stronger over time. I knew we could enjoy glimpses, but I was doubtful they could last. I felt I needed to rush in and make it happen, secure the connection, before it got stolen from us while we slept.

Some part of my cynicism was naturally lodged in my life history, but it was also grounded in good ole common sense. Even in our most courageous moments of openness, Sarah and I recognized the radical gap between the degree of vulnerability we were experiencing and the survivalist vibration of the world. There was a reason that we kept talking about moving to a mountain top, far away from the maddening crowd. With our hearts so completely open, every bit of worldly harshness felt too much to bear. Along with that, we were both opening up to startlingly new dimensions. What to do with these dazzling new worlds? How to protect them from our young, unformed selves?

And, as much as it pained me to admit it, perhaps the truth is that we are not always supposed to spend our lives with those who most deeply touch our soul. Where did that expectation even come from? Granted, some great loves do manage to sustain themselves throughout a lifetime—and I have every faith that more will as we evolve in awareness—but many don't. Perhaps they were never meant to. Perhaps those who separate should simply be grateful for the blessing that came, without tainting the memory with overblown expectations. Perhaps any step toward great love should be seen as a great success in this still armored world.

This inquiry proved creatively rich, inspiring me back to the wall with writings to share:

> We have a natural tendency to assume that a remarkable chemistry between two souls is confirmation they are meant to be together. In the heat of profound feelings, it seems counter-intuitive to imagine ourselves separate from our beloved.
> But chemistry and longevity aren't necessarily companions. Just because we feel earth-shatteringly alive with someone doesn't mean they are supposed to be our life partner. They may have come for a very different reason—to awaken us, to expand us, to shatter us so wide open that we can never close again. Perhaps they were sent from afar to polish the rough diamond of our soul before vanishing into eternity. Better we surrender our expectations when the beloved comes. (S)he may just be dropping in for a visit.
> Is the kettle on?

I spent weeks probing into the question of expectations. At first, I was hard on myself, both for projecting expectations onto Sarah, but also because I had spent so many years focused on what didn't happen, without celebrating what did. She had come into my life and opened me like nothing ever before. Our connection had transported my consciousness and given me new eyes. I had become a different human—a better human—and seen things very few humans do. Even from the separation, I had learned profound and valuable life lessons. I had learned to keep my heart open amid great pain. These were great feats within our current human consciousness. Isn't this cause to rejoice? Sure it is.

> We must be under no illusion that all soulmates are meant to last a lifetime. Some are only meant to last a moment. That brief soul-gaze with a

'stranger' at the grocery store that reminded you of your own essence was just right. That unexpected weekend encounter that sent your spirit soaring was perfect. That great love that walked away after cracking your heart open was just what the soul doctor ordered. No matter how long they last, profound connections paint pictures of possibility in the sky, expanding your lens for all eternity.

My hardness toward myself soon turned to compassion. In many ways, I had been too hard on myself for too long. It was time to give myself a break. Surely I had done my best with the challenges before me and the tools I possessed. Even if I had been flawless, we still may have fallen apart. We had neither the ability nor the foundation in place at that time. We had been given a glimpse into something beyond our present level, and it was nearly impossible to sustain it. Everything had unfolded exactly as it should have.

And yet, at the same time, there is something of value to say about how one prepares the space for great love. One thing that had become clear is the value of emotional healing work, both in one's efforts to prepare for love, and in one's efforts to sustain it. This is not to say that love cannot enter our lives when we're emotionally unhealthy—it had certainly entered mine in the heart of a troubled landscape—but it is to say that it can be helpful to do some work to clear our debris in advance. When we don't do it, it becomes difficult to recognize love, to attune to love, to hold love safe...

Clearing our emotional debris has many positive impacts. It creates more space inside for love to enter and it gives us more energy to see love all the way through. Unresolved material is like undigested food—it blocks the channel and prevents new nourishment from entering. All bunked up, we may not even notice love when it walks through the portal. Releasing our emotional holdings cleans our lens, allowing us to notice love when it comes. With a dirty lens, love is blind and we are blind to it. And working through our issues expands our awarenest, providing us with the tools we will need to manage our triggers and patterns. Of course, love will bring up new challenges from their burial ground, but with more awareness of the processes of pattern recognition and healing, we stand a better chance of staying out of our own way. If you aren't aware of the stuff you came in with, you are going to have a hard time managing the new levels of material that the love excavates.

This is the actual New Earth. It isn't a place where we imagine that merely watching our wounds will actually transform them. It isn't a place where we confuse dissociation with expansion. It's a place where we jump right into the heart of the emotional material, shaping it like clay into a newer, truer lens. Real presence is a whole being experience.

### Compassion-eyes

After spending a few days nursing that line of inquiry, I went for a long wintry walk throughout the downtown core. It had been a long day of writing. I was so immersed in the love journey that I could almost feel Sarah knocking at my front door mid-afternoon. I even went to the door to check, quickly realizing there was no one there. Maybe she was knocking on my heart from the inside out.

Snow was falling lightly, blanketing the city in a white embrace. I stopped at an all-night café and sat by the window with my latte, turning to watch the white flakes as they drifted down from the sky. I watched them change form as they landed, transformed into something else when they merged with the earth. I remembered what it was like to change form with Sarah, and wondered what it must have been like for her to change form with me.

I thought of her childhood in Colorado. A volatile family, a young

223

girl with a tree fort as her primary protection. It was no wonder she fled our union. She too had no template for kind relations.

I closed my eyes and tried to imagine her in her humanness. At first it was very difficult. Because of the nature of our connection, I had not really seen her in this way. In my eyes, she had always been elevated beyond the worldly. Even when she sabotaged our connection, she still wasn't human to me. She then became the devil, the lowest of the low. Either Goddess or Devil, ne'er the twain shall meet. A familiar thread—I had her on the same polarized projection path as I had myself.

I kept my eyes closed and remembered a series of uncomfortable events, moments of great reactivity and anger. With my awareness, I went looking for her in there—not the warrior her, but the frightened her, the vulnerable her, the tender Sarah doing her best to manage an overwhelming situation. I stayed with the memories until she appeared in my mind's eye, sitting outside my house after yet another conflict, shaking like a leaf. I saw her eyes overcome with fear. I felt her heart racing. I could hear her planning her getaway. In that moment, she was all of five years old, a vulnerable little girl, with tangled hair and a tear-streaked face, fleeing to her tree fortress with lightning in her feet, trying to escape familial madness.

I wept for her as I walked home. Interestingly, I had never been able to cry for her before. I could cry about her, but not *for* her. I was too wounded to focus on her own internal experience. But, at this moment, something was changing. Now I could hold her within the heart of compassion. Now I could see her vulnerability through empathic eyes. Now I could see the tender little girl beneath, longing to be healed. Yes, she had done her very best, too.

I stopped to brush the snow off a bench in the market and sat down. I remembered what Sarah had said to me after the betrayal: *"It was a suicidal act. I just had to kill it. I can't hold this much love in my heart."* Back then it sounded like bullshit, but now I felt the true weight of those words. I recognized that it was the truth. It was too much to handle. With a love that vastly exceeded the level of development we were presently at, the love had no safe ground. One way or another, it had to topple.

For the first time, I had no energetic charge around how she killed it. Through compassionate eyes, I understood she needed to do something so cutting and final that there was no way back. We needed a harsh event to end our impossible dream. In a strange way, the harshness of the reaction was directly proportionate to the depth of connection. Truth be told, had it been any gentler, I would probably have continued to chase Lightnin' Foot forever.

That night, I went for dinner with Daniel and his fiancée, Vanessa. Ironically, I was alone, and he was now partnered, having met his beloved on a bird-watching expedition in Costa Rica. No, they weren't watching cardinals, but they were brought together by synchronicity of a divine order. She had missed a charter flight back to Toronto and had to wait another week for the next one. While hanging around in San Jose, she bumped into an old friend who had flown down for the bird watching tour. Turns out she had an extra ticket to it because her sister had contracted mononucleosis and couldn't come. Daniel and Vanessa met the first morning of the tour and hadn't left each other's sides since. Isn't the universe funky.

While we were eating, Daniel described a forgiveness ritual that he had performed four years earlier, when he was ready to forgive Hannah for leaving him. He had flown to the beach where she had died. He wrote Hannah a long, honest letter of forgiveness. Then he released it to the same ocean that had taken her life, while saying a prayerful goodbye. He said it made a world of difference.

The following morning, I woke up with forgiveness in my heart—there was something I had yet to express. I got in the car and drove to the cave of remembered dreams. When I arrived, I found a giant ice chunk blocking the entrance. It seemed like it had been put there deliberately. Someone had either been there and left, or someone was still inside. I shouted "Helloooo," half expecting the abominable snowman to appear, but there was no response. I banged my fist against the cliff wall. Again, no response. So I moved the chunk off to the side, and climbed on in.

Everything looked as it had before, except there were ashy remnants of a small fire and a heart carefully drawn around my graffiti scrawl: Love It Forward. Looked like fresh chalk. New lovers had evidently found the cave.

I sat down and closed my eyes, quickly flooded with memories of our time together. The profound lovemaking. Tenderly holding her, nestled tightly together. As I remembered, I felt the hot tears of release begin to flow again. I also felt my hand become warm, as if aglow. It was as if Sarah was sitting right there beside me, holding it. Perhaps, somehow she was.

I opened my eyes and said that which had eluded me for more than thirteen years:

Sarah,
I forgive you for your actions.

I forgive you for the way you left.
I forgive you.

And I meant it.

I drove back with a feeling of levity in my heart. It was like an ancient stone had been lifted from my soul. I had finally arrived at a genuine and authentic forgiveness. Wondrous.

When I arrived home, I finished the chapter by writing a section on the process of forgiveness. Not the artificial, premature forgiveness that many of us know well, but the real thing—the kind that arrives only after a genuine healing process has come to an end. And, amazingly, even though Sarah and I were long gone from one another's lives, I had the vague sense that our connection was still being re-paired and re-stitched on some unseen level.

Sometimes people walk away from love because it is so beautiful that it terrifies them. Sometimes they leave because the connection shines a bright light on their dark places and they are not ready to work them through. Sometimes they run away because they are not developmentally prepared to merge with

226

another—they have more individuation work to do first. Sometimes they take off because love is not a priority in their lives—they have another path and purpose to walk first. Sometimes they end it because they prefer a relationship that is more practical than conscious, one that does not threaten the ways that they organize reality. Because so many of us carry shame, we have a tendency to personalize love's leavings, triggered by the rejection and feelings of abandonment. But this is not always true. Sometimes it has nothing to do with us. Sometimes the one who leaves is just not ready to hold it safe. Sometimes they know something we don't—they know their limits at that moment in time. Real love is no easy path: Readiness is everything. May we grieve loss without personalizing it. May we learn to love ourselves in the absence of the lover.

## Gratitude

I felt so profoundly propelled to the creative process, day after day, that I stopped caring what others thought about the condition of my apartment. The entire book was being written on its walls, just as my dream had foretold. As soon as one room was covered, I moved on to the next. It was a messy, magnificent spiritual practice, and a deep letting go of self-consciousness around how things look to others, in service of something true. Chaotic magnificence indeed.

Everything in me was transforming again. How beautiful, I didn't even need to be in a relationship for that to happen. It was happening through the creative process itself, as writing about love was somehow calling me higher, re-shaping me in the cosmic kiln. It was that powerful. My life was sparkling with sacred purpose.

As I approached the end of the writing, I felt the beloved hovering near. She was the hand I wrote with, the lens I looked through, the ankle-tackling kitty that tripped me up the stairs. Despite the distance between us, I somehow experienced myself in connected terms, united with my beloved, seemingly absent but always close at heart.

At the same time, I had finally become my own vessel and harbor. Instead of looking for meaning beyond myself, I found it right here, in the bones of my being. I was the sail that gathered the wind and I was the shore I landed upon. Perhaps this was the ultimate gift of the connection—the gift of my own encapsulated presence. After your beloved is gone, all efforts to find her outside yourself fail. You have only one choice: to find the divine deep within, to partner with yourself, to find God manifest as you.

And then I wrote:

> It's so beautiful what happens when we define relationship success solely in terms of whether we have learned from it, expanded from it, grown to the next stage on our spiritual journey. When we move from this perspective, relationship becomes a wonderful depth-charge for our own healing and expansion. If we find a lifelong partner—great!—but if we don't, we get better at partnering with our inner lover.

In a way, it had all come down to choices. There is this moment, after a beloved has left, when you have to decide. Do you close your heart to life, or do you feed the fires of deep feeling? Do you get lost in your memories, or convert them into new possibilities? Do you go blind to love, or do you see it everywhere? It helps to realize that love is always a blessed visitor. We have no guarantee it will come our way. Even a moment of it is a great gift from Grace. Better we build on our blessings...

> Love is a series of risings and fallings. We fall down, we get up. We get up, we fall down. We either see love's trip-ups as examples of our own victimhood—we are being abused by the universe—or as opportunities for self-creation, embracing love's challenges as essential lessons from the Godself

within. The gift of falling down—there's gold in them there spills. Stumbling towards ecstasy.

Years ago, in the devastation of our separation, I had the thought: *Perhaps this is why it's so very difficult to lose a soulmate. You don't just lose your companion. You don't just lose your friend. You don't just lose your lover. You lose your portal to divinity. You lose your gateway to God. You lose the whole bloody universe.*

I picked up my marker and scribbled it on my spiritual graffiti wall, like a man on a mission. There was something in that quote waiting to be unveiled...

Perhaps this is why it's so very
difficult to lose a soulmate.
You don't just lose your companion.
You don't just lose your friend.
You don't just lose your lover.
You lose your portal to divinity.
You lose your gateway to God.
You lose the whole bloody universe.

For weeks, I leaned into those wall-words, rolling them around in my heart...*You lose your portal to divinity...You lose your gateway to God...You lose the whole bloody universe...*

You lose, you lose, you lose.... and then, what?... What?

One night, it came clear. I was roused from my sleep in the midst of the night, the moon shining bright and full.

And I wrote the perfect proviso:

And then you find it again.
In your heartbreak.
In your healing.
In the learning of the lessons that expand you.
In the strengthening and rebirth of your willingness.

229

In the claiming of your own inner beloved.
Every path is a journey to God.
We just have to remember to open
our heart again and again...

With that hearticulation, I knew my story was truly complete. I had shared what I needed to share. I had made my peace. A sense of relief flooded me, as I felt into the completion of this writing journey. And it was more than the writing. It was also the end of a paradigm that had begun when I first saw Sarah in Boulder. So much time had passed since then, so many new Lowens had been birthed. I was simply not the same being any longer. My soul had been rewoven with love as its thread. The relationship had been the perfect laboratory for my own expansion.

After falling into a perfect two hour meditation, I walked downstairs and went outside. The first morning light was just shining in, enveloping me in hopefulness. It reminded me of my own inner process. Slowly, the darkness had receded. Gradually, things had become clear again. It's amazing how many stages there are to love's mendings.

I walked over to Bellevue Square and sat down on a park bench, celebrating in silence. Waves of gratitude moved through me, as I honored my achievement. Sarah's face entered my consciousness. I looked at her in my mind's eye, while my heart filled to the brim with love. Such grace. I felt oddly closer to her than ever before. A wave of wonderment moved through me, marveling at the ways that the divine had converted my tragedy into transformation. The gold in the dross. From chaotic suffering into chaotic magnificence. How Great Thou Art.

I took one of the deepest breaths I have ever taken and these words came pouring out of my mouth:

Oh Sarah, thank you. THANK YOU.
It was all a gift.
ALL of it.
And I have loved us forward.

# 23

## Signs and Signings

I wrote *Wholemates: Relationship as a Portal to the Divine* over a two-year period. It was quite the project to archive my walls of heart-speak into book form. After many edits, I finally transmuted it into a tangible document, ready for publish.

As often happens when walking your true-path, the energy of the writing had its own natural momentum. Rather than hunting around for an agent, I decided to send it to two publishers whose work I valued. Within six weeks, both responded with offers. I chose the publisher with the smallest advance. They were kind and ethical, and I wanted someone kind to publish my work.

While waiting for the book to come out, I worked hard in my mediation practice in an effort to save money for a three-month sabbatical. I had agreed in the book contract to do a 29-city signing tour throughout North America, to begin the following autumn. I had no idea what to expect, but looked forward to the adventure. In my personal life, I continued on my separate trajectory—not dating, not looking for love. I had tried it all, and nothing satisfied me like the beloved. Another may come, but I doubted she would come if I went looking.

*IOD*

Shortly before going on tour, I went looking for Dude to sit with. I missed his dear presence. I looked everywhere and finally found him sitting in front of the Asian dry cleaner that I used for my suits. Apparently he was waiting to get his Hawaiian shirts pressed.

"How you dudin', Dude?"

"Waiting on the Chinaman. He's always late with my stuff."

You had to love the dignity of this houseless man, always making sure he made an elegant appearance.

"How are things?" I inquired.

"Good. You looking for some wisdoms? Because my price has gone up."

Then he reached for a white plastic sign in his bag and showed it to me. In bold purple ink, it read:

$5 Dollars per Dudism.

No deferral plan.

Pay or adios.

Dude was getting bold.

"Got tired of promises to pay. What do they think I am—the Toronto Dudeminion bank? No, no way. It's not like I am charging a fortune. I mean, I give them the goods for a pittance. And they can take my wisdom all the way to the karmic bank and cash in. I can't tell you how many IODs I've written that never got paid."

"IOD, isn't that a contraceptive device?"

"Not an IUD, idiot! An IOD: I Owe Dude. I mean, they pay for all that detachment drivel. How many times do I have to tell all of you? Detachment's just a silly tool. It's not a life, people! At least my Dudisms actually keep people in their bodies!"

Clearly it wasn't the right moment to sit peacefully with Dude. I got up to leave, but not before handing him a $50 bill.

"What's this for?" he inquired.

"For ten people who didn't pay their IODs," I replied.

He looked a little stunned, then slowly grinned.

"Hey, now I can pay the Chinaman. Sit back down. I owe you some Dudisms."

I didn't want any Dudisms right now. I felt at peace. I shook my head no, thanks.

As I crossed the street, he shouted after me: "Well, at least YOU have gratitude in your attitude. You are living proof that my wisdom works, lover boy!"

And so I am. My pushcart guru had made all the difference.

## The Scent of the Beloved

The book tour was grueling—29 cities in 45 days. Publishers want to get their money's worth. Intensifying my discomfort was a driver who never stopped talking, despite my request that he relax and breathe on numerous occasions. He talked so effusively that we missed the correct highway exit on four different occasions. Eventually, I surrendered to the wave of words, trying to catch some shut-eye between paragraphs.

The rigors of the tour reminded me that I am not as physically vital as I once was, something that I'd failed to notice in my habitual life. I was now 50—it had been more than 14 years since Sarah and I said goodbye—and my aching back and strained eyes reminded me of my limitations time and again.

Making things more difficult were some of the interactions I had at the signings. They were often triggered by the same question, usually asked right after I read the sections in the book that celebrated the path of the beloved as a spiritual practice. A woman's hand would shoot up from the audience and she'd ask whether I was currently in a relationship. I always answered the same way, "My heart is always ready for the beloved."

She or someone else in the crowd would then express cynicism about my claiming to understand so much about soulmates without being in a successful partnership. It was always an uncomfortable dialogue. People don't understand that the greatest loves of all are often the hardest to hold together in this mad world. But, still, the question nagged at me, as it illuminated the strangeness of my path. I was talking about great love without a single prospect in sight.

Before the final leg of the tour, I took a few days to myself at Rockwood Hot Springs, the place where I had first started the healing process, in the smoldering aftermath of the relationship. Being at Rockwood seemed to bring the beloved close again. One morning, I was sure that I smelled Sarah's sublime scent on the wind. That night, I dreamed of a love that was never truly gone, as we communed with great spirit in the halls of eternal reflection. I was never alone. The beloved was everywhere...

After a few signings in Southern California, my driver picked me up before dawn for my final book signing in Petaluma, way up north. It was an eight-hour drive and he ranted most of the way. Interestingly, his rants were all about love—its impossibilities, its illusions, its disappointments. It never ceases to amaze me how much we all have to say about something so entirely mysterious, myself certainly included. And what do we know? I mean, really, what do we know about life's greatest offering? We haven't even begun to remove the wrapping paper, let alone look inside. The divine's greatest gift lies in wait, cloaked in mystery and paradox, patiently waiting for humanity to open it fully and real-eyes its treasures.

After we missed yet another highway off-ramp, we arrived one hour late for the signing. I forgave him—love does have a way of confusing our exits. When I finally got inside, I was surprised to find there were over 200 people waiting to hear me speak, our largest crowd yet. The book was moving quickly to bestseller status, catching fire in the marketplace. The beloved was well-pleased.

### Ready

I read from the book for about 30 minutes, then answered a series of forlorn questions from the broken-hearted. Goodness, had anyone been able to sustain their great love? I had been hoping for a simple ending to my tour, but it wasn't happening in Petaluma. This crowd was alive and wanting answers!

When I finally sat down to sign books, I was overwhelmed by a scrum of purchasers, most of them buying two or more copies. I went into warrior signing mode, only looking up now and then, opening and autographing books as fast as they could put them on the table in front of me.

After an hour of rapid-fire signings, I suddenly noticed a subtle shift in the energy. Although people were still presenting book after book to the table, it felt like the world around me was slowing down. A feeling of warmth overcame me, a sudden softening around my heart. Then, as if in slow motion, a book was calmly placed in front of me on the table. I reached for it to sign, when I noticed words on the hand that laid it there. The hand hadn't moved an inch. The words were unmistakable, written in bold green marker.

$$I\ am\ ready$$

I knew that hand anywhere. I knew. My hand began to shake, dropping the pen. My eyes moistened as I stared intently at those words. The hand of my beloved. As I opened the book of our love, a small tear fell on the page. No need to sign my name. This was the perfect signature.

I stared down at the book, feeling a sudden shyness. I needed a moment, I needed a lifetime. Can life change this quickly?

Yes. It can.

I looked up and deeply into her eyes. She met me there. Yet again, a bridge of remembrance formed between our souls. Not a moment had passed since our last meeting, not a bloody moment. Soon her tears fell too, landing with ferocity on the book of our love. My breath deepened, as she re-entered the chambers of my heart. The gateway opened wide, as every cell came alive. The great out-pouring, the great in-pouring. Our love was the perfect kindling for a heart-fire of ecstatic proportions. In the no-blink of an eye, our souls were set ablaze yet again.

The room went entirely quiet. People began to return to the table, as though they were witnessing a great rebirth. They could sense that this was no arbitrary encounter. The depth of presence was unmistakable. I looked at Sarah's face, as though I too was witnessing something extraordinary. And so I was. My be-loved had returned. Oh the heart, the heart.

After forever, I walked around the table to hug her, but she backed away. "Not yet," she whispered, just like the first time we met. "After the signings." *That* voice! I forgot there were people still in line. Returning to the table, I completed the signings, while Sarah sat down on one of the nearby chairs.

After the last book had been signed, my chatty driver appeared, eager to take me to the airport. With my heart now wide open, I suddenly loved hearing him talk. Sweet chatterbox, how can I disdain you now? You have driven me to meet my beloved. I took him aside and told him I wouldn't be needing his services any longer.

I wasn't flying home tonight. I had already arrived.

# 24

# Homecomings

Sarah and I left the bookstore, and began walking around town, in silence. There was so much to talk about, but not just yet. Our silence was abundantly expressive, rich in form and texture. We walked back in time and forward into eternity, keeping pace with the beat of our unified heart. Where before we bounced a little above the earth, something had shifted in our energetic field. Years removed from the roller coasters of young love, we now walked with our feet planted firmly on the ground. We hearticulated a little more sweetness with every step.

Although silent, I could swear I heard a little music in the winds. Was that a distant flute soulebrating our reunion? Had the cosmic conductor set the soulharmonic orchestra in motion? Were we being loved-up from afar?

As we walked, I noticed the changes to her appearance, as she no doubt noticed mine. A sprinkling of glittery gray hairs had replaced the blond, and her face was softer and more cherubic. Most notably, there was a prominent scar that stretched from her forehead and ended beside her left ear. And she walked with a slight limp in her right leg. It spoke loudly and clearly. Something terrible had happened. My heart longed to heal it, my lips to kiss it better.

We walked down a trail to a small river. Oh, how we loved rivers. As always, we became indistinguishable from the natural world. Soon there was no distinction between us and the sun that bounced off the river, the water that cascaded over the rocks, the trees that framed the banks. It was *all* Go(o)d. This time it really was.

Like in the beginning, I stared at our shared reflection in the mirror. Unlike in the beginning, I could now see where I ended and the other began. I saw the merging, but I also saw two formed individuals. Two distinct selves destined to touch again.

We put our feet in the water and laughed and laughed, struck with joyful amazement that we were together again, sharing a moment. It's like we had never parted ways, except that there was more peace now. Time has a way of smoothing hearts out. No need to dive so deep for soul food when the fruits of our love labors are so perfectly within reach. We reached down and touched God(dess) to our lips, parched and thirsty after 14 years apart. The rivers of essence rose up to meet us as we drank to our souls' content. We had so earned this divine thirst quenching. Heavens up.

### Right Path, Wrong Time

After the soul-quenching, we wandered back to her car. We didn't need to talk about it—I was going wherever she was going. Sarah drove us back to a small motel outside town where she had booked a room. She had driven all night from Sante Fe to get here, arriving one hour late, as I did. Yes, divine timing.

When we got inside, we lay down on the bed and held each other. Tears fell again, as years of loneliness washed away. We cried and cried, as though we were crying for our separation, for our reunion, and for all the other lovers who had lost their way. We soaked the pillow mightily, as we let it all flow through us.

We nestled together into a sound sleep. Early in the morning, I was awakened by a feeling of pressure on my chest. Sarah was up to her old tricks, writing graffiti on my skin with a felt marker. I let her finish, before standing and looking at her creation in the mirror:

Home is where the Ogdo is.

How many times I had woken up in the morning longing to see her graffiti words on my flesh. Finally, my mad artist was back at work.

"You lost your touch," I said playfully. "I never used to notice until after you were done."

"Noooo, I wanted you awake this time," she smiled.

"Tell me everything..."

She did.

After we parted, Sarah spent over five years running away from her heart. She raced from town to town, job to job, entanglement to entanglement, until her flight from reality caught up with her in Minnesota.

"I ran like the wind, Ogdo, except the wind turned into a tornado—a tornado of my own creation. Then it all came crashing down to earth, just like it had to," she said with great relief on her scarred face.

One afternoon, right after losing yet another job, she lost control of her car and smashed into a large oak tree on the side of the road. She was catapulted through the front windshield, missing the tree by inches, luckily landing on a bed of tall, thick grass. Nine vertebrae were smashed, her right leg was broken in four places, and her face was mangled. Because it was dark, no one noticed the accident until the next morning. She was in a coma for eight days, requiring seven surgeries before she could leave the hospital 22 weeks later. In her words, it was the best thing that ever happened to her. The gift of crashing down. Some people need to create a nightmare far worse than the one they came from, before they will go back down the path and heal their early wounds.

At 31, she moved back home to live with her parents for two years. For the first time in her life, she began digging deep, doing the inner work that she had been running from, committing herself to a concentrated therapeutic process. She worked at it diligently, interfacing with her demons, healing her early memories, recognizing the ways her childhood had influenced her choices, behaviors and patterns.

"The universe is very wise. No matter how things look, it always has our best interests at heart," she stated. "It made sure the injury was so bad that I couldn't take care of myself. I had to go home to heal—and not just be home like in the old days, when I could run away at the first sign of trouble, but go home and just lie there. This time I was a sitting duck, unable to move, totally dependent. Wow. I was sure I would just die—really. I felt my defenses would kill me in my sleep, but they didn't. Then, after more screaming outbursts than I can count, I realized it was all perfect. I mean, it really was. Because if I could stay *there* without running, I could stay anywhere without running. What better place to work through my issues than the house that birthed them. Not from afar, with vague, selective memories, but right on the battlefield itself where I couldn't forget anything. And my compassion for my parents deepened as well, as I really got to know all they had overcome in their own childhoods."

I was captivated by her clarity as she spoke.

With respect to us, she owned her part, acknowledging in subtle detail all the ways that she had acted out. Clearly she had thoroughly processed this, piece by piece. Whenever I tried to own my part in it, she stopped me cold with the same words, "There was nothing you could do. I wasn't ready yet."

Right path, wrong time. For her, it was that simple. If aging teaches us one thing, it's that we cannot force another's path on them. They have to learn how to walk it on their own terms.

"I wanted to contact you when I was healing, Lowen. I picked up the phone hundreds of times, but I stopped myself each time."

"Why... why did you stop yourself?"

"Because my reasons for calling were selfish. I was calling for me."

"What would be wrong with that?"

"It would be the same as it was before. Me taking from you and giving back so little. I didn't want to take without giving anymore."

"But..."

"Just because I was forced to slow down doesn't mean I was ready. Even though you were also young in your own way, you modeled something to me that I hadn't become yet. You modeled absolute devotion. I knew you would die to protect me, but I knew I wouldn't do the same for you. I couldn't inhabit my love for you yet—I wasn't ready. I realized that when I was lying in the hospital bed after the accident. I imagined your spirit entering my body, taking my pain, enduring it all so I wouldn't suffer. Even in those darker days, you were the light all along. I knew you would have gladly taken my place, but I knew that I wouldn't take yours in the same situation. I was still too selfish. I made myself a promise that I would never return unless I would take your place on your deathbed."

We sat in silence for some time before I decided to take a break and get us some breakfast. On the way out the door, I turned to ask her the obvious:

"And would you, Sarah?"

She looked at me with tremendous presence and replied, "Yes, Lowen. Yes I would."

I had never seen her so resolute.

### Mystery Stew

After we ate some delicious banana pancakes and took a long nap, she continued to share her story. Following her time at home, she went back into the world, moving to Santa Fe to complete one of the dreams she had begun and then abandoned in her non-committal lifestyle—a degree in Naturopathy.

While in school, she met a wonderful man who helped to nurture and support her as she came of age, a man she genuinely loved and valued. They were together for four years, building a joint naturopathic practice in the mountains of New Mexico. It was a meaningful and grounding time in her life.

After a few years, the beloved kept waking her up at night, demanding her attention. At first, he arose in the form of gentle dreamscapes, as she had with me. Then, when she pushed them away, he arose in the form of harsh nightmares in which she was perpetually torn away from the other half of her soul. The beloved calling to the beloved across space and time. Dial in, dial out, there really is no such thing as long distance when two hearts beat in the same direction. The only choice is to answer, or the call comes through in more obtrusive ways. We had each lived with a fire in our heart, one that burned so bright that our spirits could not ignore it.

After a process remarkably similar to mine, she let him go. She spent some time on her own, then flew to Toronto to see me, somehow knowing I would still be in the same apartment. She had come right up to the house—twice—and knocked on my door. The first time, she had heard me coming and fled down the side alley. This must have been the time I could have sworn I heard a knock at the door and imagined it was her. The second time, she sat on the chair on the rear porch for hours, waiting for me to come. But I never came.

After a visit to many of the places we had frequented together, she had rented a car and driven to Goshen Park to find the cave. After hours lost, she finally found it, our cave of remembered dreams. Once inside, she grabbed a piece of chalk from her bag and wrote me a love letter on the wall. Then she turned around and saw the words I had written. She panicked and smudged over her writing. As she was exiting the cave, she turned back and drew a big heart around my words, as a way of seconding the motion—loving it forward. Ahhh, I remembered seeing that chalk heart around my words. It was her.

She raced back to Toronto, overwhelmed with emotion. After a sleepless night in a downtown hotel, she decided to go home. She knew that it wasn't time yet. There was still more prep work to be done.

And then, two years later, she knew it was time. The catalyst was the sudden death of her mother. Jessie died peacefully in her sleep one night, of a heart attack, with Norman by her side. The intensity of the heartbreak cracked through Sarah's final layer of armor, leaving her no choice but to live with her heart wide open. The fragility of life hit her hard, and she saw there was no time to waste.

And then she searched for me on the internet. When she found out about my book tour, she organized her work vacation around my final book signing. Still living in Sante Fe, she had driven most of the night to get here. It was a smooth ride. Finally, no obstacles in our way.

After she shared her story, I hugged her long and deep, and then went for a walk alone in the magical night air. I needed to integrate all of this. There was an entrancing quality to the night, one of those California evenings that is soaked in warmth and wonder.

While walking, I noticed how calm and safe I felt in the deep within. Where the heart rate of the connection was once restless, it was now restful. Where before I would have doubted her pledge of readiness, I now trusted it. It wasn't a question of wishful thinking. It wasn't a question of thinking, at all. It was simply clear. I could genuinely and viscerally feel the transformation in her energy, in the tenor of her words, in the vulnerability in her eyes. She was now both solid and open at the same time. She had come through a long gestation period, and re-emerged in a healthier form. And so had I.

Earlier I had written, "You can look for a relationship but you can't look for love—love finds you when it's ready." Now I realize there is an addendum to that. Sometimes love finds you when it's ready... *and* when you're ready too. How that happens is anybody's guess. Love is the great mystery stew, its secrets well kept, its ingredients known to Providence alone. While both people are being prepared, marinated, skewered, cooked to readiness in the fires of life, the cosmic alchemist is turning the pot, reverently preparing the base for the lovers to meld into it. Only God knows when the stew is ready to be served. Divine timing, divine dining.

Clearly our stew was ready. A beautiful convergence of readiness. Both the universe and our inner worlds were aligned and in agreement.

Our time was now.

## Cuddlelingus

When I got back to the room, Sarah was in the shower. Soon I was too. Naked together for the first time in 14 years, we entered a state of reciprocal devotion. A far cry from the sexed-up showers we used to take, we moved cautiously, slowly and tenderly re-learning each other's bodies. We kissed one another's scars and seeming imperfections, with bhakti presence. I gently ran my tongue over the scar tissue that stretched across her face. Then, I turned her around, moving her wet hair, and found her perfect little pink birthmark on the back of her neck. I kissed that too. It was one of the most intimate experiences we have ever shared together. Although both of our bodies showed signs of aging—a little more weight, some hidden plump places, the touch of lines in our skin— there was no judgment nor retreat. There was only gratitude. Gratitude for the blessed opportunity to commune together yet again. Gratitude for the opportunity to wash the past away and begin anew. Such grace.

It was then I realized: If we age honestly, we *become* love. As the body weakens, love surges through us, longing to be released, longing to be lived. With no time left to not love, we seek authentic embrace everywhere. Our deft avoidance maneuvers convert into directness. Our armored hearts melt into pools of eternal longing. This is why we should look forward to aging. Finally, after all the masks and disguises fall away, we are left with love alone. God waits for us on the bridge between our hearts.

As I kissed her new body, I remembered the previous Sarah—a youthful, supple body bursting with life-force. Now, her body was etched with the traces of time and life-learnings. It's so interesting—when we are young, it's the illusion of perfection that we fall in love with. But as we age, it's the humanness that we fall in love with: the poignant story of overcoming, the depthful vulnerability of aging, the struggles that grew us in karmic stature, the way a soul shaped itself to accommodate its circumstances. With less energy to hold up our armor, we are revealed and, in the revealing, call out to each other's hearts. Where before wounds turned us off, they are now revealed as proof that God exists. Where we once saw imperfect scars, we now see evidence of a life fully lived.

Ahhh, what a journey it has been.

After the shower, she led me to the bed and began to gently stroke my body. In total silence, she massaged and nurtured me for hours, kneading me back to life. A lover's apology. When she was done, she lay down facing me. Still in silence, we looked into each other's eyes, interspersing tears with laughter. As the universal portal opened yet again between us, all reactivities evaporated into essence. In this moment, there had never been a betrayal. There had been no time apart. There was only God's reflection.

Some people read the heavens by looking up. I'm a different kind of astronomer. I read the heavens by looking at Sarah. In her eyes, the starlit sky. In her smile, God shining true. The entire soular system—right here before me. Perhaps this is why I seldom looked up at stars since Sarah and I first met. Why look for the divine out there, when she's right here, in the heart of connection?

The next morning, we woke up aroused and alight, ready for the next stage of deepening. I turned toward my beloved and made love to her, worshiping her soul temple with heart-free abandon. As before, she was still God's luscious fountain and I her diligent devotee. Unlike before, I approached her yoni with a tremendous tenderness, cradling it with my lips and hands, exploring it slowly and with great subtlety. Cuddlelingus. The portals of essence opened wide as I dove heart-first into her timeless rivers. The more intensely she climaxed, the more fully my thirst for God was quenched. I drank her in with bottomless delight.

We spent the next two days in the room, alternating lovemaking with deep bonding sleep. As we communed, all the forms of our lovemaking moved in new and unforeseen directions. Where before I responded eagerly to her willingness, now I moved gingerly, wanting to take such delicate care of this great gift, like a grateful virgin in delightfully uncharted territory. At the heart of it, we're all virgins when it comes to love. Where before our passion was like a rocket that catapulted us through Gods gates, it now slowed and softened in form and texture, less a bolting rocket and more a slow-moving presence, one that tenderly melted into divinity one breath at a time. Where before we would orgasm, now we would *ourgasm*—a shared climax of pure mutuality, a simultaneous soul-spasm of a unified form. We were missing something back then, often rushing to climax, in a flurry of hunger. No longer lustful, we were no longer racing to completion like two people who sensed their time together was limited. We now worshiped love as love worshiped us—with great presence.

"Oh, Ogdo, it's the same, except... quieter."

"Yes. So much stiller."

"I want to die like this."

"We will."

Although the tenor of our intimacy had changed, our access hadn't. As it was before, we cracked through the veneer between our hearts and the universal heart every time we made love. Again, this was not the same universe I saw when I touched God alone. It was an entirely different skyscape, a magnificent galaxy revealed by love alone. As we breathed in unison, one soular flare after another lit our way, inviting us deeper and deeper into the heart of God.

It was amazing to watch my sexuality come back to life with Sarah. When I was with Miriam, I had been at times sexually unresponsive. I told myself it was simply a question of aging. But it wasn't. My body was speaking my soul's truth, as it was now with Sarah. The heart-genital highway was back in business. The vitality of my erections was a direct reflection of the vitality of my love. Clearly, everything depends on where you are cuming *from*. Let there be no doubt: body and soul are reflections of the same divine mirror.

Intrinsic to the transformation in our intimacy was a shift in Sarah's participation. For her, it had always been more difficult to give. But this had changed. Now she honored my awakened masculine as I honored her awakened feminine, worshiping my body temple as I worshiped hers, celebrating each other with equal engagement. Where before my egoic power cock would have resisted, I was now more receptive—a tenderling warrior bearing the fruits of his soul's labor. Any archaic ideas of the superior man on top fell by the wayside, as Sarah took her turn as the superior woman, exploring me in the same way I explored her—reverently, devotedly, hungrily.

As familiar as we were to each other, there was a way in which it all felt entirely new again. We soon became one orgasmic tuning fork, naturally finding new ways of igniting and expressing our love. It was like beginner's heart, over and over again, as we rested in our completeness. Finally chemistry, cumistry and karmastry together, at a time when both of us were ready to hold it safe. The best kind of *ménage à trois*.

So much happened in those two days in room number 130. By the time it was over, we knew with certainty we were ready. Not ready for perfection, but ready to spend the rest of our lives crafting and nurturing our shared temple. Only death or alien abduction could separate us now.

And perhaps neither. The call of the beloved is like a call from the unseen world. It outlives the death of the body, outlives the trials of mortal life, calling out to us from our eternal resting place, reminding us that it will soon be time to come home.

# 25

## Wholemates

It is now seven years later. We have spent these last years in worship. We have made an offering of our hearts. We have lived our love as prayer. Where before we wondered if our ultimate mission lived outside of us, we now recognize that it exists between us. We have become devotees to a greater cause—Us. With unwavering commitment to the union, our love has become our primary spiritual practice, our teacher, our clarifying path.

People find their sacred purpose in many different places. Our love is ours. That's where the Go(l)d is. It has been the fire that warms us, the fresh spring that invigorates us, the temple that houses us. Even when we lose our way, we always know where home is. With our beloved under wing, we fly our hearts home.

Carved into the door to our bedroom are the words I wear my heart with you in it. On one wall of each room, there is a hand-written poem to the beloved. And there's also a wall plaque on the hallway landing that reads: When two hearts beat in the same direction, the meeting point is God. She finally gave me that one. Wherever we look, we are reminded of our blessings.

At the same time, it is radically different from our initial imaginings. It is more solid, more human, more real. If anything has held the temple safe, it has been grounding our love at every level on Mother Earth. We mutually accepted that sky-riding was our natural orientation, and that in order to sustain this powerhouse connection, we had to also ground our soles on Mother Earth. We are clearly soulmates—

a love connection sourced in essence—but we have also become solemates—a love connection that is grounded in daily life. We had sketched our legacy in the sky, and now we are sketching it in the dirt. As solemates, we stand a much better chance of lasting.

Our solemating demands a genuine integration with the practical world. This means regularly doing precisely what our merging nature resists: staying on top of our chores and obligations, remaining connected to our friends, leaving our love bubble and spending real time in the culture at large. We participate in society not to the extent that we abandon our uniqueness and morph into homogeneity, but in a way that keeps our timeless energy grounded in the flow of time.

Remaining grounded also means retaining our individuality and independence. After Sarah returned, I let go of my mediation practice. *Wholemates* had become an international bestseller, and I became a professional author-publisher, writing and administrating a small publishing business out of the house I purchased with my book royalties. Sarah was tempted to work with me, but instead got a part-time job as a naturopath in a neighborhood clinic, ensuring that we had the separateness we needed to remain healthy. When we reconnect at the end of a long day, it's the perfect balance—a fusion of sovereign entities.

Our solemating also has a psycho-physical quality to it. Recognizing our tendency to float into ecstasy, we have maintained a disciplined embodiment practice to keep us here. We practice yoga, dance and holotropic breathwork on a regular basis. And we have sustained a commitment to body-centered therapy with Sally, so we can keep our feet planted firmly on the ground and continue to develop the healthy ego and sturdy boundaries required to hold great love safe. We understand all too well how important it is to have a strong self to come home to, particularly given the fragmentation intrinsic to our merging. The more intensely we fly, the more deeply we ground. The more firmly we ground, the more safely we fly. From sole to soul. And back again.

If you really want to know someone, start by looking at their feet. How grounded is their spiritual life? What is the inner-face between their earthly and their divine life? How fully do they make contact with

Mother Earth? How present are they for the whole of the human experience? Do they come crashing back to earth when the truth hits the
fan? The eyes are a mirror of the soul, but so are the soles. If you want
to gauge how sustainable your love connection to another will be, ob-
serve the way they move on the planet. If they come crashing back to
earth when reality comes a calling, you know you will have a problem
when the romantic phase wanes and the next layer of truth arises.

It's not about giving up on the fairy tale relationship. It's about
landing it in reality. It's about giving the fairy feet. It's about peeling
away the prince's armor and loving the real being down below. It's
about wiping off the princess' makeup and loving her divine humanness. It's about finding romance in the naked fires of daily life. When
our masks and disguises fall away, real love can reveal itself. Forget
fairy tales, the human tale is much more satisfying. We just have to
learn how to get turned on by humanness.

When Sarah and I first connected in this lifetime, I was all-too-hap-
py to see our psychological issues as unreal in contrast to our ecstatic
experiences. In my mind, there was the soul's journey and there was
the human journey—and they were entirely different. But through a
more grounded lens, I have come to understand that there is no distinction. In fact, I believe our unhealed emotional issues and patterns
are actually direct reflections of the soul's state of being. Where does
spirit live, if not in the heart of our humanness? It's all an integrated
dance of sacred imagination.

It would be easier to maintain the connection if we were at a collective stage in humanity where we truly understood the expansive role
that intimate relationship can play in our spiritual lives. Relationship is
not just a manifestation of the divine: it is also a fertile field for the soul's
expansion. It is a breeding ground for the soul's emergence. It is where
many of the soul's lessons are harvested. To the extent that we learn
the heart lessons intrinsic to our love connections, we expand in karmic
stature. To the extent we resist them, we delay our own expansion.

When we turn away from our lessons, the universe jumps into action, orchestrating our return—a symphony of self-creation dedicated
to our unique expansion. This is the nature of karmic gravity—we are
returned to our path until we fully walk it.

Of course, converting our loss into expansion requires great courage and an adherence to a sustainable healing process. We have to go into the fire for as long as we need to transmute the suffering into gold. This means staying with our feelings until they are truly done with us, no matter how uncomfortable it is.

It also means being careful not to confuse analysis with healing. Dude was right—there's a meaningful difference between a cerebral interpretation of an experience ("I *know* why this came into my life") and an embodied awareness of it ("I *feel* why this came into my life"). Unless your knowing arises from your felt experience, it's meaningless. Stay with the emotional process until your soul food is digested. It will be difficult at times, but the feelings will only hurt until they transform. Once they make it all the way through the conversion tunnel, the lesson takes root. Divine perspiration.

## Sacred Loving

At the deepest level, honoring our union has been a journey into wholeness. There was no other way. When we kept it partial, it turned against us. Like many early life trauma survivors, we had overdeveloped certain threads of consciousness and avoided others. When we met, Sarah was an expert bliss-tripper. She wanted the light without the shadow it illumined. There were many ways I too was unwilling to own my shadow. In our own ways, we were both playing hide-and-seek with our own essence. Yet to honor this love right, we knew that we had to embrace all elements of reality. We had to turn on the light in every room, particularly those spaces that hadn't seen the light for decades, perhaps lifetimes.

Perhaps the most important question you can ask a potential love partner relates to their relationship with the shadow—their own, and the shadow that emerges in the relationship itself. That is: "How much work are you willing to do on yourself and the relationship when the s*#t hits the fan? Are you willing to go as deep as we have to go to work it through, or are you only interested in a breezy, low-maintenance relationship?" Few people ever talk about this during the romantic phase, because they are not envisioning the challenges to come. But it is an essential inquiry. I have known many people who were shocked to watch their 'great love' walk out the door when the connection required personal accountability and therapeutic work-through. Some of us will brave the journey; others will flee the fire. Some of us will do the work to transform our stories into the light at their source; others will run away with their 'tales' between their legs, only to find out later that their tales go with them everywhere they go. If you can determine someone's willingness at the beginning, you can save yourself a lot of trouble later.

With a quest for wholeness in mind, we agreed to work deeply with the challenging emotional material that our tremendous love excavates. We made a commitment to stand firmly in the bond, no matter what storms are passing through. Consequently, we have faced our demons in ways we never could the first time together. When our abandonment and engulfment wounds close in on us, we now bring them right into therapy. We have worked our stuff hard, massaged it, revealed it, owned it, and sometimes even healed it.

And, just as important, we have refined the art of authentic right-lessness, not caring who is right, but mutually caring for what is true. This shift seems to have transformed our dynamic the most, moving us from the egoic need to win that was borne in our warring childhoods and past life history, to the recognition that victories are a shared experience, manifest in the strengthening of the bridge between our hearts.

It's not about someone winning our heart. It's about restoring its aliveness. It's about softening its armor. It's about filling it up with light. When real love enters, it doesn't take anything from us. It gifts us with the everything.

This is every human's birthright: to know the universe that love reveals.

Our sexuality continues to transform on many levels. We had been profoundly alive to each other years ago, but there was a way in which our armor was still on when we made love. There is a meaningful difference between taking off your clothes and taking off your armor. Clothes come off lickety-split but armor can take a lifetime. I think both of us are beginning to understand this now. Intense soul-gazing has been replaced with a deepening vulnerability, one undress rehearsal after another. There is still an innocence in the field between us, but it's an informed innocence now.

When I used to go to bed with a woman in my younger days, I didn't realize there were so many of us in the bed at the same time. There was her and me, her parents, my parents, our past lovers, and anyone else we had unfinished business with. That's the thing about being unconscious, we can't help but bring our unresolved baggage into every relational encounter. Talk about an unwelcome orgy! It's a busy bed when we are unconscious. Hard to move around freely with so many projections on the mattress. One of the reasons we do the work to heal our past is so we can actually create more space for intimacy. With our patterns fallen away, we stand a much better chance of holding love safe. With our projections worked through, we can actually see the beloved with clear eyes. Finally, it's just the two of us.

Where before we had a love, now we have a relationship. Or perhaps it would be better to call it a *Realationship*, a connection that cuts a swath through all manner of authentic terrain, not only the pleasant landscapes, not only the mired, murky swampland of endless triggers. All of it. This doesn't mean we don't argue, or feel at odds with each other, but it does mean that we are committed to finding the love everywhere we can, going deeper and higher into the heart. Peeling away layers, ever deepening. Now we don't only pray to our union when it tastes sweet. We also pray to it when it tastes bitter. In its own way, it has all become sacred— every trigger, every conflict—because we recognize that it has the capacity to grow us to the next level of awareness. *Holy* shit.

It's a different thing, to make a relationship sacred. When it's just the love you honor, you are still in two different worlds. You love her, she loves you, but what stands between you? What of the bridge between your hearts? What of the world you become together? Conscious relationship is all about the third element—the alchemical combination of two souls merging, the living breathing world that you co-create in love's cosmic kiln. It's the difference between loving and serving love. It's the difference between the narcissistic quest for ecstasy and the joys of deep devotion. You serve loving. You are a devotee to the dance. The conscious-nest is a world unto itself.

Our connection is much like a never-ending mine. Although we feel so complete together, there is always the sense we've only scratched the surface of divine possibilities between our souls. Once we fully extricate the gems from one level of the mine, more are waiting at a deeper level. The deeper we go, the more brilliant the treasures we find. And the treasures aren't static, but dynamic and flowing, actively informing the next stage of our mutual expansion. Alone on my meditation cushion, the treasures had been so limited, but with my beloved by my side, an unlimited karmacopia of delight has revealed itself. Such magic.

On an individual level, I now know true peace. I see how no time was lost or wasted. Everything that came before—my early life challenges, my unresolved issues, Sarah's departure—makes perfect sense in the context of my own soul's journey. I came into this life with an armored consciousness and I needed exactly what I received in order to open it. I needed the harsh upbringing. I needed the great love. And I needed Sarah to leave so I could learn how to open my heart without being dependent on another. I am now at the point of every return.

Although I'm individually broadened and transformed, I recognize that it is fundamentally intertwined with my love-relationship. Two trees side by side, separate but connected at the roots, always connected at the roots. Two human beings sitting side by side, hearing the raindrops beating on the temple roof, feeling the presence of the other everywhere. Grateful and gracious, jointly whispering IU.

There is a path at the heart of each love connection. Each has its own karmic blueprint. It is seldom what we imagine. You just have to find the path and follow it wherever it leads you. Some connections are meant to last a lifetime, and many aren't. Expectations are like quicksand. They keep us from arriving at our true destination. Wherever we land, may we arrive with our hearts wide open.

### Birthdays

Two years after she returned, Sarah asked to go to the cave. We hadn't been there, together, for more than 16 years. It was time.

"Let's write together there, Ogdo. On the cave wall."

"Yes, let's, sweetheart. Let's."

The cave of remembered dreams, with my beloved in the flesh. What could be better?

We set out early in the morning. Spring was just beginning to peek through winter's deep slumber. There was a certain fragrance in the air, a hint of rebirth and renewal. When we arrived at Goshen, we found the park open but no one there. It was all ours. There was still crunchy snow on the ground and the air was chilly. Sarah grabbed her knapsack from the car and we began our trudge through the snow. Halfway to the cave, a large heron flew over our heads, its left leg hanging so low that it almost brushed Sarah's head. A welcoming party?

When we arrived at the cave, we stood in silence for a moment, paying homage to the memories. Some of them were still there, written on the wall. Time had protected them.

Sarah asked me to sit down against the wall. After a few moments, she came over and blindfolded me. "Just trust me, Lowen. This is not a sex thing. Too cold for that this morning. But I do have a sweet surprise for you."

While blindfolded, I heard her rustling through her bag. And then I heard the ever-so-familiar scratch of her writing on the cave wall.

"I thought we were supposed to do that together, baby."

"We will sweets, just give me a few more minutes."

When she was done, she kissed me and removed the blindfold. I looked at the cave wall directly opposite me. In green florescent chalk, she had written:

> I want to be inside your footsteps and walk with you each day.
> I want to rest within your quiet breaths at night.
> I want to whisper in your teardrops and live within your laughter.

My eyes teared up, as suddenly the contrast between her physical presence, and my memories of isolation in the cave overwhelmed me. I stood up to hug her, but she motioned me to remain seated.

"I'm not done, my love," she said with those smiling eyes of hers in full bloom.

I sat back down, as she got down on her knees in front of me. Reaching into her knapsack, she pulled out a small marble box. It looked like a family heirloom, elegant and timeless, with stories of its own. She placed it down in front of me. I reached for it and opened it to the most beautiful, simple ring of white gold.

"What's this for, Sarah?"

"It's my way of saying sorry."

"For what?"

"For all those birthdays I missed."

Now I remembered—she was reciting my original marriage proposal.

"And it's also my way of saying that I want to be there for all the rest of them... for all your birthdays to come."

Before I could respond, she looked into my eyes and said, "I love you as God loves. With nature as my chapel, and the divine as my witness, I ask you—will you marry me, Lowen Cooper?"

A surge of radiant elation filled my heart. I felt ecstatic that she asked me, too. How very beautiful—a woman asking a man. Why not—what is tradition in the face of love itself. I smiled and slid the ring onto my finger gleefully.

Then she reached back into her bag and pulled out the ring I had given her many years ago. I hadn't seen it since our reunion and hadn't asked about it. I always assumed it got lost somewhere amid our years of separation. Clearly it hadn't—she had kept it safe.

I took the ring from her hand. Two perfect hearts intertwined, forever fused. I slid it back on her finger. Still a perfect fit. And then she smiled and said, "I do." I kissed her lips softly.

We spent the rest of the afternoon writing on the cave's walls. And, when the afternoon sun warmed the day, I took out my pen-is and wrote my love inside her. What would a visit to the cave be without a little lovin'?

### Coach House

The next winter, we went looking for Dude. Our spring wedding was imminent, and we wanted him there. We checked out all the places he would frequent when the weather got bitter. No dice—we couldn't find him anywhere.

We finally found a social worker who knew him from one of the neighborhood shelters. It turned out that Dude would drop in to give pep talks to the homeless, but never actually slept at the shelters. He had a makeshift house of his own in one of the Kensington Market back alleys. She didn't know where, but there were only so many streets to choose from.

On a particularly icy day, we began the alley search. Checking behind the residential homes first, we found nothing. Then we searched the alleys behind the retail stores. Just before giving up, I spotted what appeared to be Dude's weathered Rumi book lying in the snow. We worked our way toward it and stopped dead in our tracks. There, pushed up against a fence between two fruit stores, was what appeared to be a yellow pagoda. It was made from pieces of old wood and covered, for the most part, in flattened coffee cups glued to the entire structure as a kind of protection. There were hundreds, perhaps thousands of cups. Quite a sight.

Outside the door was Dude's dilapidated street sign, half buried in snow: **$5 Dollars per Dudism. No deferral plan. Pay or adios.** Something was askew.

We knocked on the coffee cup door. No answer. I pressed it open, but there appeared to be an interior latch. I pushed harder, until the latch gave way. Inside, I found Dude lying on the cold hard ground, apparently unconscious. His face was red and splotchy, his whiskers icicles, his breath shallow. I called to Sarah to go get help. While she was gone, I covered him in my winter coat and rubbed his back. He didn't budge at all. My pushcart guru was near dead.

I looked around his place. There was little to see: a small messy cot, a toboggan with two blazers hanging off it, a giant bottle filled with untold amounts of cash. And a drawing of a young him with a long beard, and a woman donned in a bonnet. On it, were the words "Micah and Elizabeth Rasmussen's wedding." It appeared my pushcart guru was Amish. Wonders never cease. No wonder he lived such a natural life and had so little draw to civilization.

The ambulance pulled up, and we rushed Dude to hospital, in the nick of time. Just as he had always appeared when I most needed him, I had arrived to return the favor. Clearly we were part of the same soulpod, inextricably linked.

After he recovered, he finally told us a little of his story. He and his beloved Elizabeth were together for seven years, living and running a feed shop in Northern Pennsylvania. Tragically, their first child died during childbirth. A little girl they had named Robin. His wife Elizabeth never recovered from her grief. After falling into a dark depression for several years, she finally fled Micah and the community to live with a man she had met during Rumspringa, the period when Amish adolescents get to explore the world. It was her way of running away from her pain. Dude was so heartbroken that he fled the US and landed in Toronto. He had been living on the streets here for over 20 years.

We invited him to live in the couch house on my property, rent-free. He had several health conditions, ranging from type 2 diabetes to arthritis to gout—he simply couldn't continue to live outdoors. He protested mightily—"I want to earn my way"—until we agreed to accept payment in the form of snow shoveling and property maintenance.

He has been living with us for some time, tending to our small property with great pride. Now and then, when the wisdom business is booming, he leaves some cash in a rusty old can at the front door. We don't tell him, but we go right out into the world with it, loving it forward to other houseless people.

In every great love dance, there is a whole soulpod of contributing influences. It begins with the family of origin and ripples outward from there, into a whole tapestry of meaningful faces, each of them playing a necessary role. They call to us, we call to them, and our angels broker the deal. Some will be remembered as supporters, some as lite-dimmers who impede, but all are essential to the lovers' ultimate dance.

In the sunroom of our home, we created an altar that honors our love. On it are a colorful array of symbols of our connection: cardinal feathers, a birds' nest, green chalk, stones, cards. There's also a special section of pictures of everyone, alive and dead, who somehow contributed to our journey home. Every now and then we hold an early morning prayer ceremony to express our gratitude to them. Seldom are we alone. Our new squirrel friends usually appear in the window, perhaps drawn by the candle, or perhaps because they are determined to be included in our circle of love. There was a time in my life when I would never have included bushy rodents in my family—but it all makes perfect sense now. When you find a love like this, you are swimming in magic. Nothing is excluded. And, nothing surprises you anymore. Everything serves the Beloved in its own sweet way.

## Today

I wasn't quite sure where to end *An Uncommon Bond,* the story of mine and Sarah's journey. The story of love lost, yet never lost. The story of the journey from soulmates to solemates, from woundmates to wholemates. The story of a love so true that it birthed a universe of eternal enchantment.

How do I end that which will never end?

I will end it with today.

Today, just as I was about to finish this last chapter, we decided to go for a bike ride on Toronto Island. It was a beautiful spring day, with a soft and fragrant breeze. On the way back, we stopped to pick up some groceries at the St. Lawrence Market. There were too many bags to ride with, so we decided to walk the bikes all the way home. Instead of taking the main streets, we went down quieter back alleys as graffitists often do, looking for a good wall or two to ruin. When we took the last turn, we came across a young couple heatedly arguing about their relationship. They were clearly, dearly, sparklingly in love, and yet completely submerged in a trigger-fest of great intensity.

Sarah looked at me, "Oh Lord, those triggers. God protect them."

"Should we warn them, honey?"

"No. Life will take care of that," she replied knowingly.

"Think they'll make it?"

"So few do," she replied. And then her eyes lit up. "But, yes... maybe. They do have a lot of fire. That can be useful."

We stood and furtively watched them for a while. They would never have known that we were sending prayers their way.

So few couples make it at this individualistic stage of human development. I mean *really* make it, in the deepest and truest sense. But many more will as we continue to evolve beyond our perceived separateness and embrace relationship as a path to wholeness. It's not an easy path, and it's not the path for everyone on their soul's journey—but it is a gateway to wonder for those who are both destined and willing to brave the journey.

At this moment we are sitting on the couch. As I write these last words, Sarah is eating a bowl of her favorite coconut ice cream. We just finished a large dinner and both of us are feeling sleepy. And how fucking perfect it is. Because she is sitting beside me. Because her feet are touching mine. Because my heart has found its home.

I am right where I belong.

Return to Sender...

Address now known.

Our temple of mutual delight.

Here we shall pray forever.

THE END

# Words from the Author

Throughout this lifetime, I've had many glimpses of great love coming my way. I didn't see a face, or hear a voice, but I felt it there, tugging at me, waiting ahead or behind me on the path, a karmic bonfire with my name on it. Somehow I knew I had to wait for this love above all else—to polish me, to cleanse me, to stretch me so wide open that I could not help but transform. And so it did.

Before my first great love arrived, I had spent many years on the lone wolf male warrior spiritual path. Unity consciousness was primarily an isolationist endeavor. If I was going to touch God, it was going to be with my mind, or in the heart of a solo meditation journey, or at the tail end of an emotional healing process. It wasn't going to be in the presence of a woman. It wasn't going to be while having intercourse with my beloved. It wasn't going to be in the heart of vulnerability. It wasn't going to be on the wings of a love.

I met her magnificence when I was 36 years old. After twelve years of personal healing work, I was just ready to receive love's blessings. Not comfortably, not peacefully, but with a genuine hunger for the expansion at its heart. If I had consciously known what would be required of me, I would surely have declined. Great love is tricky like that. It shows you why it came long after you are so deep in the adventure that you can't turn back. At the least, I would have packed the ghost of Rumi in my travel bag, just to keep me hopeful on those deep dark dives into the mystery. There were so many of those.

It wasn't the first time I had loved, but it was the first time I had explored the universe through the portal of connection. It was the first time I had melted into longing in love's cosmic kiln. It was the first

261

time I had touched divinity in the heart of intimacy. It was the first time I had loved as God loves. I will never be the same. The call of the beloved always comes with the promise of expansion, and seldom in ways we plan or imagine. If you want to know what's coming, choose a more practical love. But if you want to grow toward God, let your soul do the picking.

With her—and this was even true in the suffering—I touched a magical universe, one I didn't know existed. It was like our love was a portal to another dimension altogether, a magic carpet ride of trans-ordinary delight. There is the head-centered non-duality and there is the heart-nest of wholeness. And they are simply not the same worlds. How to hearticulate the splendor?

Although the love between us ran ocean-deep, the intensity of our connection—mixed with our present levels of spiritual and emotional maturity—made the relationship unsustainable. By the time all was said and done, our relationship was in ruins, and I lay crumpled on the ground like a kite struck down by lightning. If shattered was what I needed to grow in karmic stature, then I got just what the soul doctor ordered. If ever there was a time I wanted to go back to a head-tripping path, it was then. But it was too late for dissociation. With my emotional armor long gone, I had no choice but to get inside of my heart and weave it back together with whatever thread of hope I could find. It was no easy feat.

In the heart of that process, I stumbled upon the work of Jeanne Achterberg, a mind-body healing pioneer and brilliant academic. I was a Masters of Psychology student at Saybrook Graduate School in San Francisco, when I noticed that she was teaching a seminar on 'Uncommon Bonds' at the next conference. Divine timing. Building upon cultural anthropologist Virginia Hine's work with 'bonded couples'—a particular kind of spiritual love relationship—Jeanne later coined the term "Uncommon Bonds" (see page 274 of this book) to describe such couples. When I heard her describe them at the conference, a light went on in my consciousness, suddenly illuminating a journey that was far beyond my understanding. Finally some clarity as to what I had experienced. Finally.

Soon thereafter, with Jeanne as my chair, I wrote my Master's thesis on my uncommon bond experience. I was so delighted to have a framework of understanding that it poured from me seamlessly: over a hundred pages in 31 hours. After it was approved, Jeanne offered to chair my PhD dissertation on the same topic. I was tempted, since crafting a map of relational consciousness felt deeply valuable, and, I suspected, part of my life-calling. But something else called me first. I wanted to write for the world, but I needed to write my autobiography first—*Soulshaping: A Journey of Self-Creation*. Love and relationship writing would have to wait.

That was more than 14 years ago. Since then, not a day has gone by when I didn't think of writing an uncommon bond love story. It nagged at me relentlessly, often waking me up in the middle of night to jot down a paragraph, or to call my ideas into my home answering machine while I was at work. One time, I was so immersed in writing notes for it that I didn't notice the parking dude writing me a ticket while I was sitting in the car—and I always notice those characters!

By the time I actually sat down to begin writing it in 2011, I already had a 55,000 word document filled with notes, sentences and complete paragraphs. Not exactly starting with a blank slate. Instead, I began with a treasure trove of ideas, insights and personal reflections, all ripe and ready to be shared. The call to write this book was that alive, that pressing, that personally imperative. An essential step on my soul's journey.

Long ago, I spent time with a group of male meditators. Despite admitting that many of their love experiences had a mystical and divine quality, they kept reiterating the contention that it was meditation—not love—that would take them to God. Despite acknowledging a profound experience of unity through the horizontal heart portal, they kept returning to their vertical head channel. For them, the kingdom of consciousness was reached through the inner road, with meditation as their primary vehicle.

I related to this perspective. But I no longer do. Yes, meditation is one path to a more expanded consciousness, but it's only one path—it is not *the* path. And, it may not even be a path that goes anywhere near as deep or as high as a relational path, as a horizontal path, as a path dripping with love-soaked connectiveness. Perhaps our experience of the 'kingdom of heaven' when we are alone with God is just the first step for humanity. Perhaps our experience of unity consciousness—a relative term if ever there was one—expands boundlessly as we deepen in intimacy. With profound love relationship as our vessel, we are catapulted to a vaster and more fertile universe, one where we are both witness and participant, one where we actually transform the cosmos with every kiss, with every touch, with every shared breathstroke.

I am tired of hearing what God is from head-tripping men. I am tired of hearing what God is from isolationists on a spiritual quest. I am tired of hearing what God is from lovers of detachment. I want to hear about a juicy God, a creative God, a relational God, a God that arises when we jump into life and stop playing it safe, watching life race by like a passing train. It's time for the dancers to tell us what God is. It's time for the artists to tell us what God is. It's time for the lovers to tell us what God is. We are not here to watch God from afar. We are here to live God from the inside out.

At the same time, I understand some of what has sourced the overemphasis on meditation, detachment and contemplation as the path. Patriarchal control systems have been put in place since time immemorial, keeping us looking to the General, or the Despot, or the Wealthy Man, for our answers. If we begin to find our answers in each other, those systems fall apart. When you add in religious control—they can't control you if you go to the love-making temple to find God—you can see that in our history, we have not had the freedom nor the invitation to explore human relationships as a pipeline to divinity.

In the words of systems theorist Dr. Kathia Laszlo "Everything feminine has been suppressed in patriarchy for so many centuries. Earth based spirituality, natural healing and childbirth, and anything that empowers women has been eliminated by men in power and presented as evil. The same is true for relationship as spiritual path. That would have made men and women equal partners, and it would have given too much power to the feminine if it recognized the uncontrollable, volatile, chaotic nature of emotional connection as valid, natural, healthy and helpful."

And perhaps we just haven't been ready. In the world I grew up in, many of us were ruled by survivalism as a way of being. We organized our personalities and chose our life path based on whatever masks were needed to get food on the table and otherwise manage reality. Since our quest for survival defined us, we picked partners who reflected that pragmatism. Love was another venue for our security issues. And in the heart of such a harsh world, the subtleties of great love simply had no place.

In the next step of our world—one that is organized around authenticity—we will choose our partners based solely on soul-sourced love. We will choose our partners from the heart outward. Soul-centered love demands that we find our nourishment in the lover's gaze, the opening heart, the deep breath of union. Our identity will be sourced in the rhythms and tides of the heart ocean, not the adaptations and disguises of the marketplace. Another planet altogether. The ultimate answer is to raise the vibration of the world so that it can meet great love heart-on.

The simple truth is that we have historically been at a very individualized stage in human development, one where it's all many of us can do to manage and heal our own emotional material and figure out who we are. To attempt to mix one as-yet unhealed being with another has been particularly challenging and exacting, especially if the relationship is more soulful than practical. This isn't to say that relationship isn't essential to our healing and expansion, but sometimes it's just been too much at once. When soulmates come together, they often excavate more than their individual pain. They also bring the pain of the collective to the surface. It's all there, in the heart of the mine. That's a lot of dynamite going off at once!

At last, something is changing, as the quest for a conscious relationship is becoming a priority for many. Whether it's because the structures of society are evolving to support it, or because we have matured individually to the point of readiness, we are more open to the possibility that love connection—in both its light and its shadow—is intended as a vehicle for transformation and divine interfacing.

With that in mind, I want to invite others to share their stories. We need to hear what you have experienced, where love has taken you, what has gotten in the way. We need to hear your reports from love's sacred battlefields. We don't need to hear any more fantasies about love—we need to hear the truth—each person's individual truth.

Once we have learned enough, we can construct a new kind of language, one that is rooted in the yearning, the wisdom, the compassion, the softening of the receptive heart. The language of the mind can be very clever, but the language of the heart has a brilliance all its own. When we hearticulate, we speak from a place of essence, the place where the divine lives. What a bountiful dictionary, with such rich and subtle textures and tones. This is the language of love.

I also invite others to craft relational models of consciousness for the world to consider. I may not have a chance to get to that work this time around, but perhaps you can. We have far too many individually-centered models and so few relational ones. We need maps, frameworks, and holarchies that speak to the stages of consciousness that arise at different stages of heart connection.

I'm not just talking about sexual relationships between heterosexuals, like the one portrayed in this book. I am talking about all forms of relationship, including platonic ones, and all forms of human sexuality—heterosexual, homosexual, transgendered. It's the heart that God is interested in, not body parts. It's what we learn within the heart that lasts for all eternity. In other words, everyone's experience is welcome, and everyone's experience will help us to more fully understand the landscape that awaits us as we de-armor and ride our love for each other into divinity. The portal is each other. So many universes await.

Imagine the next step, where we don't see relationship endings as defeats, but as victories and necessary openings—lessons on the path to wholeness. Imagine the next step, where we honor the courage it took to open to the possibility of love, where we see intimacy as a wondrous opportunity to deepen in cosmic stature. How can any failed relationship ever be a complete defeat? It took such courage to brave it all, to make love with the divine, to touch God through our vulnerable heart. This is not to say that we don't grieve loss; it is only to remind us of the opportunity that lives at the heart of every farewell. A little scar tissue can go a long way on the path to presence.

As relational models are developed, we will need individuals who can support love's travelers and shepherd them through perilous terrain. After all, the journey will take them through all kinds of vast and unfamiliar soulscapes. The further they go, the less it is about the couple alone, and the more it is about the collective. With their love as rocket-fuel, they will be catapulted right into the heart of Providence. There they become one with all that is, the light and the shadow, the healed and the unresolved, the glory and the gory. There they become more than two branches of the human tree—they become the entire forest.

This is why traditional psychotherapy often fails soul connections. Early childhood issues don't even begin to cover the vast array of triggers and shadow-material that come up when souls merge with the divine. We have to be very careful not to pathologize the challenges that arise when great love comes, or else we will miss the gifts such challenges offer. With this in mind, we need to cultivate a community of 'Love Elders,' those who have ridden love's highways into eternity. We need to commune with those who have been there before us. A definition of Love Elders can be read on page 272.

In an effort to protect love journeyers from being led astray, it would be helpful if protocols and guidelines are immediately established to ensure that those who come to call themselves Love Elders are acting from a place of genuine wisdom and integrity. We have seen what happens when confused path travelers end up in the hands of ungrounded healers with questionable depth and integrity. The path becomes muddied, and damage can be done. We don't want to see Love Elders becoming another term that's distorted and watered down by the New (C)age movement. Because of the deeply vulnerable nature of awakening love experiences, we want to be sure that those who support the process are healthily egoic, sturdily grounded, appropriately boundaried—and living with full integrity. In other words, individuals who have been down many roads and come through the other side intact, clarified and wiser.

Before Jeanne died in 2012, I had some email correspondence with her. In one email, she indicated that she intended to write a book about uncommon bonds, so much so that she was carrying the materials around with her. I remember her telling me that she had submitted the idea to some publishers long ago, but they felt that the world wasn't ready to consider uncommon bonds as a relational construct.

Perhaps they are now, for soul-sourced relationships may well be an essential step for this sinking earth ship. Jeanne surely understood their significance:

> *The telling of the story of uncommon bonds creates a new myth for relationships that involves the evolution and transformation of our being. The bonds may well be the threads in the matrix of humanity, and in the final analysis, the only thing that endures. We who have bonded experiences can see ourselves as two of the many lights in the inter-connected web of all life, and as these lights burn brighter in synchrony, we shake and move and transduce the filaments of the web so that the material universe is changed, subtly perhaps, but changed, nonetheless.*

Although I have certainly not written the book Jeanne would have written, I hope that I have written something that honors her highest vision. She knew I was going to write this book and gave me her blessings. Some of her inspiring words to me were taped to the wall in my primary writing space throughout the process, inviting me to venture a little further than I might have otherwise gone. Although the story does not factually replicate the journey I took—the characters are constructs, the details are different—it does capture many of the elements of my inner experience throughout my uncommon bond journey. As it is with many individuals who have had an uncommon bond experience, that process was more like karmic boot camp than any idealized version of love relationship. I wanted many times to soft-touch the story I was writing, both for the sake of my reader and, frankly, to make this book a breezier write. Yet I kept feeling the need to share the authentic truth of my inner journey—however excruciating it may be: darkness, challenges, warts and all. Having said this, I recognize I still don't know a thing about love. If you want to discover how little you know about love, try writing a book about it. Its unfathomable mysteries are always a little beyond reach.

And when it comes down to it, aren't we all virgins when it comes to love? One surprise after another after another. Just when we think we've found our footing, the universe sends a soulnami our way, reminding us that we were always lost at sea. Love is both our life preserver, and our sinking ship. It is an oceanic mystery, one that gives up its secrets one drop at a time.

As part of my creative process, I made a conscious decision not to spend any real time comparing types of love connection. I play a bit with definition in the Love Dictionary, but I sidestep the question of how, for example, 'twin flames' are different from 'soulmates' and 'uncommon bonds.' I have known too many people who wear their relationship characterization as a badge of honor (not unlike those who wear the tags 'spiritual,' 'yogi,' 'guru' and 'spiritual master'), and I feel it is important we avoid comparisons at this stage of understanding. It really is such a delicate art to intimately hearticulate the experiences we have, without muddying the waters by placing them in a hierarchical framework characterized by greater or lesser loves. Even when we do reach a stage where distinctions can be clearly made, it is best we view them not from a place of superiority, but see them in their inherent perfection, with tremendous gratitude. Many never taste great love in their lives. If you have, then get down on your knees and give thanks.

It is my hope that we never forget the relational and co-transformative nature of human expansion. Although the ultimate romance is with your own soul, it is our experiences together that give birth to the essential lessons. We are each here to participate in this dance of sacred imagination, stepping on each other's toes and turning each other toward God one clumsy step after another. We trip, then get back up with greater awareness. With this in heart, I'm hopeful we can learn to accept one another in our humanness. We are going to continue to make mistakes, but there is grace in that if we see our errors through to the lessons they contain.

One of the most important benefits of honoring relationship as a spiritual path is that it reminds us that we can't rise alone, that there is a perpetual linkage between ourselves and others. There's no question that the patriarchal emphasis on individual spiritual path has contributed to selfishness and even destructive behavior—particularly in unawakened men, who see advancement as something that exists independent of their connection to anyone or anything outside themselves. We need accomplishment to become a relational construct; that is, we co-create together, with mutual benefit as our shared goal. I do know one thing with certainty—if my male brethren don't de-armor their hearts soon, then much of the work that has been done by the divine feminine and awakening men to enhearten the culture will be lost. We must climb Heart Mountain together.

I often try to picture a humanity that loves freely and fully. Just imagine that phenomena. We would become a divine symphony, with the sound of our shared song reaching to the heavens to pull God right down to earth where we can see Her up close and personal. If we can touch something we call God alone, just imagine how much vaster that experience will be if we can touch Her as a chorus.

May we meet Her with our hands held together and our hearts intertwined. Grateful and gracious, forever more.

—Jeff Brown
Toronto, Canada
March 9, 2015

# Love Dictionary

**CUDDLELINGUS:** When a lover orally innerfaces with a woman's yoni (vagina) with great tenderness and presence. A kind of labial love hug that is slow, subtle and sweet. Instead of attacking the yoni with the tongue in an assertive attempt to satisfy, the yoni is attuned to—gently and devotionally, without agenda or end-goal. An intimate tongue cuddle, one where the yoni feels seen, cradled, and honored. A divine, reverential thirst quenching for the giver, and a blissful, delicate unfolding for the receiver. A cuddle party of the highest order.

**HEART-ON:** A male erection not inspired by external stimuli, but ignited from the heart outward. A heart-on indicates that the heart-genital highway is in communication, and open for travel. An erection where soul-sourced love is the sexual turn-on. When the love is true, physical arousal is God's way of showing his Divine face. The penis as a conduit to the cosmos.

**HEARTICULATION:** The language of the heart. A new love-lexicon of longing and union that flows from the tides and rhythms of the receptive heart. You don't learn this grammarless language through your mind. You learn it by letting your most vulnerable heart open and speak its truth. There are no guidelines, no limitations, no reference points for hearticulation. The more you open, the more the love dictionary expands. Soundings and utterances of an ever-deepening nature. Heartspeak.

**KARMASTRY:** Sexual and/or energetic chemistry between two people that is sourced in a karmic contract of a sacred, universal order. Traditional chemistry between two people often originates in physical attraction alone. Karmasty is chemistry that emerges from a vaster karmic backdrop—two souls drawn to each other because of a karmic, cosmic and soulular pull. This may be the first time their souls have encountered each other, or, the karmastry between them may thread forward from prior lifetimes, rippling into this present space and time. Those with karmic contracts come together to work through past material, and integrate new lessons—serving their evolution. Karmastry can reflect any side of the human spectrum—from horror to bliss, gory to glory, shadow to light and back again. Although we are led to believe that connections of this powerful a nature are intended to last a lifetime, they often are not. They may exist for the blink of an eye, lasting only as long as necessary to actualize their encoded intent. Not always a joyous visitor, karmasty often enters our lives for challenging reasons—to teach us an essential lesson, to crack through our emotional armor, to inwaken us from our perpetual slumber. Be careful what you wish for.

**LOVE ELDERS:** Individuals who have traveled love's highways and had a vast array of relational experiences. They have explored the heights of ecstasy and the depths of suffering, and, rather than turning away from the teachings at the core of their experiences, they chose to remain in the fire until wisdom was birthed. At the heart of their work is the belief that love relationship is a spiritual practice, a portal to divinity that must be nurtured with compassion and attunement if it is to bear fruit. In sharp contrast to the individual consciousness models long advocated by patriarchal thinkers, Love Elders advocate for the development of relational consciousness models that will serve humanity going forward. They move from the belief that we are not just here together to keep each other company—we are here together to show each other God. The portal is each other.

Their work is to support others as they navigate the difficulties that arise in all forms of soul-based love connection. They help guide couples over challenging terrain—making it to the other side with their relationship intact. They illuminate some of the particularly complex dynamics that can infuse soul-based relationships—providing a clearer backdrop and context, and a warm ray of hope during dark times. Hearticulators extraordinaire, they also help individuals to find healing and closure around relationships that cannot be sustained.

**OURGASM:** A climactic merging of beloveds that catapults them into God while lovemaking. Not limited to the genitals, an ourgasm permeates every cell of the body... and then, expands far beyond that, as the couple touches heaven and beyond on their love-loomed magic carpet. This is not an ordinary orgasm based on pleasure alone. An ourgasm is an essence-sourced liquid love climax that illuminates and celebrates God's face. It is a love-making so perfect in oneness and unity—a merging so total—that it ultimately consumes itself by exploding straight into divinity. An energetic love-burst that both includes and transcends the body itself. A cuming together that eclipse any notion of a distinct "you" and "me" and morphs into OURS.

**SACRED SHAFT:** A reverential term for the penis as a vessel for divinity; a cosmic missile straight into God. In the unawakened man, the penis is a pleasure-seeking—and pleasure-giving—device. In the awakening man, it is much more than just that. It is a sacred carrier that helps to transport both to a higher love-consciousness. It is a column of love-light, a holy pillar that pierces the veil of separation between lovers. AKA: Godstick, Godrod, Soul Shaft.

**SOULENDIPITY:** The inter-weave of foretellings, clues, dreams, visions, signs and symbols that demonstrate Divine Orchestration is at work. This orchestration can serve many purposes, not always visible to the naked eye. Regarding personal relationships, soulendipity is an indicator that two souls are destined to cross paths—ready to journey together here on earth. Various hints nudge them in each other's direction—a divine treasure hunt. Once the souls do come together, their journey often continues to be framed by these signs and sightings. The challenge is clarifying why they are being invited in each other's direction. That is, what is the learning, the growth, the expansion at the heart of the connection? Is it to love one another eternally, or are there other lessons waiting in the wings?

**SOLEMATES:** A higher-level love connection that is emanating from the Divine yet perfectly finds its feet here on Mother Earth. Solemates are the embodied counterpart of soulmates, the other side of the coin; the yang nested within the yin. They move and relate from the ground up, rather than from the sky downward. They don't live their love as an ecstatic flight of fancy—they make a determined effort to land it in everyday life. A mature and seasoned bond that has recognized the fact that their connection doesn't just have a place in the cosmic and divine realms, but also has a perfect place down here and now, in human existence. They have endured the many challenges of integrating their emotional material, so they can live seamlessly in love, on this plane. They put a strong emphasis on integrating their relationship into everyday life, ensuring its groundedness and sustainability. They continue to work on their psycho-emotional issues and reinforce their boundaries so their soulful connection can be held safe. They make no distinction between their spiritual and earthly lives. They participate in society not to the extent that they abandon their uniqueness and morph into homogeneity, but in a way that keeps their timeless relational energy grounded in the flow of time. And as they solidify as solemates, they are better able to impact this earth plane, touching and affecting humanity.

**SOULMATES:** A higher level connection that is sourced in essence and the call of the soul. Most often, soulmates recognize each other instantly, overcome by a sense of familiarity and shared karmic lineage in each other's presence. They sense that the other holds a key to their transformation, their very wholeness. Although they match on the higher levels, they have yet to master a grounded, balanced, practical relationship here on earth. And some may never. This may be due to their developmental spiritual-emotional maturity—they don't yet have the mutual foundation to ground the relationship on earth. Or some may not be meant to "land." They are simply meant to travel into higher realms together, for however long and deep. Soulmates are the sky-based counterparts of earth-based Solemates, and when a couple can master both realms (Wholemates), they become the Everything.

**UNCOMMON BOND:** A term crafted by author Jeanne Achterberg, arising from her own studies and the work of cultural anthropologist Virginia (Ginny) Hine. The following definition is taken from my Master's Thesis on the topic, which was based on Jeanne's writings and our dialogues:

Uncommon Bonds are love connections that are sourced in the transcendent and transpersonal realms. The couple feels destined to have met: their connection is sourced in grace. This often leads to an experience of parapsychological or paranormal events, such as synchronicities, soulendipities, and non-local communications that defy known laws of time and space. There's a knowing of pure recognition of the other—a feeling of being cut from the same cloth, a sense of having occupied the same body in a previous life, or perhaps one soul residing in two bodies. The lovers experience a prayer of gratitude and a sigh of relief as though coming home after decades of wandering: "Ahhh, there you are." A transpersonal energy dances within and between the couple. Spiritual practice is important to them, since the relationship is often experienced as the premier spiritual engagement, an outgrowth of a relationship with the Absolute. Sexuality is also experienced as a spiritual practice, holy and sacramental, a doorway leading to expanded consciousness and even touching pure consciousness. The union feels as though it transcends personal neurosis, addictions, affairs, impotencies, inadequacies, great sorrows, and the pure and inevitable facts of growing old.

A soul-crafted dynamic, the relationship polishes the rough diamond of the soul, our very essence. For this reason, the relationship is sometimes arduous, complex and often accompanied by many dark nights of the soul. During times of separation, the tether to life seems to be violently and forcibly torn apart, often experienced as a kind of abyss in the absence of the other. There's a sense that the soul work could not happen in any other way than through the relationship. There's also incredible bliss and profound ecstasy during the course of the transformative process, along with a sense of wholeness and completeness. Holding simultaneously to a sense of distinct self and connection to the bond at times feels overwhelming. Repeated dancing back and forth—now self, now disappearing, wave to particle and back—characterizes the growing, changing, polishing, and refining process. Whether experiencing separateness or union, the couple are always passionately alive.

Additionally, the couple feels bonded on all levels—body, mind and spirit. When they remain together, physical attraction and erotic cohesion last a lifetime. The couples often share in mutual life's work, or they long to work together one day. They are aware that they cannot grow to the next level without each other. Finally, many uncommon bonds do not have a sexual or intimate component. Some are linked as friends, others as teacher and student, parent and child, co-workers, or siblings.

**V-PASSIONA MEDITATION:** A term to describe intimacy as a spiritual practice, one where impassioned, heart-centered lovemaking (sexual inter-source) is an excavator of deeper truths, a clarifier of consciousness and a portal to divinity. With hearts weaving and hips heaving, the lovers ride their mutual bodyship into God. Not to be confused with Vipassana Meditation (or Insight Meditation)—a solitary meditation practice that uses mindful breathing and contemplation to gain insight into the true essence of reality. V-passiona focuses on human connection as the doorway into authentic insight, revelation, inner peace and truth. Lovers explore the universe on their meditation cushion built for two.

**WHOLEMATES:** A love relationship that spans all realms and ways of being. Both solemates and soulmates, the connection is mutually sourced in essence, and grounded in the earth dimension. Rather than living through limited threads of consciousness, the couple ascends with both feet on the ground, penetrating the everything in their daily travels: shadow and light, gory and glory, shopping list and unity consciousness. A kind of conscious in-coupling, the partners endeavor to marry all archetypes and ways of being, bridging body and soul in love's cosmic kiln. Soul-to-Solemates, they have mastered sky (the higher, deeper, soulful levels) and earth (the healthy, grounded, balanced life and personality levels), and have finally become a complete 'Realationship.' On the river of essence, everything flows in the same direction—toward the ocean of wholeness. A harmonized and mutually inclusive consciousness. The path of the Wholly Holy.

**WOUNDMATES:** Relationships that are sourced in unresolved emotional patterns, issues and holdings. The pull between the two individuals is driven by the unhealed shadow material that each of them carries, often in ways that reflect and trigger the other's wounds perfectly. The material may have arisen in this lifetime or prior lifetimes, and may reflect their individual history and that of the collective. Many woundmate connections are difficult to identify because they often have an intensely melded or enmeshed quality, lacking in boundaries and codependent in form. The wounds call out to one another in such a way that the individuals cannot distinguish themselves from the other. They are also difficult to identify because they often masquerade as heightened and expansive, as the intensity of the wound material catapults the couple into seemingly transcendent terrain. But they always come crashing back to earth with their wounds in tow. Wound-birthed passion is meaningfully different from love-birthed passion, with very different outcomes. Woundmates are not to be confused with soulmates, which can also trigger shadowy material to the surface of consciousness, but are sourced in a more promising and fertile wellspring, one that fosters real growth and progress. Soulmates are drawn to one another by a call to essence. At the heart of their connection is the opportunity to grow in karmic stature, while woundmates often just flounder in the mud, trigger after trigger, downward spiral after downward spiral, attached at the waste.

**YONIVERSE:** A term that reflects the sacred, universal nature of the yoni (vagina) as the (w)hole of creation. Properly seen and honored, the yoni is a powerful and sacred pipeline to divinity. God's love canal—the tunnel from possibility to humanifestation. The Divine Feminine as the portal to the universe, the source of Life, the first wonder of the world, indistinguishable from the Godself, Itself. When we explore the yoniverse with presence and reverence, we are catapulted to a meaning-based landscape that is intertwined with the divine. The yoniverse of meaning.

# GRATITUDES

Gratitude to those who supported this creative journey in their own unique ways: Jackie Feldman, Jill Angelo Birnbaum, Andrew Harvey, Jessica Bahr, Emmanuelle Labat, Bauble, Freeman Michaels, Adrian Sohn, Laura Beth Walker, Victoria Erickson, Leo Jacot, Brad Rose, New Leaf Distribution, Ondrea Levine, Roger Peplar, Debbie Devine, Beela, Shayna Orfus, dear friends Ryan and Lowen, Katherine Woodward Thomas, Elizabeth Lesser, Kathryn Graham Wilson, Acacia Land, Shayne Traviss, Sophie Brown, Jody Bresgi. And even gratitude to all the lite-dimmers I have known who only served to inspire me to greater heights.

Gratitude to editor David Robert Ord, for his focused and helpful contribution to this book. And to Allyson Woodrooffe for her always brilliant graphic work.

Waves of gratitude to my Facebook supporters, who have given me energy when none could be found. I am blessed by your presence every day.

Heartfelt gratitude to Randy Brown and Angela Spagnuolo for holding down the fort until I could finish this book. And to the brilliant Tarini Bresgi, for her continued support and presence on the Soulshaping journey.

Tremendous gratitude to my primary editor, Amy Gallagher, for her unwavering support and attunement to my intentions with respect to this book creation. Like love itself, creativity is no easy path. Without the right support, we simply cannot find our way. Amy was an exquisite companion on this creative journey. Deep bows to her brilliant mind and bhakti heart. Buffalo rocks.

# About the Author

A former criminal lawyer and psychotherapist, Jeff Brown is the author of *Soulshaping: A Journey of Self-Creation*, and *Ascending with Both Feet on the Ground*. Endorsed by authors Elizabeth Lesser, Oriah Mountain Dreamer and Katherine Woodward Thomas, "Ascending" is a collection of some of Jeff's most popular spiritual graffiti—quotes, soul-bytes and aphorisms frequently shared in social media. He is also the author of the viral blog *Apologies to the Divine Feminine (from a warrior in transition)* and the producer and key journeyer in the award winning spiritual documentary, *Karmageddon*, which also stars Ram Dass, Seane Corn, David Life, Deva Premal and Miten. He has written a series of inspirations for ABC's *Good Morning America* and appeared on over 200 radio shows. His third book, *Love it Forward,* was published on Valentine's day, 2014. He is also the founder of Enrealment Press and the creator of a new online school, Soulshaping Institute, which launched in January, 2015. He is presently in Toronto, working on another book of quotes and a book that reflects his lens on spirituality. You can connect with Jeff's work at www.soulshaping.com, www.soulshapinginstitute.com and www.enrealment.com.